ALL
THIS
AND
MORE

ALL THIS AND

A NOVEL

MORE

PENG SHEPHERD

WILLIAM MORROW

An Imprint of HarperCollins*Publishers*

ALL THIS AND MORE. Copyright © 2024 by Peng Shepherd. All rights reserved. Printed in the United States of America. No part of this book may be used or reproduced in any manner whatsoever without written permission except in the case of brief quotations embodied in critical articles and reviews. For information, address HarperCollins Publishers, 195 Broadway, New York, NY 10007.

HarperCollins books may be purchased for educational, business, or sales promotional use. For information, please email the Special Markets Department at SPsales@harpercollins.com.

FIRST EDITION

Library of Congress Cataloging-in-Publication Data has been applied for.

ISBN 978-0-06-327897-4 (hardcover)
ISBN 978-0-06-338732-4 (international edition)

24 25 26 27 28 LBC 5 4 3 2 1

ALL
THIS
AND
MORE

HOW TO READ THIS BOOK

This is a book about choices. Their allure, their power, and their consequences.

And so, of course, you have a choice about how you want to read it.

At certain points in the text, the story will present you with several options about what to do next. You can either allow the book to guide you along like a more conventional novel, or you can forge your own path by choosing to jump to a different chapter. It's entirely up to you.

To stay on the guided path, or, if you're ever not sure what to do next:
Pick the first option.

To forge your own path through the story:
Pick any option you like.

Have fun! And remember: you could have *All This . . . and More.*

THE SHOW

It happened one unremarkable Friday night. Without prelude, without fanfare. Almost as if by accident.

Everyone was still eating dinner or driving home from work, and had no idea the world had just changed forever—because of a television show. Probably the only people who saw the first few minutes of the premiere were the ones who already had the channel on as background noise to be ignored.

But it didn't take long.

By the first commercial break, the show had taken the entire globe by storm. Family members had called each other, friends had messaged online, and the Internet had exploded. By the time the commercials finished and the first episode returned, there were more viewers glued to their screens than for any other broadcast ever aired, by an order of magnitude. There were hundreds of millions of televisions in the United States all locked on that channel, and hundreds of millions more devices streaming it from abroad. By the ending credits, *four billion people* were tuned in.

After all, who wouldn't want the chance to change their life?

Before *All This and More*, reality TV was still considered a guilty pleasure. Something to be embarrassed about, never to admit watching. Now, no one would argue that the show is the greatest work of media ever made. A redefinition of the meaning of art. Of humankind.

It stuns, to recall how oblivious everyone was to what was coming.

A simple premise: each season, a contestant would have ten episodes to try to better themselves—whatever that meant for them. Repair their marriages, or find true love if they were single, or pursue the dream career that they'd always wanted with every fiber of their being, but had been too afraid to go after. To reach for their joy.

It sounded cheesy, overly saccharine. And it was. But it was also *so much more*. Each night, legions of rapt viewers watched the season one star, the innocent, earnest Talia Cruz, try something new to get closer to attaining her dreams. She bravely risked it all, flashing through internships, cities, bad dates, good dates, and hairstyles, happier and happier every time.

But it wasn't incredible because Talia was succeeding at the game. It was incredible because it wasn't a game.

The changes to her life weren't special effects. They were *really happening*. All thanks to the Bubble.

After the first episode concluded, millions of people became armchair physics experts in an instant, of course. *Quantum bubbling* was the official term. It had something to do with "separating observable instances and integrating particles," the scientific literature said. The concept had been discovered a few years before by a private lab, and had only been a theory at that point, something that no one outside of academia had paid much attention to.

Until *All This and More* proved that it clearly wasn't just a theory any-more.

"Look. In a nutshell," an anchor said during the next day's morning newscast, scrambling to be the first to summarize advanced quantum me-chanics to his audience, like he knew what he was talking about, "with enough power and control, you can create iterations of reality branching off from one moment, then collapse them all again once you're done. It's like being able to see the future—all possible versions of it, at once."

The broadcast desk was quiet for a moment.

"You should write the Wikipedia page," the meteorologist finally ribbed.

"It sounds like something out of a sci-fi movie," the sportscaster added, and chugged his mug of coffee.

But even though no one really could explain it, they could see it hap-pening. After every choice Talia made, everything in the Bubble would instantly rearrange itself, entire rooms or buildings or neighborhoods mor-phing into somewhere new in real time, right before their eyes.

It wasn't like magic. It *was* magic.

The entire world cared as much about Talia Cruz as her own family did. More, even. Countless souls wanted her to finally become the passionate, courageous reporter she'd always dreamed of being, even more than they wanted to love their own jobs—not to dread the instant their alarm clocks went off each morning, not to think of the eight hours that always followed as mind-numbing, as soul-crushing. They wanted her to break up with the lazy, free-riding boyfriend who'd been holding her back since college, to reconcile with her long-lost little brother, and to finally travel back with him to visit the place where their mother had been born. They wanted so desperately for her, it eclipsed all else.

Because, deep down, they understood the show's implicit promise. That if Talia could be chosen to radically, miraculously change her life, it meant that, however remotely possible the chance . . .

So, maybe, could *they*.

And when the first season ended and Talia really did finally end up free and ready to find her real Prince Charming, with her family reunited, and in her dream job—as the cheery, darling host of a women's issues talk show—along with everything else she wanted, the cry of celebration that went up around the globe could have registered from space.

Talia Cruz had really done it. She had really turned her life around, and it had stuck.

It was real.

A TV show that could literally *alter the fabric of reality* to change one's life.

No wonder everyone, everywhere was obsessed with the show. No wonder it was all anyone could talk about. No wonder people quit their jobs, gave up their homes, and moved across oceans to attend overpriced workshops to "learn the secrets of getting chosen" with millions of other desperate people, or camped out in the RealTV network parking lot waiting for open auditions. No wonder they would gladly stand in line until they fainted or even died, just for the chance to be a contestant.

Naturally, critics interrogated why such a technology would be wasted on reality TV when it could save the world. But trying to stop war or solve climate change would have been impossible—the Bubble could fit a life, maybe two, but not the entire Earth. Then, the scaremongers declared that the technology was dangerous, or unethical, or even untrue. Was whatever happened inside a quantum bubble real, if it had been manufactured? they asked.

No one listened. No one cared. Who could begrudge the legitimacy of Talia Cruz's new life, or question things like participant consent or the value of authenticity, when they all knew that if they had the chance to be on *All This and More,* they'd take it in a heartbeat?

What was a pesky thing like truth compared to *happiness*?

When season one ended, humanity looked forward to season two more than any other event in modern history.

Except for some reason, season two never came.

Halfway through filming, the whole thing shut down, and the footage couldn't be aired. Technical difficulties, or legal difficulties, the press releases said, the network promising it hadn't given up, that *All This and More* would return soon.

The world waited, restless. Every evening, millions rushed through dinners and scrambled to living rooms to flip fruitlessly through TV channels and scour websites and social media on their phones, searching for news. Days, weeks, months, and still, they waited. As if the show could be willed back into being if they refused to give up hope.

But that deliverance never came.

Until one night, after even the most loyal of fans have stopped believing, it finally did.

It's another unremarkable Friday night. Some are still doing the dishes after mediocre leftovers. More are already on the couch, scrolling mindlessly. Others have just gone to work, to grind through a night shift.

They all hear the music.

"YOU COULD HAVE ALL THIS . . . AND MORE!"

An exuberant voice cries at hysterical volume.

"LIFE is many things—good, bad, steady, unexpected—but we can all agree that each one is UNIQUE. All your experiences, all your choices, have made you the person you are today. But have you ever wondered what you could be doing instead if you'd made a DIFFERENT CHOICE?

"Pursued a different COLLEGE MAJOR?

"Married your HIGH SCHOOL SWEETHEART?

"Or what about gone for the sexy, thrilling ONE-NIGHT STAND a few years ago in that dark, seedy bar, instead of playing it safe and heading home alone?

"We're about to find out!"

Billions are at the TV at once.

Everything else has ceased to exist but those words, that music, this moment.

All This and More is finally, finally back again—and it's the start of the first episode of season three.

A new contestant. A new set of choices. A new chance at perfect.

The frame of every television seems no longer like a portal, but mere decoration.

Almost like there's no edge to where one's life ends and the show begins.

A NEW STAR

"Have you ever had the feeling you've gone down the wrong path?" Talia Cruz asks. "Like somewhere along the way you made a bad choice . . . and wish you could go back?"

The screen fizzles a little, static snow falling lightly for just a moment before the scene crystallizes. Is it the Bubble shaking off the last bits of quantum dust, after such a long break? Or merely an aftereffect added to make the footage more intimate? Whatever the case, it doesn't matter. The important thing about the preshow clips isn't the cinematography or special effects.

It's the star.

The woman in the chair across from Talia puts her hand to her chest. She's dizzy, or maybe sick, with nervousness. Who wouldn't be, when faced with this chance? This impossible dream that, somehow, a person could rewind and do it all over again. Make different choices, fix her mistakes.

That she could somehow really, as the show promises, *change her life.*

"Let's back up. First, we're thrilled you're here, Marsh," Talia gushes, clasping her hands together on top of the pristine glass table. "Can I just tell you how thrilled?"

"Uh," Marsh manages to squeak out. She's always been a bit pale, but the roiling in her stomach has made her cheeks even more blanched than usual, and the harsh studio lights turn her limp brown hair mousy.

Plain, she would say. *Too generous to spend time or money on herself,* her best friend Jo would stubbornly counter.

"Thank you," Marsh splutters at last. "For this opportunity."

Ever the professional, Talia's charming veneer does not crack in the slightest. If anything, her smile patiently widens.

"I love that. So genuine. You remind me of me, on my first day."

Marsh attempts a smile back, but it comes across like mild, embarrassed constipation. She's still not sure how she's actually in the same room as Talia Cruz—likely the most famous person on Earth at this point. It's hard not to stare. Talia is just as tall and graceful as she was in her own season, with the same bronze skin and luxurious golden locks. Her pitch is exquisite, and the conference room doesn't echo, despite being all sharp angles and hard surfaces polished to an eye-watering shine.

"By the way," Talia continues, busy with the papers in her slim folder. "How are you with motion sickness?"

Talia's asking her about the Bubble. About the reality-bending quantum physics that make the jumps through realities actually possible.

Marsh tries to nod.

The giant flatscreen on the wall screeches to life right then.

"Welcome back, folks! After an unexpected season two hiatus, the world's most popular series ever, *All This and More*, finally returns! RealTV is bringing you a season three as explosive and thrilling as our unforgettable season one premiere. There's excitement, there's romance, there's drama, and a whole lot more! Starting right now—"

Suddenly, the awful upbeat music cuts off, and the blaring colors disappear.

"Sorry about that," Talia says, setting down a remote on top of her folder. "That song will get stuck in your head for sure."

It's too late. This show is all Marsh has thought about since the day it premiered, anyway.

But she never expected to actually *be here*.

Over Talia's sharp shoulder, Marsh's reflection gapes back at her from the darkened screen. She has the same expression that she saw on Talia's own face three years ago—back when she was just a nobody, about to step into her first episode. A look of disbelief, of incomprehension. Of being unable to trust something that's too good to be true.

"So." Talia draws her back. "Let's talk about you."

With the attention back on her, Marsh's throat tightens. She blinks rapidly, self-consciously, until her eyes aren't shiny, surprised at her own reaction. Unsure of whether it's terror at being chosen for this, or guilt.

Because she's lucky. She has her daughter, who's healthy and happy. She has a home, and a job that, even if she dreads heading into the office each day, puts food on the table. That's a lot more than some people can say. She should be happy with what she's got. Everything is fine.

Talia is ready for this. "But why are you here, then, Marsh? If everything is fine?" She's using her talk show voice, a musical blend of compassion and firmness. "Why did you enter your information into RealTV's system, for a one-in-a-billion chance to be a contestant on *All This and More*? Why did you answer the call? Why did you come to the studio? Why are you sitting here with me right now?"

She leans in and fixes Marsh with her gorgeous, inescapable gaze.

"Why do you think I chose you?"

Marsh swallows hard.

Maybe she can lie to everyone else—colleagues, friends, family—but she can't lie to Talia Cruz, who knows that subtle, gnawing ache inside her better than anyone else in the world. That creeping dread that this life isn't bad at all, by any measure—but it isn't the one she's supposed to have. She just ended up here. And now it's too late.

Or is it?

"Believe me, I understand what you're feeling," Talia assures her. "How big this moment feels."

She clicks her pen.

"Don't be nervous. Just start from the beginning."

"I . . . I'm not sure what to say," Marsh stammers.

"Marriage. Divorce. Motherhood. The past. The future. Hopes. Fears," Talia offers. "Everything that happened before this that led you to this moment. Everything your loyal viewers need to know."

She points to the words that are somehow materializing in the air between them:

The Recap

The seconds stretch, uncomfortable. Marsh fidgets like prey caught in a wire trap. The option of gnawing off one's foot in exchange for escape seems at least semi-legitimate.

How can a person not even know where to start in her own life?

Maybe it is right that Talia chose her, after all.

"Well . . . my name is Marsh," Marsh finally tries.

Already, the show responds. The smallest flicker as the room seems to contract around her. Whatever Marsh is about to admit, she doesn't want to, and the Bubble knows it. She's curling in on herself, becoming smaller, and it's copying her.

"Actually, Marsh isn't my real name. It's short for Marshmallow—"

She sighs before she scrunches the first two fingers on each hand, to mimic quotation marks for what everyone says.

"Because I'm so sweet and soft."

The music does a little wah-wah.

"Someone started the nickname in high school, and it just kind of stuck," Marsh continues. "Now, my best friend Jo always calls me Marsh, and so do the rest of my friends, and my coworkers. Everyone calls me Marsh, really. No one even remembers my real name anymore. As soon as anyone hears Marsh, that's all they remember. Because I'm so nice."

And boring, she really means.

There are other ostensibly nice things people might say about Marsh, too, she knows. A good friend, for example. Kind and dependable. Always around if you need her.

She's like the best supporting character in a movie ever.

Especially her own.

Marsh winces. "I'm not very good at this."

"Who's Dylan?" Talia prompts, reading from her folder.

"Oh," Marsh says.

Talia grins.

THE RECAP

THE SPARK

The studio's stationary camera slowly zooms in on Marsh as the lights dim. Talia is still sitting across the table, but Marsh feels that she might as well be on an island, alone in the middle of an ocean. The music softens; the corners grow fuzzy.

Marsh looks down.

"Dylan, Dylan, Dylan," she says to herself, and shakes her head. "Even after everything that's happened, I still get butterflies when I think back to the first moment I saw him."

The Bubble reacts, and a soft glow begins to gently throb around them. This is why they do the recap, Marsh knows. To customize the Bubble to the star. But to feel it happening around her in real time is like magic.

The glow sharpens, until a forest scene comes into view on the flatscreen in front of her. Lush, crisp pine, the sound of rushing wind, and a helpful caption.

It was twenty-five years ago, on a camping trip Marsh's sophomore year of college at Arizona State. A bunch of her classmates had driven four hours north to the woods of Flagstaff during break.

Marsh stares at her memories as they manifest, spellbound.

"Are you ready for this?" Mateo cries on the screen, clearly more excited than almost anyone else about this. They're all on the cold, clear shore of a lake, ready to attempt kayaking in several of the little boats some of the guys had brought strapped to the roofs of their cars. The sun is high and white, and Marsh has put too much sunscreen on.

"You bet," a younger, even shyer version of her replies beside him, trying to sound convincing.

She and her best friend Jo knew Mateo from a class their first semester of college, before he changed to another dormitory. He'd invited the two of them on this camping trip because, in his words, prelaw students were more fun than physics majors. Marsh knew that he really meant that Jo was more fun than physics majors, but that the two of them came as a package deal, they'd been inseparable since they'd first met in Intro to Constitutional Law, and so if he invited Jo, he had to invite Marsh, too.

A lot of things in Marsh's life had been like that. By that point in university, she'd started turning down some of the offers and letting Jo go alone, because it was just too embarrassing. But this is one time she'll always be grateful that she let Jo talk her into coming on the trip.

Because it was this day that she met Dylan.

"Hey, there you are!" Mateo is shouting, waving at someone across the crowded, rocky beach.

There he is.

On-screen, their eyes meet. For a moment, her younger self forgets to breathe or blink. Marsh watches the moment with equal intensity.

"We've been waiting on you for half an hour! How long does it take to put on a bathing suit?" Mateo continues to tease, oblivious. Somehow, he doesn't notice that Marsh and Dylan are just staring at each other, and not listening to him at all.

"Hi," Dylan finally says.

He's a little taller than Marsh, with dark skin and a jock-ish, cool buzzed head. He's so handsome, he looks like he could have been a high school quarterback, or a prom king.

"Holy mackerel," Talia whispers as a character insight bubble appears on the flatscreen, in exactly the same adorable tone she used whenever something fantastic happened her own season—two little words that became her beloved signature catchphrase by the finale. "That guy's a scientist?"

DYLAN LEE: *Mischievous, full of life, and a physics geek through and through, even if he's quite a looker! Everyone always said that Dylan was a little out of Marsh's league when they started dating, but the two lovebirds proved the world wrong and got married! For years, things were absolutely perfect. But somewhere along the way, something happened . . .*

"I'm Dylan. Mateo's roommate," recap-Dylan finally says.

Young Marsh is trying not to melt, and mostly failing. "I'm—" she starts to reply.

"This is Marsh!" Jo cries before she can finish, appearing in a burst of laughter and thundering of giant yellow life jackets. She's a ball of energy, short yet still gangly, almost like a little spider, with skin even darker than Dylan's and a spiky black pixie cut. She drapes an arm over Marsh's shoulder and offers one of the vests looped in her fingers to Dylan.

"Marsh?" Dylan asks, taking the life jacket from Jo, but his eyes never leave Marsh's.

"It's short for Marshmallow," Jo explains to him as Marsh—both of them, young and old—wince inwardly. "Because you'll never meet anyone sweeter. She's the best person we know."

"Marsh," Dylan repeats, as if considering the word, as Jo slides a vest over Marsh's head, winks, and then spins off again toward another circle of classmates.

"It's an old joke," Marsh says as soon as she's gone.

"I like it," he replies.

"It's dumb," Marsh says.

"It's not," he insists. "It's a good thing to be known for." He smiles. "Hardly anyone is kind anymore. Especially lawyers."

Hearing him say it like that again—so quietly and intensely, while staring deep into young Marsh's eyes—makes older Marsh soften. It was the first time she'd ever felt like, for once, being herself was actually kind of cool. Like she didn't have to try to be edgier, or tougher, or more fashionable, or any of that. She could just be herself. And someone might like that self.

Marsh ends up in Mateo's kayak, so she spends the afternoon paddling around with him right next to Dylan and another friend of theirs from the physics department, who's much better than Dylan at kayaking and the only reason the two of them stay upright and dry. But even though Dylan is a terrible oarsman, he's having the time of his life. He spends the whole outing playing jokes, or pretending to fall or drop his paddle, and Marsh and his friends laugh so hard that she cries.

Marsh wants to stay right by Dylan, to spend every moment of the rest of the weekend together, but she loses track of him while climbing out of the kayaks and dragging them up onto the gravelly beach. And then, she gets roped into helping set up the plastic folding chairs in front of the campfire, and then into putting out all the supplies for the group dinner around the flames, and then . . .

By the time she's done, people are ready to start cooking and eating, and then Marsh is cooking and eating, too, and trying to look like she's paying attention and laughing at Jo's jokes instead of letting her gaze desperately wander the crowd, searching for Dylan like a pathetic, lost child.

She'd been so sure that there had been a spark, the moment the two of them met. It was there in how his eyes locked on her, in how close he stood when they had been talking. It was electric. A finger in a socket, a lightning storm.

But then where was he?

Marsh and Talia watch the party feast on hot dogs, corn on the cob, and beer when dusk falls. Afterward, young Marsh moves from group to group with Jo, letting the chatter distract her until it's dark and people start to settle into smaller, quieter conversations for the night. Eventually, she finds herself standing alone by the fire for a moment, watching the orange light dance as she soaks in the warm glow.

"Well, hello there," Dylan says as he sidles up beside Marsh. "Enjoying the fire?"

At the sound of his voice, everything else falls away from the recap for a second. The forest, the flickering flames, the laughter coming from all around the campsite.

"It's nice," young Marsh finally manages, once she looks sure that she's in control of her heart rate again. "I heard there will be s'mores, later."

"I heard that, too," he agrees.

In the background of the scene, Jo begins to head back toward Marsh from the cluster of girls she'd been talking to, slows as she recognizes Dylan, and then smoothly re-angles her direction toward another group of friends with a subtle, cheeky nod to Marsh.

"Did you have a fun afternoon, after the lake?" Marsh adds to him, trying to sound nonchalant.

"Nope," Dylan replies. He hesitates, then drops his voice. "I just wanted to be hanging out with you."

Marsh blinks, surprised and thrilled at the same time.

"But—but I didn't see you after the kayaks," she stammers.

"Yeah, I know." He rubs the back of his head sheepishly. "I was trying to play it cool."

Marsh turns and locks eyes with him at last.

"Pretty dumb, huh?" he asks, laughing. "I just didn't want to blow my chances with you by seeming overeager."

Marsh is now blushing so hard that she's lost the upper hand, but she can't help it. "I don't think you have to worry about blowing your chances," she finally says.

At that, Dylan's nervous grin gets a little less nervous, and a little more playful. He reaches behind himself, to where he must have already set some supplies down on a folding chair before he made his move.

"This is for you," he continues, and offers Marsh a thin, straight stick for roasting s'mores.

"Thank you," she replies shyly, taking it from him.

"And so's this."

Both Marshes look down. In his other hand is a little, puffy white shape.

"A marshmallow." He winks. "For Marsh."

He's leaning in, so close that the soft exhale of his breath stirs a loose curl of her hair.

"It's a dumb name," Marsh says again, too nervous to think of anything else.

"I like it," he insists again, as well. "I really do."

"That makes one of us," she tries to joke.

Dylan scoots even closer. "What if I secretly call you Mallow, then?" he asks, barely a whisper.

"Mallow?" Marsh repeats.

"You know. Marsh. Mallow. Same name, but different. It could be our thing."

Our thing. Her heart thrills.

Marsh manages to nod just before he kisses her.

Marsh watches, mesmerized, as she and Dylan talk about everything that night, huddled together at the edge of the campfire. Childhoods, hobbies, travel, future dreams. Long after everyone has gone to bed—even Jo, who was always the last one up—the two of them are still there, knees pressed together, whispering and giggling. At one point, a corner of the marshmallow Marsh has skewered over the fire catches the flame and begins to burn, which makes her shriek. She tries to save it, but Dylan just laughs, grabs her hands on her stick, and thrusts them a little farther forward, so the marshmallow is pushed straight back into the blaze.

The poor little white puff goes up in a glorious, bubbling explosion of sugar and flames as he kisses her again—just like her heart.

"I was so young then. My whole life ahead of me," Marsh says to Talia, and her young self. "It was like anything could happen."

A few years later, on a walk through Central Park in New York one balmy April morning, it even still felt that way when she turned around

from studying the flowers at Azalea Pond and saw Dylan not standing behind her, but rather down on one knee, holding a little velvet box.

In fact, it felt even *more* like that. Like her life had only expanded, not
narrowed. Like it would go on expanding forever, as long as she and Dylan
stayed together.

"Congratulations, Marshy!" Jo screams with glee as she bursts from the
foliage on-screen—Dylan had planted her in the bushes ahead of time with
her camera and a bottle of champagne, to capture the moment for them.
She practically throws the bottle at him so he can pour for them all. "I already have ideas for the bachelorette party!"

"Do you still have that picture that Jo took?" Talia asks her. "That perfect
day?"

"I do," Marsh says.

What she does not say is that it's no longer in its gold frame on the mantel above the fireplace, next to the other pictures of her and Dylan, or the
candids of the whole family together—everyone midlaugh because their
black Lab, Pickle, messed up the shot by bounding into the frame just before the shutter clicked.

She took it down and put it in the box that she then shoved at the back
of her closet, after Dylan had finished packing his things and left for the
last time.

There's a shudder, as if Marsh can't bear to think about that moment any-more, and the recap suddenly shifts backward.

Now on-screen is an even slightly younger Marsh, perhaps in her first year of university. She's wandering around her college library. The vast hall is quiet, and she's moving slowly through the towering stacks, her finger-tips brushing the spines of every book she passes. She looks bewitched, enchanted, by what they all might contain within.

"I remember this. My very first day as a freshman," Marsh says as she watches her former self, her eyes full of wonder as she relives that moment. "I went to meet my academic counselor, and then I walked to the study abroad office. By lunchtime, I had a stack of eight textbooks for prelaw, and three flyers for exchange programs—Mexico, Iceland, and Hong Kong. They were my most prized possessions."

"That's a lot of places!" Talia laughs, and so does Marsh.

"I'd been itching to get out of my hometown since I was old enough to read, and all those places sounded like the complete opposite of where I'd come from," she shrugs. "Latin America seemed so vibrant and musical, the Nordics so mysterious and remote, and Asia so huge and chaotic, like it could swallow me whole. I thought that if I could make it there, I could make it anywhere."

"Sounds more like you wanted to be a travel agent than anything else," Talia jokes.

Marsh laughs, but quiets again as she reflects. "I'd been in love with law since middle school, actually. That sounds corny, but it's true. I liked the idea of trying to find the truth at the heart of something."

She ponders that for a moment.

"Maybe that's also why Dylan likes physics so much," she finally murmurs.

"Let's stay in the scene," Talia prompts. She softens her expression until her forehead has the faintest empathetic crinkle, and her eyes peer deep into Marsh's soul as the recap screen waits for a prompt. "Dylan proposed after university, the two of you got married, you started law school . . . and then what happened?"

At that question, Marsh can't stop the smile that spreads across her lips.

"Harper," she says, as a faint beeping begins in the background of the recap. It almost sounds like a little alarm.

Or a hospital monitor.

Suddenly, the lights go down, and the suggestion of a flock of nurses—the rustle of blue scrubs, the snap of latex gloves, the squeak of sneakers on linoleum floor—swirls around Marsh and Talia.

"After I stabilized and woke up, Dylan told me about the bleeding," Marsh finally says. "They caught it in time, and everything was fine in the end, but it was really touch-and-go for a bit. I remember talking with him one minute, and the next, he said that my eyes were rolling back in my head and they were dragging him away from my bed and pushing it out the door to the surgery wing, everyone shouting and all the monitors screaming at once."

Talia is clutching her hands to her chest, both terrified and enthralled as she listens.

"It was worth it," Marsh says when she sees Talia's expression. This is something she feels absolutely, unshakably certain of, if of nothing else in her life. "I'd do it a thousand times again."

"Hello, little Harper," young Marsh says as she pulls the bundle in her arms closer to her, and a little nose peeks forth from the soft fabric to nuzzle her own. "Welcome to the world."

Beside her, Dylan is perched on the bed. His eyes are shining, huge and fierce and wet. "Happy birthday, baby girl," he whispers, his voice thick.

HARPER LEE: *Marsh and Dylan's daughter, and the light of Marsh's life. She's whip-smart, kind, and responsible, even for a teenager—the perfect kid! Harper's greatest passion is music, especially classical violin. Her dream would be to attend the prestigious Pallissard Institute of Music, the best high school music conservatory in the country, but she knows that her parents can't afford it.*

"But," Talia gently nudges Marsh, who's caught up in the recap footage playing over her head, staring so intently that she's forgetting to continue her story, "a law student with dreams of joining one of the top firms in the country couldn't take an extended recovery and maternity leave with the bar exam looming."

"She couldn't pump during training, either, or skip court if her daughter came down with the flu in preschool," Marsh agrees. "Things had to change."

Then she looks down and sighs.

"Or maybe they didn't change at all. Maybe I'm just using it as an excuse, and I never would have done any of it anyway."

"Are you sure?" Talia asks softly.

Marsh shrugs. "I don't know. But I went and got all those flyers years before I married Dylan, and even more years before Harper was born."

She looks up at Talia.

"But did I go to any of those places I dreamed that I would go? Did I refuse to give up my career? Or did I just let it all go, because that was easier, was less scary, than trying?"

Talia lets the pause linger, full of regret.

"What about Dylan? Did he consider scaling back his own career once Harper came along?" she asks at last.

"I didn't want him to," Marsh says. "He was right in the middle of his PhD at that point. He'd been working so hard for so long, researching full-time and working night shifts at a private lab all to cover the bills, just to give it up then."

She turns and looks again at baby Harper and a young Dylan holding her, and smiles.

"It wasn't totally fair, but maybe it didn't have to be, I thought at the time," she says.

"And Dylan agreed?"

Marsh laughs a little. "Dylan was so shaken by the close call that he couldn't think straight. He just agreed with whatever I said." Her expression grows a little more serious. "I've never seen him so afraid as that day at the hospital," she says. "And never have again."

"Not even once?" Talia asks.

Marsh looks at her for a long time.

There can be no secrets, no matter how painful, she knows. The Bubble has to learn everything about her life if there's any hope of her fixing it.

Talia's voice is soft, but firm. "Not even years later, on the night that you caught him in the act, and he knew that your marriage was truly, irrevocably over?"

Marsh is silent. She looks down, and then turns back to the recap. She watches the three of them in an artfully faint sepia tone as they do the little things together—Harper's first sponge bath, Harper's first word, Harper's first steps.

"That doesn't happen for a long time," she finally says.

And before that, there would be a lot of good times. The trips they'd take together as a family, the memories they'd make. Dylan would go from being hopeless in the kitchen to a surprisingly competent cook. Marsh would come in with Harper from her music lessons and find him putting the finishing touches on a meal he'd made after sneaking out early from work, just to see her smile. The notes he'd leave telling her what he loved most about her, the flowers he'd pick if he walked home through the park instead of driving. The way his voice would get soft and his eyes misty when he talked about how it would be when the two of them were wrinkled and old, together.

Marsh admits that sometimes, at night, she'd go into the living room to find him fast asleep on the couch, Harper dozing in his long arms with the exact same expression on her face, and she'd be so overwhelmed with happiness, such pure and engulfing joy, that she'd briefly worry she might be dying. Like the love was too much for her body to physically bear.

"I thought I could never want more than that moment," Marsh whispers as she watches.

"Some doors slam loudly as they close on you, and others click shut so quietly that you don't realize they're gone for years," Talia prompts her.

"This one was one of the quiet ones," Marsh says. "I didn't regret it for a long time. A very long time."

Talia nods knowingly. "Until . . . ?"

Marsh sighs. "Until Jo made partner at Mendoza-Montalvo and Hall."

As Marsh talks, a montage of scenes from a work celebration smatters the space above and behind her head. There are party hats and glasses of bubbly and trays of hors d'oeuvres going around a luxurious conference room, and everyone is crowded around Jo, who appears to be giving an impromptu thank-you speech at the front of the room as her own character insight bubble finally appears.

JOANNA HALL: *Marsh's best friend, and a force of nature. Jo's a risk-taker, a heartbreaker. She and Marsh met on the first day of college, and have been inseparable ever since, despite the very different paths their lives have taken. Jo may be Marsh's polar opposite, now a high-flying partner at the firm they both work for while Marsh is stuck as a paralegal, but she's also as loyal as they come, and will do anything to help her friend find happiness.*

A distinguished man with tan skin, silver hair, and a suit that looks like it cost more than a car joins Jo at the front of the conference room just as

Marsh, carrying a tray with a giant cake on it, bumps open the door with her hip in the corner of the shot. There's just enough time to catch sight of her expression as she looks around the party before another caption pops up beneath the same man now raising a glass to Jo.

VICTOR MENDOZA-MONTALVO: *Marsh's boss at Mendoza-Montalvo and Hall. Tough, ambitious, and with a jaw that could cut glass. Marsh has been working as his head paralegal for decades now, appreciated but invisible—can she prove her abilities to him and finally get the promotion she's always dreamed of on* All This and More?

"I set that cake down, saw Jo's name on it, and I finally realized that I had made a huge mistake by giving it all up." Marsh looks away from the montage, down at her hands. "And that it was too late to fix it. I'd lost too much time. And then . . ."

Talia leans in. "And then?"

The music changes, growing quieter, more sinister.

Marsh grimaces.

"And then . . ."

THAT NIGHT

Marsh knows where she has to go now.

She doesn't want to, but she has to. She can't just show the good, she knows a shrewd, talented journalist-celebrity-goddess like Talia would tell her. She has to show the bad, too. *That's what puts the "real" in "reality TV."*

The image on the screen has shifted. Harper is a young teenager, and Marsh is firmly middle-aged, the way she is now as she sits beside Talia. She and Dylan have been married twenty years.

"Time is strange like that," Marsh says to Talia as she watches. She tries to ignore that helpless feeling creeping up on her, of knowing what's coming but being unable to change it because it's already happened. "It all seemed so unique at the time, but in the end, what did I do, really? I went to work, did the laundry, went on vacations, had sex, had a kid, had slightly less sex. Went to work more, did more laundry, went on more vacations, and had even *less* sex. Everything and nothing happened, for two decades."

She sighs.

"You know, Dylan had this saying," she finally continues.

"He called you Mallow?" Talia prompts.

"He did." Marsh hesitates. "But he had another one, too. 'You gotta light it on fire sometimes'—the 'it' being a marshmallow skewered on the campfire stick of life, of course. We were having an argument about money, or a trip, or spicing it up in the bedroom, or something. It was funny in the moment, the first time. But over the years, it sort of became our marriage's unfortunate refrain."

Talia clucks her tongue. "Surely, Dylan wasn't perfect, either."

"No, he wasn't," Marsh agrees. "He was a little bit of a workaholic. Impatient. A nitpicker. He was always pushing for something, and I was always trying to keep it the same. I thought I was balancing him out. But now I think . . . maybe he was right."

She looks up at Talia.

"I mean, that's why I'm here now, aren't I? Because I missed every chance I ever had to 'light it on fire'?"

The background behind Marsh morphs. The recap version of her is sitting in a car, parked in the dark of night at the curb of the community college where Dylan works.

"I remember stopping at every stop sign on the drive there, and looking both ways before rolling through," Marsh says. She chuckles, hoping for insouciance, but the sound is hollow. "As if being especially good right then might have made a difference. Might somehow have made things go my way, at the last second. But of course, it didn't."

Recap-Marsh sits in the run-down parking lot with the engine off for what seems like forever, working up the courage to climb out.

Finally, the frame pans. There are only two other cars there with her at that late hour, parked right next to each other in the darkness at the other end of the lot.

One is Dylan's old Volkswagen.

The other—well.

"Our anniversary was that week," Marsh finally tells Talia. Her stomach is slick, roiling. "Twenty was such a big, respectable number. I was proud of that number. It felt like some kind of proof." She swallows. "That we were happy. That the marriage was good. That I'd made the right choice all those years ago."

The truth is, things had not been happy or good for a long time.

Marsh had never returned to school after all. She never graduated, never took the bar, never got a chance to practice law. And as for her travel dreams, she and Dylan did visit Mexico for their sixth anniversary—but Harper was just a newborn then, and Marsh was in full new-mother caution mode, panicking over every little cough or sneeze—she didn't even try the resort-guided scuba dive, within the safety of their man-made lagoon, let alone leave the beaten path to explore the vibrant cities, try all the exciting food, or take in the nightlife.

Marsh swore they'd go back one day and she'd really dig in. But of course, once Harper started school, the budget got even tighter, and time seemed to move even faster.

She never managed to visit Iceland or Hong Kong, either.

Everything she'd wanted for her life—none of it happened.

The marshmallow had never even gotten *near* the fire.

And with that, the montage swirls to reveal the scene.

The empty lobby of the community college is too bright, too revealing.

Marsh watches herself hesitate at the elevator, unable to decide if she wants to ride up or sprint out of the building.

"What am I doing?" the Marsh in the recap whispers to herself desperately. She presses the UP button again, and then jams the button a third time, frantic.

Finally, she notices the little gold-plated sign on the door.

TAKE STAIRS AFTER HOURS.

The elevators power down at night to conserve electricity.

Below the footage of herself cursing at her luck, Marsh shakes her head and manages a rueful smile.

"Now that I think about it, it's kind of funny. Dylan is actually the reason I even know about *All This and More*," she says. "He's the one who told me about it in the first place. Not just the show, but the science behind it, too. Quantum bubbling."

Most people first heard the words *quantum bubbling* the night of Talia's season premiere, but the concept had been discovered years before scientists figured out how to make it actually work as part of *All This and More*.

"I couldn't have cared less," Marsh continues. "What did some physics theory have to do with getting a kid to school on time every morning, or with eight hours of pushing paper around at Mendoza-Montalvo and Hall every day?"

"But to Dylan . . ." Talia leads her.

"His whole world was physics," Marsh nods. "To him, this was the discovery of a lifetime."

"This could change quantum theories. It could change *everything*," Dylan babbles in a quick jump cut to their kitchen, as recap-Marsh fusses with the oven and he paces the room. He's supposed to be helping with dinner, but he's so excited, he just keeps picking up utensils and setting them down instead of stirring whatever he's supposed to stir, and knocking things over as he tries to explain the news. The real Marsh almost looks away—it's jarring to suddenly see him so chatty, so intimate, again. "It's huge! A whole new reality! It's like, imagine if the butterfly effect were real. Any theory, any idea, you could test it out, infinite times!"

"Will it help me with the dishes?" recap-Marsh replies to him, snatching the spatula before the vegetables burn. The real Marsh doesn't have to look to remember how far his face fell.

"This is bigger than dishes," Dylan says as the quick shot fades out, but his voice is already quieter than before.

"You're too hard on yourself," Talia says once the screen is dark.

"Still. I could have feigned more interest," Marsh replies. "His students didn't really care, either. Quantum bubbling just seemed too abstract at the time. After a few weeks of impromptu lectures on the subject, he gave up trying to convince a bunch of budding photographers and creative writing freshmen, and me, how cool this new discovery really was."

She shrugs at her own naïveté.

"But then, about five years later . . . your first season premiered, Talia."

The screen pulses to life again, and now Harper, thirteen years old, is helping Marsh feed Pickle his evening meal when Dylan comes barreling through the front door, his eyes wild with excitement.

"It had been years since I'd last seen that look on his face," Marsh says, below the image. "I couldn't remember the last time I'd seen him at home in the evening, period. He'd already been stretching his hours at work for years by then, to avoid the inevitable, awful silence of the dinner table."

"Girls! Turn on the TV!" Dylan cries excitedly as Pickle comes crashing straight into his shins at the commotion, a big, black barking cannonball.

It turns out, earlier that day he'd run into an old colleague from his PhD studies, a physicist named Lev Hoffman, who had told him about *All This and More.*

Dylan didn't like reality TV, but this show was going to be different, Lev had assured him. It was going to be *big.* As Dylan describes their conversation, the studio around Marsh begins to glow with a particular hue of purple that she, and everyone else in the world, knows very well.

Sharp Purple.

Dylan tells Marsh that Lev works for the privately funded Sharp Labs, part of Claire Sharp Incorporated, the colossal corporate empire wealthier than most nations that had originally discovered the concept that made the whole show possible: quantum bubbling. And he's the lead scientist for the first season.

"I remember Lev!" Talia says fondly. "He was a darling. I wish he were still with the crew for you this year."

"Just watch the first episode," recap-Dylan is saying to Marsh and Harper as he pulls them toward the couch. "Then you'll see."

They all watched the whole season together, that last year Marsh and

Dylan were still married. The screen shows her, Dylan, Harper, and Pickle all huddled together on the couch, the adults with glasses of wine and Harper sharing her popcorn with Pickle, but Marsh doesn't need to look to remember it.

It was, oddly, one of the best times they had with each other, right there at the end. She and Dylan would barely talk, barely even touch each other—by that point in the relationship, an accidental graze of a hand or a foot in bed came with an actual apology—but that one night a week, he'd be home on time, and they'd settle in like a perfect, happy family to watch *All This and More*. Even though they were paying attention to the TV and not to each other, it had felt like, briefly, the show made them more present. Or perhaps not *even though*, but *because*. The show gave them an excuse, it let them pretend. It was about a different life, different choices, not their own.

"It was almost like being in love again, those nights," Marsh admits to Talia. "And when your season ended, I couldn't wait for season two to start. I thought that if it could come soon enough, maybe Dylan and I could keep hold of this new feeling a little longer. That maybe things could . . ."

But then season two never came.

"I don't know what happened, either," Talia says.

"It doesn't matter, I guess," Marsh replies. "By the time Sharp had announced that they couldn't air the season, but promised they'd return soon with another, it was too late."

She turns to the flashback footage, which has returned to the community college lobby. She watches herself pushing open the door to the stairwell, and staring up at the dark journey ahead.

"I was already here."

It's a long, awful climb. Seven flights later, Marsh arrives to the right floor sweaty, panting, and embarrassed. This was no way to confront a cheating husband! She wanted to be steely, cool. She wanted it to be his dignity that was shattered, not hers. She can't do that with her bangs clinging to her forehead and her shirt all twisted around from the climb.

Before emerging from the stairwell, she takes her compact mirror out of her purse and fixes herself.

Somehow, this makes it even more painful.

The hallway is just as long as she remembered. That feeling returns again. That she could just turn around, climb back down. Pretend that she didn't know *for sure*, pretend that her marriage was okay, or would eventually be.

As long as she didn't look at a thing head-on, maybe it didn't have to be real. But her feet won't obey, and they just keep marching her down the hall, carrying her toward his office.

She thought the door would be locked.

It was not.

"I don't need to watch it again," Marsh says, looking at her hands instead of the footage.

The recap gives only snatches of movement, a flash of arm or a glimpse across a back, but it was Dylan's eyes that stunned her the most, that night.

They were big and dark, like two black holes, as he moved on top of the outline of this other woman. Like it wasn't even him behind them anymore, like he'd gone somewhere else entirely and it was just a body there, a thrusting, throbbing tapestry of muscles and nerves and sex. No agency, no guilt, even. Those two swallowing, drowning pools. So deep that he couldn't clamor back to the surface of them before Marsh fled from the doorway, tears streaming down her face as she ran.

"And just like that, everything was over," Marsh finally says as the recap goes dark. "Everything we'd worked to build, everything we still had wanted to do. Two decades of history, thrown out like trash."

But also, she couldn't have done anything else. Once she knew, she couldn't have just kept pretending it was all fine, or would be again. Even without the affair, it had not been fine for years.

"I know what happened wasn't my fault," Marsh continues. "But I still felt like I deserved it, in a way. Because even if Dylan hadn't blown everything apart . . . I still was never going to have that life I wanted anyway. I still wasn't going to do all the things I'd dreamed about. Every year, I promised myself I would make a change, I would do something, and I never did. I just kept letting it slip by."

She looks down.

"It was my choice, every time—and I never chose myself."

"Sorry," Dylan says, suddenly back on-screen, and awkwardly clears his throat.

He and Marsh are on opposite sides of the kitchen island six weeks later, a cold pot of coffee between them. The divorce papers are open in front of her, the pen still in her hand. The ink of his signature is already drying on the left line.

In the studio, Marsh's eyes alight on the bandage on his hand. *A small burn from grilling burgers, nothing to worry about,* he'd grumbled when she asked. She'd spent weeks furious about that bandage, making herself sick imagining all the possibilities. He actually singed the skin at the stove trying to impress some new fling with his manly cooking skills. He tried to light a bunch of candles for a romantic tryst and got clumsy. Even, maybe, trying to make campfire s'mores to flirt with someone else.

It wouldn't have mattered if it had been six weeks or six years later, he was always going to move on faster than her. It's easy to be first when the other person never moves at all.

"I can leave the papers here if you want more time. It's just that band rehearsal starts in an hour, and I'm helping with snacks," Dylan finally murmurs, as if ashamed.

The two of them had agreed that the most important thing was Harper. Marsh didn't want him to let her down his first time cheering her on solo. Each of them had to be both parents now for everything, on each of their turns.

"Right," recap-Marsh replies. "You can't be late for that."

She signs.

The recap screen is dark for a beat, to let the somber scene sink in. Talia doesn't prompt Marsh for once, letting her have her space.

Finally, the area behind her begins to glow again, and eventually, Marsh appears sitting on her couch, her best friend Jo next to her, the coffee table in front of them covered in half-empty Chinese take-out containers.

"You don't have to actually go out with any of them if you don't want to," Jo insists as she offers an egg roll. "Just make a profile and message some of them."

By the end of that miserable year, our dear Marsh had finally stopped randomly bursting into tears whenever she thought of Dylan, but in place of that raw agony had settled a kind of cold, immovable numbness that was almost worse. She couldn't enjoy food; she couldn't have fun with friends; she couldn't even smile. And her job, which she already didn't love but was paying the bills, was on the rocks, because she could barely concentrate. Even Jo was at a loss as to what to do. Worst of all, sweet Harper was becoming affected, unsure of how to handle her mother's crushing unhappiness.

"You know, when she was a baby, I used to think that Harper had gotten more of my personality than Dylan's," Marsh tells Talia, avoiding most of the scrolling caption. "She was such a gentle, sweet child, even when she was upset about something. But the older Harper has gotten, she's become more and more like him."

"Is that bad?" Talia asks.

"No, not at all!" Marsh cries. "I'm glad she has some of Dylan in her, to balance her out."

It's not diplomacy. She means it. Harper is a teenager, so she's still awkward and shy, but there's a sharper streak to her now. When she's practicing violin, her eyes glow with focus just like her father's do when he's talking about physics, and she frowns exactly the same way when Marsh is annoying her.

And she seems to be annoying her more and more lately.

"Every parent of an adolescent worries about that," Talia soothes when she admits it.

Marsh gives her a polite smile. "It shouldn't be her job to take care of me, it should be the other way around," she says. "I'm worried . . . I'm worried we're slowly starting to grow apart."

She is. But it's more than just that.

Before, her daughter was too young to see Marsh as anything but a mother. But now, she's old enough to also start to see her as a woman.

And Marsh is worried that all she sees is a timid, unadventurous one.

"Fine, just *look* at their pictures," Jo bargains in the flashback. "You don't even have to send a message!"

She's talking about LoveMatch, of course. The worst, and only, place for Marsh to go to start dating again.

"Just flirt a little," Jo urges. "See what's out there."

"I don't care what's out there," Marsh replies stubbornly, but it's a lie. Maybe it wasn't at first—Marsh couldn't imagine even *looking* at another man after Dylan, let alone more—but eventually, the ghost of desire always returns.

"Not even a little?" Jo teases. "Come on. I saw the way you looked at the Chinese food delivery dude just now."

"So, he was cute," Marsh fumes back. "That's not a crime!"

"Neither is downloading LoveMatch." Jo stares her down. "I can tell you want to. You just want permission."

"Fine, I want to," recap-Marsh groans.

But it wasn't Jo's permission she needed.

"Mom," Harper's voice interrupts right then.

Both Marshes look up to see a teenage Harper standing in the hallway in the footage, staring at her mother with her arms crossed, and the recap music stops dead, just like Marsh's heart did the first time through this moment. How the world could live in a single sigh or laugh, a roll of Harper's eye.

Who knew if Dylan was still seeing whoever had been in his office that night, or if he was seeing anyone at all. But to Marsh, it didn't matter.

It only mattered that Marsh was considering dating again, and that Harper had heard *her*.

Then, mercifully, Harper giggles at Marsh's horror-stricken face, and all the color comes back into the scene.

"Listen to Jo. Sign up for LoveMatch already," Harper says. "I dare you."

"So I did," Marsh tells Talia as they sit below the recap. "I signed up. Actually, I remember as I waited for the download to finish that for the first time in years, I actually did feel the tiniest, most tentative flicker of hope."

"Just to see what's out there," on-screen Marsh tries to convince herself. She uploads some photos, and sets her profile to "active."

Talia looks inquisitively at the Marsh across from her.

She shakes her head. "It was . . . absolute hell."

The music screeches as a collage of mortifyingly awful messages from potential suitors flood the screen, hundreds of little bubbles whose words could curl hair.

"I went on probably a hundred first dates," Marsh says, her voice flat and lifeless, as the montage finally selects one such evening to play out. "Each one was worse than the last."

She sits alone as the restaurant swirls around her, an appetizer untouched. Stood up, or the guy left before they'd even ordered—they all run together. Marsh stares at the empty chair, and at the next table, a young man gasps with joy as another young man gets down on one knee and holds up a little velvet box, and the whole restaurant applauds.

She opens up her phone to delete the app.

"But there must have been *someone* good out there," Talia prompts desperately, as if she can stop recap-Marsh from doing it. "A diamond in the rough!"

"There was," Marsh admits. "Just one."

As recap-Marsh studies her phone, the embarrassing music and garish colors shift into a gentler, optimistic hue of Sharp Purple.

Talia cocks her head and raises an inviting eyebrow.

Marsh gets the prompt. "It's the reason I'm sitting here today, really," she says as a swirl of pixels crystallizes into a dramatic caption.

After a hellish, seemingly endless year on LoveMatch suffering through the worst, most pathetic dates she'd ever been on . . .

The words scrawl themselves over recap-Marsh's face as she tosses away her crumpled tissue to bring her phone closer, and her expression changes from devastated to perplexed—and then, even happy.

. . . Something miraculous finally, finally happened in Marsh's life.

Marsh looks directly into the camera, at Talia's prompting. "Ren Kurosaki sent me a wink," she says.

REN KUROSAKI: *Marsh's high school sweetheart—cue the nostalgia! If Jo is Marsh's polar opposite, then Ren is definitely Dylan's foil. He's everything Dylan is not: softer, sweeter, more adoring. From the first instant, it was love* *at first sight for Ren. By the end of high school, their classmates joked that he wasn't Marsh's boyfriend, but rather her shadow!*

Is he still the same devoted guy, all these years later? Can Marsh find new love with an old flame?

Ren is already at the bar they've chosen for a first date, and when he looks up as she walks in, he nearly falls off the stool.

"It's been a long time," Marsh says.

"It has," he agrees. She's trying to be smooth, but he's grinning at her. A real, excited smile, not a polite one. "But you haven't changed at all."

Marsh smirks a little as she watches herself pretend not to notice how nervous Ren is. How his hand shakes just a bit as he reaches for his drink, or how he stammers for a second when he tells her how nice she looks. Ren is maybe not quite as handsome as Dylan, but he's cute in his own way. And more importantly, he's *different.* So present, so happy to be with her.

"I know we were young, but I'd always thought we were meant to be," Ren admits on-screen, more relaxed now, after their second drink. "Whatever happened between us, back then?"

"Graduation," Marsh says.

Marsh and Ren dated for two years, but when he only got into a local community college in their little hometown of Beaumont, Texas, and she won a small scholarship to Arizona State University, Marsh's parents urged her to accept, even though it would mean leaving him behind. "That was just puppy love," they told her. "This is your future."

"I was so crushed!" Ren laughs at himself as the caption fades. "I remember thinking it was the end of the world!"

Marsh pushes down a tiny thrill and steals a bite off his plate with her fork to see what he'll do. He pushes his food even closer to her.

"So," she continues, encouraged, "I thought you were still living in Beaumont."

Ren shakes his head. "Finally got myself outta there. Took me a little longer than you, but who's keeping score?"

Marsh smiles. "And you're a journalist here in Phoenix?"

"Phoenix and elsewhere—wherever the story is. But say 'investigative reporter.'" He winks. "It sounds sexier like that."

"It does," Talia agrees, and winks back.

The rest comes out over another round of drinks—and then another.

The two of them stay until the restaurant closes, the last ones on the recap screen.

He graduated with some useless degree, Ren tells Marsh, and then promptly left the country. He traveled all over as a backpacker at first, but after he realized he wasn't too bad at writing, he began searching for stories he might be able to sell. The thrills, the close calls, the funny moments—she watches herself hang on every word. Even though it was a little grungy at the start, his life has been so exciting, so dynamic, so interesting. He even managed to write a big feature on the making of the *All This and More* show, which was published just after the first season concluded.

"Oh, I think I read that one," Marsh recalls in the recap, as he mentions it. "I didn't realize that was you. It was really good! I loved it."

"Can you imagine being the contestant?" Ren says, and they both laugh. "How incredible would that be."

Eventually, on-screen Marsh steers the conversation toward what she wants to know. On the romance front, Ren had been single awhile. He was once serious with a woman, but they broke it off after a few years. He was traveling too much, and she wanted children. She's happily married with two kids now, and he still sends her a Christmas card every holiday.

"Oh my God." Marsh rolls her eyes playfully at him, once he's done with his monologue. "You are literally too perfect. You must have *some* baggage."

"You," he says.

Marsh looks up at him.

"You were my baggage." His voice is soft. "I don't know if I ever really got over you."

She'd expected Ren to play it cool, but he messaged her that same night, as soon as she got home from the date. They went out again the next evening, and the evening after that. They went out every night for a week straight before Jo stomped over from her corner office to Marsh's desk outside Victor's and demanded that Marsh turn him down once, and meet her after work to spill all the details. On-screen, the two of them impatiently tap their feet in front of their work computers, staring at the clock. If Marsh was already in hot water with her boss because she'd been too sad for the last year to focus, she was equally distracted now for entirely different reasons.

As soon as five o'clock hits, they dash out of the building and to Marsh's house so fast, they even beat Harper home from violin practice. Far too much wine and Chinese takeout later, they're whispering giddily on the couch as Marsh recounts everything through an artful flashback sepia overlay.

"It was perfect, Jo!" Marsh says as she describes her and Ren's first kiss. "Just perfect!"

Jo squeals like a teenager, bouncing around on the couch like the two of them are back at a high school sleepover.

"I haven't seen you like this in a long time, Marsh," she says at last, after hugging her. "It makes me happy."

"I'm happy, too," Marsh admits. "Things are finally going right."

"What a love story," Jo gushes. "The guy from high school with the biggest crush ever on you is still just as smitten after all these years. It's so romantic!"

There's a sneaky glint in her eye now.

"Speaking of romantic . . . I have something for you."

"For me?" Marsh asks.

Jo picks up her purse, and then both of their wineglasses. "Come. We need your mirror."

Jo leads her down the hall, Marsh nervous but curious. It's the wee hours of the morning, but Marsh's eyes still dart down the hall toward Harper's room as they pass just to make sure that her door is closed. Whatever Jo has planned, it's not for a young teenager to see.

Next, she's in her bathroom, wrapped in her old robe and staring at the full-length mirror.

Below the screen, Marsh does the math again as she watches. How long it had been since she'd slept with another person besides Dylan? More than two decades. And how long it had been since she'd even slept with *him*, once things had started to get rocky? No comment.

Recap-Marsh takes another sip of wine and faces her mirror again.

Actually, she takes three more sips.

"You can do this."

Then, as the camera pans modestly up to just her face and collarbones, she drops her robe.

"Okay. Not bad for forty-five," she finally says, as authoritatively as she can.

Marsh chuckles, embarrassed but sympathetic, as recap-Marsh opens the other eye she'd been squinting shut out of terror. Experimentally cocks a hip.

"You're a goddamn warrior," she tells her reflection, nodding vigorously to inspire confidence. "You are sexy."

But some other random part of her that's supposed to be taut and toned starts nodding ever so slightly along with her, breaking the spell.

She sighs and takes a long swig of wine. "Fuck."

"Did you put it on yet?" Jo hisses, muffled through the door.

Marsh snatches up her robe again. "I'm getting there," she says.

Jo giggles. "You haven't even taken it out of the package yet, have you?"

"I . . . am doing it now," Marsh says.

She turns to the box of lingerie on the sink counter. The tissue paper is still arranged flirtatiously around it.

It's strappy. Lacy. Red.

Lasciviously, embarrassingly *red*.

The tag, which is also made of lace, says the getup is called "Le Fascination." *Is that even proper French?* She still has no idea.

"Can I see?" Jo whispers.

"One second," Marsh protests. She gingerly lifts one of the straps with two fingers, like it's a small snake.

"That's it, I'm coming in."

Before Marsh can stop the door, her friend is in the bathroom, too. Jo grins, grabs the lingerie, and begins dancing around with it over her clothes as they both chortle—and for a moment, recap-Marsh looks like she might just be brave enough to do this. To be the bold, sexy woman she wants to be. To wear Le Fascination and completely bowl Ren over. To make him hers.

To take back her life.

"Okay," Jo finally says, wiping her eyes as the two of them catch their breaths. "So it's been a while, and you're nervous. But you want to do this, right?"

Despite the blush rising on Marsh's cheeks, she nods.

Below the recap screen, Marsh turns to Talia.

"The truth is," she starts, "I'd been taking things slow with Ren not because I was nervous and out of practice."

Talia quirks a brow.

"Well, I *was* nervous and out of practice," Marsh admits, a smile escaping her lips. "But it was also because this night felt like my last chance."

"Last chance?"

"Every date with Ren had been great so far—except the last one. He seemed withdrawn, distracted. I thought the guy of my dreams was losing interest."

The recap screen cuts back to Jo and Marsh, the two of them huddled in her bathroom as they share her glass of wine, Le Fascination lying between them, as she recounts the same story to Jo.

"When I finally told him, I could tell something was wrong, I'd been bracing for the worst," recap-Marsh tells Jo. "'It's not you, it's me.' I was sure it was the end for us."

"Oh my God," Jo gasps, her hand over her mouth. "What did he say?"

Marsh grabs Jo's fingers and laces her own through them, excited. "He confessed that he was just as in love with me as he'd been all those years ago, but he was worried that my hesitation to get physical meant I was still in love with Dylan. That I wasn't ready to move on yet! And he was afraid of getting hurt." She's beaming. "Because what he wants with me . . . is serious. *Serious,* Jo!"

"I knew it! I knew it!" Talia shouts in exactly the same way Jo does in the recap at the same moment, their two voices melding into a squealing chorus, one in the past and one in the present.

"I did exactly what I thought you'd do," recap-Marsh tells Jo. "I grabbed his perfect face and kissed him hard, and told him that I was *more* than ready. And that I was going to show him the next time I saw him."

"Good girl," Jo says proudly. She holds out Le Fascination again. "Ren is going to love you in this. It's going to be the *perfect* night."

"Perfect," recap-Marsh repeats.

Present Marsh looks away from the screen, to Talia.

"I was going to light that goddamn marshmallow on fire," she tells her.

"And?" Talia asks excitedly, on the edge of her seat.

"And then, last night, I messed it all up in the worst way possible," Marsh says as Talia recoils in horror.

The music wails, tragic.

"I ruined *everything.*"

THE PIVOTAL MOMENT

Talia is staring at Marsh now with one hand clapped over her mouth, waiting for her to say something—anything—as she continues to sit there with her head hung low.

The music is shifting and the haze filter is lightening on the flashback montage, gradually inching closer to the environment of the studio, where Marsh and Talia are sitting live—the recap is nearly over.

It's only a day and a half behind the present time now. Marsh watches herself climb into Le Fascination in a bathroom stall at work, put a tight black dress that Jo loaned her over it, and then leave the office to meet Ren for their big dinner.

"Light it on fire," she whispers to herself on the elevator ride down.

"We can't just . . ." Marsh starts to ask, but Talia shakes her head gently. She sighs.

"Yeah. Okay."

The sun is just setting over Phoenix, and the skyline is golden orange. Ren beats Marsh to the restaurant, always early for their dates so he can confirm the reservation, and is waiting for her by the front door. As Marsh approaches, he glances at every passerby to see if it's her, and when his gaze finally lands on recap-Marsh, the way that his eyes light up with surprise and pleasure makes present Marsh's already fluttery heart race—even knowing what's to come.

"You look incredible," Ren whispers in her ear as the waitress leads them to their table, one of his hands resting delicately against the small of her back.

Marsh spends the meal feeling like everyone can see right through her clothes to what's underneath, but Jo was right: Ren doesn't seem to be able to tell how nervous she is. All he knows is that he's getting lucky later, and can't take his eyes off her. Jo was always right about these things. Ren eats his entrée so fast, it makes Talia giggle.

Marsh skips dessert, and Ren drives the two of them back to his place, his foot like a lead brick on the pedal. He lives downtown in a swanky industrial loft, with a funky metal cage elevator and floor-to-ceiling windows. The furniture is artfully distressed, the decor effortlessly casual. The whole city twinkles through the glass panes, the sky a deep shade of Sharp Purple in the night. Marsh's jaw actually drops when he opens the door.

"I know, kind of a bachelor pad," he says as he leads Marsh inside, apologizing.

She shakes her head. "No," she says. "That's not it at all."

It *is* a bachelor pad. And that's why she likes it.

Because it's nothing like her own boring suburban family home.

They try to make small talk as Ren goes around the room turning on mood lighting and trying to find some music—but then conversation pauses for a second too long, and all pretense drops.

They're on each other in seconds.

"Are you okay with this?" he asks as he nuzzles her ear.

"Yes," on-screen Marsh answers passionately.

She can still feel it now. Ren's lips were so soft, his skin so hot. She'd been afraid her heart was thundering so loudly that his neighbors could hear it. The recap shows his hand on her leg, slipping slowly up her inner thigh, under her skirt, and then he's drawing gasp after gasp out of her as the camera jerks swiftly back to show just their faces.

"Yes," Marsh says again. "Oh, yes."

And then she blows it.

Big-time.

"*Dylan*," she moans. "It feels so good."

Dylan.

She said "Dylan."

Below, present Marsh has covered her ears so she doesn't have to hear it again.

For a single moment, nothing changes on the recap screen. The Marsh in the scene doesn't even realize what she's just done. But then she finally does—at exactly the same time as the realization dawns on Ren as well.

She stares in humiliated agony as he freezes, and his expression goes from excited and mildly perplexed to crushed all at once.

Poor Ren is *heartbroken.*

And everything is ruined.

"I don't even know why I said it!" Marsh cries to Talia beneath the recap, her eyes shimmering in the harsh overhead lighting all over again with shame. "I hadn't even been *thinking* about Dylan! I was in the moment!"

"Old habits are hard to break," Talia soothes.

It's night again, but not the same one—it's a whole day later. Marsh is at home, standing in her bathroom wearing her same robe.

But this time, it doesn't look as fun as it did before.

She wouldn't admit this to Talia, but of course, she had been thinking about Dylan, a little. It would have been impossible not to. But there's a difference between being sad that her twenty-year marriage imploded and actually wanting it back, isn't there? Marsh could be sad and happy at the same time. She could wish that she was still with Dylan without actually wishing she was still with Dylan, and also wanting to be with Ren.

Couldn't she?

After getting home from the disastrous date, Marsh spent the rest of the night texting Ren apologies and then waiting for his response. She fell asleep late, woke up late, and missed work, so she just carried on texting him, hoping that finally, he'd reply.

"Ren was a perfect gentleman about the mix-up, but it was clear that I'd ruined everything," she finally says to Talia. "Right after, he politely insisted that he was fine, it was no big deal, but he was just so tired, and had to get up early in the morning, so maybe it was best to end the evening there."

"Oh, Marsh," Talia coos, looking distraught.

"He called me a taxi, and even kissed my hand when he put me inside," Marsh continues. "He told me to send him a text when I got home, so he knew I was safe."

Reluctantly, she gestures at the footage illuminated above her head.

"But he didn't reply back to it. So I just kept writing them."

How many times could a person apologize before it went from contrite to pathetic? Jo would say once. Talia might say two. Marsh, perhaps, would say three times, at the very most.

Recap-Marsh checks her phone again.

She's already sent *eighteen* texts since the night before.

"What was one more, I told myself," Marsh says as, in the recap, she uncorks a cabernet and grimly, nervously sips it straight from the dark green bottle. "I'd already crossed the line into embarrassingly pitiful long ago. I thought, maybe if I just kept texting him, it would prove to him just how sorry I was, and how little that slipup meant. That maybe it would show him how much I cared about him and wanted a future together."

Just as she puts her thumb on the screen to pull up the keyboard for the nineteenth time, her phone buzzes in her hand right then, as if on cue. Despite the fact that she's already holding it, Marsh bolts upright from her lean against the sink to grip the device with two hands, her heart racing.

But it's not Ren. It's an email from her boss, Victor Mendoza-Montalvo.

She's fired.

Talia howls with dismay, but Marsh just grimaces.

"It gets worse," she says.

Recap-Marsh's phone buzzes again.

This time, it's Ren.

She's already standing stiffly, still absorbing the shock of this latest disaster, but she somehow manages to straighten up even more as her fingers move to open his message.

He finally replied!

Everything's not lost!

Hey, Marsh, the text begins.

After a moment, Marsh drops the phone in her robe pocket, and reaches for the wine again. Her eyes are dead and glassy.

I had a wonderful time reconnecting, but I think it would be best if we . . .

She doesn't have to read the rest.

In another life, maybe, he'd written at the very end.

Another life.

Another. Life.

"That was it. I was done. I went straight to my laptop, opened up the application, and before I could chicken out of it, I did it. I submitted my name."

This is the moment, she told herself at the time, feverish. The moment she finally stops letting things happen to her, and makes them happen instead. The moment she finally takes control of her life. The moment she finally makes a choice.

In their chairs, Marsh and Talia look at each other, an intimate, knowing stare.

And then, like a divine sign from the heavens, her phone rings on-screen in her pocket, startling her.

"Marsh," a familiar voice greets her over the line, perky despite the late hour. "Do you have a minute to talk?"

She'd recognize that caller anywhere.

There's no one in the world who wouldn't.

"I'm calling from *All This and More*," Talia Cruz's voice says.

ALL THIS AND MORE

THE FIRST CHOICE

As the recap finishes at last, the screen recedes and the studio brightens slightly. Box lights glow on the periphery, creating an intimate, quiet halo effect.

Across the table, Talia is sitting perfectly still. She's a statue, not blinking, not even breathing.

At first, Marsh is nervous for her reaction. But the longer the silence goes on, the less afraid she becomes. She doesn't like to disappoint, of course. But when you always expect to fail, there's a comfort in it when it finally comes.

She knew all of this was too good to be true.

"I'm sorry," Marsh begins, wringing her hands nervously. "I just—"

"Holy mackerel," Talia finally says, in her trademark adorable way.

She's grinning now, her eyes sparkling. She looks happy.

No.

Hungry.

"That was *quite* a recap."

"Really?" Marsh squeaks.

She waits for Talia to thank her for her time, to wish her the best of luck and point to the door, unable to comprehend that this isn't the end of her audition, the terminus of her last and only chance, but none of that happens. Talia keeps sitting there, and the cameras keep rolling.

Marsh stares, dumbfounded.

She was prepared for this to be the end. Not the beginning.

For once, she doesn't know what comes next.

"I'm . . ." she finally manages. "You really want . . . me?"

"You don't agree?" Talia asks. She sticks her bottom lip out a little bit, feigning disbelief that Marsh doesn't trust her. It's clearly just some light ribbing, but it's unbearable, the idea that the most beloved woman on Earth might be even playfully upset with her.

"It's just, out of all the applications . . ." Marsh rushes to clarify. She lowers her voice, even though there's a microphone pinned to her blouse. "Out of the mountain of papers, the millions, the billions, of people begging to star in season three, who would give anything to change their lives . . ."

She doesn't know why she has to be like this. Why she has to spend every day wishing for something, only to sabotage herself if she ever gets close. But it's easier to give up than to want.

". . . Why did you call *me*?"

"Are you kidding?" Talia gasps. "Marsh, you're perfect for this—as you've just proven. Middle-aged, recently single, desperate for a change. You're the everywoman that everyone can get behind. And we've got a possible path for every facet of your life! Romance! Career! Parenting! The choices are endless. We have *so much* to work with."

It shouldn't be a compliment, but it lands that way anyway for Marsh. She breathes a sigh of relief, perversely happy that her life is pathetic enough to please Talia. That she can see so many things wrong with it. So many things she could help her change.

Talia, however, mistakes her silence for hurt feelings instead of relief. She leans in, like they're friends sharing a secret.

"Look. I know in the movies, the protagonist is always super unique, super special. But this isn't the movies. This is reality TV. Normal is good," she says. "Viewers have to be able to relate. They have to see themselves in you. And they will. They're going to *love* you."

"But—"

Talia puts a gentle hand on Marsh's.

"Your job is to be the story. Let me and the studio take care of the rest."

"I'm the story," Marsh repeats, trying to sound confident.

Talia checks her expensive watch and stands up. "Marsh, are you ready to get this show on the road?" she asks, as Marsh's heart leaps into her throat. "We're due in costume and makeup in five. We've got to get moving if we're going to start your first episode on time!"

"Oh!" Marsh cries, scrambling after her. She tugs uncomfortably at her mousy hair, her somewhat-fitting clothes. They don't stand out, and that's always been the point. "Do we, I mean, is all that necessary?"

"Of course it is!" Talia replies. "Remember, you're not just Marsh now. You're the star of season three of *All This and More*!"

Marsh nods jerkily as they hurry. Talia walks twice as fast as she does, even in her stilettos. Marsh tries to summon a comfortable expression, but the frantic rustle of her pants makes it clear that her legs are moving twice as fast as Talia's just to keep up.

"Silly me! We should do the boring fine-print stuff on the way!" Talia exclaims as the two of them lurch abruptly out of the gleaming corridor and into a backstage area—suddenly the lights are warmer, everyone's wearing all black, and interns carrying clipboards are scurrying everywhere.

"The fine print?" Marsh repeats, trying not to pant.

There apparently was a very slim tablet device in Talia's folder, which she hands to Marsh now, a slideshow already cued up on its glass screen.

"It's all right here—everything you could want to know about the Bubble!"

Talia clearly has a speech memorized, which she delivers as Marsh grips the device nervously. They're walking so fast, she has no idea how she can hold it upright in front of her without dropping it, let alone actually read what's on the screen.

"Quantum computing is so advanced these days, the small section of reality that we section off is very stable," Talia trills as Marsh tries to flick through each incomprehensible slide, not even bothering to pretend to read the huge mathematical equations blinking by in between pictures of RealTV's offices, a high-tech, purple-accented laboratory with a big purple SHARP LABS sign, and scenes from season one, of course. "One hundred percent safe, comfortable, and separate from the actual world. The Bubble constantly streams footage back to the studio from every angle, where we can rewind it, fast-forward it, replay it, tweak it. A completely controlled environment. At the finale, your new life will slot right into the world, with minimal interruption. You might have slightly different hair than before, or have attended another school, but that's all." She winks. "No rips in space-time, no collapse of dimensions."

"That's . . . comforting," Marsh finally replies, trying to look comforted.

"Trust me," Talia says. "It's totally safe."

"I believe you," Marsh says.

"Wonderful! Sign here."

She presses Marsh's hand to the tablet, where a blank signature line is waiting. One smudge of her finger later, a rough squiggle appears and the whole presentation disappears. *Congratulations!* the screen says, before Talia snaps the tablet away again.

"This is so exciting!" she cheers. "Do you have any other questions, before we go live?"

"Actually, yes," Marsh replies.

Talia glances sidelong at her without breaking stride.

"Where's Alexis?"

She means Alexis Quinn, Talia's producer during season one. *All This and*

More sent her into the Bubble with Talia, to guide the then-timid Miss Cruz through her choices. She was the epitome of a partner—as tireless and dedicated as her star, always ready with advice and encouragement, sometimes before even Talia knew she needed a friendly shoulder to cry on during a tough scene. By the finale, Marsh loved Alexis almost as much as she loved Talia.

But so far, Alexis has been nowhere to be found.

"Alexis isn't with the show anymore," Talia answers, with a delicate balance of sadness but optimism for her old friend. "Now that we're on a new network this season, we're starting over with a totally new crew."

"Oh," Marsh replies. Whatever happened during the second season must have been messy, artistically or legally, for an entirely new crew to be required. "Then who . . . who's going into the Bubble with me?"

Talia does a little spin.

"Me, Marsh!" she cries.

"What!" Marsh gasps, stunned. "You're going back into the Bubble?!"

"I know, right?" Talia says excitedly. "It's perfect! The veteran season one contestant serving as a guardian angel for the new season three star. I can't wait!"

"I—whoa! That's incredible. I'm so grateful," Marsh stammers.

She can't believe her luck! If there's anyone who knows the show better than Alexis, it's Talia.

"I'll be with you every step of your journey. Which is good news, because I have one more fun surprise," Talia continues as a portable wardrobe whizzes past, a dozen different kinds of fabric grazing Marsh's arm. "*All This and More* is airing live this season!"

"Wait, what?" Marsh chokes, horrified. "Everything I do is going to be live?!"

"Yep!" Talia gushes. "Every victory, every obstacle, every choice— *everything*! How exciting, right?"

Marsh's head is spinning. She was already starting to panic from the pressure of revisiting every significant moment in her life, but now she'll have to do it—and figure out how to fix her past mistakes—with the entire world watching her in real time?

But Talia is hustling her ever onward. "Trust me, it'll be even better this way!"

As they continue their speed walk toward hair and makeup, they pass a man, dressed not in all black like the backstage crew, but rather in a simple cotton button-down and plain slacks, and who looks vaguely familiar. He's leaning against the wall and doesn't make a move to speak to Marsh. He just looks up from his feet and studies her intently as she walks.

When Marsh looks back, he's gone.

"Who was that guy?" she asks, meekly interrupting whatever Talia was saying.

"Who? Oh. That was our resident physics genius, who will be running your Bubble this season," Talia answers. "Ezra Hoffman."

Something pings in Marsh's brain at that. Didn't Dylan say he went to school with a Lev Hoffman—one of the two brothers who together helped discover the quantum bubbling concept that made the show possible?

That's why Ezra looked so familiar!

"Wow, he and Lev could practically be twins," Marsh says.

"They are, in fact," Talia replies, smiling.

"Twins who are both physics geniuses," she muses. "They must really love working together."

Talia's flawless face clouds for just a moment. "Unfortunately, the brothers had a bit of a falling-out when *All This and More* was pitched to Sharp Labs, where they were researchers. One wanted to work on the show, and the other didn't want to apply quantum bubbling to TV and media. Ezra quit to go into academia, and Lev stayed on at Sharp to help us. But after season two collapsed and Sharp Entertainment folded, Lev resigned with the rest of the old crew, and I guess no one's heard from him since. That's why we've got Ezra this year. But hey"—she leans in and giggles adorably—"they look so similar, it's almost like Lev's still here!"

Marsh chuckles for Talia's sake, but even as she's whisked onward, she remains curious about the physicist. What a chance to get some answers! She wants to go back and ask Ezra about how it all works, not that she'd understand, but then two more women appear in front of her and cry, "Three minutes!" Then she's in a chair, and there are hands in her hair and a soft brush flitting across her face. "Hold still! We're going for something casual and fun."

Talia gives Marsh an excited thumbs-up. "I know this is a lot, but you're going to do great," she says to her, as if able to see that Marsh's heart is racing in her chest.

"Places!" a woman sporting a head mic shouts, and Marsh lurches out of the chair. The adrenaline is hitting her now, cutting through the shock.

"I don't know if I can do this," she admits. She's trembling, her throat so tight she can barely speak.

"Stage fright?" Talia asks.

Marsh nods.

There it is again, the briefest flash. The musty dark of a school auditorium, the itch of gauzy fabric costuming. The shrill, raucous laughter of her classmates that night. The humiliated burn on her cheeks. That day she'd meant to finally break out of her shell, to leave her mark on the world. The first time she'd tried, and the only one.

"Always had it," she manages to eke out. "Ever since I was a kid."

"Well, don't you worry!" her host purrs. "We'll fix that. By the finale, you'll be a star. I promise!"

It was true for Talia, Marsh tries to tell herself. Who she was at the start of her season and who she was by the end was like apples to rocket ships.

But Marsh is not Talia.

Talia winks. "Not yet."

"I'm afraid," Marsh whispers, ashamed.

"It's okay," she replies. "So was I."

"What if I make it worse?"

Talia waits until Marsh meets her gaze again.

"What if you make it better?"

"Places!" the woman demands again, but Talia holds up a finger, and instantly, an intern appears at a dead sprint to deposit a three-ring binder in her hands. It's only about a fourth of the way full, a neat stack of printed papers hole-punched and fed onto the massive metal loops.

"This will help," Talia says.

"What is it?" Marsh asks.

"Have you heard of a Show Bible?"

Marsh shakes her head.

"This is how we track everything that happens in the show," she explains. "Character backstories, key scenes. That's why we call it a bible! *Stranger Things, Breaking Bad, The Walking Dead*—all shows have one, to help the writers stay consistent across episodes and seasons."

She flips to the first page, a list of names and bios. Next to Marsh's, it reads, "Get that popcorn and those tissues ready, viewers! You'll be rooting for our star from the very first minute. Marsh is forty-five, smart, sweet, funny, and trying to figure out where it all went wrong . . ."

"Uh," Marsh says.

"Do you remember those old kids' books, where you found your way through the story by making choices?"

Marsh nods, thrilled to know what they're talking about, for once. Those old paperbacks were all the rage when she was young. Endless scenarios in which you would start on page one as a generic kid with no backstory, and then depending on the choices you made, you'd end up saving your middle school from vampires, fighting zombies on a pirate ship, searching for lost treasure in a jungle while outrunning aliens, or something else just as impossible.

Talia grins and holds the binder a little higher.

"This is nothing like that," she says.

Marsh chuckles despite her nerves.

"The kids' books were fun, but the point was to get as zany as possible, even if it didn't always make sense," Talia continues. "Our Show Bible is exactly the opposite. There are no random options, no unrelated paths. Every choice here will be a *real possibility* from your actual life, Marsh."

Marsh swallows hard at that thought, exhilarated and terrified. It already had been impossible to read the old books as she was supposed to—she'd constantly second-guessed her choices, dog-earing every page where her path split so she could go back if she got a bad ending—and those choices didn't even *matter*.

This is her actual life she's about to play with!

"Don't worry," Talia assures her. "Think of the Show Bible more like a map or a guidebook. Each time we make a choice, I'll write down everything important here, so we won't forget a single thing. That way, if we need to change course, or even rewind, we'll have a perfect record."

"We can do that?" Marsh asks. "We can go back, if we need to? That's not cheating?"

"Not at all! With the Show Bible, we can do anything." She smiles. "Feel better?"

Marsh, grateful, touches the cover.

"Places, *please*!" the woman yells again, and Talia gently pushes Marsh forward.

Suddenly, the stage is even *more* chaotic than it already was. Everyone is moving, getting into place, getting ready, and she's swallowed up.

"Right here, love," another tech says, and tugs her toward a red X on the floor. Marsh spins around, but Talia is already there, right beside her.

"Remember to breathe," she says as she checks Marsh's clothes, looking serene even though billions of people all over the world are about to be staring at their faces on live TV.

"Talia," Marsh begs. "I have to know. Tell me the truth. Why me?"

"I already told you!" Talia says. "You're perfect for this! Your relatability is off the charts. You're the modern everywoman."

"No," Marsh insists. She makes Talia stop moving for a moment. "Please. Don't feed me the network line. Billions of applicants entered the lottery. There are people in jail for crimes they didn't commit. Parents who have lost their children. Patients dying of terminal illnesses. Why was *I* chosen over someone like that?"

For just a moment, Talia looks at Marsh as if she's really seeing her, as a person and not a fun project. Suddenly, Marsh gets the sense there might be something Talia's not telling her—about the show, or about why she was somehow miraculously selected—but she doesn't know what it is. Maybe *Talia* doesn't even know what it is.

Or maybe it's nothing at all.

But she can't shake the ominous feeling that there was something there, in that instant.

"Mic check!" a tech says suddenly.

Then Talia is off again, dancing gracefully around Marsh as she gives her hair one last delicate fluff and pats her back in a hug that won't wrinkle her blouse.

"Marsh, honey, sometimes we just get lucky," she says as she swoops into position beside her, on a little green X on the floor. "When it happens, you don't question it. You just grab it." She winks. "That's what this show is going to help teach you, remember?"

Marsh takes a deep breath.

Talia's right. In the end, it doesn't really matter how she got here—it only matters where she goes. And she's not going to let this last chance slip through her fingers. Not this time.

She is going to *live*.

"Ready to be a star?" Talia cries as the lights flare, and a red ON AIR sign blinks on and off a few times, warning. "You're going to be fantastic! Look at that smile!"

Marsh knows she isn't so much smiling as just baring her teeth like some kind of trapped prey animal about to be devoured, but Talia is saying to leave everything to her, she'll do all the talking, Marsh just has to keep standing there until it's her cue.

"My cue?" Marsh whimpers.

"Your first choice!" Talia replies. She's handed the Show Bible to an intern, who's standing just off camera, at the ready.

"I don't know how to even *begin*—"

"Don't worry! I know it's a little overwhelming at first, so I've already selected two options for you to help us get started."

A huge robotic arm swings low across the front of the sound stage like a swooping vulture, then does a circle around Marsh.

"But—" she starts, but a mic screech cuts her off amid the chaos.

"We're a go in sixty seconds!" the sound engineer blares over the intercom.

Marsh's heart lurches into her throat.

"Look at me," Talia says to her. "I'll be right here. As soon as you get going, you'll see how easy it is. You'll know what to do."

"Fifty seconds!" the intercom yells.

"What's my first choice, then?" Marsh splutters. She realizes she's clutching Talia's arm, but Talia's still smiling patiently at her.

"We'll start really general," Talia says. She motions quickly for the Show Bible, and holds it open to the first new page, where two lines are scrawled in neat, Sharp Purple ink.

> **Ren didn't break up with Marsh last night**
> **Marsh never dropped out of law school**

Marsh looks up at her, a deer in headlights. "This is starting general?" she shrieks.

Talia grabs her shoulder with her free hand to steady her. "It's all right, Marsh. You're going to be great! And remember, we can even backtrack and redo your choices in some cases, so nothing is set in stone until the finale."

"Ready for the countdown!"

Marsh stares at her two options desperately—waiting for one of them to reveal itself to her as the correct choice. But the game is different now, and none of the old rules apply. The only person who can choose is her, this time.

"Wait, what about Dylan?" she asks. "Shouldn't he also be an option?"

Talia shrugs, a little jump of her shoulders. "Don't worry, Marsh!" she chirps. "All in good time. We'll get to him, I promise. But let's take it one step at a time."

She puts a hand on Marsh's arm.

"You can do this."

Finally, Marsh nods.

The intercom shrieks. "Okay people, we're on in ten! Nine!"

The set begins to freeze, black-clad tech crew fading away to shadow, crane mics and light diffusers floating into place. The spotlights get even brighter, the music even louder. The main camera's lens fidgets into focus, a bottomless black eye, and little light on the front of the rig turns yellow for standby.

This is it. It's happening. Marsh's pulse is racing so fast that she might faint.

"Just go with your gut. The first choice that springs to your mind," her host says confidently—but she's not looking at Marsh. She's looking directly at the camera now.

"Lights!" someone shouts. "Camera!"

"Hey, Marsh," Talia whispers as a familiar tune rings out across the studio, and winks.

Marsh knows how this moment goes from Talia's own season. It's how every choice happens. First that musical jingle, and then Alexis would sing-song the first half of the show's title to Talia, and Talia would always answer with the second half.

But this time—somehow, impossibly—it's happening for Marsh.

"You could have *All This* . . ." Talia begins, just like Alexis used to.

Marsh swallows hard, knowing that's her cue, and tries to look brave.

"*And More*," she manages at last.

"Action!"

If Ren didn't break up
with Marsh last night:
Turn the page

If Marsh never dropped
out of law school:
Go to page 429

EPISODE 1

Slowly, Marsh opens one scrunched, terrified eye.

She's in a house.

Her house.

"Okay, good," she sighs, relieved.

She opens the other eye and looks around.

It's before lunch, judging by the light. Marsh is in her living room, standing beside the fireplace mantel. Pickle is napping on his dog bed on the floor beneath the bay window, snoring softly.

Did it work? she wants to ask.

Everything seems the same so far.

Marsh waits for a moment. For something to happen, for someone to tell her what to do. She's supposed to be forging ahead down this new path, but old habits are hard to break.

"Hello?" she finally calls.

Pickle's ear flicks once in his sleep, but the rest of the house remains silent.

"Harper?" she tries again.

Her eyes leap across the room to the hooks on the wall by the front door—*Harper's backpack isn't there*—but as soon as the panic jolts through her, it's gone again, replaced by a meek foolishness.

The show did not erase her daughter. It's simply late morning; Harper's already at school.

"Hi, Marsh," a voice says, and Marsh nearly jumps out of her skin.

"Oops." Behind her, Talia scrunches her shoulders apologetically. "I didn't mean to surprise you."

"Sorry," Marsh manages, once her voice won't give away how fast her heart is racing.

It comes out as a mumble, but Talia has more than enough pep to carry the scene until Marsh gets her act together. "Welcome to your first choice!" She beams and executes a twirl. "How do you feel?"

"Uh . . ." Marsh trails off, still disoriented. "Well, so far . . ."

But she jumps again as her phone buzzes in her pocket. She pulls it out and looks at the text message now on the screen.

Hey babe, the tapas restaurant is booked up already, so how about Vietnamese tonight instead?

The name above the message reads: Ren Kurosaki.

Marsh looks back up at Talia, speechless.

Is this real?

She stares at her phone again.

It can't really be real.

Talia grins at her dazed expression. "It is."

Marsh turns to the row of picture frames on the mantel, desperate for more evidence. Some of the ones she used to have there are missing—the portrait where Harper's in her prom dress, her arm looped through Dylan's, and the other where Marsh is holding a fish she caught while camping with him years ago—but there are others in their place now. Marsh and Ren at some kind of fancy dinner. Marsh and Ren in bathing suits at the beach. Marsh and Ren smooching as he takes a selfie of the kiss, the two of them smiling into each other's lips.

"It . . . it *is* real," Marsh repeats, struck with wonder.

Ren didn't break up with her last night after all.

Her phone buzzes again, startling her a third time, and Talia can't help but giggle.

Nam Phuong was about to book up too so I grabbed a 7pm spot, but if you want something else, just let me know and I'll call them and cancel!

"What should I do?" Marsh asks.

"I think you should answer," Talia says.

Marsh's fingers fumble across the screen clumsily.

Nam Phuong sounds great, she types. *Thanks for getting us a reservation!*

No problem, Ren replies. *Gotta run, work meeting, but can't wait to see you tonight.*

As soon as his message reaches her, he's typing again, and another one blips up right underneath it.

Love you

Marsh stares at those words, lost in them.

He said it so quickly, as if he didn't have to think about it. As if they've already been saying it to each other for a while now.

"Ren loves me?" Marsh repeats, like the words are magical.

Ren loves her.

Love you too! she scrambles to answer, before it can get weird that she hasn't said it back. Her head is swimming and she has no idea what to think right now, but she'd rather not ruin everything with a fumble before she even has a chance to figure out what "everything" is.

"Ren loves me."

Marsh is smiling now. Grinning, even. Grinning so intensely, it's making her eyes shimmer.

"It's real," she whispers. "It's really real."

TopFan01: <Here we go, y'all!>

The words appear in the air right in front of her face, a stream of hearts exploding all around them, and Marsh screams, nearly dropping her phone.

"The chat roll is online already!" Talia exclaims, delighted.

YanYan242: <TopFan01, you're back!>
Fortunata111: <Our favorite moderator!>
JesterG: <All hail the voice of reason!>
TopFan01: <Thanks, y'all. Happy to be here, too! Are you all ready to root for Marsh as she makes her life perfect??>

"The . . ." Marsh pauses. "Chat? Roll?"

"It's a new feature this season, now that the show is live!" Talia sings. "It's amazing. Sharp Entertainment used to host an Internet forum where fans could gather, but this year, RealTV has created a direct line between you and your millions of dedicated, passionate viewers! You'll be able to see their comments in real time during key scenes." She clasps her hands together. "Amazing, right?"

"Uh." Marsh stares at Talia long enough that any normal person's smile would waver. "Y-yes," she stammers at last. "Amazing."

Talia rewards her with a comforting squeeze on her arm as more hearts flood across her field of vision.

N3vrGiv3Up: <I can't wait!>
Schneckchen: <Ich liebe diese Sendung!>
Moms4Marsh: <Go, Marsh, go!>

There are hundreds of posts every second, far too many to catch, let alone remember, every name. But inevitably, some stand out.

Notamackerel: <YAWN! I can already tell this is going to be the most boring season ever!>

Thousands of cartoonish middle fingers obliterate Marsh's view, until she nearly staggers.

Monsterrific: <Oh, of course. Our favorite troll had to find his way here, too>
StrikeF0rce: <Couldn't find any friends of your own during the hiatus?>
Notamackerel: <Got tired of your mom!>

The thumbs-downs overwhelm Marsh so quickly that she actually swipes at the air in front of her. "How do I . . ." Every word is like a fleck of dust stinging against the jelly white of her eyes. "How do I make it stop?"

Talia giggles. "We never want our viewers to stop, Marsh! But of course, they'll understand that sometimes you need a private moment. If you ever do, you can just go like this"—Talia closes her eyes for a second, a slow, deliberate blink—"and the comments will minimize for a little bit."

Marsh copies her, and everything goes mercifully silent.

"Wow" is all she can finally manage.

Talia, unfazed, tugs Marsh to the couch and settles them both on it. "So. Talk to me. What do you think of your new life so far?"

"Well, I've only been here for about five minutes, but Ren and I just texted. He, we . . ."

Talia clasps her hands when she sees the grin spread across Marsh's face. "That's a good sign," she says.

Marsh jumps up, too excited to hold still. "We're seeing each other tonight."

"Looks like you've already been seeing each other quite a bit," Talia replies, winking at Marsh as she looks around.

Talia's right, she realizes. Ren's stuff is all over the house. One of the coats on the hooks by the door looks like his, and the shoes beneath them are the ones he wore on his first date with her. The last scribbled note on the notepad on the coffee table—something about the timing for a lunar eclipse—is in his handwriting.

Talia is watching Marsh pace like a proud mother. "So, you're happy with this first choice?"

"It feels good," Marsh says. "It feels . . . right."

SagwaGold: <我哋愛你呀, Marsh!>
LunaMágica: <She is so adorable!>

Talia grabs Marsh's hand before she can bat the words away on instinct, and Marsh manages to smile appreciatively instead.

Her host winks at her, and Marsh blushes.

You're getting the hang of this, it means.

"You know what we need to do now," Talia continues as she pulls Marsh down the hall. "We need to pick out a dress for your date tonight!"

The dinner is amazing. Ren is amazing. He's even *more* thrilled to be with Marsh than before, if that's possible. He's so enthusiastic about every little thing she does and says that it's almost cartoonish—Marsh has to try not to laugh at times.

It's perfect, she wants to tell him, even though he wouldn't understand. It's just like it was before she ruined everything, like that terrible night never happened, and the two of them just kept going. But there's a deepness to it in this version, an intimacy that comes with time. The way Ren puts his hand on her back as he guides her to her seat is practiced and comfortable. The way he watches Marsh openly when she fixes her hair or tries an appetizer, eager to see if she likes it, instead of trying to hide his glances. And the more relaxed he seems about their relationship, the more excited it makes Marsh—which then starts to make him more excited, although he can't tell why. He can just feel the energy in her glances, the way she's sitting closer to him and constantly touching his arm.

"Someone's a little frisky tonight," Ren whispers teasingly into her hair in the taxi on the way home.

"Just you wait," Marsh whispers back. But as their driver eases into her driveway, Ren pulls back and climbs out of the car to go around and open Marsh's door.

"As much as I want to, I gave you my promise, and I intend to keep my word," he says.

"Your promise," Marsh repeats, confused, as Ren extends a hand to help her climb out.

"That I'd get you home in time for you to get a full eight hours of sleep before your early morning tomorrow." He checks his watch and grimaces. "It's already eleven."

"Well, maybe if we were really quick . . ." she suggests, but Ren shakes his head with a smile.

"I'll take care of locking up and turning all the lights out. You can just go straight for your toothbrush," he says as he takes her keys and opens the front door for them—which for some reason is on the other side of the house than usual, Marsh realizes.

That's odd, she thinks.

Why would the Bubble do that?

But Ren is still talking. "This is your first huge exam," he's saying. "I know you're going to ace it, but you should be going into it as well rested as possible."

What exam? Marsh is about to ask, but as soon as the two of them step inside, her eyes fall on the pile of open books spread across the dining table, and she understands.

Criminal Law I, Legal Research and Writing, Constitutional Law I.

She can't stop staring.

In this new reality, she's restarted law school, too.

She's doing it.

She's finally doing it.

An excited shiver runs through her as Ren comes up from behind and gives her a hug and a peck on the cheek.

"I'm in law school," Marsh says, amazed.

"Yes, you are," Ren replies. "And you're doing amazing at it." He smacks her butt gently. "Which is why we need to get you to bed, before it gets any later! If it's my fault that you don't get the best score in the class because you were tired, I'll never forgive myself."

"Okay, okay." She laughs, heading down the hall for her bedroom with her hands up in a gesture of surrender.

Marsh trusts Talia's assurances that the Bubble's camera angles are set to "modest" inside her home as she gets into her pajamas. She brushes her teeth as she listens to Ren move around the house, dutifully making sure every window and door is secured. As she rinses the sink, there's a polite rap on the wall, and Marsh looks up into the mirror to see Ren leaning against the doorframe.

"All done," he says. "Safe and sound for the night."

"You're the best," Marsh replies.

He follows her back into the bedroom, talking about plans with friends that they must have for later in the week as she sets her alarm and climbs into bed. Even as new as this reality is to her, everything seems so easy, so natural. They're practically perfect together.

"Sleep well," Ren says as he kisses her good night. "Call me as soon as you're done tomorrow and tell me how it went."

"I will," she agrees as he heads out of the bedroom to go back to his own place, even though what's running through her mind is the complete opposite.

Wait! she wants to shout. *Stay!*

As if he can hear her, just before Ren steps into the hall, he pauses and glances back at Marsh.

"I know nothing but sleep would be happening tonight, but Harper *is* still at her dad's until tomorrow afternoon . . ." He trails off.

Marsh pats the pillow beside her. Ren grins. He pulls off his jeans and shirt so he's just in his boxers, then climbs into bed.

"I promise to let you sleep," he says as he snuggles contentedly into the comforter.

"I know," Marsh says, clicking off the lamp. "Good night."

"Good night," he echoes in the dark.

It's about ten seconds before she's climbed on top of him, and his hands are all over her.

This time, Marsh makes sure it's definitely Ren's name that she cries out.

Marsh doesn't get enough sleep, but it doesn't matter. Her new life is so fresh and exciting, she's already awake before her alarm goes off. She cancels the timer so the blare won't wake Ren, who's tangled up adorably in the blankets and still snoring, and then slips downstairs to make coffee.

There's the sound of a car pulling into the driveway, and doors slamming. Marsh puts the carafe back in the machine and peers through the kitchen window to see Harper bounding across the driveway—and Dylan following behind.

Oh boy.

Talia did say that they'd get to Dylan eventually. How does a happily independent new woman act around a former partner? How does one be blithe but still charming while wearing the same old robe that said former partner once bought for her? How does one convey that it's entirely about the softness of the fabric and not the identity of the giver without making it seem like exactly the opposite? She can't help but wish for a commercial break, or that Talia were there with her right now to tell her what to do.

Notamackerel: <Oh, look, the guy who dumped Marsh because she's so pathetic!>

Moms4Marsh: <Just you wait. By the season finale, Dylan will be kicking himself for leaving her!>

"Hi, honey," Marsh greets her daughter as she unlocks the door.

"Uh-oh, someone's going to be late to class," Harper says, surprised her mother is home. She sticks out her tongue. "Not setting a very good example, are we?"

Marsh resists rolling her eyes. Plenty about this life is already better, but Harper is still definitely a smart-aleck teenager.

"I'm not late," she replies. "I'm leaving in an hour. But aren't *you* going to be late?"

"Well, *ex-cooze me* for trying to chat with my own mother!" Harper whines, and skips down the hall toward her room, probably to retrieve something she forgot. "Don't fail your test!"

"Thanks," Marsh sighs, just as Dylan arrives at the stoop, carrying Harper's backpack. Despite her nerves, Marsh's eyes catch on it—it's slightly different from the original. Outside the Bubble, Harper's backpack is red with stripes. But in this episode, it's Sharp Purple with butterflies, and the logo says CHRYSALIS in embellished calligraphy.

Another odd detail for the Bubble to alter.

"Her friends want to go swimming after school today," Dylan is explaining. *Straight to business—no good morning, no hello.* "I'll drop her off at the bus stop after she grabs her suit."

"Thanks," Marsh says, just as Pickle, having heard the commotion, launches himself out the door and Dylan laughs and groans at the same time as sixty pounds of Labrador slams into his shins.

"Hey, buddy," he says, trying to hold Pickle still so he can't jump all over him. "Okay, calm down, calm down. This dog really needs some training, you know. They have weekly classes at the park . . ."

"Yeah, I'll be sure to get to it, with all my free time." Marsh sighs.

Dylan looks like he's about to give her some unwanted advice on managing her schedule, but the sentence fades from his lips as he catches sight of Ren coming into the kitchen.

Ren is fully dressed now—but it's seven thirty in the morning.

"So, he spends the night now," Dylan says to Marsh as Pickle shoots back inside after Harper, still barking.

"Never when Harper's here," Marsh replies.

Dylan's gaze shifts pointedly over her shoulder back toward where their daughter's gone, as if to say, *Well, she's here now.*

"I didn't know you'd be bringing her by before school this morning," Marsh says. "But I'm sorry. I'll be more discreet about it."

Dylan shakes his head. Marsh is already mustering a rebuttal to whatever he's going to nitpick next, but his expression takes the heat out of it. It almost seems like it's not the fact that Harper will see Ren that he's upset about. Or at least, it's not the only reason.

It almost seems like . . . he's a little sad?

"I'll, uh, be in the living room," Ren announces to no one in particular. He disappears around the corner, and the television turns on, to give Marsh and Dylan some privacy.

"I am sorry," she repeats.

"No, I'm sorry," Dylan says, waving it off. "I shouldn't have said anything."

His hand comes to rest on the doorframe, and after a moment, he moves it up and down, like he's testing the wood.

"Is this door different?" he asks, staring at it with a frown.

Marsh pauses. She looks at the backpack, then back at him.

"Different how?" she asks at last.

He sighs. "Never mind. It was hectic this morning. We woke up late and were rushing, and then I spilled coffee all over the car—"

"Yikes." She snorts. Good, casual. "Well, I hope it didn't stain anything."

"Oh, yeah, everything's fine," he replies. He slaps his palm a couple times on the wooden frame of the door, giving it one last, unsettled look before shrugging. "Sorry. Everything just feels a little off today. The important thing is, she'll make it to the bus on time."

"Harper! Hurry it up!" Marsh shouts, remembering that she's still here, and Harper throws a dramatic, irritated groan down the hallway from her room.

When she turns back, Dylan is looking at her guardedly.

"I know this is probably . . ." He trails off, giving up on whatever excuse he'd prepared. "I have a gift for you, but you can do whatever you want with it. It's completely up to you."

"A gift?" Marsh asks, surprised.

Dylan lowers Harper's Sharp Purple butterfly backpack, and she can see that he's also holding a medium-sized rectangular box behind it, sort of like what a dress shirt might come in.

"It's actually really old," he says. "I bought it for you a long, long time ago, but the timing was never right to give it to you. And then, well." He shrugs.

Marsh takes the box. "Thank you," she says cautiously. "Can I open it now?"

"If you want."

She unwraps it, and a smile catches her as she sees what's inside.

"It's a briefcase," Marsh says softly. "For a lawyer."

"I finally got around to unpacking the last of the boxes I took from here when I left. It was inside one of them." He gestures to the gift. "I know it's super old now, I don't know if that makes it vintage or just outdated, but it felt wrong to throw it out. I just wanted you to have it—whatever you decide to do with it."

Marsh touches the gold front clasp on the leather, moved.

Dylan must have bought this when she was pregnant, probably for a fortune they couldn't afford at the time, and planned to give it to her after Harper was born and she'd returned to finish law school and taken the bar.

He'd kept it all this time. Even after she'd dropped out. Even after things had started to go wrong for the two of them. Even after he'd blown up the marriage. Even after he'd moved out, and the divorce, and she'd gotten together with Ren. He'd still kept it.

Marsh looks back up at him, at a loss for words.

"I really am happy for you," Dylan says. His voice is low, vulnerable. "I know how much you wanted to do this, and how much it cost you to give it up, for our family. I'm really glad you're doing it now. I—I'm proud of you, Mallow. I think Harper will be, too. Once she grows out of this stage."

A sudden prickle in Marsh's eyes catches her off guard. Has she ever heard Dylan talk this way before? She'd done such a good job of hiding her disappointment over her lost career from him while they were married. It was a point of secret pride for her—as if hiding it from him could also hide it from herself. Knowing that he'd still glimpsed it somehow was almost more startling than even the affair.

"So, all ready for your exam?" Ren asks brightly when Marsh comes into the living room, his voice raised slightly over the faint rumble of Dylan's car easing out of the driveway to take Harper to the bus stop. "What's that?" he adds, when he sees the briefcase in her hands.

"Nothing," Marsh manages after a moment.

His face slowly changes as he watches her, shifting from excitement to concern. He looks as confused as she feels.

"Are you okay?" he asks.

Marsh looks down at the briefcase. "I . . ."

But the doorbell rings.

"Talia," Marsh cries, overcome, when she gets back to the door and sees that it's her host this time.

"Talk to me," Talia says, sweeping her into a comforting hug. "Talk to our viewers. Tell us how you're feeling."

Marsh glances back quickly, to make sure Ren is still in the living room.

"I don't know! Everything was going so well at first, but now I'm worried that maybe I started off with the wrong choice. Ren is wonderful, but I have decades of history with Dylan. A whole life, and a daughter." She swallows raggedly. "Maybe I gave up too easily. Dylan did do something terrible, but how bad the marriage got before he did it wasn't entirely his fault. I—I'd stopped trying, too."

Talia nods sympathetically. "It's all right. These are big changes! A little panic is normal in the beginning. What are you thinking?"

"Well, if he is really this sorry that it all ended, as sorry as I was, maybe if I could go back to before things got really bad between the two of us, I could save our marriage," Marsh whispers nervously.

"Or, maybe you should have focused even *more* on your career than this," Talia offers as an alternative. "Even though you're back in law school now, and Ren is clearly very supportive, you've lost out on a lot of years. Jo's been a partner for a decade already, and you're still just in your first year of the degree." She steps closer. "But if you'd never given it up in the first place, where would you be now?"

Marsh's grip on the briefcase tightens at that.

Classic Marsh.

She'd been thinking only about what was right in front of her, but maybe Talia's right.

There's more than one way to change a life.

Marsh looks up as the show's familiar jingle cuts gently in, coming from who knows where. It's the music that plays whenever she has the chance to make another choice. To push herself closer to the life she's always wanted.

"Remember," Talia says, and Marsh turns to see Talia smiling. "You could have *All This* . . ."

Marsh smiles back. It's taken her a moment to wrap her head around it all, but she's getting into it now. Starting to feel just how many possibilities are at her fingertips. Just how easy it is to snap them and ask for something new.

"*And More*," she replies.

To have focused on
Marsh's career all along:
Turn the page

To try to save Marsh's
marriage with Dylan:
Go to page 95

CAKE

Marsh's heart is thudding in her chest as the camera fades up from black and the scene crystallizes around her.

No, that's the beat of party music at full volume, she realizes as her eyes find their focus.

Marsh is standing in the boardroom of her law firm, Mendoza-Montalvo and Hall, crammed in with a bunch of other employees. It's a party, from the looks of it. And a roaring one, at that. Someone's cranked up the stereo in the corner, and the entire ceiling is covered in balloons. Everywhere there isn't a bottle of champagne or a platter of hors d'oeuvres on the great oak table, the lacquered wood is sparkling with confetti.

This is what Marsh knows the attorneys all do on Friday nights at the firm—celebrate whatever landslide case one of them just won. She's not been to all of them, just the ones where Victor asked her to stay late to help set up the champagne and hors d'oeuvres, but she's seen enough to know that this particular celebration seems even *more* lavish than they already are.

"Marsh!" Talia says as she pushes through the crowd. "Can you believe this?"

"What's going on?" Marsh asks, but the room erupts into applause and whistles, drowning her out.

"Our champion has arrived!" one of the first-years shouts.

Marsh turns around, expecting to see everyone cheering for either Jo or Victor. But they all seem to be clapping and looking at *Marsh*.

"Just go with it! Enjoy yourself a little," Talia grins, letting the crowd overtake her as she scoots back into it. "I'll be here, don't worry."

Still trying to get her bearings, Marsh spins back toward the giant table, where the congratulatory cake is sitting. She looks to see whether Victor's or Jo's name is written in colorful frosting on the side of the towering pastry.

But this time, the letters spell out *M-A-R-S-H*.

The party is because *she's* the one who just won what seems to be the biggest case their firm has ever had.

Marsh is not just a lawyer for Mendoza-Montalvo and Hall now, she realizes.

She's a superstar there.

"You're looking very starry-eyed." Jo chuckles as she appears and hands her a glass of bubbly. "The victory's finally hitting you?"

Marsh finally stops staring at the cake and toasts her as nonchalantly as she can manage. "Used up all my steely veneer in court," she says.

Jo takes an appreciative sip. "I'll say. I've never seen a jury come back so fast in my life. I hadn't even finished my lunch when we heard they were filing back in, and I had to stuff my face and run. I was still chewing a bite of sandwich as I slid into one of the pews!"

Marsh bursts out laughing as Jo mimes how she tried to hide her mouth as she huddled in the last row of the courtroom earlier that afternoon.

"I can't imagine what Judge Chopra would have thought if he'd seen me, but I wasn't going to miss the verdict for anything," Jo finishes, still chuckling. "I'm so proud of you, Marsh."

"We all are," a familiar voice says, and Marsh turns to see Dylan standing behind her.

What's Dylan doing at Mendoza-Montalvo and Hall? She gasps.

Her left thumb darts furtively forward to stroke her ring finger, to confirm there's no ring there. How could there be? In this episode, because Marsh put her career first over everything else, her path would have followed Jo's much more closely than it followed her original life. She and Dylan would have divorced just after Harper was born, and she would have gone on to finish law school and become a lawyer, like she'd always wanted.

Already, her head's starting to spin a little keeping track of the details. When she and Dylan split up in each reality, how old Harper is, if there was ever a Ren. Marsh is glad that Talia has the Show Bible to make sense of it all.

"Our woman of the hour," Victor Mendoza-Montalvo declares, then a friendly thump lands on Marsh's shoulder as he joins their little circle. "Ah, a visitor?" Victor asks, seeing Dylan.

Marsh freezes for a moment, unsure of how to introduce him, because she still doesn't know who Dylan is to her in this reality, but Dylan is already shaking Victor's hand.

"I'm Dylan, Marsh's ex," he says casually, as if he's completely comfortable with it.

"Oh, yes," Victor replies, as if he faintly recollects this information— Marsh's suspicion that she and Dylan have been divorced a long time must be correct, then. "The two of you have a daughter, right?"

"Speak of the devil," Dylan replies as Harper appears from the crowd at the same moment.

"Hi, Mom," she says as Marsh joyfully cries, "Harp!"

"I wanted to bring her by for a little bit," he explains as Harper, self-conscious around so many adults, gives her mother a shy hug. "I thought you might like for her to see what an incredible job you did."

The rush of pleasure at his words surprises Marsh. She'd always told herself that Harper's passion for the violin was proof that she'd been a good parent, wasn't it? That she'd taught her daughter that she could have anything she wanted, if she worked hard enough.

But it was one thing to tell her, and another thing entirely to be able to *show* her.

"Thank you," Marsh says to him, and means it.

"Speech! Speech!" the junior associates are chanting now.

Marsh tries to wave them off, but the cheers just get louder, and Jo is pushing her forward gently, until she finally gives in.

"I . . . uh . . ."

An embarrassed blush is threatening at her cheeks. She can feel the cheap stage makeup on her face again, hear the whisper of the old drama teacher giving directions from the wings. So many eyes on her, so much attention.

But it's different this time.

They're not all staring at her with ridicule.

They're looking at her with *awe*.

"The very first day of my Introduction to Constitutional Law class . . ." Marsh finally stammers—and the whole room leans in. They're smiling, waiting for the funny anecdote, ready to laugh.

They *want* to hear what she says, she realizes.

And when the crowd erupts into whistles and thunderous applause at the end of her speech, Marsh is stunned to find that she's not shrinking away anymore, not hunching her shoulders and casting her eyes down. Instead, she's actually *grinning*.

Maybe she really can do this.

"You've outdone yourself this time," Jo says as Marsh rejoins them. "We should have told the interns to get even more balloons!"

"I'll have to give the cleaners a bonus this year, for all the times we've destroyed this room with a party." Victor winks at her. "It's worth it, though.

Keep on winning like you are and I'll happily hire a full-time second cleaning crew just for your celebrations."

"That's our Marsh," Jo says. "Any more landslide verdicts and we're going to have to change the name of the firm."

Marsh almost chokes on her champagne—*Is she that close to being considered for partner?* She's afraid to even *hope* that it's already possible for her so early in the season, but Victor is looking at Marsh expectantly. Her stomach loops itself into excited knots.

"I'll leave you to catch up," Victor finally says, nodding politely to Marsh, Dylan, Harper, and Jo as he starts to move toward another cluster of lawyers. "Enjoy the party, Marsh. You've earned it!"

"I'm off, too," Jo says as she first air-kisses Marsh's cheeks, then Harper's, which delights the girl.

"Take care," Dylan says to her, shaking hands.

"You too. And Marsh, I'll see you later!" she shouts at Marsh over the crowd as she departs. "This is your night. I'm not letting you stop celebrating until dawn!"

As Jo waves from the door, Marsh spots a little poster hanging on the bulletin board beside her—it's a sign-up sheet for a company retreat to Hong Kong.

Is that a clue? A teaser for what's still to come? Her heart flutters with excitement.

"Meet me in an hour! You better be there!" Jo says, and disappears.

"Does she ever slow down?" Marsh laughs.

Dylan shrugs back. "Do you?"

There's no trace of jealousy or bitterness in his voice, but still, the words catch Marsh off guard. She looks at him more closely, trying to see this version of his life instead of the original.

"So, how's your work going?" she asks.

"Good," he says. "And it's been fun to have Harper in my class this year."

"What?" Marsh asks, confused. Harper is only in her teens—does this mean Dylan doesn't teach at the college level in this life, but rather at a high school?

"Yeah." Harper shrugs. "I was going to take biology for my science requirement, but physics is kind of interesting."

"She's doing well so far," he says proudly. "Maybe she'll even get the PhD I never did!"

Marsh laughs at his joke, but the sudden drop in her gut makes the sound come out funny.

Dylan never finished his PhD in this life?

In the real world, Marsh was the one who gave up her career to raise Harper, both because it felt cruel to ask Dylan to do it and because she'd thought she wanted to, at the time. But in order for this reality to have worked out the way it has for her, it must have been Dylan that had to pick up the parental slack when they separated.

Did he choose it happily?

Or does he regret it here, just like Marsh does outside the Bubble?

"Do you ever wish you'd finished your PhD?" Marsh asks him, softer.

Dylan smiles. "Oh, I don't know. It was so long ago. And Meadows High is great."

"And he gets to see me all day," Harper teases, then grows awkward once more.

"Want some of the cake?" Marsh offers as she studies her.

"It's eight o'clock! She'll never sleep tonight," Dylan cries.

"But we're supposed to be celebrating," Harper counters, giving him puppy-dog eyes. "You're saying that Mom's big win isn't worth just *one* sugar high?"

Dylan chuckles. "Touché. You really drive a hard bargain, missy. Clearly you learned from the best."

She smiles, shy all over again at this reference to her mother.

Marsh frowns. Now that the show has softened her daughter's sarcastic, surly adolescent edge, she can clearly see the difference between how Harper is with her father and how she is with Marsh. She clearly *likes* her mother—but isn't as comfortable with her as she is with Dylan.

It seems that in this life, Marsh has been so busy climbing in her career that the two of them didn't spend enough time together to grow as close as they should be.

"Fine, but no extra frosting!" Dylan insists as Harper scampers off.

Marsh wants to ask him more about her, but once she's gone, Dylan's gaze unfocuses, his thoughts drifting somewhere distant.

"You know, sometimes, it sort of feels like I did," he says, almost more to himself.

"Did what?" Marsh asks.

"Finish my PhD. There are these moments . . . of course, they never happened, but they feel so real that sometimes, I forget they actually didn't. Almost like in some alternate universe, I managed it, or something. I don't know if that makes any sense."

Marsh tries to come up with a response, but she doesn't really know what to say to that. In another version of this moment, she might find it funny that her own personal physics expert is talking about quantum bubbling without any idea how relevant the subject really is, but in this version, she can't summon the humor. Not when he looks so lost in it.

Dylan laughs, his gaze returning to the present. "Who knows, maybe it's just a coping mechanism. But it works. I'm happy with my job."

"Hey." Marsh waits until he looks at her. "Your job is important. Seriously."

He taps her glass gently with his own. "Well, thanks. But we're not here to talk about me. We're here to celebrate you. And speaking of that, I have something to show you."

"A gift?" Marsh asks.

"Sort of." Dylan is chuckling to himself and shaking his head as he unzips the backpack he must use to cart his teaching materials to and from the high school. His smile is infectious, and Marsh can feel the corners of her lips tugging upward, but as soon as he pulls out the present, the grin fades from her face.

Dylan is holding a medium-sized rectangular box. Sort of like what a dress shirt might come in.

Marsh stares at it, unnerved.

She already has a very strong suspicion of what's inside.

Hasn't this moment played out before already? she wonders as she tries to unwrap the gift as casually as possible. *Or is it new, because this is a new path?*

"It's a briefcase," she says as she uncovers it, feigning surprise. The words sound strange in her mouth. "For a lawyer."

"Okay, there's a story to this, I promise. I didn't just buy you a super outdated, cheap messenger bag earlier today as a joke." Dylan laughs. "I originally got it to surprise you when you finished law school and got hired here with Jo. But then—well, you know." He shrugs.

"You kept it all this time," Marsh replies.

"At first, I think I was holding out hope we might reconcile. But then after I realized we wouldn't, I started to get another idea." He nods at the box. "I watched you do so well here, climb the ladder so quickly, and I knew you were where you were supposed to be, doing what you were supposed to be doing. Even though things didn't work out how we planned, they're still pretty good. We've got Harper, and we're still friends."

"I'm so glad we are," Marsh says. Her voice is genuine, earnest.

"Me too," Dylan agrees. "I know you've got a much better briefcase now, probably one that costs as much as my car, but Harper's birthday is next month, and I was just thinking, maybe we could tell her that I bought this for you when you were just starting out, and now we're giving it to her, to use for school if she wants. Kind of like a good-luck talisman. Something to remind her that she can go as far you have, if she works just as hard."

Marsh looks at the bag again, overcome. She touches the tacky, gold-plated front clasp on the leather.

"If you use it for just one day, it'll technically be true," Dylan says, mis-reading her expression. "You don't even have to take it out of your office, so no one will see it."

Marsh shakes her head. "It's not that."

She looks back up at him, unsure of what she wants to say. Her throat is tight, and she's on the verge of tears.

"I really am happy for you," Dylan says. His voice is soft, and without a trace of defensiveness. "I know how much it cost you to achieve this. The choices you had to make, the sacrifices you had to endure. I'm proud of you. Harper is, too. Even if she's too embarrassed to admit it."

Marsh flinches as a sudden prickle stings her eyes. She's certainly made some hard choices, and a lot of sacrifices, to be who she is in this new version of her life.

But was it really worth it?

"It was," Dylan says then, almost like he's reading her mind.

Marsh tries to nod, but she's looking down at the bag again instead of out at the party. "Do you ever . . ."

In response, Dylan clucks his tongue and holds his glass up to her. "All the time. But that's what I do, not you. Don't go soft on me now, Mallow. Not after all it took for you to get here. Besides, there are no redos in life anyway, right?"

Marsh doesn't quite trust herself to speak. She steels herself and accepts the toast, and hopes Dylan can't see the tightness in her lips as she tries to smile.

As Marsh takes a sip of her champagne, her phone lights up suddenly, jolting to life where she's got it pinned between her thumb and the briefcase in its box with her other hand.

"It's Jo," she says, skimming the text message. She clears her throat quickly. "She's over at Chrysalis now, and is demanding I join her."

Chrysalis?

She's seen that word before.

"Of course your celebration continues at the most exclusive bar in the city," Dylan says. "Those views must be to die for."

So Chrysalis is a bar now, Marsh muses. And if it's the most exclusive bar in town, it must be on top of the Vanguard skyscraper, and is called Skyline outside the show.

She knows because, outside the Bubble, that's the bar where the two of them celebrated their last anniversary, before everything fell apart. It was make or break, and Dylan had gone for the grand gesture. But Skyline was so exclusive, he couldn't get a reservation, and they had to wait in line for two hours outside. Then, they couldn't afford seats, and had to huddle at the standing-room-only bar, where they paid so much money for just one round of drinks that it pretty much ruined the whole evening.

And look at her now.

She's a regular at this place, in this life.

Even so, she can't help but wonder what subtle ripples this choice sent through the Bubble to have caused the bar's name to change in this reality. But perhaps it doesn't matter. If her life ends up perfect, who really cares what one exclusive bar ends up being named?

"Chrysalis! You should go," Victor says as he passes by Marsh and Dylan again. "What good is a private table on the balcony if you never use it?"

Marsh blinks. Not only does she have enough power to get past the red velvet rope at Chrysalis, but she also has a private table there, apparently.

A phone buzzes again, but it's not Marsh's this time.

Victor pulls his own phone out of his pocket, and then chuckles at the screen. "Jo's texting me now, to tell you to get your workaholic ass over there."

"She never gives up on a good time." Marsh rolls her eyes, but inside, she's glowing to be so familiar with a titan like Victor that she and Jo would be on social text chains with him.

"Seriously, go," Victor is saying as he pockets his phone and waves at someone across the room. "We'll carry on here for another hour, but you deserve far more celebration than that for this case. Jo will make sure you get it."

"I'll think about it," Marsh says. "I will."

"I don't want to see either of you roll in here tomorrow until at least eleven o'clock!" he demands as he departs.

"If you're on your way to another party, I've got to get my congratulations in now!" another voice says, and Marsh looks up to see Dylan's jaw drop open as Talia joins them.

She enjoys watching him cycle through his emotions. It's the same process she went through the first time she saw Talia in person: surprise, disbelief, shock, euphoria, shock again.

"Dylan, this is—"

"Talia Cruz," he says, starstruck.

"Charmed," Talia says.

"It's an honor," he manages as he shakes her hand. "Wow, the people you rub shoulders with these days," he adds to Marsh, and she tries not to flush with pride.

"We're old pals," Talia adds with a little wink. "But Marsh is really the star here tonight! What a victory!"

As they chat, Marsh's phone buzzes impatiently once more, a string of emojis from Jo lighting up the screen. Marsh deduces from Jo's choice of pictures that the crowd at Chrysalis tonight is very attractive.

"Looks like you're going to have a good night whether you stay or go," Talia says as she sees what Jo's texted, and winks again. "That guy's also been looking at you all evening."

Marsh glances over her shoulder to see a man about her age in a sharp blue suit standing with another group of colleagues.

Adrian Jackson is looking at her. One of Mendoza-Montalvo and Hall's best lawyers, after Victor and Jo. Although in this episode, maybe he's also behind *Marsh*, now.

Moms4Marsh: <Omg, he's gorgeous!>

He *is* gorgeous. Tall, athletic, with dark brown skin and a goatee. When he sees Marsh meet his gaze across the room, he raises his glass subtly to her and winks without missing a beat of conversation.

Marsh whips around again, flustered. She glances at Dylan, unable to help it, but he's shrugging casually like this is entertaining for him, not hurtful or embarrassing. In this life, they've been amicably separated since Harper was a baby, after all. Any sadness over their divorce has long since faded, and been replaced with a comfortable co-parent relationship, she supposes.

But flirting right in front of him feels like a step too far.

Talia, however, seems to have other ideas.

"Well, I think I'll go freshen up my drink," she says pointedly, and Dylan takes the hint.

"Here, allow me," he offers. "Would you like anything, Marsh?"

Marsh shakes her head, even though her mouth is suddenly cotton.

As Dylan heads to the bar, she stares at his back. He's always carried his stress in his shoulders, and after decades, she could read his mood in the slope of his trapezius, the pinch of his scapula. Sometimes his mouth would say one thing, and his deltoids another. One could hide things, but the other never could, she knew well by now.

Talia clears her throat and nudges Marsh gently. "So, is this night just perfect, or what?" She giggles.

She looks surprised when Marsh throws up her arms.

"I don't know!" she cries. "Everything feels so strange!"

"I understand," Talia says, giving Adrian another appraising glance from across the room. "It must be hard to fully enjoy yourself in this scene with Dylan hanging around."

Marsh's gaze follows Talia's, to Adrian's blue blazer, his dark goatee—

Wait a second.

She looks again, confused.

Is that . . . ?

"What?" Talia asks.

"Sorry," Marsh shakes her head. "It's nothing."

For a second, she thought Ren was at the party—even though that would make no sense.

But it was just her imagination.

Her phone buzzes again. A string of joking profanity has unfurled itself across the screen, along with a pair of lips and a bunch of hearts.

That's right! Jo's still waiting for her at Chrysalis!

"What if we go to the bar?" Talia chirps, seizing the opportunity. "You can spend some time with Jo, let loose a little, enjoy yourself without your ex peeking over your shoulder . . ."

"It's more than just that," Marsh says. "I'm finally a lawyer now, but at what cost? Harper's whole childhood was with us separated, and Dylan's career is totally rewritten. This is too far."

"It's all right. These are big changes! There are going to be a few kinks to work out in every path," Talia says.

"But this?" Marsh shakes her head. "I wanted to make my life better—not ruin Dylan's. It's not fair to him."

N3vrGiv3Up: <We love you, Marsh! Always thinking of others!>
Notamackerel: <She's just a coward!>

Marsh pushes away the comments, frustrated.

It *isn't* fair—that she put two decades of labor into something now not over but erased, that Harper didn't get to grow up with the family she had outside the Bubble, that Dylan's life is hollow, diminished.

It isn't fair that even if she'd choose to leave this path for all those reasons, the trolls still may be right.

Talia holds her gaze calmly. "A little panic is normal in the beginning, but let's not jump the gun. You've wanted to be a lawyer for so long, and now you finally are! You want to give it up again so easily?"

Marsh frowns, but finally shakes her head. "I don't," she says.

"Of course not!" Talia agrees.

Marsh looks up as the show's familiar jingle cuts gently in through the party's stereo speakers, announcing her next choice.

"This is all part of the process," Talia promises her. "You're so early in your season. Just give this path a little more time. See how you like being a lawyer at the top of her game! And then if you *still* decide you want something else, we can do that. Deal?"

Marsh nods. "Deal."

Talia knows what she's doing. And she's right. What *would* be the harm of staying in this version a little longer, even if things are a little skewed? Hasn't she had to skew her own life for everyone else's, for years? What's another episode or two?

"Remember, Marsh—"

Marsh turns to see Talia wink at her.

"You could have *All This* . . ."

Marsh smiles back. "*And More,*" she replies.

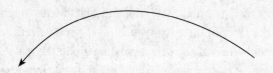

EPISODE 2

SHAKEN, NOT STIRRED

The Chrysalis bar is packed to nearly bursting.

"Right this way," the maître d' says, and Marsh tries to ignore the looks of envy on the faces of the patrons behind the red velvet rope as she's led straight through, toward the private seating along the glass overhang balcony. She gapes at the opulence, trying not to think about her and Dylan's disappointing night here.

As Marsh moves deeper into the bar, the lights grow invitingly dim, and the delicate jazz from the band playing inside mixes with the rumble of laughter and tinkle of crystal. Everything is glittering, adorned with either delicate string lights, candles, or chandeliers, the bar mimicking its view of the nighttime city far below.

"You made it," Jo exclaims as the maître d' stops and does a little bow. "I was beginning to wonder if I was drinking alone tonight."

"Never," Marsh says. Another waiter is already there before Marsh is even fully settled, holding a cocktail she must order often.

"Cheers, darling," Jo replies, and they clink glasses.

Their two-person table is the best in the entire bar, with a view out over both the western and southern sides of Phoenix, and Marsh can't help but stare at the desert landscape as she takes a sip. The cocktail is so smooth, it goes down like water.

"This place is gorgeous," she murmurs, once she puts her glass down.

Jo quirks an eyebrow. "That's why we always come here. It's been your favorite place for years."

"Of course," Marsh replies. "Just admiring."

In this new life, going to Chrysalis on a regular basis is not only something Marsh and Jo do, but something they nearly take for granted at this point.

"Do you have that blush I like so much with you?" Jo asks her as she touches up her lipstick.

Marsh opens her designer clutch to see, and blinks at the packets of condoms inside. She's now the kind of woman who's so potentially open to an adventure at any possible moment, she carries her own condoms around. Everywhere, all the time.

The wrappers even match her purse. She wants to laugh at that.

"You look like you've seen a ghost," Jo says. "You should dust some on your cheeks, too."

"It's just a little strange," Marsh admits. "So different from being married."

That's the wrong thing to say—*different version, different life*—but the words are out before she can stop them.

"Married?" Jo repeats, baffled. "That was a *lifetime* ago. A blip. Only good thing that came of it was Harper."

"I know," Marsh agrees, trying to imagine what that would actually feel like.

She takes another drink, and tries not to let Jo see her thumb slide gently over the bare skin where her wedding ring would have been. It shouldn't even matter—that ring isn't there in Marsh's original life anymore, either. But still, it's strange to think that now, it hasn't been there since Harper was an infant. Her whole life, Harper grew up with both Dylan and Marsh. In this one, she's never known them together at all.

"Sometimes, I just wonder . . ."

Jo snorts. "Who wants a white picket fence when you could have a corner office?" she asks, and this time, Marsh can't see a glimmer of the secret yearning that she knows is always there, beneath Jo's constantly buzzing exterior.

Outside the Bubble, she and Jo have always had what the other's missing, and missing what the other has. *No woman wants a part-time wife,* Jo would sigh, each time she had to recount yet another painful breakup to Marsh. *And no law firm wants a part-time lawyer,* Marsh would reply as she listened, while rocking Harper to sleep on her chest. But now, it seems that Jo is wholly satisfied by her career, and really doesn't wish she could find a long-term partner.

Marsh doesn't know if she likes that the show has changed that about her best friend or not. It certainly makes things simpler for Jo, but life can't be *only* about one's career.

Can it?

"I'll be right back. I'm going to call Harper real quick," Marsh blurts out then.

Jo looks surprised. "Why?" she asks.

Why?

That's an odd reaction.

"What do you mean, why?" Marsh asks. "Because she's my daughter."

"She'll be back in town in another month or so, when the trimester ends," Jo replies. "You can see her then."

"When the what ends?" Marsh repeats, confused.

"I know, I don't know why they do it that way in LA. They think it makes them sound fancy," Jo says, but Marsh gasps.

Harper is going to high school in Los Angeles now?

That's six hours away from Phoenix by car!

What just happened, over that last episode break? Marsh wants to cry.

"Dylan never would have agreed to something like that," she says, before she can stop herself.

"Dylan knows how much the violin means to her. And he really has no say in anything when you're the one footing the bill." Jo laughs. "Besides, she's at his place whenever school is out, so he sees her plenty."

Marsh nearly buries her face in her hands, miserable.

It sounds like Harper is now enrolled at a music conservatory, which is good news—except that this conservatory is in another state. And worse, when she is home, she doesn't even live with her mother?

"Come on. Let's get another round," Jo says.

"I'm going to call Harper first," Marsh insists.

"Just text her. She'll reply at some point, I'm sure." Jo shrugs.

At some point.

Marsh takes a deep breath and tries to stay calm.

Jo has to be wrong about this. She has to be. She's Marsh's best friend, and still is in this reality, but she's also different. Sharper, tougher. Maybe so is this version of Marsh, but never where Harper is concerned. She never would let that happen. Ever.

"One call," Marsh says. "Also, that brunette by the crystal fountain is staring at you."

Jo's eyes flash. She casts a subtle glance across the bar, where her eyes land on a curvy woman with a blunt bob, cute freckles, and a killer tight dress. Her type, at least, is one thing consistent across realities.

"On second thought, maybe do call." Jo winks. "I'll be right back."

As Jo prances off to flirt, Marsh dials Harper. She waits for her daughter to pick up, but the call goes to voicemail. She leaves a message saying that she was just thinking about her and wants to say, *I love you.*

She waits five minutes, but Harper doesn't call back.

Hmmm.

Marsh sends a text message to the same effect, and asks Harper to shoot her back a quick reply so she knows that she received it.

She waits another five minutes, staring at her phone's screen. The little check mark goes from gray to blue—Harper has read the text.

Five *more* minutes later, she still hasn't replied.

At last, Marsh puts the phone back in her purse, lips tight.

She chose this path because she's always dreamed of being a lawyer, but also because of Harper. Because she's the best thing in Marsh's life. Because she wants to give her everything.

And she has, in a way. She's an ambitious, accomplished role model for her daughter, and she can afford to send her to a music conservatory, where she can pursue her own dreams. But instead of bringing them closer, this choice seems like it's pulled her daughter even further away.

"Well, well, well," a voice says.

Marsh turns around to see Adrian standing there. Again.

"Fancy running into you here. Celebrating your big win?" he asks.

It's the same man, but she can't tell if he's still flirting with her like he was at the office yet. Is this a continuation, or a reset?

"I am," Marsh allows, playing it safe. "And you?"

"Drinking away my sorrows." He shrugs. "There are worse places to do it. And also, worse lawyers to lose to," he adds roguishly.

Adrian must not be a colleague, but rather her competition, now, Marsh realizes. The opposing lawyer for the big case she just won.

"Nothing personal," she says, as blithely as possible. "Just doing my job."

Adrian nods. "Well, I'm glad for the chance to finally talk to you. I've been trying to catch your eye for years from across the courtroom, you know. Ever since the first day you joined Mendoza-Montalvo and Hall."

Marsh snorts privately. She can't help it.

"Really. Ever since the first day?" she replies, incredulous.

This Adrian doesn't know it, but outside the show, where Marsh has been a paralegal at their firm for decades, he's never spoken to her even once.

He sighs, but as if he's pleased, not disappointed. "But that's the problem with people like us."

"... Lawyers?" Marsh guesses.

"*Hungry.*" Adrian grins. "Neither one of us was willing to be the one to slow down for just a second, not until we got to the top."

"The view is good way up here, I have to say," she says.

Adrian chuckles. "I gather you'll be moving into the office next to Jo's now, after this win."

He takes a sip of his cocktail.

"I hear that desk is . . . very sturdy."

Marsh chokes on her drink.

Adrian laughs. "I meant because of all the case files you'll have sitting there waiting for you. What did you think I was insinuating?"

Marsh tries to come up with a clever retort, but Adrian is even more handsome in this episode, if that's even possible, and she can't think. His cologne is intoxicating, a subtle poison.

Adrian steps closer, and Marsh's heart skips a beat.

"Next time we're up against each other, I won't make it so easy," he purrs.

"Well, I look forward to it," she finally manages. "What fun is life without a rival?"

"Agreed. But who says rivals can't also be friends?" Adrian winks.

Marsh swallows and tries to bat her lashes. Is this how a powerful, sexy person seduces someone? Does she look alluring, or like she has something in her eye?

"I can drink to that," Marsh finally replies, and Adrian's grin grows wider.

"I'll be right back," he says, disappearing toward the bar. He doesn't even ask Marsh what she drinks. He probably already knows.

Marsh casts about for a slightly more private section of the balcony, where she can practice this new sex vixen identity without too many people overhearing her bumbling attempts, and as she does, her eyes land on a familiar face.

Talia is at one of the tables nearby.

"Look at you!" she squeals at Marsh as she slides into the open seat, touching Marsh's stylishly coiffed hair and running a finger admiringly along the hem of her apricot-colored blazer like the fabric must cost a million bucks. "Gorgeous. Who's the designer? I've got to get myself one."

"Oh, stop," Marsh says, but she's flattered. By the end of her season, Talia Cruz looked like a totally different person. She'd been cute before, but at the finale, her wardrobe had become a whole fashion show in and of itself. But it wasn't just her stylists—it was also her confidence, Marsh knows, and sits up straighter. The clothes *do* feel better this way. As if tailored to encourage power poses.

She has to admit, she could get used to this part, at least.

"So, now that you've been here a little longer, how's it going?" Talia prompts. "Is your career everything you dreamed it would be?"

"I'm definitely a . . . high flyer," Marsh replies. "But . . ."

"But what?" Talia waggles her eyebrows. "I saw Adrian around here a moment ago. You're not still thinking about your old ex, are you?"

Marsh shakes her head. "Harper."

Talia grows more serious. "Something's wrong with Harper?"

"No, she's great, I think," she says. "But that's the problem! Apparently, I hardly even know her in this life. She goes to a music conservatory in California, and then when she's back here, she lives with Dylan! I work so much, then party with Jo every night, and I barely see her. I just . . ." Marsh snorts, disgusted. "It sounds like I just pay for everything, and that's it."

"You have a very important job," Talia says comfortingly. "And it's enabling Harper to pursue her dreams."

"I know," Marsh says. "But I just thought . . . I just thought all of this might have brought Harper and me *closer,* too." She sighs. "I did want to be professionally fulfilled, and I love that Harper can attend a music school now, but I also want to be a good mother to her. I can't do that if we're practically strangers! I mean, how often do I even see her, in this life? Like four times a year?"

"Marsh," Talia coos.

She frowns. "Maybe I gave up too much by choosing this path."

"There are a million reasons why Harper could be hard to get ahold of, other than that you're not close," Talia suggests. "It's late in the evening already, for one. Or she might be studying for an exam, or preparing for an upcoming concert."

Marsh tries to believe. But she can't shake the way that Jo said what she did when she wanted to call her daughter. Not like Harper was busy right now, but like she's busy all the time. Because they *aren't* close.

"Just give it a little time," Talia is saying.

Marsh frowns. "I already have."

Talia watches her for a moment, and then reaches into the huge leather satchel beside her.

The Show Bible thumps heavily as she sets it down on the cocktail table.

"Look, things might not feel perfect right now, but the longer you stay here and make choices, the more data we'll have, and the better final outcome we'll be able to achieve for you," Talia says. "By the end of the season, we're going to have so much to work with, it'll be a cakewalk. Even better than the incredible one Mendoza-Montalvo and Hall just made for the party in your honor!"

Marsh watches the pages whiz by, wondering what's on each one. It's larger than it was in the first episode. Much larger. Talia has taken so many notes. How can she possibly have written so much, let alone actually use it all?

"Plus," Talia continues with a wink, "it's already so late. Wouldn't it be better to just have a little fun tonight, and then get more serious in the morning?"

Marsh glances up at that, just in time to see Jo near the exit of the bar. One hand is on the waist of the woman she'd been flirting with, and the other is giving Marsh a smug wave goodbye.

"She's going to have a good night tonight," Talia says.

She leans in.

"Maybe this episode isn't perfect, but maybe it *is* exactly what you need, for once," Talia suggests. "To get out of your head a little, to just have some fun instead of always trying to do the right thing. Don't you deserve it?"

"There you are," Adrian says then, his timing exquisite. He's back with two drinks, and an expectant smile on his face.

Marsh stares at her cocktail.

Adrian has brought her the drink she ordered the night she came here with Dylan.

"You don't like the Chrysalis Twist?" he asks.

"Chrysalis Twist?" she asks.

"The name of the drink. It's their signature cocktail. One sip and you're supposed to leave your old life behind, they say."

Leave your old life behind.

The words were meant flirtatiously, but here and now, inside the *All This and More* Bubble, they seem a little *too* on the nose.

What's going on, exactly?

Why does that word, *Chrysalis*, keep following her?

Marsh casts about for an excuse not to take a sip. "Adrian. This is, uh . . ." she starts, trying to come up with some kind of plausible backstory for why she's friends with Talia.

But everyone at Chrysalis is powerful and famous, including Marsh, now. Adrian likely doesn't think it's strange at all that she's sitting with a celebrity like Talia Cruz.

"A friend," she settles on at last.

"A friend who's stayed out far past her bedtime," Talia replies, sliding off her stool, the Show Bible tucked under her arm.

She gives Marsh's shoulder a squeeze as she passes, and Marsh just barely catches the words under her breath.

"Let go, have fun, for once. There are always more episodes. Remember, you could have *All This* . . ."

"*And More*," Marsh returns quietly, as Adrian smiles and her heart begins to nervously quicken.

Tourn3sol: <Elle ne le fera pas>
BenzinhoGatinho: <Sim, ela fará isso>
YanYan242: <Come on, have some faith in Marsh!>

Adrian tips his head politely as Talia leaves, and then looks back at Marsh—Talia, the giant binder in her grip, and the drinks already utterly forgotten.

"So," he asks. "Your place or mine?"

Marsh had been hoping that this version of her, the cutthroat lawyer at the esteemed Mendoza-Montalvo and Hall, would know how to ask for exactly what she wants in bed and always get it, but it turns out, she doesn't.

Apparently, the Bubble can only do so much.

She fumbles through the whole thing and fakes two orgasms, both of which Adrian seems to believe are real, then breathes a sigh of relief when he finally passes out before he can suggest round three. Hopefully, the darkness and tasteful angles Talia promised made it look hotter than it actually was.

Marsh wasn't sure she'd able to sleep after such a disappointing advancement, but eventually she must have drifted off, because in the morning, her conquest's light snoring wakes her before her alarm does.

In this path, she lives in a modern downtown apartment with high ceilings and cool exposed brick. It's almost like Ren's trendy loft that she saw that one disastrous night, come to think of it, but decorated more to her taste. Her gauzy curtains are slightly parted, and in the morning light, the room is almost too bright.

Marsh sighs, ragged. She'd kill for a shower and cup of coffee, but definitely *not* with Adrian. She stifles a yawn, trying not to move too much in case it wakes him, and wonders what polite excuse she can come up with to kick him out as soon as he stirs.

She's still drowsy, but her eyes finally focus on the sleeping face on the Sharp Purple silk pillow next to hers, and at first, she doesn't understand.

She recognizes it, but something's wrong.

It doesn't look like Adrian's face.

Because it's Ren's face.

"What the fuck!" Marsh yells, bolting upright in shock.

"What! What's happening?" Ren says blearily, startling out of sleep so violently that he falls off the bed.

JesterG: <Holy mackerel!>
Notamackerel: <Lol, WHAT>
Moms4Marsh: <I'm so confused! Where's Adrian??>
Monsterrific: <What a twist for the show to pull off!>

"What the hell are you doing here?" Marsh shouts.

"What are you talking about? You invited me!" Ren shouts back, clambering to his feet. "Last night. We had a drink and were flirting, and you brought me back here! Remember?"

"No, I most certainly did not bring you back here last night!" Marsh stabs a finger at him. "I brought back Adrian Jackson!"

Ren massages his face roughly, and then bends down to snatch his clothes from the floor. "Jesus, lady, if you wanted a one-night stand, you can just say that. You don't need to invent a whole thing so I won't offer to cook you breakfast or ask for your number."

Marsh is scrambling through her dresser for something that's not a designer pantsuit. Does Ren not know her in this reality? "I'm not inventing anything!" she cries.

Am I still dreaming? she wonders deliriously. The comments are going haywire, obliterating her vision with laughing emojis and jokes, but she ignores them, blinking them off three times in a row before they finally shut up.

Did the show do this? Did they bring Ren here to do some kind of late-night switch? Or did Adrian somehow . . . morph into Ren?

Did the Bubble . . . glitch?

"You have to go," Marsh says.

"Yeah, no shit," Ren replies.

"No, I—" She shakes her head. "I'm sorry."

Ren is heading for her bedroom door, his fingers hooked on the heels of his shoes. "Whatever. Thanks for last night. I think."

Marsh watches him leave, speechless. She jumps as the door slams.

What the hell is going on?

As she leans against the wall, waiting for her heart rate to return to normal, there's a little rustle. A dark shape darts out from beneath the dresser and shoots across the room. Marsh screams, until she realizes it's just a cat.

"How on earth did you get in here?" She asks it nervously.

She's never had a cat, and has always assumed they're all skittish. This one doesn't seem to be, though. It's black and silky, with round yellow eyes, which are currently staring at her like two big moons.

Marsh sidles up to the cat as slowly as possible, trying not to spook it, but it just watches her from its new perch on the corner of the unmade bed, its tail swishing placidly. It doesn't seem to be planning to go anywhere now that she's not shrieking. At last, Marsh reaches out and touches the little silver tag on its collar.

Pickle, it reads.

She drops the tag and lurches backward.

This is getting really weird.

Pickle the cat hops off the bed and pads across the floor to where Marsh has stumbled. He threads himself in between her ankles in figure eights, purring. Then he trots away and jumps onto a little decorative side table, where there are two small bowls, one filled with water, and one empty. He sits expectantly beside the empty one.

This animal doesn't seem like a plant from the show. A cat would never cooperate like this for any human boss. He clearly knows Marsh and this apartment very well. As if he belongs to her, as her pet.

Her Pickle.

Marsh keeps staring at him until he meows, irritated.

"Sorry! I'm just trying to get my head around this," she says, rushing to locate a bag of cat food. "Why am I talking to a cat? It's not like you can understand me any better than you could as a dog. Why am I still doing it?!" Frazzled, she pours some kibble into the bowl, and watches Pickle happily crunch his way through it.

Think, she admonishes herself. There has to be an explanation for both Ren and Pickle.

She had a few drinks last night, but she definitely wasn't drunk enough to have completely misidentified Adrian as an entirely different person in the previous episode. And even if she was a little tipsy, she's certainly not drunk now, staring at this animal, which is clearly not a dog.

Actually, the longer she observes this Pickle, Marsh realizes that he does remind her of the original, canine version of Pickle. He cocks his head the same way, and scratches at things with his little front left paw just like he does as a Lab.

Maybe in this version of her life, a dog would have been too much for a single career woman to properly take care of, she considers. Maybe a cat was all she could handle.

But that still doesn't explain why Adrian turned into Ren.

Briefly, hesitantly, Marsh blinks the comments back on to skim them to see if anyone else is wondering the same thing. But it seems they've taken it in stride, as part of the show, and are now cooing over Pickle the adorable cat.

She stifles a groan and minimizes the scrolling texts again.

She needs to talk to Talia.

A few minutes later, Marsh has thrown together a presentable enough outfit and whizzed down the elevator from the penthouse to the parking garage. Even as rattled as she is, she doesn't miss the conspicuously placed flyer for a winter holiday taped just above the panel of buttons.

Your future awaits in Iceland, a white and blue ribbon of text beckons in front of an imposing mountain peak, as she stares.

The elevator dings, and Marsh tears her eyes away from the poster to rush through the sliding doors, but then stops cold once she enters the garage.

She doesn't know what her car looks like in this life.

But as she's digging through her purse to see if her key ring will give her a hint, a soft squeal of tires on concrete interrupts her, and a sleek dark sedan with impenetrable tinted windows pulls up in front of her.

Marsh stares at it for a few seconds, wondering what's going on, until the driver opens his door and pokes his head over the top of the roof. He's young, barely a teenager, in a white dress shirt with a red vest.

"Good morning, ma'am! Will you be taking your car now?" he asks Marsh politely.

Marsh blinks. In this reality, her luxury building apparently has a full-time valet for its residents.

"Yes, thank you," Marsh recovers, and darts over to the driver's side.

"Have a wonderful day," the valet says as she clambers behind the wheel, and shuts her door for her.

Marsh waves to him, and then hits the gas. The car lurches into motion with feline grace.

"Talia!" she cries as Talia picks up just after the first ring.

"You sound tired," Talia says. "Must have been a good time last night!"

"The opposite," Marsh replies. She puts her phone on speaker and tosses it onto the passenger seat so she can drive with both hands. "However bad you're imagining, triple it."

Talia laughs. "Better luck next time."

Marsh can't even think about a next time right now. "We need to talk," she says. "Something really weird is going on."

"What do you mean?"

"Well, I went home with Adrian last night, and then in the morning . . ." She fumbles, at a loss as to how to explain the strangeness. "He was Ren!"

Talia coughs on her end of the line, like she might have just choked on her breakfast for a moment. "What? What do you mean, he was Ren?"

"Exactly that! Like the show replaced Adrian with Ren, for some wild reason!" Marsh takes a right turn too fast, and her tires squeak. "And it turned Pickle into a *cat*, and—"

"Okay," Talia says, trying to calm her. "Remember, we're making big changes to your life. Some surprises are to be expected."

"Surprises!" Marsh wails, incredulous. She's not sure if she's relieved that she didn't imagine everything that just happened, or unnerved that the show really would play musical chairs with her romantic partners with such whimsy.

"The Bubble is an incredibly complex system. There are a million side effects to every single choice that it has to track, and some of them have to be streamlined to make your new reality work," Talia explains. "Sometimes, the change will be obvious, like becoming a lawyer. Other times, it will be less so, like Pickle becoming a cat."

Or Ren taking Adrian's place, Marsh muses.

But even if this was just a side effect, why did the Bubble insert Ren, and not Dylan?

Even in this reality, in which Marsh has been divorced far longer than she was ever married, Dylan still did propose to her. Dylan still was with her through pregnancy, and childbirth, and took care of her while she recovered, before it all went south. And he's still Harper's father, even if he's not her husband. Surely, the Bubble must know how significant of a person to Marsh that makes Dylan. He seems like the obvious choice.

Or maybe that's the reason? she ponders.

Is the show trying to push Ren and her together?

Or . . . trying to keep her and Dylan separated?

"Marsh, I need you to trust the process. We're going to make everything perfect by the finale, just like I promised you," Talia is assuring her. "Where are you now?"

"I'm in my car," Marsh replies. The light ahead of her turns red, and as she brakes for it, it finally occurs to her that she actually doesn't know where she's going.

Yes, she does, she realizes as her gaze settles on the neighborhood outside her tinted windows.

She was driving to her house.

Well, it's not her house anymore, in this episode. But in real life, it is.

Marsh wonders who lives there now, within those familiar, unfamiliar walls. Originally, she and Dylan bought it when Harper was about two—before that, they'd been in a two-bedroom apartment closer to downtown. That's probably where Dylan still lives now, with their daughter. In this version of reality, Marsh has probably never set foot in this house. It never belonged to either her or Dylan at all.

She pulls past the driveway a bit, so as not to creep out the residents, and puts the car in park along the curb. It seems smaller, somehow, but in a cozy way. The windows have the same wooden shutters, and the front is painted the same cheery light blue. There's a little plastic sign poking out of the grass on the corner of the property that says, CHRYSALIS REALTY: MAKE YOUR DREAMS COME TRUE!

Chrysalis.

That word again.

She stares at the sign for a long moment, trying to ignore the twinge of dread in her gut.

This is getting really, really weird.

"We have to make some changes," she finally says to Talia. "I'm so glad I'm finally a lawyer, but there have been . . . a lot of unintended consequences."

"That's okay," Talia replies. "We've got plenty of time to get it all straightened out! But overall, your life is getting better and better. Don't you agree?"

Marsh frowns. It's definitely true that she's drastically improved things already—at least professionally. She's found her passion again, and become the lawyer she always wanted to be. She's winning cases and rising fast at Mendoza-Montalvo and Hall, and everyone there finally sees her as the smart, ambitious woman she's always known she could be.

But was it really worth what happened to Dylan's career, and her marriage, which now barely ever was? Or what happened to her relationship with Harper? She still loves her mother, but it's obvious that the two of them are even *less* close than they are in the real world. They're nearly strangers—and no wonder. Harper lives with her father, and Marsh works herself to the bone and then goes drinking every other night with Jo or brings home a warm, faceless body to fill her bed.

Talia's car keys jingle on her end of the line, drawing her back. "I'll meet you wherever you are, and we can go over everything," she says to Marsh.

"No need," Marsh replies. "I know what I want to do. My career is on track, but I need to focus on my personal life now."

There are two ways to go about accomplishing that, though. She could try to make things better with Dylan and Harper, to give him one last chance to have their family back together again. She's not sure how many last chances a person deserves, but maybe it doesn't matter. In the Bubble, she has infinite tries to get it right. Or at least until the season finale.

On the other hand, is the show trying to tell her something important? Is that why Ren keeps popping up in her life, no matter what path she chooses? Because she *is* supposed to be with him after all?

"I love this new, take-charge attitude, Marsh! You're doing a great job pursuing everything this show has to offer," Talia gushes. "Remember, Marsh, as we like to say—you could have *All This . . .*"

"*And More,*" Marsh replies.

To go back to before Dylan cheated on Marsh: Turn the page

To pursue Marsh's burgeoning relationship with Ren: Go to page 125

EPISODE 3

PALLISSARD

Suddenly, Marsh is back in the master bedroom of her house now, teleported like magic between the end of the last scene and the opening of this new one. The room is quiet and still, and everything is bathed in a gentle pink glow from the early sun through the blinds.

She's under the covers, but her eyes are wide open, and her heart is racing a little, despite the peacefulness and familiarity of the scene. These quantum jumps still feel like the lurching moment of a roller coaster's first dip. She takes a deep breath, willing her pulse to slow.

She's here now. Right where she wants to be.

This new setting is so nostalgic, but maybe that's a good thing. This time through, she knows exactly what she wants to do. She won't let this chance go to waste.

Marsh nestles into the blanket and yawns. The clock shows that it's after nine, and that makes her smile.

She missed these lazy mornings with Dylan so much.

Marsh pats the duvet beside her, searching, but his side of the mattress is already empty, the sheets thrown back. She can hear the soft sounds of bare feet padding around the master bathroom, and then the shower turns on.

Dylan is almost incapable of getting ready quietly in the mornings, no matter how hard he tries. He's a noisy tooth brusher, towel fluffer, sink splasher, just like a little boy. The only time he ever managed to be as hushed as he is now was early on in their marriage, just after Harper was born, when he would try to get downstairs without waking Marsh on the weekends so he could cook breakfast and bring it to her in bed.

The smile lingering on her lips grows even bigger at that memory. She buries her face in the pillow and curls her arms to her chest to pantomime sleep, so as not to spoil Dylan's surprise.

Everything is finally back to the way it's supposed to be.

Everything is right again.

The shower turns off just as Marsh realizes that her wedding ring is not on her finger.

What?

Confused, she lifts her head to study her hand. She's still staring at that bare expanse of skin as the footsteps leave the bathroom and enter the bedroom.

Marsh looks up—but it's not Dylan standing there in a towel.

It's Ren.

She bolts upright in bed.

"What the fuck!"

"What?" Ren jumps, startled. "What's wrong?"

Moms4Marsh: <Whoa!!!>
JesterG: <I was so ready to see Dylan!>
TopFan01: <Same! That caught me off guard!>

Marsh is naked just below the camera frame, she realizes. She grabs the blankets up around herself.

What's happening?

She chose to go back to before Dylan cheated on her. None of it happened! That horrible night, her careening drive home from his office, furiously locking him out of the house by changing the alarm code, the call she made to a lawyer the next morning, the divorce—

So what's going on now?

Where is Dylan? Why is Ren here?

And why isn't she wearing her wedding ring?

"Did you have a nightmare or something?" Ren asks, coming over to her side of the bed.

Marsh takes a deep breath. "Maybe," she finally allows.

He leans forward to kiss her forehead. She lets him, trying to play it cool until she has more context. "Coffee?" he asks. "We could drink it out on the back porch, and let the sun chase away the bad dream."

"That sounds good," Marsh says.

Ren hops up and heads for the kitchen still in just his towel. Why is he so comfortable half-nude in her home in this episode? She wants to ask.

Then a gut-wrenching thought strikes her.

"Oh no," Marsh moans, a hand on her forehead.

Is *she* the cheater this time around?

Are she and Ren having an affair instead of Dylan and his mistress?

Marsh scrambles into a shirt and leggings. Her hair is a mess, but she doesn't care. She tears out of the bedroom, then returns and snatches Ren's jeans draped casually over the top of the dresser before rushing downstairs.

"Oh, thanks," Ren says as he sees Marsh round the corner. He tosses the used coffee filter in the trash—*he knows right where the trash is, in the cabinet beside the sink*—and reaches for the jeans. He whips off the towel without a thought, right in the middle of the kitchen, like Marsh has seen his body a million times before.

Moms4Marsh: <Yowza! Starting a Ren fan club!>

Marsh feels the heat rise on her face as she flicks the block of scrolling text away, and tries not to peek as Ren hops into each pant leg.

She should be figuring out what happened with Dylan!

"I just, you know, with Harper still being pretty young . . ." Marsh starts, her voice low so that Harper can't hear from her room, if she's already awake.

Ren gives her a funny look. "We dropped her off at her dad's last week, though."

Marsh looks down at her bare finger again.

She still doesn't know entirely what this means, but two things are now starkly clear: that even without his infidelity, Marsh and Dylan *still* couldn't make it work and divorced anyway, and she also still met Ren in the aftermath.

Marsh is not sneaking around on her husband with Ren. She's just *with* Ren. Because her marriage is over. Again.

She tries to cover a wave of frustration by turning to the cupboard to pull out two mugs.

Was this a sign from the universe, that she and Dylan were never supposed to be together? Or that she and Ren are? Or did she just not choose right, last time? Should she keep going down this path, or try again?

As Marsh frets, she turns the mugs over in her hands. They're cheap, free swag that Dylan got at an academic event; both are bright Sharp Purple and have the same cheesy logo.

Her eyes narrow as she notices the text.

Tenth Annual Intercollegiate STEM Fundraiser
Chrysalis Conference
Reach For New Heights! Change Your Life!

Notamackerel: <Is it just me, or is that word following Marsh around?>
Moms4Marsh: <Shh! We're going to miss their conversation!>

"I definitely will be fully dressed outside the bedroom once Harper moves back, though," Ren is saying as he pours the pot of coffee first into Marsh's mug, then his, oblivious to the logos on them. "That goes without question, obviously."

"Moves back?" The words are out of Marsh's mouth before she remembers she already should know.

Ren eyes her oddly again. "Harper's staying with him all summer, because Pallissard is right around the corner from his apartment. Remember?"

Pallissard.

The Pallissard Institute of Music. The best high school for music in the country. To be good enough to audition and be accepted to that school has been Harper's unwavering goal since she started the violin at seven.

"Are you okay?" Ren asks, concerned by Marsh's expression.

"I'm great," Marsh insists.

She's still in limbo, free-falling through all these choices as she scrambles to open a parachute, but this news about Harper is beyond her wildest dreams. Her marriage still flopped, and Harper's still a little distant, but she's now attending Pallissard's summer program—a miracle Marsh didn't even know could happen in this show—and she herself seems to have landed on her feet with Ren.

Maybe that last choice didn't lead to exactly what Marsh expected, but this life is definitely not *bad*.

She nods decisively, starting to smile. "It just sometimes still feels like a dream."

Ren smiles back and wraps her in a hug. "A good one, though?" he asks.

"Are you sure you don't want anything?" Ren repeats, looking concerned.

"I'm just not hungry," Marsh says.

He frowns. "Okay. It's just, you're the one who suggested we go to brunch in the first place."

Marsh did. She took one sip of her coffee, and then poured the rest down the sink and declared that she wanted to go to brunch as Ren stared at her in bewilderment, still waiting for his own mug to cool. She wasn't hungry, she was just too full of energy. There are so many differences in this episode, and she wants to explore them all. She wants to drive straight to Pallissard to watch Harper practice. She wants to call Dylan and ask him what the hell happened this time, that the two of them still couldn't make it work even without the affair. She even wants to jump right back into bed with Ren to see how good things are on that front in this reality. Most of all, Marsh just wants to get out of the house, to start experiencing this new life. Brunch was the first thing she thought of.

But here under their table's striped umbrella, their ice waters sweating in the warm morning, some of the earlier exhilaration has worn off. If anything, she feels even more unmoored than before, and just as antsy.

She should have chosen somewhere else, is the problem.

This is the brunch spot that she and Dylan used to go to every weekend, when Harper was a baby.

Those were some of the best days. The waiters would set Harper up in a high chair and she'd gleefully demolish a whole plate of pancakes while Marsh and Dylan watched in delight. He'd tell Marsh about a camping trip another teacher took his family on the other week, suggesting maybe the three of them could buy a little tent and show Harper the stars, and Marsh would tell him about an experimental pop-up restaurant she'd passed, and wanted to try.

There was so much fun still, back then. So much more to look forward to.

"Marsh?" Ren coaxes.

This life is good, she knows.

But also, she chose this option because she was trying to her find her way back to Dylan again. Because maybe what she wanted was to be married. To still be a family.

"I have to go to the bathroom," Marsh pronounces, and lurches up from her chair as Ren jumps halfway out of his.

"Do you want me to get a to-go bag?" he asks.

"Sure," she says as she dashes toward the inside of the café. "Actually, no. Never mind."

It might not even matter in a few minutes.

In the bathroom, Marsh lets the sink run and listens to the water.

"Am I being ungrateful?" she whispers to the mirror. "There's just so much here that's different than it was before."

But isn't this the point of this show? Not to get something different, but to get exactly what she wanted?

There's someone in one of the stalls behind her, Marsh realizes just as the lock begins to slide open. She turns off the faucet and pretends to fix her hair, embarrassed that whoever's there might have heard her mumbling, but when their eyes meet in the reflection, she spins around in relief.

"Thank God you're here!" Marsh exclaims as Talia joins her at the sink.

"Sorry I'm late. I didn't know you two were going to shoot off to a café so quick," she says. "Catch me up! How are things in this new life?"

"I'm not sure," Marsh replies. "Things are definitely *different,* but not the way I expected. I was trying to give Dylan one more chance, but he's still gone anyway."

"You've got Ren," Talia offers. "And Harper's doing so well!"

"She really is," Marsh agrees enthusiastically. This Pallissard development is incredible. She's truly grateful for that. "Her music studies are something I want to protect. Can we do that, even if we keep tweaking other things?"

"Of course! I'll make a special note of it," Talia replies. She opens the huge leather tote bag on her shoulder and pulls out the Show Bible again. "Let's see what we're working with for this episode."

Talia checks to make sure the counter is dry, and then lays the Show Bible down and opens it up. Marsh can't help but stare at how much it's grown since the last time she saw it. Each choice has to be carefully documented, but has she really already changed so much? It feels like she's barely begun.

"Interesting," Talia pronounces as she looks up from the page. "It looks like we could try again to repair your marriage with Dylan by jumping even *further* back than the night he was unfaithful, to some other pivotal moment in your relationship. Can you think of one?"

Marsh shakes her head—and then freezes as a memory occurs to her.

Talia's eyes practically glow with hunger.

"What is it?" she asks excitedly.

"Uh. Never mind."

She shakes her head, but Talia is like a hound with a scent. There's no getting out of it now.

At last, Marsh swallows and looks down. "When Harper was about five, that was when Dylan and I hit our first rough patch. Not a rough patch, just a bit of a rut, I guess. Things weren't bad, they just weren't as new as when we were dating. And with a young kid, we'd fallen into kind of a routine."

"Believe me, we all know how that feels," Talia sympathizes, and the comments flood in to agree. "So, what happened?"

"Well, Dylan's birthday was coming up, and I wanted to do something big," Marsh answers. "Book a trip, go to a really nice restaurant, whatever he wanted. I asked him if he had any ideas. I thought he would be excited, but he seemed reluctant at first. He just kept telling me whatever I wanted would be great. I couldn't figure out why. Finally, I got it out of him."

She hesitates, nervous.

"What did he ask for?" Talia's beautiful face shines at her like the sun, urging her on.

"He said . . ."

The words get stuck in her throat for a moment, and then she spits them all out at once, an awkward jumble.

"He said he had this fantasy and wanted to try a threesome, if I would be into it."

LunaMágica: <No way!>

JesterG: <Our sweet, innocent little Marsh—in a threesome?!!>

MeiMei22: <不可能! No way this isn't scripted!>

"How adventurous!" Talia giggles as Marsh whips back to the sink and washes her hands vigorously, just to have something to do. Talia sidles up next to her. "What did you say?"

"I sort of said yes that night, but took it back the next morning," Marsh admits. "I think he knew I wasn't serious, just stunned, and honestly, I don't know if he was totally ready, either. I don't think he expected me to agree in the first place, let alone stick to it. We laughed it off over breakfast, and it never came up again."

"Do you think it changed anything?"

"I don't know," Marsh muses. "But even though we didn't go through with it, he'd been vulnerable to me, and I hadn't embarrassed him. I thought that was worth something." She pauses for a moment. "But I do wonder sometimes what would have happened if we'd tried it."

"You think it might have helped bring you closer?" Talia suggests. "Made things better?"

"Or made things worse," Marsh argues, but she's mostly saying it because she knows she's live on a billion screens right now, not out of any real conviction. What she'd actually admitted to Jo in the weeks after, and privately to herself for many years after that, was that she really *did* wonder. Who hadn't really, who had been in a monogamous relationship for decades? But she also knows that she never actually could have screwed up the nerve to do something that adventurous, no matter how curious she was.

Well, not in *that* life, anyway.

But isn't that why she's here now, on the show?

"That certainly does sound like a very pivotal event in the relationship," Talia says slyly. "What a perfect moment to revisit, to try to save your marriage again. If you want."

Marsh is blushing even more now. "But—"

"Don't worry," Talia says. "The cameras will be very tasteful, as they always are, if you do go there. Just hints at what's happening. And I promise I won't barge in for an interview midtryst." She giggles.

Marsh nods, but she's still mortified. After all, she just admitted to everyone in her life—*and the world*—that their meek little Marshmallow once considered turning things upside down in the bedroom.

And if she keeps going this way, she's going to have to consider it all over again in the next episode.

"Take your time," Talia offers generously.

Marsh tries not to think about Ren still out there on the patio, waiting for her to come back with that concerned look on his face. If she goes back in time, it'll sort of feel like erasing him, in a way. He was so sweet earlier this morning, so happy to just be with her, making coffee.

Almost *too* happy, honestly. Dylan had never cared that much about the little things, had he? Or was it just that after so many years, it was harder for her to recall all the good moments?

But Talia is still grinning at Marsh.

It's clear what she wants Marsh to do. What everyone wants her to do—the corners of her vision are literally vibrating from the effort of containing the screaming comments pane—but she's surprised to find that the pressure to say yes, this time, is more comforting than terrifying.

Maybe what she'd been wanting back then wasn't an easy way out of the encounter, after all.

Maybe what she'd been wanting was permission.

"I know this might feel like a big choice, but you can make as many of them as you want. Or unmake them. That's the whole point." Talia tilts her head a little as she winks, the way she always does right before she says the phrase she knows Marsh, and everyone else in the world, will recognize. "As we all know—you could have *All This* . . ."

"*And More,*" Marsh finishes, the first hint of her own shy grin tugging at the corners of her mouth.

LIGHT IT ON FIRE

Marsh has been staring at her reflection in the mirror for five solid minutes already, unable to look away.

She looks so young.

She *is* so young.

The show has sent her back *ten years*.

Of course it did, because this is the moment of her life she chose to jump to, but she hadn't thought about what else it would mean. That some of the wrinkles would evaporate, some of her bits would lift a few millimeters. Her hair would get a little shinier, her cheeks a little plumper—both sets.

This is *incredible*.

She had no idea *All This and More* could do this.

"My God," Marsh mumbles, watching herself touch the smooth skin around her eyes, where there should be a feathering of crow's-feet.

The first time through this age in her life, all she was worried about was her little leftover pooch from her pregnancy with Harper, and the first fine line threading itself across her brow. At forty-five, she can't believe how good that body was, how she hadn't known it then.

Well, she's not going to waste it this time.

Then another realization hits her. In this path, Harper's still just a kid. Not only does Marsh have a fresh chance to start over with Dylan, but with her daughter, too! Now, she can make sure they build the mother-daughter relationship they deserve, and never grow apart.

Overjoyed, she finishes brushing her teeth with her eyes closed so she won't keep gawking at the mirror, then hurries downstairs. Marsh had forgotten what her house had looked like, so many years ago—the bones are the same, but the walls are bright, happy yellow instead of sensible, suburban white, and everything is a little more cluttered. Harper's toys everywhere, dishes waiting in the sink, a pile of clean laundry that still needs to be folded on the couch. The endearingly chaotic home of two busy parents with a young child.

There's more life, more love, in this decade.

She remembers how this day goes. She woke up before Dylan, or perhaps he was pretending to still be asleep to avoid an awkward conversation, and was already in the kitchen when she told him she didn't want to try a threesome after all. It seems important to preserve some of the logistics, for some reason. Enough is already changing, or about to.

At the fridge, Marsh pulls out the carton of eggs and a jar of fruit jam. She's putting some bread into the toaster when she finally hears footsteps thudding down the stairs.

Her heart soars as Dylan comes into the kitchen.

He's really here.

She's found him at last, and they're together once more.

"Morning," Marsh says casually.

"Morning," he replies, not quite making eye contact.

Marsh has the coffee ready, but he looks a little less hungover than he seemed the first time around. Or maybe she'd remembered the two of them as drunker than they were, because it had made it easier to blame the wine for his bold fantasy, and her initial agreement to it.

"Sleep well?" he asks Marsh as he plants a chaste kiss on her cheek. He kept some stubble in his thirties, and it tickles her slightly.

"Mm," she replies.

His shoulders say that he's nervous. He's not sure if Marsh is upset this morning. If she took what he said seriously last night, or if she even remembers.

Harper skips in and climbs into her seat at the kitchen table, greeting the animals on her place mat as she does so.

Her daughter! Marsh's heart sings. Her baby girl!

But she does a double take when she sees her. Harper's only five now, of course, but that's not what it is. In the real world, and in every other episode so far, her hair has always been curly like Dylan's, but today it's straight, just like Marsh's.

Before she can remark on it, Dylan is next to her at the cutlery drawer, and the clink of silverware provides cover for a quiet conversation.

"About last night," Marsh starts.

"Yeah?" Dylan responds. He was getting out the forks and napkins, but he's stalled now, waiting for what Marsh is going to say. He's attempting to look casual and doing a terrible job at it.

Marsh turns on the burner, and the little blue flame roars to life under the pan.

"I've been thinking . . ."

"You don't want to do it?" he asks, voice low.

Her heart flutters as she hesitates. This is the moment when she said no, she wasn't sure. The moment she started giggling nervously, and then he started giggling nervously, and suddenly it was over, before it had even started. A bullet dodged, a potential disaster spared. It would never come up again.

She still wants to say no. It just feels too scandalous, too dangerous. Maybe if they'd just been dating, but this is their marriage. It's a much bigger risk.

But then again, she didn't do it the last time, and her marriage ended anyway.

"I do," Marsh whispers, so quietly she's not even sure she actually said it.

But the look on Dylan's face makes it clear beyond a shadow of a doubt that she did.

"Wait." He's staring at Marsh in disbelief. "What?"

"I do," she repeats, a little more confident this time.

Moms4Marsh: <Goooo Marsh!>
JesterG: <Woot woot!!>

Dylan leans even closer, so that they're both hovering over the pan now, their voices completely garbled by the sizzle of the eggs. His eyes are huge. Every part of him is tuned to her, like he's an antenna in the cold vacuum of space and she's a mysterious, distant pulsing signal.

"Are you serious?"

"Sure," Marsh replies.

She's smiling, enjoying this now. Dylan is normally the smooth one of the two of them, but here he is staring open-mouthed at her as she calmly stirs the eggs, a flirty smirk creeping across her lips.

"After all, you gotta light it on fire sometimes, right?" She winks.

Dylan is still so gobsmacked, he just keeps staring. Then a laugh escapes him—a boyish, uncontrolled snort that makes them both giggle harder.

"What's so funny, Daddy?" Harper calls from the table.

Dylan stammers, trying to come up with some kid-friendly excuse as Marsh flips an egg onto a plate and delivers it to Harper's butterfly place mat. The butterflies look different than she remembers. Or, were they not supposed to be butterflies at all? Weren't they always fish?

"Well, honey . . ." Dylan is fumbling miserably.

"It's a secret," Marsh says to her, and winks.

"A secret? What kind of secret?!" Harper asks excitedly.

"It's for his birthday," Marsh continues, back at the stove scooping up another serving for Dylan. "I have a surprise present for him."

"Is it a good present?" Harper asks, picking up her fork.

Marsh glances sidelong at him. She lets her eyes pan subtly down, then back up again, the way she's seen actresses do in movies. Dylan is frozen in place, his eyes locked on her as if it's the first time he's ever seen her. Perhaps it is—this more adventurous, sexier version of her.

"I think he'll like it," she finally says.

"Okay. But you're *sure* sure?" Dylan clarifies again, later that night. Harper's in bed, the dishes are done, and the two of them are on the couch with some wine, whatever's on television in front of them long forgotten.

"I'm *sure* sure," Marsh says. She smiles pointedly at him. "For once in your life. Stop. Nitpicking."

"Yes, ma'am," he concedes, and holds out the wine bottle. "Refill?"

"Are you getting frisky with me?" Marsh teases, noticing how close he's leaned to her to top up her glass.

"I can't help it," he replies, stealing a kiss. "I can't get enough of you right now."

Maybe Dylan was really right about all this, the first time around, she has to admit. It's unconventional, but who can say what works in any relationship except the people in it? Maybe a little bit of risk and thrill was exactly what they needed. Maybe this would make them grow closer, and keep them that way, rather than let them slowly spiral apart again. Maybe Marsh can have both things—romantic excitement *and* a happy family with Harper.

"Was Harper's hair always so straight?" she asks suddenly.

Dylan pauses, confused by the abrupt change of subject. "What?"

"Nothing," Marsh says quickly, wincing at her mistake.

That was the wrong thing to bring up. She doesn't want to lose the vibe.

"Cheers." She raises her glass. "Tell me about how this works."

"I don't know," Dylan replies, fidgety with excitement. "I guess the first thing is we find someone?"

"How? Not from either of our jobs. I don't want it to be anyone we know."

"No, no one we know," Dylan confirms. "There must be an app or something."

Marsh is laughing now. "A dating app for threesomes?"

"Why not?" He grins goofily.

It takes a little bit of Googling, but a few minutes later, a new little colorful square is downloaded on Dylan's phone, and they're both snickering as they input a profile and choose a sufficiently anonymous photo of the two of them together.

"Not our faces!" Marsh cries, rejecting one he's just picked.

"I know!" He laughs back, still scrolling. "This one—no, *this* one, you look really hot in this one."

Marsh glances at him as he selects the picture of them on a beach and crops their heads out of the frame. It's been a long time since he's said something like that—marriage and the baby made it easy to be lazy—but the casual way with which he tossed it out now is somehow more exciting than if he'd delivered it like a pronouncement. Like he still thinks it's true that she's attractive, not like it's something he feels he needs to say to be a good husband.

"Ready?" Marsh asks him nervously.

Dylan looks down at the phone again. His thumb hovers over the JOIN button.

"Do you want to look through people together?" he asks.

Marsh considers this for a moment. "I want you to choose," she says.

"Really? All on my own?"

Marsh nods. It feels right. She's already been in charge of so much, thanks to the show. Because she said yes to the threesome this time, their relationship has changed dramatically. It's only fair that Dylan gets to make this choice now.

"I trust you," she says.

She means it. She really does. In this life, things are still good between them. They haven't grown apart, haven't started neglecting each other, haven't given up trying, even after they realized that they needed to, or they were going to lose it all. Dylan hasn't betrayed her yet, and hopefully never will.

Dylan explores the app, trading messages with other people and showing Marsh some of their pictures. For the first few days, everything seems perfect. He's so excited he can barely sit still, every look they give each other turns flirtatious, and the petty domestic arguments have dwindled to almost nothing.

But after about a week, things start to go downhill.

"They're all so *young*," Dylan complains to Marsh quietly at the coffeepot as he assembles Harper's school lunch box. "They're just not interested in us."

"Are you saying we're old?" Marsh asks, pretending to be affronted. She sneaks in an extra peanut butter cup for her daughter when Dylan's not looking.

"No!" he groans. "But they're infants, practically. Not married, no mortgage, no desk jobs, no kids of their own. I guess being in your thirties is ancient in the hookup world."

Marsh stifles a laugh. If only this Dylan knew that both of them are actually in their *forties*, outside the Bubble. But still, she has to find some way to make this work. It might be the key to saving their marriage.

"I'll keep looking," Dylan says. "Maybe I'll expand our search parameters a bit."

And he does. He sends more messages, spends more time scrolling. Marsh starts to worry that she might not actually be able to follow this path to fruition. Can it really be that hard to find another adventurous woman who isn't more than a decade younger than her and Dylan? Has life really gotten so boring for them already? Does she need to go back *even farther* to have a chance at fixing things?

But one day at last, Dylan comes home from work with a mischievous grin on his face, and she knows he's finally found someone.

"That's just it," he says that night as he and Marsh recline into the couch together, twisting the wine cork off the metal spiral. "*They* messaged *us*."

"Ooh," Marsh says, a bolt of flattery pinkening her cheeks for a moment, and then pauses. "Wait, did you say 'they'?"

Dylan nods nervously. "It's not just a woman. It's a couple."

Marsh stares at him, then takes a long, deep drink of wine.

Hmmm.

This was not what she was expecting.

She's not really into women, not like Dylan is, but she could imagine that kind of a night, if necessary. Both of them flirting with each other to excite him, touching each other softly, maybe kissing a little, and then letting him take over and lead the encounter.

But now it wouldn't be just a woman there.

There would also be a man.

A man who would be doing things to Marsh. In front of Dylan.

"Too much?" Dylan asks, studying her hesitantly.

"Well," she starts to say.

She's about to tell him that it is too much, that she's not sure she can do this anymore, but she bites her tongue at the last moment.

It's true that a couple is a lot more than she bargained for. But that's what this show is about, right? Not letting chances she'd been too meek to risk the first time around pass her by again?

If she's not going to try it now, when will she ever?

The look on Dylan's face when Marsh agrees to change the threesome into a foursome is almost reward enough all by itself.

"The couple's username is Chrysalis," he whispers to her later, after the two of them are snuggled into bed for the night.

She nearly sits upright.

Chrysalis.

She doesn't like this.

She doesn't like it at all.

Why does that word keep appearing, over and over, no matter where she goes?

"Are you okay?" Dylan asks.

"What kind of a username is that?" Marsh replies, putting her head on his shoulder so he can't see that her brow is furrowed.

"I think it's the little cocoon caterpillars transform into butterflies inside or something," Dylan replies.

Marsh tries to roll her eyes. "So poetic!"

"Oh, stop." Dylan laughs. "Everyone has a cheesy username."

It's true. The username the two of them chose is Kurremkarmerruk, which is a character from an old book they both love that they were sure no one else on the app would know—especially if they're all mostly as young as Dylan insists.

Marsh allows herself a quick blink to glance at the comments, to see if any of the viewers have noticed that strange word, *Chrysalis*, has cropped up again, but everyone is too busy discussing just how much skin they'll get to see in the upcoming scene to notice.

Or, maybe it's not as big of a deal as she thought. Maybe she's blowing this out of proportion.

Still, Marsh can't shake the uneasy feeling.

"Okay, okay. What's this other couple like?" she asks instead. She cuddles closer, trying to stay in the moment.

"About our age, somewhere in their thirties. The woman is tall and redheaded, and the guy has dark hair," Dylan says, nervously but with excitement. He looks at Marsh, trying to make sure she's still up for this. "I think . . . I think you'll like him."

Marsh is surprised that even though she's still nervous, the jitters seem as much from anticipation as they are from fear.

She's actually looking forward to this, she realizes, starting to grin.

Dylan and Marsh decide on Saturday night. They'll have a sitter come over for Harper and go to dinner first, just the two of them, and then their amorous guests will meet them at home. Marsh considered booking a hotel, but at the last second, she backpedaled. If she was going to do this, she wanted to do it on familiar turf. A place where she felt confident and in control. Harper's bedroom is on the other side of the house, and she's always slept like the dead, even at five years old. Dylan, the original Dylan, once burned some popcorn and set off the smoke alarm, and Harper didn't wake up the whole time the two of them were fanning the kitchen with towels to make the screaming wail stop.

Harper never heard Marsh sobbing into Jo's shoulder late at night in the early weeks of the divorce either, no matter how anguished her cries became, she can't help but also remember.

The date with Dylan is weird, of course. Tense, flirty, nervous, silent, then a rush of conversation, then more fidgeting. They tip the waiter way too much, then drive home a little over the speed limit, staring at each red light. Dylan sends the sitter home while Marsh peeks in on Harper, who's snoring soundly, and when they both meet back in the bedroom, they have fifteen minutes to get ready before their guests arrive.

"I bought a little something," Marsh admits. "To wear, I mean."

Dylan's eyes light up. "Oh yeah?" he asks.

She winks. "I think you'll like it."

He watches Marsh slowly saunter into their small walk-in closet and flick on the soft light with stunned captivation. It's so funny how just a few days ago, or fifteen years in the future, depending on how she looks at it, Marsh was mortified to try on Le Fascination with Jo. Now, as she holds up this set of lingerie—which oddly does look *a lot* like the original Le Fascination, just pink instead of red this time—she's not intimidated at all. Maybe because this young body still doesn't quite feel like hers yet. Or maybe because this time, she has the power, rather than the other way around.

Once she's closed the door, Marsh reaches up to the top shelf, where she stashed the shopping bag with the lingerie earlier that day. As she pulls it down, she accidentally dislodges the things stored beside it and almost dumps them onto her head.

As she starts to shove it all back into place, she pauses, and then takes down a box from the clutter.

It's medium-sized and rectangular.

Like what a dress shirt might come in.

"Oh, yeah," Dylan says when she comes out of the closet with her robe on, the lacy pink getup hidden underneath it, and he sees what she's holding. "I forgot about that old thing."

He takes it from her, and then opens it to show her what's inside, even though she already knows.

"It's a briefcase," he explains.

"For a lawyer," Marsh finishes, barely more than a murmur.

Is it strange that she's found this box here, and now? Or does it not count because she's years in the past in this episode?

Does that mean this is the first time it's happened?

Slowly, Marsh reaches out to touch the soft leather.

Or not?

Dylan has misread the quietness of her voice for sadness, rather than apprehension, and steps closer to her.

"I should have told you," he says. "I bought it just after we found out you were pregnant. Cost me my whole grad school paycheck. You were so happy, though, both about our daughter and about becoming a lawyer, and I wanted to surprise you."

"You don't have to explain," Marsh says. "It was a sweet gesture."

He scoots closer to her. "I know a lot of things changed after Harper was born—and that's okay. But, it felt wrong to throw it out. For me to be the one to do it, I mean. But you can do whatever you want with it."

Marsh nods as she listens, studying the briefcase. She lets him tuck a lock of her hair behind her ear.

"You know, sometimes, I wish I could leave something behind," Marsh starts.

She's thought about telling him this over the years, many times, but she's always stopped herself. The sting of humiliation, the shadow of that drab student auditorium, always stilled her tongue. And then eventually, it was so late, and she and he were so old. All the plans already long made, all the roads already started down. It seemed like it would be embarrassing, or ungrateful, to say.

But this is a new chance, and a new Marsh. It's ten years earlier. This time, maybe she will.

"A mark of some kind on the world, I mean."

"Like Harper?" Dylan asks.

She shrugs. "Yes, but something else, too. Or, maybe now, it's that I wish that I could leave something behind *for* Harper."

She gives the briefcase a little shake.

"I used to think maybe it could be a groundbreaking case, or a new precedent, but it doesn't have to be law, even. Just *some* kind of mark. Something for her, and for me. Something to show her that she can do anything she wants to do—because I did, too."

When she looks up, Dylan touches her cheek.

"Well, now I'm really glad I kept this old thing all this time." He smiles. "It sounds like you might need it after all."

"You'd *really* be okay with that?" Marsh asks softly. "If I did want to restart law school, all these years later?"

"Of course," Dylan says. "I love you, Mallow. I want you to be happy."

Marsh looks at him, at a loss for words.

Maybe this choice really was the right one, after all.

With perfect timing, Dylan's phone buzzes. Their guests have texted rather than rung the doorbell, as planned.

"They're here," Marsh says.

For a moment, Dylan doesn't know what to do. He just stands there, excited and nervous, until Marsh starts laughing.

"Go get them!" she urges. "Before the neighbors see."

"Right!" Dylan jumps into action, awkward. "So, this is it."

"This is it," Marsh says.

Dylan smooths his hair down and then musses it again as he rushes to the bedroom door. But as his hand touches the handle, he pauses, his eyes unfocused, as if momentarily lost.

"What is it?" Marsh asks.

"It just feels like . . . I already *did* give you the briefcase, somehow," he muses. "But that's impossible."

Marsh shudders at a sudden chill.

But then Dylan shrugs, unconcerned again.

"Must have been a dream," he says.

"Must have," Marsh finally agrees.

He winks, then disappears, closing the door behind him. "Be right back."

Marsh waits in silence, trying to push the unsettling exchange away. She attempts to lounge sexily. Tugs her robe open a little, just enough to show a flash of pink lace, rearranges her legs. *Get back in the moment,* she urges, but there's so little time. Before she's even counted to ten, she can already hear Dylan returning from the front door.

"Sometimes, you gotta light it on fire," she whispers desperately as two more sets of footsteps begin to echo softly down the hall after him. "You gotta light it on fire."

She can do this. She wants to.

Dylan slowly opens the bedroom door, and beckons in these mysterious strangers to meet Marsh. A shadow falls across the rug, and another man's hand appears. Marsh is so full of butterflies, she worries she might float off the bed.

But as soon as she locks eyes with the mysterious man, her stomach hits the floor.

It's *Ren.*

"What the fuck!" Marsh shrieks, scrambling to her knees, trying to get off the mattress.

"Whoa!" Ren gasps, jumping back at her outburst.

Moms4Marsh: <OH MY GOD!!!>

C0c0drilo: <¡¡¡Puta madre!!!>

The comments scream.

LunaMágica: <PLOT TWIST!>
StrikeF0rce: <Okay, this is hilarious!>

"What's wrong?" Dylan asks, rushing toward Marsh protectively. "Are you okay?"

"You . . ." Marsh says to Ren. She's fighting with the sheets for her robe and wrapping it around herself as fast as she can. "Why are you here?"

Amid the chaos, Marsh vaguely notes the poor woman, tall and red-headed, looking equally bewildered as she hesitates in the darkened doorway behind Ren, but she ignores her. She's not important right now.

"Because . . ." Ren falters, looking at Dylan. "The app. I thought . . ."

"But how?" Marsh hisses. "Why does this keep happening?"

She wants to laugh, or cry, she's not sure which. Was this really what would have happened if she'd gone through with the threesome, in the real world? Was Dylan always going to have unknowingly found Ren? Or is this the show, pulling the strings again?

"Why does what keep happening?" Ren repeats, unsure of what's going on.

Does he just not recognize her yet in the semidarkness of the bedroom, because the app hides their real names, and this version of Ren hasn't seen Marsh since high school? Or has the show changed something else, and this Ren really doesn't know her?

It doesn't really matter, she decides. All of this is just *wrong*.

"I'm sorry," Dylan is saying to Ren and his partner as he urges Marsh toward the bathroom. "Just give us a second."

"Totally okay," Ren replies, still rattled.

"Are you all right?" Dylan asks her as he closes the door.

"I'm so sorry," Marsh stutters, gripping the sink.

"No, don't apologize," he says. "I knew this was a bad idea. It was too much. Way too much. We should have started with holding a match to the marshmallow, instead of shoving it into a house fire, or—"

"Dylan, please, stop," Marsh says, before he can turn it into an argument. She rubs her temples and sighs. "Enough with the goddamned metaphor already."

He winces. "I only meant, we don't have to do this, if you don't want. Really."

"I know," she replies. "I'm okay. I just . . ."

She stares into Dylan's face, searching for a sign. Disappointment, or relief, or something else.

"I just need a second," she finally says. "I want to call Jo."

"Oh," Dylan replies. "Okay, yeah. Maybe that's a good idea."

Marsh nods. "Go back out there so our poor . . . *friends* aren't stranded alone in our house, and I'll come out after I talk to her and tell you how I feel."

Dylan kisses her, then slips out, closing the door behind him. As he awkwardly reassures Ren and the other woman, Marsh snatches her phone from the pocket of her robe.

But it's not Jo she's calling.

"Marsh," Talia says when she picks up. Her voice is a little teasing. "I just got settled in for a long night on call here at RealTV. I thought I wouldn't hear from you for hours—"

"What is going on?" Marsh hisses, cutting Talia off. "What is Ren doing at my fucking *orgy*?"

Talia's office chair squeaks sharply over the line as she sits straight up. Even amid her confusion, Marsh is vaguely pleased that this curveball seems to flap even the unflappable Talia.

"Is something wrong with the Bubble?" Marsh asks. "Because I don't remember anomalies like this happening to you in season one!"

"*Nothing* is wrong with the Bubble," Talia promises. "It's totally stable. But even if it wasn't, the network would pull us out immediately. That's the first rule of the show."

Marsh is still pacing the tile floor, but talking to Talia is working. She's starting to calm down.

"Remember, what you're doing here on *All This and More* is monumental, Marsh. A few anomalies are inevitable along the way," Talia continues. "But put that aside for a second. This is what you want, right?"

"Yes," Marsh agrees.

Talia *hmm*s, prompting Marsh to give more.

"I guess, despite this complication, my relationship with Dylan has never been better," she adds. "Things are really great with him."

"I couldn't agree more," Talia says. "You're doing great. Even better than I did!"

Marsh manages to laugh a little at that.

"So, which way are you leaning?"

"I don't know!" she cries. "I have no idea which is the right choice."

"Why, that's easy," Talia gushes. "It's the one that will get you closer to perfect by the finale."

"Perfect." Marsh repeats the word, clinging to it like a life raft.

Yes. That *is* the point of this incredible show. That's why she chose this moment to go back to. For the chance to save her marriage, and make it perfect. She'd been willing to try, at least. But the partners Dylan brought in weren't supposed to have made things this complicated. On the other hand, turning down Ren now means that this night will end up just like it was in her original life.

Marsh shifts the phone to her other ear, stalling Talia.

"Come on," Talia needles charmingly. "Admit it. You still kind of want to go through with this, even with this surprise."

"I—" Marsh gasps, affronted.

"Think about it. How often does a person get to both have their cake and eat it, too?" Talia cuts her off. "In the real world, you can only have one—either Dylan or Ren. But here, if you can get over the bizarreness, you can have both tonight."

Marsh frowns.

It's a good point.

But on the other hand, she can't shake the feeling that something is just *too* off about all this. Both emotionally and quantum-ally. It's like the harder she tries to get back to Dylan, the more the show pushes her toward Ren, in some way. Is it simply because the show can see everything, and is smarter than her? Or because something else is going on?

"I have the Show Bible here," Talia says. Pages fan over the phone line as the all-important soundtrack starts to jingle. "I'm ready."

Marsh looks at the bathroom door again, where Dylan, the redhead, and Ren are waiting for her on the other side.

"Me too," she finally says.

To go through with the encounter:
Turn the page

To decline the encounter:
Go to page 367

Marsh comes back out of the bathroom. Dylan, Ren, and the redheaded woman all look up at the sound, unsure of whether they should be excited or apologetic. Dylan is perched on the edge of the bed, fiddling with the belt of her robe that got left behind when she bolted, and the woman is still standing near the door of the bedroom, twirling a ringlet of her fiery hair. Ren is beside her, his arms crossed awkwardly.

"Sorry about that," Marsh says. "I'm just nervous."

"Nervous . . . but in?" Dylan asks.

Marsh allows a tiny nod.

The change in the room is immediate. Both Dylan and Ren relax, hands unclenching and legs loosening, like big cats preparing for a hunt. The woman comes over to stand next to Marsh, and Marsh exchanges a shy glance with her.

"Just relax." She winks at Marsh.

Does she look familiar?

But the room is dark enough that Marsh can't be sure. It doesn't matter, really. She's beautiful, from what Marsh can see. And confident. She's wearing a slinky dress and heels, but whatever she's got on underneath is very strappy.

What are the rules of an orgy? Marsh blushes. She obviously knows Dylan's name, and also happens to accidentally know Ren's, although it seems that no one else but Marsh realizes that—but is she supposed to exchange names with the woman before they all do this? Would that be polite or super weird?

The woman seems to sense Marsh's hesitation. "We'll let them take the lead tonight," she tells her.

Okay, then.

Dylan and Ren look at each other, then look at the two women flirtatiously. Hungrily. Marsh suddenly understands what a gazelle must feel like.

She might kind of like it.

Dylan goes to her and kisses her first. Hesitantly to start, almost like they're dating again, and everything is new. His hands stutter across her waist, exploring shyly. Then there's another hand on her shoulder, and

Marsh and Dylan both turn to see Ren standing on her other side, his fingers trailing slowly down her arm.

Dylan gives Marsh a gentle nudge toward Ren, and then sidles over to the other woman.

YanYan242: <Omg, this is actually happening!!!!>
LunaMágica: <Marsh's greatest fantasy come to life!>

Ren starts slow, touching Marsh's hair first. He brushes a silky lock from her eyes and tucks it behind her ear as she bends gently into the caress, and his gaze roams her body. Nervously, he opens her robe to reveal Le Fascination, and his eyes smolder. He leans in as his hand trails down her stomach, inch by inch—and then just as his fingers slip beneath her lacy underwear out of the camera frame, Marsh and Ren's lips touch.

Marsh gasps, her body shuddering with surprise and pleasure. Ren's touch is electric, lighting her up and then shocking her with every motion. Her cheeks burn hotter with every moan, until she's sure she's glowing crimson.

Next to Marsh, Dylan is all over the other woman. Shirts are being thrown to the ground, trousers are being peeled off. Then they're all on the bed, a writhing, shuddering mass barely discernable in the semidarkness. Lace rips as Ren plunges into Marsh, over and over, or maybe it's Dylan now, but none of them care, and none of them stop.

Everything is happening too fast. She wants to analyze this, to pause the scene and play it back over and over from every angle, but her brain is no longer processing. All her thoughts are turgid, stagnating, turning to a white-hot mass sinking lower and lower in her abdomen, until it gathers like a fine point of light ready to explode.

Just as a low, guttural moan escapes her lips, the door to their bedroom creaks open.

"Mommy?" a tiny, frightened voice whimpers.

Oh no.

The whole world freezes.

Harper was always a scarily deep sleeper—but that had been in Marsh's original life. In this reality, it turns out that maybe she isn't. Maybe the sounds of two couples fucking are enough to stir her from her slumber, and to frighten her enough that she would run from her bedroom to her parents' to see what was wrong.

"Harp," Dylan starts to say, hoarse from exertion.

But the room is dark, she's groggy, and all she can discern in the moment are shapes. Her mother pinned down on the bed, crying out, and strangers hovering over her.

"Honey," Marsh whispers.

Harper turns and runs, sobbing in terror.

"Shit!" Marsh curses, scrambling up in a panic. "Shit, shit, *shit!*"

"Fuck, I'm so sorry!" Ren lurches off the bed with his partner.

"There's a kid here?" the woman asks, mortified.

"I thought it would be fine!" Dylan says, diving for his slacks on the floor as Ren also does the same for his jeans. Harper's cries echo as she runs, and now Pickle is awake and barking in the living room because she's upset, forcing Dylan to shout to be heard. "I thought she'd just call out for us if she woke up, not come in!"

"*What?*" Marsh shouts back, incredulous. Everything is chaos—she doesn't even have clothes, she was already in lingerie when Ren and his partner arrived. "Where the fuck is my robe?" she yells.

"She's always too scared to leave her bed at night whenever she has a nightmare!" Dylan cries. "I figured this would be the same!"

Marsh tries to say something, but it just comes out as a string of foul sounds. She doesn't know who to be angrier at, Dylan or herself. Why the hell wouldn't he have pushed for a hotel if he knew Harper doesn't sleep deeply in this reality? Why did she assume everything about this life would be the same if the whole point of *All This and More* is to make things different?

Hasn't she learned anything from the other episodes?!

"We should go," the redheaded woman says, practically crawling out of her own skin to get to the door. Ren's got jeans on and nothing else—no shoes, no shirt—and Marsh doesn't care which neighbors might see a random half-dressed couple leave her house in a beeline for their car, or whose fault any of this is anymore. She just needs to get to Harper.

The four of them dash down the hall, falling over Pickle in the dark. Harper's sobs are bouncing off every surface in the house, like she's in all the rooms at the same time. Marsh and Dylan continue to call for her as Ren and the woman break for the front door, but Pickle is all over Ren, barking and nipping at his heels, unsure if he's supposed to be playing with him or chasing him out. Ren trips, and Pickle dives at him as he goes down with a yelp.

"Pickle! Shit! Leave it!" Dylan orders the dog. "Harper, where are you?"

"Come to Mommy, Harp!" Marsh begs. Finally, she spots her daughter hiding under the dining table between the chairs, and relief washes over her. "Harp!"

She pushes the chairs out of the way and pulls Harper into her arms as Dylan tries to pry Pickle off Ren, who's still barking wildly, now apparently sure this is all a game.

"It's okay, honey, it's okay," Marsh tells her over and over.

"I'm sorry, he's still kind of a puppy," Dylan says to Ren as he continues grappling with Pickle.

"I'll get the car started," Ren's partner says as she whips the door open and practically throws herself out of it. As she goes, the porch light glances off her face, and recognition strikes Marsh.

Was that . . . was that Alexis Quinn?

Talia's season one producer?

But that's impossible.

Why would she be here, in this scene?

But before Marsh can be sure, the woman's gone, and Ren is still struggling to get himself out from underneath an exuberant Labrador as Dylan grabs ineffectually at the wriggling mass of fur.

"Just get his collar!" Marsh urges impatiently, so Ren can be gone that much sooner. The moment is slowly curdling from frantic into pathetic, and everyone can feel it now. Harper is still clutching onto her mother for dear life, but her sobs have calmed, and she wipes her tears on Marsh's robe as Dylan peels Pickle off Ren at last.

"I thought a bad guy was trying to hurt you!" She hiccups as Ren struggles to his knees.

"Oh, no, honey, I'm safe, see?" Marsh says, brushing Harper's hair free of her eyes. "You don't have to worry. Ren isn't a bad guy, he's a friend—"

"Wait," Dylan says.

The room goes silent, aside from Harper's sniffles. Even Pickle is frozen, startled to stillness by the sudden shift in mood. Marsh looks up to see Dylan staring at her tensely—and Ren, too.

She's still so shaken, she doesn't get it yet.

"What?" she asks.

"You called him Ren," Dylan finally says. "How do you know that's his name? We never said them to each other."

Notamackerel: <Oh, shit>

Dylan looked concerned before, during the chaos of trying to find Harper, but he's properly freaked out now. He glares at Ren, and then Marsh, growing more agitated by the second.

"What's going on? Is that why you panicked when he first came in?" He turns to Ren again, suspicious. "Do you know each other?"

"No!" Ren insists, looking at Marsh. "Not at all!"

And then, finally, despite the darkness and the disorienting circumstances of the night, his eyes widen in shock as he stares at her.

"Oh my God," he whispers. He peers closer. "*Marsh?*"

"What the *fuck* is going on right now?" Dylan shouts, nearly hysterical.

Pickle starts barking again, spooking Ren anew, who bumps into the couch and falls over it as he backs up. Harper returns to sobbing, unsure of why her father is so upset, and why he's raising his voice to her mother. The roar of a car engine lurching to life thunders in through the still-open door, and the other woman honks the horn outside, but now Dylan is moving to block Ren from leaving until he gets answers.

Marsh hugs Harper closer as she wails, trying to keep her calm, and puts a futile hand up as Dylan and Ren both start screaming at each other, unsure of whether they want to figure out what the hell is going on or to never think about it again.

"Everyone, just . . ."

She's about to explain high school, but would that information actually make this better, or would it make things worse? Would it make her seem like some kind of obsessed stalker, and make Ren even more horrified and Dylan even more repelled?

"Tell me what's going on!" Dylan cries. "Are you *cheating* on me?"

A laugh bursts out of her at the absurdity of that statement. A dry, exhausted chuckle.

"It doesn't matter," Marsh finally says.

It really doesn't.

Because none of this is real. Not until the finale, anyway.

"What does that mean, 'it doesn't matter'?" Dylan asks, staring intensely at Marsh, desperately trying to understand.

She rakes her hands through her hair, frustrated. She'd thought this was going to play out so differently, when she first came back to this moment in her life. She tried her absolute best to salvage things with Dylan, but no matter what she changes, everything still fails. Maybe no matter what she does, she'll never be able to make the two of them work.

She can imagine what Talia would say. That maybe Marsh isn't actually supposed to fix her marriage. Maybe Dylan is the very thing that's been holding her back from the best version of her life.

Maybe, as terrifying as it is, she's supposed to let him go—for good.

EPISODE 4

The colors of the next scene are heavy and dark, like the fullness before a satisfying storm.

Marsh is in the front passenger seat of a car. It's not her car—the color is different—but Marsh is still gaining her bearings. Absentmindedly, she reaches to unclick the seat belt.

"Hon, the light just turned green. What are you doing?" Ren asks her from the driver's seat.

Marsh jumps, surprised, as the vehicle eases into motion and glides through the intersection.

Okay. So far, so good.

The car doesn't look like the one Ren owned in the real world, but that's a minor detail. Ren is here. That part is right, at least.

"Hon?" Ren asks, glancing at Marsh before returning his eyes to the road.

"Uh, the belt was just tight," she says.

"It's your dress that's tight," Ren whispers with a wink.

She *is* wearing a tight dress, she realizes. A very nice tight dress.

Definitely an improvement over the clothing situation from the last scene's utterly disastrous tryst.

She winces at the thought, and pushes the memory away. There's no point in trying to understand what went wrong there. That version is over, as good as forgotten. Marsh has made her choice. She's here now, with a new chance to try again with Ren—the *right* way.

"You look good, too," Marsh says to him, noticing at last that he's wearing a suit.

"Not even in the same league," he replies.

"I think a storm's coming," Harper says from the back seat, surprising Marsh. Her voice is loud, too loud. Marsh turns to see that her daughter has her headphones on, and is looking up at the evening sky through the moonroof. The faint echo of classical music from the little speakers reaches Marsh as Harper sits back, closing her eyes and twitching her fingers in time to the song's violin.

They must be on their way to a concert, Marsh guesses. This is how Harper always prepares.

"Glad I brought the patio furniture in," Ren says. "Did you turn the house alarm on before we left?"

"I'm not sure," Marsh confesses, because she really has no idea.

"Oh, it's fine. We only got it installed last week. I'm still learning to remember to do it, too."

So, she and Ren live together now, Marsh deduces. And maybe also own this car together. It looks like an SUV—a very practical model. A family car. Maybe she and Ren bought it when they moved in. His old one was too small to fit her, him, Harper, and Pickle comfortably in it.

A fresh start.

Grinning now, Marsh opens the overhead mirror to put on a dash of lipstick. Then she leans closer to her reflection. For some reason, the wrinkles around the outside corners of her eyes are a tiny bit deeper.

She frowns and touches one fine line. Is she more stressed in this version of life?

There's a newspaper folded into the middle console between them. She tugs it free and looks at the date on the front page.

No, not stressed.

It's just two years into the *future* this time.

Marsh isn't forty-five in this episode. She's forty-seven.

Notamackerel: <Ha, she's OLD now! Look at those wrinkles!>

The outburst is downvoted a million times before she closes the chat.

"Weird," Marsh says.

"What's weird?" Ren asks.

"I—thought I grabbed a different shade," Marsh says, capping the lipstick again.

Actually, she doesn't look bad for forty-seven, she realizes, the longer she considers her face in the mirror. Honestly, she looks pretty much just as good as at forty-five. Maybe a little *better,* even. All the incremental improvements from every path she's tried so far are building on one another. Her body feels a little firmer, like she might be eating healthier or exercising more frequently, and there's a glow to her that wasn't there before at forty-five. It's already tugging at her lips, like she's so used to smiling that it's odd to have a neutral expression.

Maybe those crow's-feet are a little deeper because Marsh spends more of her time in this life grinning, rather than fretting.

Ren brakes for a turn, and Marsh looks out to see that they're pulling into the parking lot of a somewhat run-down apartment complex.

The starter apartment where she and Dylan lived before they bought their house.

"All right, kiddo, don't forget your tuba! I mean, your trumpet! What instrument do you play again?" Ren teases as they cruise through the parking lot. "Gotta be the bassoon!"

Harper laughs politely at his attempt at a dad joke. "Violin, Ren, violin."

"Violin!" He smacks his head, feigning amazement.

In the real world, Marsh hadn't yet introduced Ren and Harper, but she'd begun to wonder about how it would go—before she'd ruined everything on that disastrous night. Would Ren want to be a stepdad, someday? Would Harper accept him? Even *like* him?

Seeing them together now, it's all right. Her daughter seems comfortable enough with Ren around, but she's not her full, relaxed self yet. Warm enough to be friendly, but still too guarded to goof around.

Their relationship is off to a good start, but it's not perfect.

Not yet, she thinks.

"Thanks for the ride," Harper says as soon they park. She pops the door, jumps out, and grabs her violin case. "See you guys at the theater!"

"Love you!" Marsh replies enthusiastically, craning her neck to catch a glimpse of her daughter. As she does, she catches a flash of color on the back seat—of course Harper's remembered her beloved instrument, but in her excitement, she's left her jacket.

"Wait, Harper! You forgot your—" Ren cries, but her headphones are still on. Her door slams closed, and she skips across the asphalt toward Dylan's apartment.

Marsh leans over and grabs the rumpled fabric with a loving sigh. "Hang on, I'll be right back."

"Don't take too long," Ren warns. "We'll miss our dinner reservation."

Marsh blows him a kiss. "I'll go as fast as I can in these heels."

He waggles his eyebrows. "I'll stay here and enjoy the view."

She gets out of the car with a little bit of extra wiggle, just for fun. Harper was right, though—it really does look like a storm is coming, and she picks up the pace. Ahead, Harper's darting up the stairs to the second floor, and knocking on the third unit in. Just as Marsh reaches the landing, Dylan opens the door. He gives Harper a hug and then lets her inside, not seeing Marsh.

"Dylan!" Marsh calls, and he leans back out. "Hold on a sec."

His eyes widen as he catches sight of Marsh—she can't tell if it's because of the dress and stilettos, or because he just wasn't expecting to see her, period.

"What's wrong?" he calls out, his voice strangely formal.

"Harper forgot her jacket," Marsh says as she reaches him. "Do you mind if I give it to her?"

Dylan hesitates. He seems tenser than usual in this episode, she observes. Maybe they're not amicably divorced in this reality, and things are frostier between the two of them than they've been in other versions?

"It's just, it looks like rain," Marsh finally adds.

Dylan glances up at the sky for a long moment. "Sure," he says at last.

He opens the door wider so Marsh can slip in, and she stands there awkwardly just inside the entrance of his modest place. It looks mostly the same as when they lived there as newlyweds, with the same budget furniture and cheap curtains, except the photos of the two of them are all gone now, of course. Dylan hasn't gotten around to replacing them with anything, and the walls look sadly bare.

She's unsure of what to do. He clearly doesn't want her to go farther in or make herself more comfortable. He's waiting stiffly, one hand on the still-open door, trying to catch a read on her expression and also trying not to make sustained eye contact.

"How . . . are you?" Marsh asks.

"Fine," Dylan says, like he'd rather be talking about anything else. "How's Harper? Nervous for tonight?"

"I don't think so," Marsh replies.

He smiles a little at that. "I'm glad. She's going to do great."

Marsh's eyes fall on the side table beside where they're standing, and she spies a single ticket next to his keys—a seat for tonight at the Mirabel Theater, for a Pallissard classical music concert.

"I still can't believe it," Marsh says as she picks the stub up as if the paper itself is precious.

"Me either. She's the best first chair violin they've ever had, she told me yesterday," Dylan says. Despite the tension between them, he's beaming with pride for Harper.

First chair violin.

A grin breaks out across Marsh's face. Improving her own life is one thing, but it means even more that she's also making Harper's dreams come true.

If only there were some way to right things for Dylan, too.

Marsh knows he's not her responsibility anymore, but still. She doesn't want him to suffer. Can things really be perfect for her if they're not so great for him?

"Are you all right?" he's asking, she realizes suddenly.

She sets his ticket down and nods. "I'm just so proud of her."

"So am I," Dylan replies, but he's not smiling anymore. The happy expression has faded from his face and been replaced by something else. Unease, maybe.

"Are *you* all right?" Marsh asks him back.

"Yeah, yeah."

He pauses too long.

"It's just, Harper's always loved violin, but first chair? You've heard her practice. She's good, damn good, but not *this* good. Not yet. She only just got into Pallissard this year, off the waiting list! Then it's like, I wake up today, and suddenly she's *first chair*? On a full scholarship? How is that possible?" He points behind him, toward the living room. "And then Pickle—"

As Dylan says their dog's name, Marsh realizes that he hasn't barked once, despite Harper ringing the doorbell, running through when Dylan opened the door for her, and then Marsh's arrival after her.

Where is Pickle?

Dylan sees the question slip across Marsh's face for a split second before she hides it again.

"Right?" he accuses, pointing at her.

"Is something wrong with Pickle?" Marsh asks, trying to cover. "Is he sick?"

Dylan lets out a frustrated sound. "No, he's not sick. He's fine."

"Then what is it?" she asks, relieved.

"Pickle is a *rabbit*, Marsh," Dylan snaps. He grimaces in frustration. "We hate rabbits. Dirty, timid, moody little things. No better than fluffy rats, we used to joke when Mateo got one. Why would we ever have bought Harper a pet rabbit?"

He's right, she knows. Marsh and Dylan *did* hate that rabbit his room-mate Mateo brought home senior year of college. It was always scuffling around in its cage, making a mess, and would bite anyone who tried to pet it.

But how can Dylan vaguely sense that Pickle ever *wasn't* a rabbit, in this episode?

How did he notice the other anomalies, too?

Marsh tries to think through it, but all she can picture is Pickle as a little black bunny, hopping around in shredded newspaper in his cage in Harper's room, nibbling on some carrots.

Dylan, meanwhile, must be taking her perplexed silence for irritation, or dismissal. He shakes his head. "I'm sorry. But I don't know, Marsh. I don't know. It feels wrong. It's not him. But he's right there in Harper's room, in his cage, with two big ears. How could he be anything else?"

"He can't be," Marsh says at last. Her expression is right this time. Certain, confident, calm. "Pickle's a rabbit because Harper wanted a rabbit. We'd do anything for her. Even buying her a no-better-than-a-fluffy-rat pet."

Things are silent between the two of them for a long moment. Dylan hesitantly takes a step closer, until he's near enough to touch Marsh.

"Hey," he says. The quiet urgency in his voice makes her look up at him. "Tell me that it's not just me. Tell me that you're also feeling it. That something weird is going on." He looks so desperate. "Something really wrong."

"I . . ."

"*Please*," he whispers. "You know something is off, too, don't you?"

Marsh swallows, stalling.

It's clear that in this episode, maybe she and Dylan don't talk to each other at all, outside of Harper's scheduling logistics. They're not faintly wistful for what they've lost, or even friends, in this version. They're just barely, coolly civil. Telling him what's really going on would either just confuse him even more, or destroy the already tenuous peace there is between them, all for nothing.

And after all, even if Dylan knew what was going on, this is her season. Maybe if he wanted the chance to try to fix his life, he should have signed up for *All This and More* himself.

"Here," Dylan says then, and turns around to a duffel bag on the floor by the door. "Just look at this."

Marsh glances down, perplexed, but as soon as he pulls out what's inside, her stomach lurches.

Dylan is holding a medium-sized rectangular box. The kind like what a dress shirt might come in.

Marsh's hand is over her mouth, and she's shaking her head slightly.

Something is wrong.

Very, very wrong.

Not just that this moment has played out before, but that it just *keeps happening*, no matter what she chooses.

"Look," he says as he opens the package to show her what's inside.

"It's a briefcase," Marsh says at last, trying to sound surprised. The words are clumsy in her mouth. The metal clasp looks cold and dull beneath her fingers as he hands it to her.

"I finally got around to unpacking the last of my boxes from the divorce yesterday," Dylan says, his tone strange, like he's reciting a script rather than simply speaking, or like he knows he's said it before. "I found it inside one of them."

"You kept it all this time," Marsh replies stiffly, too.

She knows all this already, but he's still talking anyway. Dylan bought the case when she'd gotten pregnant, and planned to give it to her after Harper was born and she'd finished law school and passed the bar. Then after she dropped out, after things in their marriage went south, after the divorce, and after she'd gotten together with Ren, he'd still held on to it. The same, the same, the same. Unable to throw it away for some reason—in *any* version of their lives.

Dylan's voice is lost, helpless. "I went to throw it out, and I couldn't. I needed to see your face when you opened it. To see if you recognized it, somehow." His eyes are pleading. "Do you?"

Marsh is staring at him now, unable to make her mouth work. She's clutching the briefcase so hard, it's starting to warp. She feels sick, light-headed and unbearably heavy at the same time.

"Mallow," Dylan whispers.

But before she can say anything, Ren's voice interrupts from behind.

"Harper also left her student ID in the back," he says apologetically, and a moment later, he's standing in the doorway, too, just behind Marsh. "Can't get into the theater without that!"

"Wow, I really have concert-brain." Harper sighs as she emerges from her bedroom in Dylan's apartment. "Can't believe I forgot this, too."

"That's what I'm here for," Ren replies. "You're going to do great."

"Thanks to all the extra lessons you drove me to," she says to him, and then hugs Dylan, perhaps worried her father might be jealous. Dylan, however, barely notices. He's clammed up now that Ren and Harper are present, but is still staring pointedly at Marsh, begging her to think about what he said.

"Can we go to the theater a little early, Dad?" Harper asks him. "I want some extra time to prepare."

"Of course," Dylan says at last.

He gives her a kiss on top of her head.

"First chair," he repeats. "I can hardly believe it."

He's speaking to Harper, but the words are clearly meant for Marsh more than their daughter.

"The two of you raised a gifted musician, and an incredibly hard worker," Ren replies kindly. His hand gently, reassuringly comes to rest against Marsh's lower back. "She's very special."

Dylan's given up, knowing the moment is lost. He nods humbly to accept the compliment, and then Harper is dashing down the stairs and toward the parking lot of the apartment complex, her violin case, jacket, and ID card clutched in her arms.

"I guess we're heading over *really* early," Dylan says to both of them. "Enjoy your night. And congrats again, Marsh."

Congrats again? What is he congratulating Marsh for? But all three of them are outside on the landing now, and Dylan has shut and locked the door and is already heading off after Harper before Marsh can ask.

Ren waits until they've walked down the steps, too, and are making their way back toward their own car before he plants a kiss on Marsh's cheek. "We've got to get a move on, too, if we want to finish our meal before her show." He glances down at the briefcase in her hands. "What's that old bag?"

Ren has picked the fanciest restaurant in the city. Marsh gawks at all the dark lacquered oak, moody red drapes, and gleaming brass fixtures as the hostess leads them between candlelit tables toward a private booth near the back.

"How much is this dinner going to cost?" she whispers to him shyly after the waitress fills their delicate water glasses and departs.

"It's worth it," Ren says. "It's not every day your incredible girlfriend passes the bar and becomes an attorney at the best firm in the city."

A surprised grin spreads across her face at that news.

And another flash of realization—that's why Dylan gave Marsh his gift in this episode. Although the briefcase felt less like a present this time, and more like a piece of evidence. Or a compulsion.

"I'm so, so proud of you, Marsh," Ren says to her, pulling her back to the present. Their waitress has returned with a chilled bottle of extremely expensive champagne. Ren takes the two flutes from her and hands one to Marsh. "You're going to do incredible things, and this is just the start. I'm so glad that I get to be with you on this journey."

His words are so serious, so intimate. He's talking like the two of them aren't just having fun, but might already be discussing a long-term future together, and are working toward it.

"I'm a lawyer," Marsh finally says.

She's already doing the math in her head. Marsh is only two years ahead of her normal life, which means that she had to have studied at an accelerated, full-time program to already have taken the bar and gotten a job by now. But the only way she could have accomplished that is if she hadn't needed to also work.

Which means that Ren must have taken over all the bills. He must have supported her for the last few years, so that she could get started on the life she's always wanted as fast as possible.

"Marsh," Ren says softly.

Marsh takes his hand. "I couldn't have done it without you."

Even if not every single detail is right yet, things are finally starting to really feel truly right. Maybe Marsh isn't the big-shot attorney that Jo is, but she is a fully qualified, practicing lawyer now—*and* with a loving, supportive partner this time. One who not only encouraged her, but stepped up to help instead of just complaining at how much harder it would make things in the short-term. And now Marsh's life is really on track. Her career is on its way, and she's building a future with Ren. Things really are better than ever—everything she's ever wanted, and more.

"Congrats, again," Dylan had said to her. But why not just "congrats," then? Why "again"? It almost seemed like he didn't realize he'd said it, either. Was he so mixed up, he also half remembered that Marsh already had the option to try out a different version of this high-powered career in another episode, somehow?

"You okay?" Ren asks her.

Marsh pushes away the clouds hanging over her expression as decisively as she can.

She knows what Talia would say. She has to stop caring about everyone else more than she cares about herself. She's finally doing what's right for her for once. And as soon as the season is over, the changes will stop, and everything will settle into place. There won't be any more confusion, and everything will be the best it can be, for everyone. Marsh won't have to worry about Dylan. He'll be okay. And so will she.

"I'm just . . . really happy," she says.

"Me too. Our life is perfect," Ren replies.

"'Perfect' is a big word." Marsh laughs.

"Okay, fine, Ms. Smarty Pants Lawyer," he concedes. He sticks his bottom lip out in a comical, exaggerated pout. "Nothing is perfect."

Marsh kisses him. "But it's pretty damn close."

Marsh and Ren finish dinner with enough time to share a dessert, and then Ren drives them over to the theater where Harper's performing. After he parks, he climbs quickly out of his side of the car and jogs to hers before Marsh even has her door fully open, so he can help her out.

Is Ren really so gentlemanly, even after two years together? She swoons.

"Your dress is so beautiful, I don't want it to get torn," he says as she loops her arm through his. "At least, not until we get home."

Marsh blushes at that.

At the entrance, Ren hands their tickets to the usher, and they waltz into the auditorium to find good seats.

"Near the front. I want to be able to see Harper clearly," Marsh urges, and Ren leads them to a pair of seats at the right distance.

"She's so brave!" he exclaims as they get settled. "I would never have had the guts at her age to get up onstage like this. Did you?"

Marsh sighs. She'd rather not, but Ren is still looking at her, waiting for her answer.

"I did," she finally admits.

He grins. "Well, there you go! She gets it from her mother."

Marsh tries to smile back.

"What's wrong?" he asks.

Marsh doesn't want to think about it, but she can't help it. Too much is similar not to notice. The curve of the stage, the cheap red curtain.

"Let's just say it didn't go well," she finally says.

There had been months of preparation. Begging her parents to buy her the expensive materials for the costume she'd envisioned, hours of sewing by hand, weeks of practicing the song and dance she'd made up herself. Fifth grade was the first year students were eligible to enter the annual school talent show, and Marsh was not going to waste the opportunity.

She would be a fluffy cloud, who, through a performance that would include rain from a spray bottle and lightning from a flashlight and two cymbals, would transform into the sun by flicking on the battery-powered string lights she'd sewn into the gauze.

It had seemed artistic and deep at the time, to a ten-year-old.

This was supposed to be her big chance. To show her classmates that she could be talented, could be interesting.

But when the curtain finally went up, the glare was so bright. The auditorium was so full. So many, many eyes. All watching, all waiting, all judging. All of them, on her.

Marsh did try.

The audience of students erupted into cruel laughter. Boos and spitballs flew from the front row. She pushed on for a moment, hoping eventually they might quiet down, but the heckling continued, merciless. It didn't stop until she finally ran from the stage, tears of humiliation streaming down her face, blurring with the harsh lights.

Lesson learned, she thought as she tripped, picked herself up, and kept running.

If only that had been the end of it.

"You okay?" Ren asks, as he studies her.

"Yes," she replies, desperately pushing away the memory. "Just glad it's Harper up there this time, and not me. I'm better in the audience."

Typical Marsh.

"Nonsense." Ren takes her hand. "You're a star to me."

He kisses it with a gallant flourish, which makes her laugh.

The parents sitting on Ren's other side ask him for the time, and as he chats politely with them, she peruses the paper program, hoping to find her daughter's name in the violinists' list. A rush of pride fills her as she spots Harper in first place, right where she should be, just beneath the song she'll play.

Her daughter's first mark on the world.

Maybe Marsh couldn't manage to escape her shell as a kid, but somehow, she managed to help raise a daughter who seems too brave to have grown one at all. She clutches the page tightly, even more joyfully determined to make sure *All This and More* is as good for Harper as it is for her.

Just before she closes the program, her eyes catch on one of the local business ads at the bottom of the page.

Chrysalis Life Insurance, the little bolded text reads. *"Protect What You Love."*

That word—*again.*

Marsh closes the program and puts it on the floor.

This must be at least the fifth or sixth time it's appeared, in some form or another.

Is it just some kind of weird, weird fluke?

Or something else?

Marsh really needs to ask Talia about this the next time they see each other.

She looks up then to see Ren studying her with mild concern.

"You *sure* that you're okay?" he asks.

"Yes," Marsh lies. "I . . . just wish I could take photos."

"Well, this way you'll have no distractions. You'll be in the present moment, and experience it fully."

Marsh tries to push away her lingering unease. As she glances around the rapidly filling room, she spots Dylan sitting at the far end of the same row as her and Ren.

"Oh," Marsh says. "Dylan's in our same row."

Ren winces sympathetically. "Maybe the lights will dim soon, and he won't notice us."

But at the same moment that he says it, Dylan glances up from his paper program. Marsh whips her head back to face forward, but not before their eyes might have met by accident for a fraction of a second.

She sighs. "I think he just spotted us."

THE POCKET

Marsh fidgets, wondering if it would be better to pretend to ignore Dylan for the next fifteen minutes even though he's just a few seats away or better to go over and make awkward small talk for the sake of appearances, but Ren comes to her rescue.

"I saw a little theater lounge off the hallway right before we came into the auditorium," he says. "We could hang out there until the curtain call, then slide back into our seats just as the lights go down. Shall we?"

The lounge is small but artsy, a green 1920s art deco retreat with black and gold accents. Marsh and Ren pick two stools at the bar as they admire the decor.

But before they can order, there's a rustle of movement behind them.

"Excuse me."

Marsh turns, and nearly squeaks as she sees Dylan standing there.

"Sorry," he says. "I don't mean to interrupt."

"It's okay," Marsh says. "Is everything all right?"

Dylan nods. "I know this is weird, but I was wondering if I could have a word with you."

This is about what happened at his apartment a few hours ago, she's certain. Dylan didn't get to finish his questions, and didn't get to hear her answer. He's never been able to let anything go—why would he start now?

"As long as it's fast," Marsh replies at last. "I don't want to miss Harper's big moment."

"Oh," Dylan says. He looks at Ren. "I meant you."

Oh!

She wasn't expecting that.

"It'll be quick," Dylan promises.

Marsh studies him, trying to figure out what Dylan could want with Ren. Maybe he just wants to clear the air between them, and say that he's happy Harper has another good role model in her life, without Marsh there like a supervisor?

Is that naïve to think?

"It's okay," Ren says to her, rising. "I'll just be a minute."

"I appreciate it," Dylan says to Ren.

Marsh puts on a calm smile and waves after the two of them as they disappear around the corner.

"This is fine," she mutters to herself. "Everything is fine."

Just then, a dull chime echoes faintly overhead.

"Five minutes until they dim the lights, ma'am," the bartender says helpfully.

"Thank you," Marsh says. "I guess I'll go back to our seats, then."

She looks down as she slides off her stool—Ren has accidentally left his jacket draped over his own. He must have been so surprised by Dylan's request, he forgot to take it with him.

"Could you tell my partner if he comes back that I'm already in the auditorium, and that I've got his jacket?" she asks the bartender.

"Of course." The man nods.

Marsh is trying to keep the falsely confident smile plastered on her face, but as she picks up Ren's coat and tucks it over one arm, something firm and bulky inside catches her attention.

There's something in one of the pockets.

Not in the main outside pocket, but within the inner one, that can be fastened closed with a button.

Carefully, she feels the object through the layers. Then she gasps.

"Shouldn't you be in the audience?" a voice says on her right. "The show will be starting any minute."

Marsh jerks around to see Talia now sitting where Ren had been moments ago, sipping a martini.

"Thank goodness you're here!" Marsh cries, grabbing her arm. Talia's drink sloshes slightly, a few drops splashing on the counter.

"What happened?!" Talia laughs, struggling not to spill any more on herself. "Do I need to call for a close-up?"

"Ren accidentally left his coat here." Marsh is babbling as she digs around in the inner pocket. "I thought I felt something when I picked it up, so I put my hand in, and . . ."

As her fingers close around the object, her stomach flip-flops all over again. Slowly, Marsh pulls the thing out and holds it up.

"Look."

Talia's eyes go wide.

Marsh is holding a small, Sharp Purple velvet cube.

It's a jewelry box. A very specific kind of jewelry box.

TopFan01: <Whoa!!!!!!>
Moms4Marsh: <I knew it! I knew it!>
GeceKuşu: <Bu heyecan verici!>

"Holy mackerel!" Talia gasps, too, as the comments go wild. "That's a *ring box!*"

"I know!" Marsh scream-whispers. "I think he's going to propose!"

The bartender, who has been half listening like all good bartenders do, sets a flute of champagne in front of Marsh, where it's covered instantly by a barrage of throbbing hearts and bursts of confetti from the comments. Marsh downs the fizzy liquid gratefully as Talia takes the box from her and looks at it. She's grinning for Marsh, but the expression falters slightly as her eyes catch on the little words gilded onto the velvet, just above a small, calligraphic butterfly logo.

Chrysalis Jewelers.

The hairs on the back of Marsh's neck prickle to attention.

Not only is that word back yet again, but in every episode, it seems to get a little closer to her. It's gone from a bar to a dating app username to a sign on her old house to appearing on Harper's music program, at least.

And now, this is *definitely* too close for comfort.

"Is something wrong?" Marsh asks Talia, watching closely for a reaction. If this anomaly is truly something to be concerned about, Talia surely will have noticed it—she's the only other person in the Bubble with Marsh who knows they're on *All This and More.* Does she think it's strange, how it keeps coming up? Does she know it's been following Marsh around ever since the first episode?

But Talia just looks back up at her from the ring box, her face bright. "Not at all. It's just an interesting name for a jeweler. And the butterfly is pretty. It's like the ring is a metamorphosis from love to marriage, or something."

She hands the box back to Marsh.

"More importantly, what are you feeling right now?"

Marsh tries to ignore the subtle unease simmering in her gut. There's not a lot of time left in this episode, and she's going to have to make a very big choice at the end of it. But if Talia herself doesn't seem to think anything is amiss, maybe Chrysalis really isn't a problem after all?

"I don't know what I'm feeling. Too many things," Marsh finally replies.

"Are you happy?"

"Happy, shocked, in disbelief, all of it," she says.

"So you want to let him go through with asking you, then," her host prompts.

Marsh hesitates, still rocked from discovering the ring. After all, even though she and Ren have been together two years in this episode, she's technically only had about two *hours* with him, in real time. That's not very long at all to make a decision like this.

LunaMágica: <Say yes, Marsh!>
Monsterrific: <Yeah, say yes! Ren is a dreamboat!>
Moms4Marsh: <He's literally PERFECT!>

Marsh smiles at that. Ren is pretty perfect, she has to admit. Almost *too* perfect, it sometimes seems. In the real world, she'd say he was too good to be true.

But this isn't the real world.

Not yet, anyway. She smiles.

"You look like you just got a little more certain," Talia observes.

Marsh is still overwhelmed, but finally, she throws up her hands and shrugs.

"I mean, why not!" she cries.

"That's the spirit!" Talia laughs.

They clink glasses as an excited burst of trumpets plays over the bar's speakers.

"Well, like you always say, that's the whole reason I'm here, right?" Marsh asks after a sip of her champagne. "I might as well just try this path and see. After all, I can always just go back if I don't like it."

"Actually." Talia's martini pauses halfway to her lips, and she sets it back down. Her delicate earrings tinkle as she shakes her head. "Some things you can't undo, Marsh."

"Not even in a quantum bubble all about exactly that?"

Marsh sort of meant it as a joke, but Talia doesn't laugh. She leans in to convey the gravity of what she's about to say.

"It's true," she pronounces. "The next episode is the midseason special."

"What does that mean?" Marsh asks.

"It's a milestone episode," Talia explains. "Certain things can become a little more 'set' in the Bubble, going forward."

Marsh blinks. "You mean like my choices? We won't be able to go back and undo them? I thought you said that was the whole point! That we could redo anything, until it was perfect!"

"We can!" Talia says, placating. "We absolutely can—until the midseason special. That's why I'm telling you now. Because if there's anything else you want to experience again, or change, we need to do it before the special. Then, once everything is just how you want it, we can keep going forward."

Marsh sits back, startled.

"So, what you're saying is that if I go ahead and let Ren propose now, there will be no going back from it?" she finally asks.

"It's likely," Talia says. "So I just want you to be sure you're ready for it."

"But what if I *am* ready for it?" Marsh groans, frustrated. "What if maybe nothing will work with Dylan, no matter how many times I try? What if I want Ren to propose, so I can see how perfect our life together could be?"

"Then we can let him propose!" Talia replies. "If you're sure that you've tried everything you wanted to try, and you're happy with the way your new life is, then let's continue forward. But if there's something you're worried you missed, we can always come back to this moment later."

The camera is tight on the little velvet box in Marsh's palm as she stares at it, but a thump on the counter tells her that Talia has taken the Show Bible out of her giant leather bag and set it on the bar. Her hand rests protectively, reverently, on its cover.

It's positively gigantic now. How have that many pages been added since the last time she saw it?

"I didn't know about all this," Marsh finally says. "I'm . . . scared."

"Don't be scared! You're doing great, and everything is already going so well for you," Talia replies encouragingly.

"Does it really . . ." Marsh hesitates as she watches Talia flip through, looking for their place in the book. "I know the Show Bible has a record of everything I've already chosen and what's changed, but does it really also have all the future paths written for what I might choose *next*?"

"Technically, yes. But don't think of it as real," Talia rushes to say before the magnitude of that admission can overwhelm her. "None of those pages are real yet. They're just a guide. And as soon as we do choose something, then those pages get scrapped or revised to fit your actual reality."

"But there is a *potential* reality," Marsh says, her voice a mix of nervousness and wonder. "For every choice I might make."

"How is that different than before?" Talia asks. "That's true of any life."

"Because it hasn't already been *written out* somewhere," Marsh replies, a little loudly, and then cowers as some of the bar's patrons glance over at her.

Talia gives her a reassuring nod before returning to the Show Bible. "Marsh, these pages don't make those possible futures real. They're just possibilities. What makes them real is if you choose them."

Marsh sighs, trying to let Talia's words sink in. "Could I read through the pages for this next choice with you?" she asks. "This is such a big episode, I just want to make sure we choose the best option."

But to her surprise, Talia shakes her head. "I wish, but it's against network policy. I know it seems like it would be helpful to be able to flip forward and see what each choice will lead to down the line, but if a contestant is exposed to all that data, exactly the opposite happens. They become too concerned about tiny details they might not have even remembered otherwise. They get so overwhelmed that they become too afraid to choose *anything*."

Marsh frowns.

It sounds logical. She can easily imagine Dylan agreeing with that, citing some behavioral basis from one scientific article or another about the paradox of choice. But on the other hand, this is Marsh's life. Normally, no one has a user's manual, but in this twisted version, she actually does.

Shouldn't she be able to see it?

But Talia's perfect smile is back on. "And remember, this is just the beginning! Once we have the midseason special under our belts, that's when things can *really* take off. The second half of your season will be even bigger than the first!"

Marsh's eyes widen. "How big?" she asks.

"The sky is the limit!" Talia crows. "You've turned your love life around and taken control of your career again, but aren't there any other experiences you wish you'd had?"

"Uh . . ." Marsh stalls, both a little excited and nervous.

"Come on, Marsh! Let's dream! You've made a strong start, but do you really want to spend the rest of your season here, in Phoenix, Arizona, working for the same small law firm and going on dates to the same coffee shops and restaurants with Ren as you did with Dylan?" Talia leans forward earnestly. "Remember what you said in your recap. There were so many places you wanted to explore, as a college student! Countries to travel to, cities to live in, experiences to have! You could try *anything* in the second half of your season. Heck, do you want to join the circus—even for just one episode?"

Despite her nerves, Marsh has to laugh at that.

Talia lets the joke linger for exactly the right amount of time before growing serious again. "Talk to your viewers, Marsh," she says, in her daytime talk show voice. "Tell them what you most hope to accomplish in the latter half of your season. Fame? Wealth? Success? Or perhaps . . . something else?"

Marsh knows what Talia is talking about.

Her mark.

It was already an impossible gift just to be able to fix the mistakes she'd made in her past. It almost felt too greedy to wish for more than that.

But maybe what was *really* greedy was not daring to dream even bigger than her small world. To not use the show to its full potential. This was a once-in-a-lifetime opportunity. Why squander it by being satisfied with moderation? Why settle for good, when she can have more?

When she can have *perfect*?

Marsh finally nods. "You're right. This first half was great, but I came here for a reason. To . . . to light that marshmallow on fire."

"That's the spirit!" Talia cries. "Things are about to get very, very exciting for you, Marsh. Even more exciting than they already are." She's so ecstatic, she's practically hovering on top of her stool, rather than sitting on it. "I can't wait for you to see!"

She and Marsh each raise a glass. And right then, the jingle at the end of the episode begins to play.

"I'm ready when you are," Talia says as the music swells. "You could have *All This* . . ."

Marsh swallows nervously. Excitedly.

"*And more,*" she says.

| To move forward with the season and allow Ren to propose: Turn the page | To go back to before Dylan cheated on Marsh, to try to save their marriage: Go to page 95 | To go back to put Marsh's career ahead of any romance: Go to page 68 |

EPISODE 5

Marsh stares at Talia for a few more seconds, then at the little velvet box again.

"I think . . ." she starts to say.

But before she can finish her sentence, someone shouts her name, and everyone turns as Jo hurries into the lounge, out of breath.

"Jo! Harper's going to be so happy you came," Marsh says, before she remembers what she's holding. "Wait, I have to tell you something!"

"Later," Jo says, beckoning, not noticing her hands at all. Finally, Marsh realizes that her best friend doesn't look excited, but flustered.

"What's wrong?" she asks.

Jo points down the hall, back toward the auditorium. "Dylan's gotten into a little bit of a tiff," she says. "You better come quick."

"Good lord, what now?" Marsh groans, sliding off her stool.

"Go ahead, I'll catch up," Talia says, taking her wallet out to cover the drinks with her RealTV corporate card.

Marsh shoves the ring box back into Ren's pocket, and takes his coat with her as she hurries down the hallway after Jo. "What's the matter with him lately?" she's saying, dodging other guests as they rush. Her ankle wobbles a little in her tall shoes, and she nearly bumps into an usher—

Huh?

She stumbles.

Was that Alexis Quinn again?

The moment was lightning fast, but she could have sworn it was!

Marsh cranes her neck, but Jo is leaving her behind, and the crowd has shifted.

"Marsh!" Jo calls, and Marsh hurries to catch her again.

Maybe she was wrong.

But she doesn't think so.

Something weird is going on.

"How bad is it?" Marsh asks once they're even again.

"When I left to find you, pretty heated." Jo reaches the door into the auditorium and pushes it open.

Marsh bursts into the theater, searching the room. She spots Dylan standing in the middle of one of the aisles, making angry, clipped gestures—at *Ren*.

"Unbelievable," she sighs angrily.

The lights are about to go down, the show is minutes away from starting, and the two of them are in the center of the audience, arguing like two immature teenagers as the other guests give them strange, surprised looks.

What has gotten into Dylan? He could be a little grumpy sometimes, but Marsh never would have believed he could be this rude, to cause a scene at his own daughter's first concert.

She dashes over as fast as she can, furious.

"Marsh," Ren says as he spots her. "There you are!"

"What is going on?" She gasps. "Have you both lost your minds! This—"

But Dylan cuts her off. "Marsh, listen to me." He looks desperate and unmoored again, the way he looked at his apartment earlier. "I don't know what it is, but something is wrong with Ren. He—"

"Dylan, stop," Marsh pleads. "This is ridiculous."

"It's not! You know it's not! And now"—he points at Ren—"he's up to something, I know it."

"No, he's not, he—"

"No, listen! Ren just said, 'Marsh can't find out!'"

"Dylan—"

"Marsh!" Dylan insists. "He's got a secret! I'm telling you, something is going on!"

"I know something is going on!" Marsh shouts in frustration, and jams her hand into Ren's pocket.

Dylan still looks confused, but Ren's face changes from shock to panic as he realizes that Marsh is holding his jacket—and has accidentally found the ring—at the same moment that she yanks the little box out.

"Nothing is wrong with Ren," she finally says, her tone weakening with each word.

She'd been so focused on getting the two of them to stop fighting, but now the adrenaline is fading, and the drama of the thing she's just done is dawning on her. Everyone is watching, gripped by the moment. She's still not used to the idea of billions of viewers watching her on their screens, but somehow, an auditorium of a hundred people staring at her from a few feet away is more intimidating, in this moment.

"He's just . . . nervous."

"I realized I'd forgotten to take my coat," Ren finally says, equally bash-ful. "I was rushing to get back to you. I was so worried you were going to notice it in there."

"Sorry," Marsh says. She holds the box up higher, and laughs. "I did."

Slowly, Ren takes the little velvet cube from her and holds it with both hands, as if it's an anchor. He swallows hard, looking very nervous, but determined.

"Well, this was not the way I had planned to do this, but . . ."

He's sinking to one knee, and Marsh is staring at him. People are gasp-ing and aww-ing for her, and the world is starting to spin. No—she's just hyperventilating!

TopFan01: <This is it!>
Fortunata111: <It's happening!!!>

Ren puts his finger on the clasp.

"Marsh," Dylan says, trying to cut off Ren's all-important question, but Marsh ignores him. *"Marsh!"*

"You shut up," she says to him, still staring at Ren. "For once in your life, just shut up."

Ren takes a deep, trembling breath. He's so nervous, his bottom knee wobbles a little as he balances.

"I knew from the moment I met you, when we were just teenagers, that you were the one for me," he says, stammering a little. "I let you go once because I was stupid and young—and I've spent decades regretting it. I'd always wondered what it would be like if, somehow, in some way, we could have had a do-over."

Moms4Marsh: <He has no idea how literal that statement is!>

Ren swallows again, but his eyes are shining.

"I can still hardly believe I have a second chance now, but I'm not going to let it go to waste this time."

He opens the box, and the diamond dazzles on its band.

"Marsh, love of my life, will you marry me?"

As Ren stares up at her, and Dylan stands just behind him, holding his breath as he waits with the rest of the crowd for Marsh's answer, her gaze drifts up and across the room, to the auditorium doors. Talia is there now, clutching the Show Bible tightly. She's waiting for the next choice. A choice that's going to alter the course of the rest of Marsh's season—and her life.

"I will," Marsh finally says.

"What?" Ren is staring up at her from his kneel. "You will?"

"I will." A grin bursts across her face. "I do."

A burst of cheers erupts all around Marsh from the audience. Ren laughs with delight as he staggers to his feet, and then he kisses Marsh deeply as his arms engulf her.

Moms4Marsh: <SO ROMANTIC!!!>

LunaMágica: <True love!!!!>

Someone in the audience exclaims, "That was perfect—just like a movie!" And it makes Marsh laugh, even as she dabs her eyes. The crowd is still clapping as Ren pulls back and fumbles with the box to get the ring out.

"I was so nervous," he says to her, clumsy with joy. "I'm still shaking."

The ring comes free, and Marsh holds out her hand. It's a solitaire on a platinum band. *The diamond is huge,* she thinks as Ren slides the ring delicately onto her finger. Almost embarrassingly so. How did he afford something like this? Did he spend his entire savings on it? He's too good to her.

"It's beautiful," Marsh says.

As Marsh and Ren, and the entire theater, marvel at her new ring as she holds it out, tilting her finger back and forth so it catches the light, another hand suddenly clamps down on her wrist.

"Hey!"

Dylan has grabbed Marsh and is practically dragging her toward the door out of the auditorium.

"Dylan!" Ren cries, outraged, but Dylan doesn't slow. The crowd titters, and whispers fill the room at the drama. "*Dylan!* Let her go!" Ren shouts, starting after her.

"It's okay!" Marsh calls back.

This is not okay at all! is actually what she's thinking. To be letting Dylan drag her away, moments after she accepted a marriage proposal from someone else! But things are so complicated. Dylan isn't her husband, but that doesn't erase the decades of history they have together. And he's clearly breaking down from the anomalies he's noticed, and is only going to get more frantic and disruptive unless Marsh can set him straight.

"I'm sorry, Ren. He's—he's Harper's father," she pleads. "Just give me one second."

Ren stares after Marsh, fuming, but finally nods and lets her go.

Dylan pulls her away as fast as the two of them can walk. He bursts through the doors with a bang and lurches into the hall, still going strong.

"Thank you very much for ruining Ren's proposal!" Marsh snaps as he hurries them along.

"Yeah, he's a real Prince Charming," Dylan sneers. "The clingy, desperate guy from high school who won't give up finally wears down the girl."

Marsh snorts at him. "Oh, now you're jealous? I haven't seen him for decades, and our paths just crossed again. And Ren is amazing! He's romantic, and fun, and—"

"Romantic and fun." She can practically hear his eyes roll as he hustles. "Wasn't he the one who started the whole Marshmallow thing you hate so much?"

Notamackerel: <What?? Damn!>
TopFan01: <That was Ren, who came up with her nickname?!>
LunaMágica: <The recap didn't mention that!>

"I don't hate it!" Marsh snaps back, furious. She doesn't know if she's angry because he's throwing it in her face, or because now the world knows.

He chuckles. "That's a lie."

"He meant it as a compliment." Marsh growls. "Not that I ever got any from you!"

"Oh, you'd rather I had been—how did you put it? Cloying? That was how you described him when we first got together, I think," Dylan sneers. "Smothering. A cringe boyfriend. We'll see how long you two last this time through."

Marsh gasps at him, livid. "Unbelievable!"

She hadn't hidden this from the recap, she wants to tell her viewers. She hadn't hidden anything! She'd merely been protecting Ren. What was one silly nickname? Who deserved to be dragged through the mud, on live television, no less, for their first, fumbling attempts at teenage romance?

And he's fantastic now, she'd add. So fantastic, it's like the show engineered him itself!

By now, Dylan has pulled her down the hall, into the lobby, and almost through the doors leading out into the parking lot.

"Dylan!" Marsh flings him off, refusing to move. "What the hell is the matter with you? You're the one who blew up our marriage. That was your choice, not mine. Now I'm not allowed to be happy again?"

"This is not about Ren," he insists. "Not really."

"Well, then what *is* it about?" she snaps. "Because if it's all right with you, I'd rather be spending the first moments of my engagement with my new husband-to-be, not my *old* one."

That barb finally lands, and despite how upset he is, Dylan laughs dryly for a second.

"That's exactly it, though," he says at last. "I just keep feeling—I'm not sure. We're divorced, but it doesn't seem real. I feel like just yesterday, we were still together. Or things were different. Or something!"

"What are you saying?" she asks.

"I don't know!" he cries, but his telltale shoulders say he does. "I have this memory of bringing Harper to see you at work, and I helped you flirt with someone, and because we'd been divorced for so long, it was just fun. But I also remember seeing Ren in your kitchen for the first time after an overnight, and feeling so . . . sad about it. It was so fresh. But both of those things can't be true. Did I dream them? Were they nightmares? Am I going insane?"

"Dylan," Marsh says, but his hands are on her arms, holding her gently in place. Even though she's furious, there's a disarming familiarity to his touch. Or maybe because of it.

This was the last way he did touch her, in the real world. Four days after she'd discovered him, when she finally allowed him to come over and take some of his things.

She couldn't stop crying, even though she made no movement, no sound. It wasn't even like crying, it was more like her face was simply leaking. Like a tap was broken somewhere in her body. He'd known that if he moved closer, she'd shake him off, because she'd have to, even though she wouldn't want to. So he'd just stayed that way, his hands on her arms, for nearly an hour. The two of them both near and far from each other at the same time.

"And what the hell is up with that word?" Dylan says suddenly, startling her back. He's pointing at the ticket window. Not at the window, but at the announcement for tonight's show adhered to the glass.

Marsh doesn't know much about classical music—but the song Harper is supposed to play is called "Chrysalis in D Minor."

That gets her attention.

"What do you mean?" she asks, unnerved.

"It's like . . ." He trails off. "It's familiar. I've seen it before, a bunch of times."

LunaMágica: <See, something is going on! Dylan has noticed it, too!>

"Where?" Marsh asks, struggling to remain calm.

"I don't know!" He throws up his hands. "But I swear, I know it."

"Maybe you do. It must be a popular piece, if Pallissard has chosen it."

Dylan groans. "No, not like that. Like it wasn't a song, always."

"Of course it is," Marsh replies, even though she knows what she's saying isn't true. "Maybe you've heard it before in movie soundtracks and—"

"Don't do this. Don't try to play this off." Dylan takes her shoulders again, more firmly this time. "I have a memory that you were never a lawyer." His voice is quieter, even more urgent. "That you never finished law school. Isn't that impossible?"

"You gave me the briefcase," Marsh says, even though she's no longer sure which episode that was, or if it happened at all.

"I burned that briefcase the weekend we signed the divorce papers," Dylan says. "I went on a guys' camping trip to clear my head, and got too drunk after everyone went to sleep. I threw it into the campfire." He looks down at his hand. "I burned myself getting it back out, but it was too damaged to save. I'm supposed to have a scar here. You asked me what it was the next time I came to pick up Harper for band rehearsal, and I was so embarrassed, I lied and said I did it grilling dinner for myself."

Marsh is staring at his completely unblemished hand, unable to turn away.

She does remember that scar. Remembers assuming he was curt because he was trying to show her that she wasn't supposed to worry about him anymore now that he was single, that it was no longer her job, and that had hurt almost as much as imagining him playing out his ridiculous bachelor fantasies, trying to impress some new woman.

"See?" Dylan says, seeing how intent Marsh's gaze has become. He's sweating, almost sick with fear. "What the fuck is going on, Marsh? What's happening to us?"

He could have said "what's happening to *me*," or "what's happening to *you*," but he didn't.

It's the "us" that finally breaks her.

"It's the show," she admits.

Stupid, she thinks.

Too late now.

Dylan doesn't get it at first. "What show?"

"*All This and More,*" she says. "The reality TV show."

Dylan is still staring at her, completely uncomprehending. "What?"

Marsh gestures feebly around the empty lobby. "We're in the show. It's happening right now."

Dylan doesn't move for a moment. Then he blinks. "You're telling me . . . you're saying . . ."

Marsh smiles nervously. "I'm the season three star."

As Dylan continues to gape at her, there's a flurry of movement around the edges of the lobby. Now that Marsh has outed them, the Bubble's cameras emerge from the periphery to capture the reaction scene up close, in relentless, automated symphony. Suspended rigs unlatch themselves from chandeliers and ceiling panels, lights flare. Lenses and mics flank the two of them from every side as Dylan spins around, a horrified look on his face.

"We're . . ." Dylan swallows hard. "We're in the Bubble?"

Marsh nods.

"Mallow," he says.

His voice is wounded, betrayed.

TopFan01: <Uh-oh>

N3vrGiv3Up: <This is not good . . . >

Marsh's heart falls. She'd been hoping maybe Dylan would be intrigued.

But clearly, he's not.

"How could you?" he asks.

"How could I what?" she retorts. "Do something for myself, for once? Take control of my life? Go after all the things I wish I'd tried, if I hadn't been sacrificing my dreams to take care of our family?"

"But it isn't just your life," Dylan argues. "It's *my* life, too! It's Harper's life! Hell, it's even Ren's life. You're changing things for all of us. And we don't have a say."

"Well, now you know how I felt, our entire marriage," Marsh replies.

She doesn't quite mean it, not to that degree, but the comment lands hard on Dylan—and she hates that she's a little pleased at how guilty he looks.

"I'm trying my best to change my life without hampering anyone else's," she finally continues. "That's why there have been so many quirks. I'm trying to make sure every detail is right—not just for me, but for you and Harper, too. There's this book Talia is using. It's called the Show Bible. She's tracking everything that happens for me, so we can have a perfect record to refer to at every choice. I can—"

"What are you even talking about?" he yells. "Like she's been spying on me?"

"No!" Marsh cries. "I only meant . . ."

She groans, frustrated. This isn't going the way she wants at all.

"I'm not trying to hurt you while I do this," Marsh finally says. "I just want to make things better for myself."

She tries to touch his arm.

"You can understand that, can't you?"

Dylan shakes his head. "Not like this."

"I thought you'd be excited! I remember the first time you heard about quantum bubbling, you were so fascinated, you—"

He jerks away. "I was fascinated with the *concept,* Marsh! As a theoretical experiment!"

"But you loved the first season of *All This and More*!" she says. "We watched every episode together. We talked about it endlessly. You were obsessed with it!"

"Who *wasn't*?" He throws up his hands as he shouts, so loud Marsh bristles, and the urge to shout back swells. He knows all the buttons, exactly how hard to push them. "But that doesn't mean that I wanted to do the same thing myself! And *especially* without me even knowing what was happening!"

He glares at her, bracing for the comeback. Begging for it, it almost looks like.

But Marsh knows even more about his buttons than he does hers.

"Well," she finally says, once the silence has lingered a few seconds too long. Dylan has deflated like a sad carnival balloon, his fury absorbed into the cold sponge of her patient, reasonable tone. She could kill him with her tolerance, she knows. "Now you do know."

"Yes, I do," he says, but it's a whine. "And I don't consent."

"Well, I'm not stopping the show." She takes a slow breath. "This episode is only the midseason special."

Dylan shakes his head, as if he can't believe her.

Marsh thinks he might be about to say something else, but instead, he just gives her a long, terrified look. Then he turns and walks toward the lobby doors, to go out into the night.

"What are you doing?" she yells, surprised. "I meant it when I said I won't stop! You can't force me to!"

"You can have your show, then!" Dylan replies, shouting back at her again because she's shouting at him. "But I want no part of it."

"What does that mean?" Marsh snaps. "You're just going to ignore your problems, or blame them all on me, just like you did before?"

"Not ignoring them," he says. "Quitting."

"What?"

But his gait doesn't slow, and he doesn't turn around. "I quit the show."

The cameras rush in on Marsh, and the comments explode with exclamation points.

TopFan01: <Can he actually do that??>
JesterG: <Is it even possible?!>

"Dylan, wait!" Marsh calls.

He storms out.

WE'LL BE RIGHT BACK, FOLKS!

"Holy mackerel!"

In a burst of Sharp Purple, Talia appears in front of an *All This and More* backdrop, grinning as she exclaims how she can't wait to see what Marsh will do next.

"What a fantastic start!" she coos. "In just the first half of her season, our beloved star has gained the courage to reach for her passions at last. She's become the talented lawyer she always dreamed of being, and chosen Ren as her ultimate dream guy! Our two lovebirds couldn't be more adorable, and we here at RealTV couldn't be happier that Marsh finally has found the romantic, devoted—*dare we say, perfect?*—partner she deserves at last. Will there be wedding bells before the season finale?"

Moms4Marsh: <Yes, yes, yes! This is the greatest season of All This and More ever!>
LunaMágica: <More like the weirdest season ever>
StrikeF0rce: <Seriously! Marsh is definitely making progress, but she's had some really strange occurrences, too>

"Plus, a midseason bonus offer!" Talia continues. "We know how much you all loved our 'Holy mackerel!' T-shirts, so don't miss our new 'You gotta light it on fire' sweaters, complete with a darling little campfire and roasting marshmallow graphic! Head to our online store to get yours now. Order before the finale for a ten percent discount!"

She flashes an especially charming smile, and holds up something soft, round, and black.

"And, an extra-special surprise—your own Pickle bunny stuffed animal!"

Monsterrific: <OMG!!! I NEED ONE!!!>
Nv3rGiv3Up: <That's the cutest thing I've ever seen!!!>
Fortunata111: <I'm buying ten right now!>

"Now, who's ready for the second half of this season?" Talia cries, to a burst of ecstatic trumpets and exploding confetti animations.

JesterG: <Okay, is it just me, or is it weird that Talia hasn't mentioned Chrysalis yet?>
Notamackerel: <Right?! Or the briefcase that keeps appearing, or how Ren pops up in every episode, even when it makes no sense. Nothing like this happened to Talia in her season! Why is she avoiding the topic?>
Fortunata111: <Maybe because the anomalies aren't a big deal?>
Notamackerel: <Or maybe because she's trying to obscure them?>

"Yes, it's true that there have been some bumps along the way," Talia acknowledges, unable to avoid the commenters any longer. "Even though Harper has really blossomed, going from aspiring musician to first violin at the prestigious Pallissard Institute of Music, we know Marsh is still trying to rebuild the close relationship they once had, and help her daughter bond with Ren as he becomes an even bigger part of their lives."

The background behind her cuts to a dramatic still shot of Marsh, Ren, and Dylan in the theater.

"And if you're just tuning in, in a dramatic twist, Dylan discovered during Ren's proposal that he's part of the show—and he didn't take it well *at all*," Talia continues, shaking her head with disappointment at Dylan. "He left her alone and stormed off set, refusing to participate in the show any longer." She leans in. "Will he come back to apologize to Marsh for his rude behavior? Or is this really the end of their long history together?"

TopFan01: <Head to our Marsh fan page to send Dylan a thumbs-down!>

Behind Talia, a montage of key scenes from the first half of the season begins to play. Talia *oohs* and *ahhs* at each moment, even though she was present for practically all of them. She's just as bubbly and excited as ever. Confident that everything is progressing as it should, and there's nothing to worry about.

"Marsh has already come so far, and accomplished so much. But if anything, it's only made her even more determined to keep working!" she declares as Ren gets down on one knee behind her in the final frame, his eyes full of hope. "After all, why settle for good enough when you can have *perfect*?"

Moms4Marsh: <See? Stop trying to drag the show down. Everything is fine!>
TopFan01: <We have to trust Talia. As she always says, it wouldn't be a meaningful journey without a few speed bumps along the way!>
YanYan242: <That's right! We're only partway through—give Marsh time to make everything right!>

Satisfied, Talia angles herself slightly to the camera, and puts her winning grin back on. The music flares, triumphant.

"Remember, you could have *All This* . . ."

EPISODE 6

PARADISE

The second half of the season opens dark. The first thing Marsh can sense is sound. A gentle, rhythmic shushing, almost like waves on a beach.

She is on a beach, she realizes as the frame brightens.

A gorgeous beach.

Caribbean? Hawaii? She's not sure she's ever seen sand this white, or water so pristine, or jungly leaves so green.

Fortunata111: <Is this place real? It looks like heaven!>

Another gentle crest of crystalline water rolls in, just reaching her toes. The sand is cool, and the breeze is warm. There's a hand in hers, and it squeezes gently now.

"I think I just saw a dolphin," Ren says.

Marsh turns to look.

She can't spot anything leaping on the horizon, but it doesn't matter. Everything is so beautiful—the waves, the sky, the palm trees, the little grass beach huts where other couples gazing deeply into each other's eyes are scattered. As she marvels, she spots Harper, too, standing with a bunch of other teenagers at the edge of the water, all of them holding up sets of goggles and fins as a snorkeling instructor explains how to use them.

"This is incredible, Ren," Marsh says at last.

"I'm so glad you like it," Ren replies, and then somewhat teasingly adds, "I knew it was going to be hard to top that big Mexico vacation you told me you took with Dylan, but I hoped Tahiti might do it."

What?! Marsh gasps, shocked.

Ren took her and Harper on vacation to . . . Tahiti??!

TopFan01: <Amazing! Ren is really pulling out all the stops for her!>
Moms4Marsh: <He's so romantic!>

She can hardly believe it. He's flown them around the world, to a place she probably would never have been brave enough to travel to, either because of the cost or the distance.

Before Marsh can protest—before she can become her old, worrying self again—Ren takes her hand, where his engagement ring sparkles dazzlingly on her finger.

"More than worth it," he says, staring deep into her eyes. "It's not every day you get to propose to the woman of your dreams, and she says yes."

Marsh leans in as their lips meet, and she drapes her arms over his shoulders to pull him close.

He's right, she knows Talia would tell her. She's allowed to enjoy this.

She's surprised to find that for once, she actually can let it go.

"Well, if all I have to do is whisk you away to a tropical island to get a kiss like that, we're going to have a lot of flights in our future!" Ren jokes when they finally pull back. "Although, now that you accepted Victor's offer, vacations like this really might be able to be more than just once in a lifetime for us."

"Victor's offer?" Marsh asks.

"To help start up the Asia division of your firm," he replies, giving her a funny look.

JesterG: <What a promotion!>
TopFan01: <Wait. WAIT. Ren just said Asia Division. That must mean . . . >
SagwaGold: <佢住香港㗎!!!>
YanYan242: <HONG KONG!!!!!>

The comments explode. The ecstatic cheering and confetti animations obliterate her view of the gorgeous beach, and Marsh is grinning like an idiot, she knows, but she doesn't care.

Not only is she still a lawyer, but she's gotten a huge promotion. And not only that—she confessed to Talia in the recap that she'd always imagined Hong Kong as the ultimate test for herself. That if she could make it in such a vibrant, chaotic, beautiful place, she'd finally believe that she could make it anywhere, do anything she wanted.

Now she's going to get the chance.

"And you like it? Our new home?" she asks Ren at last. "And Harper does, too?"

"Are you kidding? I don't know who loves it more, me or Harp!" he replies. "She's got one of the best violin tutors in the world now, she's getting to see a whole new continent, and I'm finally doing *real* journalism. No more fluff pieces or pitching things just to meet the bills. With my own column, I can really write about the things I care about. The things that are important."

Ren is positively exhilarated.

"Things really worked out for us, Marsh."

"They really did," Marsh agrees, just as thrilled.

Things really *are* bigger and better in the second half of this season already. And not just for her, but for Harper and Ren, as well. Because this is about all of them. She might be reaching for the stars, but she's not going to leave anyone behind.

Well.

Except for maybe Dylan.

Marsh sighs. Things really ended badly with him in that last episode. And since her engagement has continued into the second half of her season, this must mean that that Dylan has permanently relegated himself to sad, minor background character in her story. He'll probably appear to visit Harper from time to time, and gaze longingly at Marsh from afar as she does something adorable with Ren, but no more than that.

But it was his fault, just like it was in real life. He's the one who quit the show, not Marsh. And Marsh refuses to give up. She's forging ahead.

She's going to make her life everything she's dreamed of.

With or without him.

"What now?" Marsh asks Ren after another passionate kiss.

"Now we just have to figure out how to spend the rest of our lives together." Ren grins. "It's going to be even more amazing than before. In fact, I think we've gone from *pretty damn close* to *actually perfect* now," Ren says, winking as he calls back the phrase Marsh used at the dinner just before he proposed. "Don't you?"

"I'd say it's definitely *super super super damn close*," Marsh replies with a laugh.

She meant it as a joke. He's just so earnest, so romantic, all the time, everything a grand gesture, every moment a Moment. But Ren is so wrapped up in his enthusiasm, the jest catches him off guard.

"What do you mean?" he asks, looking confused and hurt all at once. "Are you not happy? What's missing? Is there something I'm not doing?"

"Oh, no! I didn't mean—no!" Marsh cries. "Nothing's missing."

But Ren still hasn't realized she was trying to be funny. "Something could be different, then?"

"No, no! I'm sorry, Ren. I was trying to make a joke and it was stupid. Pretend I didn't say any of that at all. I wish I had a 'rewind' button."

In fact—her eyes dart for a moment—but no, Talia isn't around yet.

"Please, Ren," Marsh says. "I didn't mean it at all."

"But you must have, on some level," he replies, wringing his hands together. "Otherwise, the joke wouldn't even have occurred to you."

"Ren."

She waits until he looks up at her.

"Forget what I said. Our life really is perfect."

Ren studies her for a long moment.

Then he smiles.

"Well, then I'm going to make sure it's even *better* than perfect!" he vows. He has that same determined glint in his eye that she's seen many times before—in the bar on their first date, when he was proposing—basically anytime he's around her.

Moms4Marsh: <Ren is so romantic!>
YanYan242: <He loves her so much!>

"*Better* than perfect," Marsh repeats, shaking her head at him with admiration.

Ren puts his hand on his heart. "I promise."

She takes it from his chest and holds it. "I can't wait."

Their last day in Tahiti is just as idyllic as the rest—and the night just as steamy. Marsh spends the last languid, content moments of post-lovemaking bliss before she drifts off wondering how even the most agile of cameras would have been able to keep things to a prime-time-appropriate rating, with every angle and position Ren excitedly whipped them into. After the fifth one, Marsh had almost thought to check for a list under his pillow, along with his estimations of her favorites. She wouldn't have put it past him.

In the morning, their flight is early. Marsh and Ren are canoodling in line at the gate to their flight home as Harper rolls her eyes beside them.

"Blech! Gross! I don't want your cooties!" she wails dramatically, mortified by their affection. She unzips her backpack and pretends to barf into it, which draws a chuckle from the passengers behind them.

"Sorry, honey," Marsh says, but inwardly, she's a little annoyed. She just got engaged to the man of her dreams! Can't Harper be happy for her mother? She's clearly comfortable with Ren now, but Marsh wants her daughter to be as thrilled that he's joining their family as she is.

"We're just showing you how cringey you'll look when you get your first crush," Ren replies jokingly, and bats his eyes at Marsh. "Is it working?"

"Good morning!" a familiar voice chirps, and Marsh turns to see that the gate agent at the desk is Talia. She's wearing a navy-blue airline uniform and tropical silk neck scarf, but somehow still manages to make it look like high fashion.

"Good morning!" Ren replies. "We wanted to check our seats."

"We just got engaged," Marsh adds. "This is our first family trip."

"Congratulations!" her host gushes. "That's so wonderful. I'll make sure we put you all together."

"Perfect," Marsh replies.

"Isn't it?" Ren asks her—again.

She kisses him. "You're ridiculous," she says.

Talia cheerfully types into her little computer terminal behind the counter as they canoodle. "How's near the wing?"

"Sounds good," Marsh replies.

"Is it weird to say that I'm actually excited to leave paradise to go home?" Ren asks Marsh.

"Aw," she coos. "Can't wait for our lives to start together?"

"Obviously," he says back to her in the same sweet tone, and pulls her into another hug so he can plant a kiss on her forehead. "But also, I'm looking forward to getting back to the office. This piece I'm working on, it's huge. Gigantic! Honestly, I can't believe they chose me. There must have been thousands of journalists pitching them for the profile." He squeezes his fists. "This feels like *it*. My big shot."

"That's amazing," Marsh replies. "Which piece is this again?"

"The Chrysalis feature, honey," Ren says.

Notamackerel: <Uh, what now??>

A sudden clatter from the gate agent desk startles them.

Talia scrambles back into a calm, professional pose.

"Sorry about that," she says.

Her grin is a Cheshire cat crescent moon.

"Dropped my pen."

"Looks like someone could use a vacation, too!" Ren jokes, and Talia laughs politely.

"The . . . Chrysalis feature?" Marsh finally repeats, once Talia has gone back to typing.

"Yeah. You know." He makes air quotes with his fingers. "The big 'secret project' you've been giving me hell about because I haven't come to bed at a decent hour for weeks now." He chuckles. "They're launching a revolutionary new product soon. Top secret until the announcement—and they want me to be the one to break it! All I need is one more piece of research, and then I should be able to give a draft to my editor."

He's on a tear now, too excited to explain anything.

"I'm close," he says, making an excited fist. "So close!"

Interesting, Marsh muses as he continues to babble.

Chrysalis must have been one of the bits of the show that carried over past the midseason special, into this second half of the season. And it seems bigger and more involved than before. Now it's not just the name of a song, or a jeweler. It's the maker of some big invention that Ren is hoping to announce to the world.

That thought sends a little chill racing down her back.

Something is off about this, she can't help but think.

Why does Chrysalis keep appearing?

And what does it want?

"Great news!" Talia says brightly. "I managed to get you three seats together."

"Awesome!" Harper replies.

Marsh stares at Talia. But her host is still grinning broadly at her, her eyes sparkling.

"Yes, that's great," Marsh finally says. She takes the newly printed boarding passes from Talia. "Thanks for your help."

"Enjoy the flight!"

The three of them walk back to their luggage and get settled in their seats. Ren disappears to the kiosk a few gates down to buy coffee and pastries.

After a moment, Marsh stands up again.

"Harp, stay here and watch our bags," she says. "I'm going to see if we can get upgraded."

At the counter, Talia beams again, radiant. "Welcome to the second half of your season, Marsh!" she sings. "It's already super amazing, isn't it? What a perfect vacation, and a perfect guy! Also, wow, your suntan is positively golden. This life is really working for you, I have to say. And let's talk about that promotion—"

"Talia, what's going on?" Marsh cuts her off.

Talia clears her throat, plasters her smile back across her face.

"What do you mean?"

"With Chrysalis."

"The article Ren just mentioned?" she asks. "He'll do a great job with the piece."

"I'm sure he would." Marsh grimaces. "But I don't want him to write it."

"Why?" Talia gasps. "It sounds like a great opportunity!"

"Because it's not just the article," she says. "I don't know *what* Chrysalis is, but something weird is going on. It's like—"

Marsh gulps.

"It's like it's following me."

Talia laughs. "I think you're worrying too much."

"No! Listen!" she insists. "I don't know when it started, but I swear, if I look hard enough in an episode, I can find Chrysalis. No matter what path I choose, it keeps appearing in all of them, changing shape each time. Getting bigger, closer. Now it's pulled Ren into it."

"Why, Marsh." Talia pauses. Marsh can't tell if she looks surprised, or almost—*a little irritated*? "Have you been . . . tracking this silly thing?"

Immediately, Marsh is embarrassed. "I didn't know what else to do."

"You should have just asked me," Talia says. "You should always come to me with any concerns. That's why I'm here!"

"I know. At first, the instances were so subtle, I didn't want to seem paranoid or ungrateful," Marsh admits. "But I'm worried something bad is going to happen."

"Nothing bad is going to happen," Talia says. "I swear. There's absolutely nothing to worry about. Little anomalies like this happen all the time in the Bubble! Remember, no life can be transformed without a few quirks."

"Even so." Marsh swallows. "I don't know if I want this path."

"What?" Talia cries, dismayed. "But this is everything you've ever wanted, isn't it? A career as a high-flying lawyer, a movie-worthy romance, and an exciting place to live? Not to mention your stunning makeover, and Harper's musical success. Why would you want to leave all that behind?"

Because something's not right, Marsh wants to say.

"Because I still have time," she answers instead. "You said right before the midseason special that this is my one and only chance to change everything I want about my life. Shouldn't I use some of my remaining episodes to go anywhere I want, try anything I can imagine, before choosing a final path?"

Talia finds it hard to argue with that.

"This is so brave. I'm so glad you opened up to me, Marsh," she gushes. "And you're one hundred percent right! We have plenty of episodes left before the finale to get everything just right. Let's take full advantage of that! What do you want to change?"

Marsh takes a deep breath. "Well . . . do I *have* to go home to Hong Kong right now?"

Talia's laugh is like a musical chime. "I mean, your flight boards in four minutes, silly!"

"But what if the flight didn't go to Hong Kong?" Marsh asks. "What if it went somewhere else instead?"

Talia's eyes flash, already scheming. A thump rattles the entire gate agent desk—she's pulled out the Show Bible from some hidden shelf, and begins flipping through it.

"Let me see what we're working with."

Maybe, with the right path, she can escape Chrysalis for good, Marsh hopes. She can go somewhere else entirely, where they can still be happy, but Ren might not be writing this article. Where their lives can be even *more* perfect—just like he promised.

"I see an excellent option," Talia pronounces at last, looking satisfied.

Fortunata111: <I love this surprise shake up!>

JesterG: <Me too! She can always go back to Hong Kong at the end, if she really wants!>

The comments are screaming at her, a million a second.

SharpTruth: <C:\ATAM\Bubble\access>

A new user catches her eye.

What? Marsh blinks. *Bubble? Access?*

But then the line is pushed from the chat, lost almost instantly as a thousand more comments flood in after, taking up the finite space.

N3vrGiv3Up: <Let's go, Marsh!>

GoluGolu: <हम तैयार है!>

TopFan01: <Everyone, head to our poll to enter your guess for where
    Marsh will end up next!>

Talia folds the crushing weight of the Show Bible over the finger she's left stuck in the pages, to keep her place. "Ready for some *real* adventure?"

Marsh holds up her plane ticket. Instead of the words *Hong Kong*, the destination field is blank now.

"I'm ready," she says.

Talia grins. "You could have *All This* . . ."

"*And More*," Marsh replies, and closes her eyes.

FIRE AND ICE

The next scene opens quietly. Marsh is lying down, a pillow soft beneath her head, and her eyes are closed. She's not really asleep, but she's supposed to be, so she lets her lids stay heavy, savoring the peaceful moment.

This is just what she needed. *A real adventure,* as Talia said. She can always finish her season in Hong Kong, if she really wants to. But why not push for even more, before then?

The only thing that could be more perfect than perfect would be *more* of it.

At that, she lets her eyes flutter open. The curtains of her bedroom are thin and gauzy, and the light is filtering gently through. They're an odd color—bright yellow. As the first rays of sun fall across her pillow, Marsh realizes why.

She isn't in a room. She's in a tent.

Is she camping? Another vacation?

She sits up to look around. Even though it's first thing in the morning, her hair falls in loose curls, even fuller and lusher than before, and her skin has kept its warm tan from the Tahitian sun.

Marsh shrugs to herself, pleased.

Finally, she climbs out of her sleeping bag and stretches in the cozy tent. Another one just like it is to the left of hers, with Ren's watch and belt curled up on top, and a third one on her other side, its pillowcase covered in rumpled sheet music.

Good. She smiles.

The tent rustles as a breeze rushes past outside, and the sound draws Marsh's attention toward whatever lies beyond. She stuffs her feet into a pair of hiking boots and grabs a sweater—even inside her tent, the air is crisp enough that she can see faint white puffs when she exhales—and takes a deep, excited breath. Then she unzips the flap of the tent and steps out.

The landscape that unfurls before her is the most beautiful thing she's ever seen.

The overwhelming green. The vastness. The mountains, the black cliffs, the pristine blue-white ice. It's like Marsh stepped out of her tent and into a fantastical, untouched Arctic wilderness! Everywhere she looks is a contrast. The dark soil and rocks glimmer like obsidian beneath a layer of mossy, emerald cover. The sea is brilliant blue, the looming peaks are covered in ice, the sky gleams like polished silver. And everywhere—*everywhere*—are millions of tiny purple wildflowers, like a delicate periwinkle blanket covering the land.

TopFan01: <Holy. Mackerel.>
Frónverji: <Hún er á Íslandi!!!!!!!!!!!!>

"The Nordics seemed so mysterious and remote," Marsh remembers saying to Talia during the recap. "The farthest away place in the world from where I was."

She puts a hand on her heart, overcome.

And now she's made it. She's in *Iceland*.

Marsh's eyes are sparkling, and not just from the flood of exclamations as viewers from the Arctic island celebrate in the comments. She was right to push Talia for another path, she knows without a doubt now.

She's living every single one of her dreams.

She stares at the landscape for a few more seconds, still starstruck, until her eyes blur. Then, in a flash, she whirls around and ducks back into her tent. Inside, she puts her hair into a bun and pulls on her windproof shell and scarf as fast as she can, eager to start soaking up every second of this amazing trip. As she rushes, the toe of her boot catches on a pebble beneath the tarp, and she bumps the small table at the foot of the sleeping bags, where a huge map is spread out.

At first, she thinks it must be for whatever article Ren is working on now, but then she realizes that all the writing on it is in her handwriting.

The map is a close-up of the southeast of Iceland, covering a swathe of seaside cliffs and icy foothills. Little towns and landmarks dot the region—Höfn, Jökulsárlón, Skaftafell, Kirkjubæjarklaustur—and a giant glacier of ice, Vatnajökull, looms over it all. And just to the south of Vatnajökull's imposing, white-ridged border, right along the coast where she must be now, she's circled one tiny, jutting cape in decisive red marker.

The word is small, but Marsh's script is neat.

Ingólfshöfði.

When she picks up the map to see what's beneath, a surprised gasp escapes her.

Photographs, dozens of them, cover the table. Of the landscape, the roiling sea, the menacing clouds, but mostly of the wildlife. There are leaping seals and cresting humpback whales, puffins soaring midflight, wild horses at a gallop.

They're breathtaking.

And at the bottom right corner, where the photographer's credit appears, they all say *Marsh*.

Hoskistrong: <Marsh er dýralífsljósmyndari!>
Frónverji: <Til hamingju, Marsh!>

The Icelandic viewers are right. Marsh can hardly believe this episode.

In this life, she isn't just traveling Iceland. She's *working* here—as a world-famous wildlife photographer!

Moms4Marsh: <The second half of this season is even better than the first!>

A stream of hundreds more repeat the same sentiment.

Marsh couldn't agree more. She might not be a lawyer in this path, but this new career isn't all that different, in a way. She's still fighting to bring attention and justice to important issues, but from an ecological angle, this time. And what better mark to leave on the world than such beautiful, timeless photographs?

Her heart racing, Marsh sets the images down and launches herself outside again into the overcast morning. Thanks to Talia, she's now in the most incredible place, and with an equally incredible dream job. This new life is even more amazing than she could have imagined herself!

She opens her arms and spins, desperate to drink every moment in. She can't wait to see what beautiful, unique shot is waiting for her to capture at Ingólfshöfði. It's going to be something incredible.

No. It's going to be *perfect*.

"*Svafstu vel?*" a voice says, and Marsh turns around to see Ren walking up to her from a much larger tent a stone's throw away. There are several tents, she can see now, most of them the same size as hers, all clustered around the big one, from which a tendril of smoke is curling through a chimney sticking out of the top. This must be their base camp, where Marsh and her crew have set up to have easy access to their desired shoot location.

"Come again?" Marsh asks him when Ren reaches her.

"Means *Did you sleep well?* in Icelandic," he answers with a smile. "Learned that from the cook this morning."

He gives Marsh a kiss, and then takes in the landscape with a deep, appreciative sigh.

"God, the air is so clean here." He whistles. He pops a dark berry into his mouth from the pile he has in one hand. "And these are delicious. Straight off the bush!"

Marsh, however, is studying Ren, rather than the view. If he was perhaps just a little too doting and domesticated in Tahiti, he's much more rugged-looking now. His stubble is a little overgrown, there's dirt on his hands, and he's dressed in explorer's gear, with tools and straps hanging from his belt and vest.

What kind of story is he writing now? she wonders.

He looks good, though. Marsh wouldn't have expected it, but for a journalist, Ren is really pulling off the outdoorsy adventurer look.

Just then, a little keening wail pierces the silence, and Ren slips and falls comically to his knees as something whizzes past him, low to the ground.

"What! You little rascal, come here!" he shouts playfully as he gets to his feet and gives chase.

"That fluff ball is always such a goof in the mornings," Harper says as she comes running across the grass, a dog leash looped through her hands, and Marsh laughs as they both duck around the back of the tent to follow Ren and Pickle.

Except it's not Pickle, Marsh realizes as she stops dead in her tracks.

Or rather, maybe it is—but Pickle is not a black Lab.

He's a white . . . *fox?*

"Yeah, you are a goof, aren't you, Súrkrás?" Ren says, trying to get Súrkrás to high-five him, a trick Pickle knows well, as he continues wriggling excitedly on the ground.

"Súr . . . krás?" Marsh finally asks.

"Yeah! I changed it after I got to lesson three in my *Icelandic Basic Phrases* book," Harper answers. "After all, shouldn't an Icelandic fox have an Icelandic name?"

Ah, Marsh realizes. "Súrkrás" must mean "Pickle" in Icelandic.

The comments are more hearts and exclamation points than words by now.

Monsterrific: <Now I need a Súrkrás plush collectible, too!>
MrLoki: <Það er ekki löglegt að eiga ref á Íslandi!>
Fortunata111: <Who cares if a pet fox is legal or not, it's ADORABLE!>

"I think he's really taking to it," Marsh replies at last, and bends down to cuddle the fluffy white mass. She'll get used to it, she knows. The most important thing is that they're all together in this new, wonderful life.

"Want a bilberry, buddy?" Ren asks Súrkrás, showing him the enticing bundle.

Súrkrás dances with delight.

"Okay, wait," he says as he holds one out, testing the fox. "Waaait . . ."

"C'mon!" Harper cries, giggling as Ren draws out the word.

"Boy, the two of you need to learn some patience!" he jokes as the bilberry eases excruciatingly forward. "Waaaaaait . . ."

"Gotcha!" Harper laughs—snatching it right out of his two fingers with her mouth.

"Hey!" Ren cries, pretending to be horrified. "That was for Súrkrás!"

"Too late!" She cackles as he wrestles her to the ground, demanding the berry back. Súrkrás jumps on top of them, squeaking with delight as they laugh their heads off together.

Marsh is laughing, too, overjoyed. If she'd been worried before about Harper and Ren's relationship, this single moment convinces her that the show has outdone itself yet again.

"Okay, okay, you win!" Ren says once Harper and Súrkrás have released him, and gives her the rest of the berries to share with the fox. He brushes off his pants as he stands. "I have to head out. Got an interesting lead."

"Oh?" Marsh asks. "For an article?"

Ren blinks. "Article? What article?"

Ren must not be a journalist anymore.

"I, never mind," she tries to cover. "What's the lead?"

Ren hefts a beat-up backpack onto his shoulders and adjusts the straps. "Magnús called. He said that the ice on Mýrdalsjökull is solid." He looks excited. "It's rocky, but if I can find just the right place to start the climb, I could set a new record!"

Ren is a professional mountain climber in this life? Marsh deduces, amazed, as she tries to pretend he's always been this rough-and-tumble version of himself.

"It's all right," he says to her, teasing. "You can tell me it's pretty sexy."

LunaMágica: <It is!>

Several thousand comments agree as Marsh chuckles at him. The Bubble has done a good job in this episode.

"I mean, it is, right?" he asks—almost like he's a little unsure now.

"*Very* sexy," Marsh says, wrapping her arms around him and giving him a peck on the lips. "I kind of wish I were going with you instead, so I could sneak a few shots of you bravely scaling that cliff face."

YanYan242: <Oh, sweet Ren! He's so in love with her!>

"Súrkrás, come back!" Harper yells, and chases after the fox as it darts off into some bushes. "See you guys later!"

"Love you!" Marsh calls after her.

"This is it, Marsh. Your big break." Ren steals another kiss from her before heading toward a row of muddy jeeps parked at the edge of the campsite. "I *know* it!"

As Ren's tires crunch on the gravel, there's a rustle behind her, and a voice calls, "There you are! You want coffee?"

Marsh turns to see Talia ducking out of the main tent.

"Talia! I can't believe you're here!" she says, happy to see her.

"I can't believe it, either!" Talia replies, and gives her an excited hug in return. "I mean, *Iceland*! It's beautiful!"

"So, what's your cover this time?" Marsh asks as they both marvel at the breathtaking landscape.

"A documentary, of course!" Talia winks, and holds up a handheld microphone. Despite the rugged conditions, she looks like a model who just stepped out of an outdoorsy clothing photo shoot. "Women and nature."

As Marsh lets out a snort of a laugh, the tent rustles again, and Jo pops her head out.

"Marsh," she says, and holds up a beat-up tablet device. "Did you see these readings?"

"Jo!" Marsh exclaims, thrilled that her best friend is here, too, and apparently still her coworker. "I mean, not yet." She takes the tablet from her.

"Öræfajökull is showing signs of volcanic pre-eruption activity," Jo explains, after giving her a funny look. "Our sensors picked it up last night, and the Icelandic Meteorological Office confirmed this morning."

"But Öræfajökull's been coded green since 2018," Talia helpfully replies, checking her notes in her fake documentary folder.

"I know," Jo agrees. "But the monitors are showing that activity's ticked up suddenly again."

"What does this mean for us?" Marsh asks.

"It means we're going to have to make a hard choice," Victor answers her as he joins, holding his own half-empty mug of black coffee and another full one, which he hands to Marsh.

"Hard choice?" Talia prompts, leaning in with her mic like she's interviewing for the documentary as Marsh downs the scalding liquid all at once, too impatient to sip it.

"I know today is our only chance before the snow hits and we lose our window, but the IMO has advised all research around Öræfajökull be halted immediately." Victor turns and points at the massive white-capped mountain behind them. "Ingólfshöfði is within the danger zone."

"What!" Marsh cries, dismayed.

How will she ever manage to capture the precious photograph she's come here to take, if they can't go to Ingólfshöfði? Just when things were showing so much promise, the weather has to change on her—literally!

"We've come so far," she insists. "We can't just give up now!"

"We have to," Jo sighs. "The IMO ordered the shutdown."

"An official estimate for anything is always conservative," Marsh argues. "There's always a buffer, for safety's sake."

"Marsh . . ." Victor says warningly.

She ignores him—something she never would have dared doing just a few episodes ago.

"How much time does the IMO think there *really* is, before an eruption?"

Jo shakes her head. "You can't be serious, Marsh. This is life and death."

"Exactly!" Marsh replies. "Life—our life's work! To capture the world before it disappears! When could that be more important, if not this very moment?"

Is this what it's like, to feel a speech coming on? she wonders. She's not thinking now, just speaking, every word the perfect one, all of them in the perfect order, with no planning. Every sentence is urgent, gripping, destined.

Everyone in the camp is staring at her as she speaks, captivated by her passion. She feels even more exposed than she did giving her first talk as a lawyer at Mendoza-Montalvo and Hall, but somehow, even more confident this time. This time, so many eyes on her isn't withering, but emboldening. Energizing. She can feel their energy as they listen to her.

And it's *good*.

"This is why we came," she proclaims, gesturing to the looming volcano. "To take chances. To leave our *mark*!"

Marsh clenches her hands into determined fists.

"Oh no," Victor says. "I know that look."

"You can either come with me or not," Marsh declares, as Talia nearly dances with proud glee beside her. "But you can't stop me."

Moms4Marsh: <That's our girl!>

For just an instant, Marsh falters. She waits nervously as her words sink in, afraid the camp is going to laugh at her.

But this is the new Marsh, and a new life. This is *All This and More*.

Like magic, the crowd goes from completely silent to a tornado of activity.

"All right, people! She's going full marshmallow again," Victor cries over the whirlwind. "I want our jeep loaded and on the way up the foothills in ten minutes, and the rest of the camp cleared and on the road down to the IMO safety line in thirty. We have no time to waste!"

Everyone is moving now, full of purpose and excitement. Someone rushes to put the camera bags Marsh will need into the back of one of the jeeps, another makes sure she's got double backup walkie-talkies, and Jo is synching the eruption countdown timers in the vehicle to the camp's clocks. Amid the chaos, Marsh barely has time to appreciate that in this new life, *marshmallow* isn't a comment on her sugary pushover sweetness, but rather her propensity to burst into adventurous flames at the slightest opportunity.

"Harper!" she calls as Harper runs to her. "You stay with the camp and take care of Pick—Súrkrás. I have to do this, but I'll be back. I promise."

"I know," Harper says, as Marsh hugs her. "You always say that."

Marsh doesn't know what it is—excitement, terror, pride that courage is now her default—but all she can do is cling fiercely to her daughter, unable to speak, as the comments flood her vision with hearts.

"Now get going!" Harper says, and pushes her gently toward the jeep. "Súrkrás and I will be waiting."

"I love you!" Marsh shouts, three times. Harper can't hear her over the din, but she can see her mouth moving, and waves back in response.

Marsh watches the churning camp until she's sure that Harper and Súrkrás are safely in an evacuating jeep, along with all of their gear. She's so full of adrenaline, she can't feel her feet. Finally, she clambers into the driver's seat of her jeep as Jo and Victor hustle themselves into the back.

"You ready for this?" Victor asks her.

"She's always ready," Jo says.

Marsh catches a glimpse of herself in the rearview mirror—even in rough clothes, no makeup, and her hair scraped back into a functional bun, she has to admit, she's positively glowing.

Just as she turns the key and the engine roars to life, the passenger door opens, and Talia leaps into the seat.

"No way I'm missing this!" Talia says as she slams her door closed. "What can I do to help?"

Marsh grins.

"Hang on," she replies.

"What?" Talia blinks.

And Marsh slams the gas pedal to the floor.

The jeep peels out of camp in a spray of black gravel that elicits a cheer from the remaining crew.

"Okay," Talia finally continues as they begin the precarious climb up the icy trail. She finds her microphone rolling around the floor bed, and assumes the air of a serious documentarian. "So, what do you hope to accomplish on this shoot?"

"Well," Marsh begins, as she puts the jeep into a lower gear as if she's been off-roading her whole life. "For the last few years, our team has focused intensely on Arctic and sub-Arctic conservation. We're trying to use wildlife photography to draw attention to the melting ice caps and the loss of habitats for several endangered species."

She can almost feel the knowledge filtering into her as she reaches for it. Talia explained that the longer she stays in a given path, new memories and experiences will start to backfill, until it's like she was here all along, but to feel it happening so quickly now is a bit like magic. It's like the pleasant warmth from an early summer sun. Or slight radiation from a quantum bubble.

"Fascinating!" Talia crows. "Iceland is the perfect place for such a noble mission."

"In more ways than one," Victor chimes in from behind. "There was a famous Norse Viking named Naddodd, who discovered Iceland by accident in the ninth century. He was trying to sail to the Faroe Islands, but he and his crew got lost at sea, and ended up finally coming aground at Reyðarfjall. It's about two hundred miles east along the coast from where we are now, where modern-day Reyðarfjörður is."

"Vikings!" Talia nearly drops the mic as they hit a bump. Volcanic gravel crunches beneath their tires, sharp and hollow. "But what do Vikings have to do with wildlife conservation?"

"Everything, actually. All of our work here in Iceland has been leading up to this very moment," Jo says.

She leans forward to Talia, dramatic.

"Our pursuit of the first-ever shot of the legendary Ísvængur."

Ísvængur?

Marsh lingers on the word, intrigued. She's never heard it before. What could she and her team be after?

TopFan01: <Can someone translate?>
Frónverji: <Já! It means "Ice Wing" in English!>
Hoskistrong: <¡Ala de hielo!>

The Icelandic viewers happily oblige, translating into every language requested.

Marsh is trying to imagine what those two words could mean—a predatory bird? A huge fish of some kind? A *dragon,* even?—but Victor is still lecturing, his artistic voice just as sonorous as his courtroom one.

"The skaldic songs from Naddodd's era sing of the first time he saw the Ísvængur, and he's credited as the person who discovered it, but it's only rumored to actually exist. Every few years, a hiker will claim to have spotted one, but no one has ever been able to capture it on film, so it can't be proven. The things are as rare as unicorns."

Talia turns to Marsh, whose heart is thudding excitedly in her chest. "Until now," she says, grinning back.

"Marsh has been working tirelessly to follow Naddodd's historic trail, and we have good evidence that the Ingólfshöfði cape may be the fabled place of the songs where Naddodd first spotted the Ísvængur," Jo agrees.

Marsh concentrates on the rocky path, trying not to blush as she listens.

"If she's right, this will be the first confirmed photograph of an Ísvængur in the world."

"Amazing!" Talia says. "That would really be a mark to leave, for sure."

Marsh can't help but glance at her host, and they share a private, exhilarated wink.

This new path is almost too perfect to believe. If she and her team can succeed in finding this mystical Ísvængur, and capture the first-ever photograph of it, they'd go down in history forever! Decades from now, when Marsh is old and gray, and Harper is somewhere far away, living a hopefully equally fulfilling life, and even long after, she'll always be able to look at her mother's photos and remember this time they had together in Iceland, and the legacy she's left behind.

She can't wait to see what this "Ice Wing" is.

As the jeep rounds the corner, it passes through a menacing cloud of steam from a crack between two obsidian boulders. It billows and curls, a thick white column buffeted by the breeze. It looks like there's a dragon living beneath, its molten breath smoldering as it slumbers.

"Uh, is that normal?" Talia asks warily.

"Totally normal," Victor replies. "You'll see these steam pockets everywhere."

Jo grits her teeth as they bounce over a rock. "Iceland sits on the Ring of Fire, and right on a couple of seismic fault lines, and the constant pressure from the moving plates and the heat from the Earth's mantle forces its way out through these fissures. The whole island is basically a cauldron of geothermal power!"

"That's . . . comforting," Talia says, not entirely convincingly. "So long as it doesn't mean the volcanic eruption is going to happen right now."

Marsh suddenly turns the wheel hard, and the jeep bounces off the trail and onto a little rock landing.

"Let's hope," she says, and cuts the engine. "Because the rest is on foot."

Marsh pops open her door and steps out onto the dark sand. Just beyond the headlights is crisp, endless air, then a dizzying drop back to the earth.

TopFan01: <Yipes!>

An army of laughing face emojis agree.

And in the other direction, there's a little trail cutting through the wind-beaten grass—and a treacherous, gravelly climb.

Ísvængur, here we come.

ÍSVÆNGUR

The hike is long and arduous. Ingólfshöfði cuts between the ocean and the looming Vatnajökull glacier like a black stone knife, battered by the waves from the bottom and the icy wind from above. Marsh and her crew make their way across the grassy top of the cape toward the edge of the sheer black cliffs, where a colony of puffins have burrowed nests into the little rocky nooks.

Even just the sight of the colorful little birds makes Marsh want to stop and stay for hours with her long lens.

But she's seeking something even more precious.

"Do you think we'll find the Ísvængur before the volcano erupts?" Talia asks her as they pick through the tangled green, shouting over the wind.

"We have to," Marsh replies. "I didn't come this far just to give up now."

"Ahead," Victor says, consulting his GPS device. "We're at the start of Naddodd's path from the songs. We should prepare."

The team stops and makes ready. They move in efficient harmony, as if they've been doing this all their lives. Bags unzip, gear passes back and forth, all without a word uttered. The ease of it is even more thrilling to Marsh than if it had been their first shoot together. She's an expert at this, in this life. She's done it a million times before, and she can do it now, too.

Marsh slings her camera over her shoulder and takes a deep breath.

"Time to make some history," Talia says to her.

"Time to leave a mark," she agrees.

Moms4Marsh: <This is it!>
Frónverji: <Shhh!!! Hafðu hljótt!>

They move forward as one, inching across the cape. Each blink feels like a minute, each step like hours. With every crash of waves from below, Marsh's breath catches. Will this be the moment she discovers the near-mythical creature she's been pursuing for years in this life? Or will she run out of time before the volcano, and her one precious chance will be lost forever?

Suddenly, Marsh freezes.

"What?" Talia asks excitedly.

But she can't answer. Her eyes are locked on something in the distance.

Slowly, carefully, she goes to one knee. She raises her camera to her eye.

Far across the grass, there's a stirring in the wind-battered green. A tremble, then a flurry of motion. A flash of polar navy, and a streak of bright cerulean blue. Then pale ice, deep ocean. The blues swirl together, mesmerizing, as something takes flight.

Ísvængur.

She found it.

It's real.

Marsh has only a moment before the chance is gone. The world shrinks to the size of her lens. Everything she's been seeking, everything she's wanted. As quickly as she can, she presses the shutter.

For an instant, its faint, fleeting click is the only sound in existence.

"Marsh . . ." Talia whispers, once the meadow is quiet and still again.

That's it.

Her mark.

Slowly, as if in a dream, Marsh turns back to her team.

"This is . . ." Jo stammers, overcome.

"This is it. This is what we've been searching for," Victor finishes.

Marsh looks at Talia with misty eyes. From the millions of hearts exploding in her vision, she knows the Bubble has captured her moment of glory in crystalline high definition. The glint of the high-altitude light against her tears, the pink of her cheeks in the cold, the faint ghost of her breath as she grins.

"We did it," she says at last. "We found the Ísvængur."

SagwaGold: <What a shot!!>

MrLoki: <Fullkomin ljósmynd!>

Talia, Jo, and Victor huddle around Marsh as she turns her camera over. Eagerly, they lean over the glass screen to preview the image she just captured.

Every pixel is in crisp focus. It's the perfect picture.

The Arctic backdrop is somber and breathtaking, a gorgeous balance of sea, land, and sky. And at the center of the frame, the brilliant kaleidoscope of blues. Two arcing slashes of color, and a small body of deep obsidian where they meet in the middle.

The commenters all realize what the Ísvængur is at the same moment Marsh does.

JesterG: <It's . . . a butterfly?>

TopFan01: <"Ice Wing" makes so much sense now!>

Frónverji: <I've never seen anything like it! We don't have many butterflies in Iceland!>

Ragnarocker: <Ný tegund! A new species, perhaps?>

SharpTruth: <C:\ATAM\Bubble\edit>

Even as awestruck as she is, that last comment catches Marsh's eye. The username, the odd string of what looks like code, is familiar. That's the second time she's seen something like that, she's sure. But as soon as it appears, it's gone again, lost in the endless stream of posts.

Marsh squints as the comments keep rolling, confused.

Is someone trying to do something to her Bubble?

But before she can ask Talia, a deep, prehistoric groan rumbles down from Vatnajökull, echoing across Ingólfshöfði.

Marsh and the crew spin to each other, eyes wide—then toward the ice-capped volcano.

"Talia, grab that rucksack," Marsh shouts. "We've got to get out of here!"

Marsh and the crew scramble through the meadow back toward the jeep as quickly as they can, too breathless to speak. She's so panicked, time warps—everything happens in fragments, a series of still shots with nothing in between. Marsh hefting her camera bag onto her shoulder as she runs, Marsh rushing across the uneven field. Marsh finally abandoning the heavy equipment and keeping only the all-important film, to save them invaluable minutes. Marsh's determined, heroic expression.

Finally, the jeep comes into view, and they all rush even faster, buoyed by hope. Marsh slams into the side of it, then jerks open her door and throws herself into the driver's seat, her key scrambling for the ignition. "Everyone in?" she asks.

"I'm in!" Talia says as she jumps in beside Marsh, somehow instantly seated in a photograph-worthy pose.

The doors slam in the back. "Us too!" Jo shouts. "Hit it, Marsh!"

Marsh drives the pedal to the floor.

From how amped up the comments are becoming, she knows the Bubble must be cutting between Talia's faux-nervous gaze—*surely, they're not in real danger, right?*—and Marsh's passionate stare in between teasing clips of Öræfajökull's brewing peak. Every time the dark jutting shape comes on everyone's screen, Marsh's view fills with prayers for the mountain to wait just one more minute, just one more, before it explodes. She doesn't know what's more dangerous at this point—the volcano, or trying to drive without being able to see the road.

"Almost there!" she says as they round a bend and the road straightens out. She floors it, desperate. "Almost!"

"I see orange!" Talia cries, her eyes glued to the rear windshield. "It's bubbling!"

"We'll make it!" Marsh says. "The IMO safety line is two miles away!"

Her eyes jump frantically to the dash. She has no idea what 128 kilometers per hour is, but it feels dangerously fast on this rocky mountain road. They've got to be within two, maybe three minutes of safety.

"Something is happening," Jo yells over the roar of the engine. "Something is *happening*!"

Stones clatter against the undercarriage and whip up to crack against the windows and windshield, sometimes so loud Marsh is sure the glass is going to shatter, but she keeps going.

"There it is!" Marsh points.

Straight ahead, a burst of color. Several bright yellow emergency services vans, and more white pickups, probably from the Icelandic Meteorological Office, are parked in a wide fan with their back bays open. Satellites and other gigantic pieces of equipment are set up around the clearing, monitoring Öræfajökull. And just behind them are all of Marsh's crew's vehicles, each one with several people standing on top of them, binoculars glued to their faces.

Even with the racket inside Marsh's jeep, she can hear the cheers as they catch sight of her whizzing down the path.

"We're going to make it!" Marsh says—just as the top of Öræfajökull blows off.

MrLoki: <Andskotinn!!!>
Hoskistrong: <Fokk!!!!!!!!!!!!!>

Marsh screams as the world goes white for an instant, and then bright, nuclear orange.

Öræfajökull has turned into a fountain of bubbling, roiling magma, red and yellow and white and angry black where the lava and glacier meet. It's the most intense, terrifying sight she's ever seen.

But it doesn't matter.

Because just as the eruption finally starts, Marsh's jeep crashes past the wooden pickets the Icelandic Meteorological Office has placed at the head of the trail to mark the safety line, and skids to a stop as the crowd rushes to her in a flood of celebration.

"Never again, you hear me?" Victor is shouting as they all spill out of the jeep, and pulls Marsh into a crushing hug. "You never get to do that again!"

"She doesn't have to!" Jo says as she grabs her next, then turns to the crowd. "This goddamn fool nearly died, but she got the shot!"

She snatches Marsh's hand and holds it up high, like she's a boxing champion.

"We have a photo! We found Ísvængur!"

"Marsh! Marsh! Marsh!" Everyone is howling now. There are tears as the crew swarms her, and whistles, and dancing. Someone has started up an ancient skaldic song about some brave Viking warrior, and the others join in, twisting it so that it's Marsh's name they sing instead of some historical hero. Harper is holding Súrkrás and jumping up and down beside her, shouting, "You did it, Mom! You did it!" Marsh spins around, taking it all in, trying to remember to breathe.

And then there's Ren, jumping out of his jeep as it careens in from the opposite direction, sprinting for her through the crowd, his tousled hair shining beautifully against the bright, fiery sky. As he runs, his arms go wide, his knees bend a little as he draws close, and when he reaches her, he sweeps her into a spinning embrace and kisses her passionately.

Even as it's happening, Marsh almost can't believe all of this is real, and how far she's come. She could barely get a sentence out without blushing during her life's recap, and now, she's standing below a volcano, laughing and singing along as her friends and colleagues scream her name. She's full of joy, alive with victory, not a trace of timidity or caution or worry left.

She's *perfect*.

"You know what this means, don't you?" Ren asks her once he's finally let her go.

"What?" Marsh asks, breathless.

"Everything," Ren says. "You're going to have complete access to any nature preserve in the world. Antarctica, Pu Luong, the Galápagos, Ngorongoro—anywhere! And the awards you're going to win! With these shots, you're going to be the star of the annual international wildlife conservation gala tomorrow!"

"Whoa, Mom!" Harper says. "That's amazing!"

A gala!

Marsh gasps, excited. She can't wait to see herself there, shining bright as the guest of honor!

"Can we go?" her daughter begs.

"You must!" Victor agrees. "They'll probably name a conservation grant after you. You're going down in history."

"We all are," Marsh says.

"No, this victory is all yours," he insists. "An accomplishment worthy of a deputy director of eco photography."

Marsh blinks, shocked.

Is Victor hinting that he wants to promote her?

This is incredible! It has to be a step up the ladder from when she became a lawyer at his firm in the first half of the season. Now she's not just a member of the team, but might be its second-in-command soon!

But what does that mean for Jo?

Before she can say more, Ren pulls her away with a wink. "Come on, there's something I have to tell you."

Harper waves them off, and Marsh lets him lead her to the periphery of the crowd. Dusk is falling, but even after sunset, there will still be plenty of light from the glow of Öræfajökull's eruption, so the party shows no signs of letting up.

"So, while I was out at the cliffs, I found the perfect spot," Ren says as soon as they stop.

"The perfect spot?" Marsh repeats. "The perfect spot for what?"

"For the ceremony!" Ren cries giddily.

What ceremony? she wonders—and then it hits her.

Ren means the *wedding* ceremony!

"It's gorgeous," he's saying. "There's a green mountainside covered in wildflowers, and a little waterfall, and cliffs in the background . . . it's just perfect!"

JesterG: <Wow! The show is really moving things along!>

The comments seem as surprised as Marsh is.

YanYan242: <I thought their wedding would be the finale!>

She'd been expecting the same, Marsh has to admit. More time to build up the excitement, more time to set up the fairy-tale happily ever after. Isn't that how most romance movies end, with the wedding?

"That's—wow!" Marsh finally says to Ren, trying to smile. "It's—I—that's great, Ren."

Ren is too full of adrenaline to notice. He's talking a mile a minute, his hands waving, unable to contain himself. "You're going to love it. I took a picture on my phone to show you. It's only two hours from here. We could do it tomorrow, even!"

"Tomorrow?" Marsh repeats.

He sweeps her into another Hollywood-esque twirling hug.

"I just feel like, why are we waiting?" he says once he sets her down. "Why *not* tomorrow?"

"Well, because the conservation gala is tomorrow, where my best shots will be on display," Marsh replies. "It's back in Reykjavík."

"The gala!" Ren smacks his forehead. "Of course. We have to be there to celebrate you."

He looks down at his muddy boots and hiking pants and frowns.

"Think they'll let me wear this?" he asks.

Marsh manages to laugh, instead of roll her eyes a bit.

Rugged Ren is handsome—but maybe this is a little *too* rugged.

"Yeah, I guess not." He shrugs. "I can't remember the last time I ironed a shirt. Good thing the wedding will be outdoors!"

Marsh gives him a kiss, and pats his chest. "Go get your phone, so I can see this special spot you found. I'll be right back," she says.

As Ren heads back to their tent, Marsh sneaks out of the celebration and weaves her way through the cluster of jeeps in the falling darkness.

Near the back, Talia is sitting in the open bay of a big van full of cameras and monitors, where she's traded some autographs with an awestruck news crew from Akureyri for a small bottle of Icelandic aquavit. Somehow, her hair is still delicately curled despite her having been hiking for hours and then thrown around a jeep.

"What a day." She smiles when she spots Marsh. "Can you believe it?"

"Not yet," Marsh replies. She sits down on the bumper beside Talia and accepts a cup of the stiff liquor. "I've barely had a chance for everything to sink in yet, with the excitement of imminent volcanic obliteration and all."

Talia laughs. "Honestly, and I don't mean to brag, but I'm not sure how we're going to top this episode. It was pretty spectacular."

"Just call it the finale right here," Marsh jokes, and they tap rims.

"Would you, though? If you could?" Talia asks her after they each take a tentative, burning sip.

Marsh's eyes drift down to where she's resting her cup on one thigh. Her engagement ring glints faintly on her finger in the distant glow of the eruption, the diamond turning a soft orange.

"It's really a lovely ring," Talia says.

"It is," Marsh agrees.

"And I heard that Ren might also have found a special place just as lovely, for the ceremony," she adds, her voice sparkling with excitement. "Your viewers are going to *love* seeing you in a gorgeous white dress!"

Marsh nods, but she doesn't look at Talia. Her eyes linger on the ring, slightly out of focus, almost as if she's looking through it.

Ren is a true romantic, in every sense of the word. Can she imagine Dylan ever being out at a physics conference and noticing something sweet for her? He was so focused on his work, too settled in his marriage with her, too comfortable and complacent and bored.

Well, probably there aren't very many romantic things at a physics conference compared to the Icelandic countryside, she allows. Ren did have an advantage there. But as romantic as Ren is, sometimes it's almost a little too much. Although, after decades of not enough, wouldn't she rather have a little too much?

Talia looks concerned. "Are you not happy with this life?"

"Oh, I am," Marsh says quickly, which pleases Talia. "It's beyond anything I could have ever dreamed."

"What?" Talia asks. "What are you thinking?"

Marsh holds up her hand, to indicate the ring. "Actually, I was thinking about Ren."

Talia nods. "So devoted to you and Harper. And in this episode, I have to say, he's quite the hunk. Very sexy."

Marsh blushes slightly. "He is." But her smile fades again. "But it just feels kind of rushed. Or maybe not quite right. I don't know exactly."

Talia cocks her head, looking a little alarmed.

Marsh shrugs helplessly. "Could we . . ." She hesitates. "Could we put the wedding off?"

Talia gasps.

"But, Marsh! I thought you were happy with Ren. And especially after that romantic midseason special, and the vacation in Tahiti . . . Plus, can you imagine the ratings boost we'd get, with you in all white?"

She fights to keep her voice light rather than shrill.

"You really want to scrap this path, too, and leave your Iceland life so early?"

"No!" Marsh cries. "It's the complete opposite! I'm thrilled with this new path."

Talia looks relieved, but still confused. "Then what is it?" she asks.

Marsh is suddenly shy. "This life is so great, there's just so much more I want to do first. I want to get my photos developed, and see what I created today. I want to curate a gallery."

She lowers her voice a little, embarrassed.

"I . . . I want to go to the gala."

Talia takes a breath, and is careful to keep her face trained in a patient, benevolent expression. But Marsh can't help but think that underneath the polished veneer, she looks almost a little . . . disappointed?

"I'm sorry," Marsh says. "I just—"

"Don't be sorry, Marsh!" Talia cuts her off. She's smiling again, looking as diplomatic as ever once more. "Believe me, I know better than anyone how difficult this process is. I want you to finish this season with everything you ever wanted. I want you to be as happy as I am. For your life to be as perfect as I managed to make mine."

She gives Marsh's hand an affectionate squeeze.

"This season is about *you*, Marsh. What you want. Right?"

"Right," Marsh agrees.

"Now. Let's go to the gala, then!" Talia chirps. "It might not be a wedding dress, but I bet our viewers will still love you in a glamorous gown! And I can't wait to see your beautiful photographs on display, either."

A heavy thunk rattles the news van as she pulls out the Show Bible from one of the cargo trunks.

It's positively gargantuan.

It looks more like a guest book for visitors to sign at an event than a reference text. There are *thousands* of pages—so many that Marsh isn't sure how it's even humanly possible for Talia to have read through them all, let alone written them, between each episode.

"I've been keeping track of all the good stuff, but is there anything else about this life you want to change before the next scene?"

Marsh hesitates.

"I mean, Ren is really exciting in this episode," she finally says—and means it. She can still see the ropey lines of muscle rippling in his tanned forearms as he played with Súrkrás, or picked up his heavy hiking back-pack. "But do I really want dirt and rocks all over the house all the time, or a guy who doesn't own a pair of trousers that aren't made of waterproof outdoor endurance material, for the rest of my life?"

Talia nods knowingly. "I think I see what you mean."

"I just . . . maybe it would be nice if he were also a little more . . ."

"Sophisticated?"

Embarrassed, Marsh winces.

"I don't mean he isn't now!" Talia laughs. "But if the goal is your happi-ness, why not let the Bubble make a few tweaks to him?"

Marsh hesitates. She's already gained so much, it feels selfish to ask for more.

"I know what you're thinking," Talia tells her. "And yes. You deserve it. That's what this show is about!"

"I'm just worried that—"

"We're not talking anything major, silly!" Talia laughs again. "Just a little softening around the edges. A few more showers, a few nicer shirts, maybe a job done indoors instead of hanging off the side of a mountain."

Marsh finds herself nodding as she listens, unable to help it.

Ren is already so wonderful, a few touches like that would make him a literal dream come true. And maybe, if she's really honest, even a bit of suave sprinkled on top. Maybe the smallest nudge like that would truly take him from amazing to perfect.

And Ren *did* tell her that she should have perfection, after all.

Talia grins. "I love this newfound determination, Marsh! Look at you blossoming."

She pats the cover of the Show Bible.

"Let's go see more of this fabulous new life of yours, shall we?"

HIGH BIDDER

The forty-third International Wildlife Conservation Gala is an elegant affair held over every floor of Reykjavík's grand Harpa concert hall, a futuristic glass structure that glitters beneath the navy-blue sky. The Harpa sits along the harbor at the northeastern edge of the city, and just beyond its sheer walls, the ocean churns in dark, foamy waves.

At the entrance, Marsh stares up at the sparkling, diamond-like façade in awe, and breathes in the salty evening air.

"You look beautiful," Ren says beside her.

A smile breaks out across her face at that, and she looks down. She's wearing a fancy gown, a sweeping deep green number that she would have been terrified to try before *All This and More*, but now looks like something she was born wearing, and Ren is dashing in his tuxedo.

He really *does* look more polished in this episode. He stands straighter, and his hair is combed back and his face cleanly shaven. He seems as comfortable now in the dressy clothes as he did in his outdoor wear. If Marsh handed him a snifter of Scotch, he could be James Bond.

She's so glad she talked Talia into letting her come to the gala—and let Talia talk her into tinkering just a little bit with Ren. He's going to fit in so well. She can't wait to see him charm the crowd.

"And so do you," Ren adds, turning to his other side.

"Thanks!" Harper laughs and does a little spin. She's in all black, the way a concert musician might be. "This is so cool. I'm kind of nervous to go inside."

"Of course you are! This is a big night for you," Ren replies, looking lovingly at her. He squeezes Marsh's hand. "For both of you."

Marsh's heart soars. Is Harper also performing at the gala?

"I bet Mom's photograph is going to be the star of tonight's charity auction," Harper says, staring at the imposing building with awe.

"If it is, it'll all be thanks to your music," Marsh replies.

That makes Harper grin.

"Let's do this," she declares, and raises her arms, as if she's stroking a bow across the strings of an instrument. "I'll see you guys after the opening sonata. And good luck, Mom. You're going to crush it!"

Her daughter scampers ahead, excited, her dress shoes clicking on the concrete walk. Guests are trickling in, the path a tapestry of silks, satins, furs, jewels. Ren turns to Marsh, and gallantly extends an arm to escort her to her grand entrance.

"Ready to make history?" he asks her.

Marsh excitedly takes his elbow.

Inside the glamorous hall, she's greeted by a standing ovation, which makes her blush. The attention has her heady, almost drunk. The room is full of photographers, biologists, conservationists, museum directors, and more from all across Europe—they all know who she is, and the daring discovery she just made. Onstage, the curtains are closed so that the gala can project rotating images of various endangered species onto them, interspersed with quotes from various important people, in order to drum up excitement and prestige. Amid stunning shots of breaching whales and soaring Arctic eagles, Marsh spies her photograph of the elusive Ísvængur.

"This is the most important discovery of the current century," a scholar of Arctic ecology studies has said of her picture.

"Our field of understanding has irrevocably changed," a Pulitzer Prize–winning conservation author has written.

Even the prime minster of Iceland has submitted words of congratulations to her.

"A national treasure—and the foundation of our new national gallery, if we're lucky enough to win Marsh's Ísvængur at the auction tonight."

That last one makes Marsh gulp.

Moms4Marsh: <Amazing!!!>

Notamackerel: <This is totally unrealistic. Iceland is going to build Marsh her *own* gallery for one photograph?>

YanYan242: <Wow, jealous much?>

SharpTruth: <Everyone, listen to Notamackerel! They're on to something. I know what I'm talking about.>

StrikeF0rce: <Yeah, right. Isn't SharpTruth the wannabe hacker? Can we ban them for disruptive behavior?>

SharpTruth: <Just listen! I have insider knowledge about the show, and—>

[Automatic security filters have deleted this account]

Notamackerel: <Nice, guys. Ever heard of free speech?>

The comments abruptly snap shut as Marsh sends them away, relieving her of the argument.

She wishes she could roll her eyes at her trolls, except the cameras would pick it up. Obviously, this turn of events is outrageously over the top—and so what? That's the whole point! The whole reason she's here. If she wanted normal, she could have just stayed in her original life.

If anything, this makes her even more determined to knock this episode out of the park.

The show isn't about facts. It's about happiness. That's why everyone watches, and what everyone wants.

And her *happiness* is certainly real.

"Oh my, it's an honor," a man standing near Marsh and Ren says as he recognizes her, shaking Marsh's hand. "An absolute honor!"

"Tell us about the shoot," another woman begs. A crowd is gathering around her now. "We heard it was quite harrowing!"

Marsh regales them with the story of Öræfajökull, a little shyly at first, but with Ren's charming encouragement, she grows more enthusiastic. The room is rapt, hanging on every word. Every time her photo of the Ísvængur appears in the rotation against the curtains again, they all gasp and coo at it.

"Just fantastic!" an elderly gentleman cries. "What a thrilling adventure."

"And what a priceless treasure," his wife adds. "I can't believe the detail on its wings."

Marsh tells a few more stories, and Ren jumps in at just the right moment every time with a funny quip or well-timed laugh.

He really is a fantastic date. Although, now that she's had some time to observe him, maybe he's almost *too* fantastic. He's so concerned with supporting Marsh and making her look impressive, she's not sure she's heard him say one original thing all night. He's almost more like a butler than a partner.

That might need another tweak or two.

Just as Marsh finishes her last anecdote, a distinguished ding intones over the hall's intercom.

"Good evening, everyone. *Velkomin til Reykjavíkur!*"

Talia is onstage now, holding a microphone and waving to the crowd. As usual, she looks like she was created for the part—her makeup is flawless, her artfully draped black gown is without a single wrinkle, and her hair probably took an entire day to pin up.

"Tonight is a historic night, not just for Iceland, but for wildlife and environment conservation efforts around our world. We thank all of you for being here with us."

The curtains begin to open behind her as she speaks, revealing a stage full of teenagers and young adults holding their instruments. Marsh's eyes dart quickly, then fix upon their target, spellbound. Just to the left of center, in the very front row, is Harper—sitting in the first chair's seat.

Talia sweeps her arm.

"But first, to open the auction, the Icelandic Symphony Youth Orchestra has prepared a very special piece that they will now play live."

The audience applauds, and Marsh pushes to the front, to be as close to Harper as possible. This is the concert she never got to in the midseason special, and she won't miss it again.

Her daughter does look nervous, but not in a way that diminishes her. It's made her sit taller, made her eyes even sharper. Her fingers look even longer against the delicate neck of her instrument—not a violin this time, but an Icelandic langspil, Marsh can see, since they live in Reykjavík now.

Marsh ignores that detail. She doesn't care about the instrument. Only her daughter.

And Harper is ready.

Marsh knows she is.

The audience holds its breath as the conductor raises his baton, and Harper sets the thin, straight bow against her langspil's strings.

The first note begins softly, then grows. A high, keening wail that fills the room but leaves no echo, like the wind from Vatnajökull. Every inch of flesh on Marsh's body prickles, a cold rush from her toes up to her neck and out through her cheeks at the beauty of it, followed by a warm wave that makes her eyes sting. The ballroom contracts around Harper, rapt.

"Amazing," Ren murmurs, as she touches her bow to the strings again.

No, Marsh thinks.

Perfect.

"Marsh!" someone whispers, and Marsh turns to see Victor and Jo making their way toward her through the crowd.

"She's incredible," Jo hisses as she hands Marsh a glass of champagne, and they clink rims. "Even better than the last time I heard her! You've got a prodigy on your hands."

"Like mother, like daughter," Ren agrees proudly, and accepts a glass from Victor.

Marsh turns back to Harper with a huge grin on her face, and watches her daughter strike another piercing, mournful note with her bow that sends a shiver rippling through the gathered patrons.

"Harper is the real prodigy," she says to her friends. "My photograph was all luck."

"Chance, hard work, genius—whatever it was that got us that photo of the Ísvængur, I'll take it," Victor says softly. "Keep winning cases like you are and I'll happily hire a full-time second cleaning crew just for these celebrations."

Huh?

Marsh startles, confused.

Didn't Victor say that exact line before, in a previous episode? Back when she was a lawyer at Mendoza-Montalvo and Hall?

But she's not a lawyer now, in this new path.

How could Victor ever remember she was?

Something's wrong.

"Cases?" Marsh asks him nervously. "You mean photo shoots?"

"What?" Victor looks puzzled.

Marsh quickly glances at Jo and Ren, but they're busy watching Harper, absorbed in her solo.

"You said 'cases,'" she repeats softly to Victor.

"I did?"

"Victor, are you all right?" Marsh asks, taking his arm.

He quietly clinks his champagne with hers. "Of course! I'm just so happy that you're going to be our deputy director of eco photography."

Marsh gapes, stunned, as Victor sticks out his hand.

"Congratulations, Marsh," he says. He's beaming at her. "It's yours if you want it."

In her real life, she's fantasized about this moment so many times, as she sat at her small desk outside of Victor's door, watching important attorney after attorney stride into his luxurious corner office for meetings, even though it would be impossible for him to promote someone to lawyer who hadn't finished law school or passed the bar. She added to it year after year, like an imaginary personal highlight reel—Victor calling her into the boardroom, Victor asking her to take a seat across the table from him and all the other partners. Victor telling her that he'd seen her potential since the day she began at the firm. Victor pushing his beloved box of celebratory cigars toward her as he stretched out his hand to her in just this way.

And now it's finally within reach. Maybe it isn't exactly the same, but it's close enough. Victor has finally noticed her, and he's impressed. He's inviting her onto the path, to someday be equal to him and Jo.

Marsh stares at his palm for another long moment, still in disbelief. Then she lunges, grabbing hold and shaking hands vigorously.

"Thank you, Victor," she says, and Jo wraps her arms around and hugs them both as Ren whispers congratulations. "Thank you."

Just then, the orchestra's sonata ends, and applause engulfs the ballroom. They all turn toward the stage to see Talia gesturing to the bowing musicians, her compliments to them drowned out by the drone of clapping.

"What a magnificent performance!" she's exclaiming. People are tossing roses overhead to the stage, up to Harper's feet, and she's grinning so hard her cheeks are red. "The perfect way to open tonight's main event."

Behind the orchestra, against the black background, Marsh's sapphire Ísvængur appears, and the musicians all turn toward it as they clap, too.

"Marsh," Ren shouts over the drone, and she turns to look at him. "I just want to say how proud of you I am. And how happy I am that this is our life." His eyes look misty. "I mean, can it ever get any better than this?"

Marsh takes his hand and squeezes hard. "I'm not sure it can, Ren," she replies.

Ren kisses her cheek, and when he pulls back, an usher has arrived beside them, whispering directions to reach the backstage area. Talia wants all the wildlife photographers in the wings, so the winners can give a speech once the final bid comes in, he explains.

"This is it, Marsh!" Ren says. "Your moment!"

"Go!" Jo encourages. "We'll be cheering you on from here."

Marsh leaves them, heading for the unmarked door at the far corner of the ballroom that the usher indicated. Another usher opens it, touches her headset, and then waves Marsh through and up a short flight of stairs to the wings of the stage. Everything is more muted here—the lights dimmer, the sounds softer—and the dull roar of the crowd beyond as the auction begins makes Marsh's heart beat faster in anticipation.

"There you are," Talia says, appearing behind her. "Congratulations on your promotion!"

Marsh whirls. "You heard?" she asks excitedly.

"I did! And with the way I'm sure this auction is going to go, this is only the start!" Talia claps her hands. "I can't wait to see what you'll do next! Go on another daring shoot? Open a new gallery? Maybe even create a foundation in your name?"

A burst of applause punctuates the question, exquisitely timed.

"I can't even imagine," Marsh says, awestruck.

Talia elbows her playfully. "Well, by the sound of how well it's going out there, I think you'd better start."

Marsh turns to peek out at the stage, hoping to steal a glimpse of the bid tallies from their odd angle. Her eyes go misty as she listens to the cheers. What could a foundation in her own name be like? Not only would she be able to leave her mark on history, but she could also help other young, bright women like herself break out of their shells and find their way to their passions. Maybe she could join with a library in London, or a charity in Oslo, a museum in Reykjavík, a university in Stockholm . . .

SharpTruth2: <Everyone, this is important! I'm trying to tell you that
    something's wrong!>
[Automatic security filters have deleted this account]
JesterG: <How is this guy back? He's more annoying than Notamackerel.>
Notamackerel: <Excuse me!>

A huge gasp and burst of applause from the audience startle her, and Marsh accidentally snaps the comments shut as she blinks.

"Sounds like someone might have just placed an unbeatable bid," Talia says with a wink.

"For my photo?" Marsh asks, a rush of adrenaline making her giddy.

A bell sharply clangs over the commotion, old-timey and jarring like one aboard a ship, signaling the end of the auction. The applause is so thunderous, Marsh can feel it in her gut. She's too excited to wait any longer. She steps out of the wings—just a few feet, just enough to see the giant list projected onto the back of the stage, to see the winners and the final bid tally.

It takes no time at all to find her photograph in the list. "Ísvængur" has the highest bid of all.

The amount of money Marsh's winning bidder has offered is eye-watering. More than anyone else in the world could match, it seems.

But as surprising as that is, it's not the price that freezes her in shock.

It's the name of the bidder.

The word hovers in elegant, Sharp Purple serif font beside her lot.

Chrysalis

It's here.

It's followed her to Iceland.

"Incredible, isn't it?" Talia cries, over the roars of the audience. "Look at those numbers!"

SharpTruth3: <PLEASE LISTEN!!! Chrysalis is not part of the show!>
[Automatic security filters have deleted this account]
TopFan01: <Mods, is there a way to ban this guy permanently, so he can't keep reentering by making a new account?>

Marsh fights the comments away nervously.

It was one thing when Chrysalis was no more than an Easter egg, a prop merely inserting itself into her episodes just to be there, but ever since the midseason special, there's no denying it's becoming more powerful. Now it's taking action, attempting to directly influence events or change things inside Marsh's Bubble. Almost like it's trying to make choices *for* her.

But to what end?

And why does it want a photograph so badly?

She doesn't know. And she doesn't want to.

Talia keeps grinning for a moment longer, but finally, she sighs.

"Oh no," she says. "I know that look."

Her host seems astounded that she's not thrilled with the auction—and exhausted.

"I'm sorry," Marsh replies. "I know you said not to worry about how many paths it takes to find the right one, and I know how hard you worked on this one—every one!—to make them everything I could want. I just—"

But as soon as she glimpsed Talia's weariness, it's gone, and she's her usual, boundlessly energetic self again.

"I don't want you worrying about me for even one second!" Talia insists adorably. "This season is about you, and that's who I'm here for. And this is what the show is all about. I'll make a hundred lives, a million lives, for you to try, if that's what it takes."

"You're not mad?" Marsh asks.

"I'm not mad at all," she assures her. "Just the opposite. Watching you blossom, asking for what you want—I'm thrilled for you. And we're going to find you that perfect ending before the finale. I just know it."

Talia opens her arms, and Marsh falls gratefully into the hug as the comments overflow with hearts, until there are so many little red shapes crowding her view that Marsh can hardly breathe.

As she finally pulls back and turns to dab her eyes, feeling optimistic again, a big thump echoes across the backstage. Talia has pulled the Show Bible out from somewhere and set it on a giant cargo crate, which nearly crumples under its weight. It's so large, it's almost grotesque at this point, like some kind of medieval tome that requires a pedestal to read. Talia can barely maneuver it by herself.

"Well, even if you don't remain a photographer, you've made amazing progress in your professional life! We can preserve that, no matter what your career becomes next," her host says. "And Reykjavík is beautiful, but how about somewhere more urban and bustling? A big city, perhaps?"

Marsh nods eagerly.

"Is there anything else you want to improve?" Talia asks.

"Ren's still not quite right," she admits, a little embarrassed. "He's got no . . . edge."

Talia giggles. "We can definitely fix that," she says. "And Harper?"

Marsh smiles. "Things are much better between her and Ren now, thank goodness. And she's definitely proud of me—but I still miss our special bond. I think Harp misses it, too. I want us to be as close as we were when she was younger."

Talia solemnly peruses the Show Bible. After a moment, she looks up at Marsh, and taps the open page near the middle of the book, where some new, amazing path is scrawled, and Marsh's hope soars.

A path where she can be just as successful, but even *more* happy.

And most importantly, a path where there's no Chrysalis.

"You could have *All This* . . ." Talia sings cheerily as the end of episode music begins.

"*And More*," Marsh replies, hopeful and relieved.

EPISODE 7

LA ESTRELLA

The next episode opens with Marsh sitting on a green couch, in a white room.

Wherever Talia has sent her, it's much quieter and smaller than the glamorous Harpa. The applause is still ringing in her ears, even though this new setting is completely silent. The ghost of her victory is still pricking at her heart rate, making her feel breathless, fidgety.

She shakes her head to drive away the last scene. At the midseason special, she didn't think life could get any better than she'd already made it, and then she ended up in the remote Arctic, where she had more fun than she could ever have imagined. Whatever's waiting for her here in this new path, she can make a life *even better* than the one in Iceland.

And hopefully, one free of Chrysalis, too.

Resolute, Marsh surveys the room. At first, she thought maybe she was in a house, but now she can see that the space is far too small to be a room in a home, or even an apartment. But although it's tight quarters, the place is well decorated. There's a cozy bedroom through the little door to the left, a kitchenette off to the right, and a tidy, modern bathroom with a full shower past that. There are four windows, all drawn closed with shades.

It almost looks like a luxury trailer, or a fancy motorhome, she muses, confused.

Why is she living in a trailer?

Only one way to find out.

Cautiously, Marsh rises from the couch and walks over to the door. She touches the lock and takes a breath, steeling herself.

Then she opens it.

At once, a burst of color and movement obliterates her view, and a swell of energetic, slightly cliché mariachi music rushes into her trailer from outside at overwhelming volume. Marsh gasps, covering her eyes for a moment, and when she looks again, a massive, chaotic, beautiful city fills every inch of the frame.

The sky is bright, the buildings a rainbow of shapes and colors and styles, all crammed together in a charming crush. There are parks on every corner, little food stands selling mouthwatering snacks, and musicians strolling up and down the plazas, holding out their hats for coins as they play.

And there's green everywhere. Trees shading sidewalk corners, bushes overflowing from the street medians, flowers bursting from the balconies of every café and shop.

LunaMágica: <¡Es México! ¡Está en la Ciudad de México!>
Pollito: <¡Bienvenida, Marsh!>

The comments are pinging excitedly, her viewers everywhere in Latin America thrilled with this latest turn of events.

ChilangoCool: <¡La mejor ciudad!>
LoboAzul: <¡Marsh, te amamos!>

Marsh keeps staring through the erupting hearts and confetti, exhilarated. She can't believe she's here, in Mexico City. The place she's been dreaming of returning to someday after her failed trip with Dylan, to prove to herself that she could do it after all, she could be open-minded and brave and try new things . . .

Now she can.

As Marsh continues to gape at her gorgeous, intense new home, a passerby glances at her—and then stops dead in the middle of the sidewalk as he stares.

"*Dios mío,*" the man yelps, shocked. "*¿ . . . Malvavisca? ¿La mismísima Malvavisca?*"

"Huh?" Marsh blinks.

The chaos is immediate.

Out of nowhere, the street is suddenly mobbed with people, all crowding around Marsh. Some are laughing, some are screaming, and they're all reaching for her.

"*¡Malvavisca!*" they're shouting as they press in. One woman in the frenzied throng looks like she's sobbing. "*¡Malvavisca! ¡Malvavisca!*"

"What's happening?!" Marsh panics.

She wrenches herself free and scrambles back up the metal stairs of her trailer, and then throws herself inside and locks the door. She leans against it, panting, as the clamor continues outside.

"Hi, Marsh!" Talia says from the couch, and Marsh nearly has a heart attack.

"For goodness' sake, Talia," she groans, putting a hand on her chest. "You have *got* to give some warning before you do that."

"Sorry, again," she replies. "I got so used to it after my season, I forget sometimes."

Marsh waits for her heart to stop racing, and then points behind her, indicating the pandemonium on the other side. "It's fine. What I'm more curious about is *that*."

Talia nods. She goes to the counter, where a stack of papers is sitting.

"What's this?" Marsh asks, taking them from her.

There must be at least a hundred pages, she estimates. It almost looks like a slim manuscript or something.

"I think you're going to like this life," Talia answers excitedly.

Marsh looks down and reads the title.

```
             UN JUEGO PELIGROSO
             ("A DANGEROUS GAME")
             Guion cinematográfico
```

It's not a manuscript, she realizes with a start as she skims the next paragraph in the same telltale boxy font.

It's a screenplay.

Marsh must be a film writer in this episode!

```
Un Juego Peligroso: the world's most popular vig-
ilante justice romance telenovela! A woman whose
father was murdered by an especially bloodthirsty
cartel in a case of mistaken identity vows to take
down one of the most dangerous gangs in all of
Latin America—but when she finally comes face-to-
face with the infamous leader, she isn't prepared
for the sudden, undeniable spark that threatens
her delicate heart . . . and her desperate quest
for vengeance.
```

Moms4Marsh: <Ooh la la! Marsh writes telenovelas?>
JesterG: <Obviously! She lives in Mexico now!>
Monsterrific: <I love telenovelas! This one sounds spicy!>

But something still seems a little off.

Marsh is clearly involved in the film industry in this life, but the crowds outside weren't shouting at her like she was a screenwriter. Except for cinematography fans, she'd bet that most people would have no idea who wrote a given script.

They were shouting at her like . . .

Marsh looks up at Talia, who's now not standing right beside her, but rather near the open door to the bedroom. She pushes it shut, revealing a giant movie poster on the side of it that she couldn't see before, because it was flush against the wall.

It's a dizzying collage of faces and action scenes on a dark background, framing the head and shoulders of the woman at its center. She's gorgeous, her hair luxurious and her eyes smoldering and her skin as smooth as silk. Her face is turned three-quarters to the camera, and her gaze is focused toward the top left corner of the poster, where the title *Un Juego Peligroso—¡la telenovela mas popular del mundo!* threatens in dramatic font.

"Whoa!" Marsh cries. "That's me!"

She can't stop staring. She looks almost as good as Talia does, by this point.

Then it hits her.

Marsh isn't writing the telenovela . . .

She's *starring* in it!

Outside, the commotion briefly intensifies, as if to underscore her thoughts. Through the trailer's thick walls, she can hear the faint echo of the crowd chanting, that same word over and over—*Malvavisca, Malvavisca, Malvavisca*. Except this time, it's not frightening.

It's exciting.

Marsh—*Malvavisca, Marshmallow*—is a beloved, world-famous actress in this new life.

"Holy mackerel," Marsh murmurs, which makes Talia laugh.

LunaMágica: <Now we get to watch Marsh's episodes AND her
    telenovela!>
TopFan01: <She's the star of a show within a show—very clever>

Talia winks at that last comment. "I couldn't help myself," she says. "But what do you think, Marsh?"

Marsh's insides are a mix of elation and terror. "I can't believe it," she manages to say.

"Better than the first time around, eh?" Talia chides.

Marsh nods, still dazed. "I did always want to come back here, after that disastrous vacation with Dylan. To prove to myself that I could enjoy Mexico the way I wanted to the first time, instead of just hiding in the hotel." She swallows. "But . . . international movie star?"

"You can do it," Talia says confidently. "Just think of how far you've come since the recap. Every episode, we've watched you grow braver, stronger, more alive. You're not just surviving now, but flourishing. You've given a speech at Mendoza-Montalvo and Hall, and charmed a crowd at a gala in Reykjavík. Now, you're back where you've always dreamed of returning— and I know you're ready to step into the spotlight and shine like you always should have . . . on an even grander scale than ever!"

Marsh finds herself clinging to Talia's words as she listens. An award-winning drama, a timeless story for the ages that viewers will watch for decades, even centuries, to come . . . Marsh has to admit, this version of leaving her mark could be really incredible.

"You're right," she says to Talia, admiring herself on the poster again. "I *am* ready."

There's a sharp knock at the trailer door. But before Marsh can protest, Talia opens it.

"*Tengo a la* Señorita Harper," a security guard says as he blocks the crowd, and Harper hops up the stairs into the trailer before he snaps the door shut again.

"Harp!" Marsh says, overjoyed.

"Hey, Mom. Hey, Talia," Harper replies, seemingly unfazed by the activity outside. In this life, she must have grown up used to having an incredibly famous actress for a mother, and thinks being surrounded by other famous people and followed by a hysterical, worshipping mob at all times is normal, Marsh supposes.

"I'll leave you two to catch up," Talia says, steeling herself to duck out of the trailer. "See you on set, Marsh."

"Yes, see you there," Marsh promises as Talia departs. "How was school?" she asks Harper as she takes off her backpack and flops onto the little couch.

"Eh, Profesora Juarez gave us *another* pop quiz," she says, as if Marsh knows all about how sneaky her teacher is. "But band practice was awesome! I had a breakthrough on that new piece I've been working on."

"That's great, honey," Marsh replies.

"I'll play it for you later and show you," Harper continues as she wiggles both sets of her fingers in the air, like she's playing a guitar. "It's such a tricky passage, but I think I've got it down. Señor Lopez says he's never seen anyone master the *requinto* so quickly."

"I can't wait to hear it," Marsh says, taking her instrument change in stride. What's more exciting is how chatty her daughter is. Like they do this all the time, and know everything about each other.

The trailer door opens a third time, and Ren ducks inside and slams it shut behind him quickly.

"Whew! It's like an obstacle course, trying to get through your fans!" He chuckles and sets something down on the floor. "Someone even offered me twenty thousand pesos for this little sausage. I almost said yes!"

A fuzzy blur shoots by and lands on Harper's thighs a second later, and she giggles as she cuddles Pickle. He's a tiny black Chihuahua instead of a Lab, but at this point, Marsh is long used to his little metamorphoses.

"I forgot to tell you, I found a date for your premiere," Harper teases her mother as she holds Pickle's front paws up so he's standing on two legs in her lap. "He's so handsome!"

"A date?" Marsh teases back. "Excuse me, young lady, you're far too young for a date!"

"But we're in lo-ove," Harper sings, and then plants a kiss on Pickle's adorable little face. "Aren't we, Pepinillo?"

"Oh! That reminds me, I have to pick up my tux before the tailor closes." Ren winks flirtily at Marsh. "I think I'm gonna go with the open shirt one. Gotta keep up my look, you know?"

"A tuxedo! Excuse me, young lady, you're far too young for a date!" Harper repeats Marsh's line to her in a joking mom-ish tone, and they all laugh again.

The longer they talk, the bigger Marsh's smile gets. She's fully confident now that she was right to leave Iceland and come to Mexico. This Harper is not just Harper—she's the Harper who Marsh has been desperately trying to find her way back to. A Harper who is both as talented at music as she's always been, but also as close to her mother as she was before the divorce upended their lives and the teenage hormones set in. They finish each other's sentences, and have inside jokes with each other—they're not just mother and daughter now, but real friends.

It's everything she's wanted.

Ren, too, has received a few upgrades in this path. His hair is extra shiny and thick, and his skin is so smooth it almost looks airbrushed. He's taller, and so well-groomed, he almost looks like a Ken doll, with a rakish bent. Almost like he's taken to this new glitzy Hollywood life even more enthusiastically than she has.

"I can't wait to see what they serve this time for the dinner after the screening," Ren is saying. "Talia told me that they booked Chef Enrique Olvera himself!"

"I bet Mom could introduce you," Harper suggests. "He's sure to come around and meet the stars after the dessert course."

"That would be a dream come true," Ren muses. "He's so badass."

"Since when are you so into food?" Marsh asks.

"Ever since he portrayed him in flashback scenes for Talia's documentary on Mexico's food scene last year," Harper replies. "*Temerarios de la Cocina*. Remember?"

Not only is Ren a little edgier in this episode, but he's also an actor. That's interesting! Marsh didn't expect that change. She scrambles for a response to cover, but she's not quick enough, and a beat of silence falls over the scene.

"What?" Ren asks. "I thought you liked that documentary."

"I did!" Marsh cries. "You were wonderful in it."

But Ren can still tell something's off. "I know I take more artsy, experimental roles, but I thought that you thought it was kind of cool we're both actors," he says quietly. "We can understand each other's work the way most couples can't."

"Definitely," she agrees. "I just meant . . ."

Marsh falters. She's just trying to make sure he likes his job in this new path, but she doesn't know how to ask him, because he wouldn't understand.

Ren sighs. He looks hurt, but it almost seems like he's also . . . frustrated?

Moms4Marsh: <Poor Ren. He tries so hard to make her happy!>

"Well, if you don't like it, I can always change!" he finally declares.

JesterG: <If only he knew how possible that might be!>

"Don't be ridiculous," Marsh says as the comment window bounces with laughter at that last remark, but Ren snaps his fingers and leaps into a pose.

"Why not? I've always wanted to be a helicopter pilot, too." He snaps them again. "Or a firefighter!"

He says it a little testily, but the more jobs he suggests, the funnier the moment gets. By the time he's on the fourth career, he's grinning toothily and starting to dance with each one, and the whole thing has become a joke rather than an argument. Marsh starts to giggle as he makes up increasingly ridiculous professions: assassin veterinarian, celebrity nostril hairstylist, artisanal cheese puzzle-maker. Harper is on the floor laughing, tears in her eyes, and little Pickle—Pepinillo—is barking joyfully as he stands on her belly.

"You're ridiculous," Marsh says at last, hoarse from laughter. "And I love that we're both actors."

Ren takes a pleased bow and sweeps her into a kiss.

YanYan242: <Ren is so wonderful!>

It's true. He's always been a true partner, which is one of the best things about him. No matter what else changes about him episode to episode—his job or appearance—that never will.

There's a knock at the door to the trailer, and a page sticks her head in.

"Ah, Malvavisca," the young woman says. "We're ready for your scene."

Marsh is still smiling as she and Ren leave Harper to do her homework and follow the page to the set. They weave through the adoring crowds along Avenida Insurgentes Sur, flanked by security guards. Marsh waves and blows kisses, which makes the exhilarated shouts grow even louder.

The page pushes open a heavy metal door to a warehouse a few buildings down. Just before Marsh and Ren duck inside, she turns to look again at the city—the screaming fans, the invigorating bustle—taking it all in.

"What a day," she whispers to herself. The first of many more to come, she hopes.

"Malvavisca, *por favor*," the page says kindly.

Marsh heads inside, eager to get to work. Everyone else seems just as passionate. On the way to hair and makeup, she greets the tech crew, the writers, and a gaggle of young extras clustered around the food table, who all want her autograph.

"Malvavisca! Ren!" a familiar voice calls, and Marsh spots Jo in a chair in front of a mirror and Victor beside her, going over the script and talking into a headset.

"Hi, you two!" she says, thrilled to have found them in this new path. "Ready for today?"

"I hear we have a guest director for this next episode," Victor replies.

"Let me guess," Marsh says. "Talia Cruz?"

"How did you know before me!" He laughs.

"Perks of being the star," Ren teases as he lights a cigarette.

Ren smokes?

Marsh blinks, surprised.

Well, he is *more of a bad boy now,* she supposes.

"I can't wait! I just hope she doesn't change all my lines up on me at the last minute." Jo shrugs, obediently holding still for a dusting of blush. "Remember that episode when they wanted a whole endangered species collection in the cartel's house, and I was suddenly supposed to be a blackmailed wildlife photographer in Iceland or Antarctica or something?"

Marsh does a double take, then tries to cover it up as they all glance at her. *That was weird.*

"Well, I just don't want to play *another* secret evil twin," Ren finally adds, which makes Jo crack up. "I've done so many by now, I must have been from a family of octuplets!"

Marsh looks at Victor, but he's laughing, too, unconcerned. They all are. She's the only one who noticed the strange callback—but then again, she's the only one who should have. Perhaps she's overreacting.

Although that doesn't explain why it happened in the first place.

"Good morning, everyone!" Talia calls from the entrance to the warehouse.

"Ah," Jo says, hopping out of the chair. "Time to get this show on the road."

Marsh rushes after her, pushing through the crowd that's gathered around

Talia to ask her various questions about angles, sound, edits, and more.

"There's my star!" Talia cries, and gives her air-kisses that are somehow charming, not cringey. "Ready to shine?"

"Not yet," Marsh interrupts. "Something just—"

"Concerns about the show?" Talia asks, and Marsh knows which show she really means. Not the telenovela, but the one bubbled around it.

Marsh nods. "I'm worried things are a little off."

"All part of the process," Talia says. "We can never judge a piece of art by its rough draft, can we? Revisions will be made. I promise. Everything will be perfect."

Marsh takes a breath. She knows what Talia's trying to telegraph. After such a big jump, everything needs a little time to settle. She's only been in Mexico for one scene—she's barely had time to see how she likes being a world-famous actress!

"Let's do this," she finally agrees.

Talia claps her hands to quiet the busy crew. "All right, everyone, let's make some art!"

She winks at Marsh.

"Let's leave our mark."

LIGHTS, CAMERA, ACTION

"Action!" Talia shouts as a production hand clacks the black-and-white-striped clapper right in front of Marsh, and then dashes off.

The set is a grand mansion. Marsh stands in the foyer, marveling at the tall windows, the walls covered in gorgeous paintings, the rich wood. The scene is dimly lit, and everything has a moody, sensuous cast. The curtains are drawn, and the chandelier overhead glows softly to give the impression that it's nighttime, and Harper's *requinto* lilts softly over the mansion's speakers as background music.

All around, the extras playing guests are dressed for a masquerade ball, draped in beautiful gowns and tuxedos and wearing feathered, bejeweled masks. Marsh pretends to study the brushstrokes of a giant mural of a galloping white horse as a spotlight illuminates the intricate beadwork on her exquisite dress. Subtly, she touches the edge of her own winged disguise, adjusting it against her cheek. She hopes the gesture looks sultry, but she's really just glad that it's there, like a little scrap of armor. She has gotten used to knowing that the Bubble's cameras are on her 24/7 by now, but the whole point of *All This and More* is that she *isn't* acting, because it's real. Having to remember lines and pretend to be someone else in *Un Juego Peligroso* is a whole new challenge.

She can practically hear Talia giggling to herself, pleased with her cleverness. Not only does Marsh get to try out the life of a famous actress in this path, but also the life of any other movie role she takes.

It is genius, Marsh has to admit.

But is this really what she wants? A life of pretend?

"*Buenas tardes,* señora," someone says then, a sonorous purr, and Marsh turns to see a tall, handsome stranger now standing behind her on the discreet red X on the floor.

"*Buenas tardes,*" Marsh replies.

The cartel boss studies her as if she were one of the pieces of fine art in his collection. He's chiseled like a sculpture, and his tux fits like a second skin.

"I haven't seen you here before," he says.

Marsh bats her lashes. "It's my first time."

The cartel boss steps closer and takes his mask off.

"In that case, I hope you're enjoying the party," Ren says.

Marsh hides a surprised gasp as the music flares dramatically.

Moms4Marsh: <Ren is playing the villain?? HOT.>

If Talia had asked her before filming started, Marsh never would have thought Ren could pull off the part. But actually, seeing him now in character, it's clear that Ren is really working it. He's somehow become even taller since the scene started, and much more muscular. His shoulders are broader, his face is sharper, and his hair is long and pulled into a sleek, low ponytail at the nape of his neck. There's a seriousness to him that there wasn't before.

He looks good.

And also a little scary.

Marsh grins.

Actually, maybe a little pretend is *exactly* what she wants.

The telenovela script calls for their chemistry to be electric, despite the danger—or perhaps *because* of it—and with cartel boss Ren, Marsh doesn't have to try very hard. The two of them are standing close, talking softly, like they're just waiting for an excuse to fall into each other.

"The moment you arrived, I saw you. A mysterious guest at my party. I was captivated instantly," Ren is saying as they clink their glasses together. "I've been hoping to find you in the crowd all night."

"Me too," Marsh replies. She's also removed her mask, and as she raises her drink to take a sip, Ren catches the tip of it where it hangs from her wrist. He runs his thumb over the painted lips, never breaking eye contact with Marsh.

She shivers.

"I would very much like to continue our conversation, and get to know each other better. Would you, perhaps . . ." Ren turns and glances down the hallway. "I have another painting, in my private collection. I think you'll find it quite special, indeed."

Marsh smiles nervously.

"I would very much like to see it," she says, hitting exactly the right combination of shy and excited.

As she follows him down the hall, passing painting after painting and little statue after little statue on fancy display podiums, Marsh pretends to have second thoughts, and then steel her nerves again, as her lines call for.

"This is my best chance," she says aloud to herself—a voice-over that

Ren's character can't hear, but the *Un Juego Peligroso* audience can. "My one shot at getting close to the leader of this cartel and taking the whole thing down from the inside."

Her eyes dart to the back of his head and linger there a moment.

"I just didn't know he was going to be so handsome," she admits, biting her lip.

Ren opens the door at the end of the hall, and ushers Marsh into a gigantic bedroom. Somehow, there are also lit candles twinkling in here, and rose petals scattered artfully across the rug.

"Well, here we are," he finally says, and gestures to a tapestry on the wall. "My pride and joy."

Marsh swallows and looks at him. "It's beautiful," she replies.

"So are you," Ren says.

They stare at each other for another moment, the music suspended tensely—and then suddenly they're kissing.

Notamackerel: <Cheesy>
Moms4Marsh: <SHUT UP! Do not ruin this for us!>

Ren is luring Marsh over to the bed, leading them across the room toward its inviting softness, and Marsh eagerly follows. Dimly, she's aware that she's supposed to be shedding her clothes in a specific order, at a specific speed, but she's caught up in the scene, and the details are a blur. Her discarded designer heels on the expensive rug. Her mask and shawl tossed against the wardrobe. Dylan's briefcase on the dresser—

Marsh chokes.

What the—

"Do I take your breath away?" Ren asks flirtatiously when she pulls back from the kiss, startled.

"That," she sputters, pointing.

"Ah, I'm a, how do you say, a businessman, señora," he replies, still in character, thinking she's improvising. "It's mine."

But Marsh shakes her head and stumbles back as he reaches for her again.

The room is dark, but she's sure of it. It's the same shape, the same style. The same cheap gold clasp, the same grain on the leather.

"No," she says. "It's not. It belongs to—"

CUT!

"Cut!" Talia calls, hopping down from her director's chair.

"What's wrong?" Ren asks as he sits up in bed. The set is full of chatter now, crew members refilling extras' drinks with fake champagne and tech hands resetting the lighting and music. "Forget your lines?"

"No," Marsh says. "I just—"

She scrambles off the mattress and rushes over to the dresser just as Talia reaches her.

"Malvavisca," Talia says, but Marsh beats her there and snatches up the briefcase.

"Look!" she says, thrusting it toward Talia. "Just look! It's—"

But then she falters as she stares at it.

"It's what?" Ren asks, now beside her, too, looking at the case.

It's sleek, classy, with fancy metal hardware and the smoothest, most supple leather she's ever seen. But that's not why Marsh trailed off. Not because of what it is—but because of what it's not.

It's *not* the one that Dylan tried to give her a million times in the first half of this season, after all.

"That was incredible," Talia is saying to Ren, fully embodying her film director role, as he nods along intently. "But I want us to run it again. I want more! More smoldering looks, more thrill of danger, more passion." She smacks one hand into the other palm, punctuating her words. "I want *perfect*."

LunaMágica: <Marsh can definitely do it! She just needs another take>
TopFan01: <She can have as many takes as she wants—this is All This and More, after all!>

As everyone hustles back into place and the set readies itself to redo the scene, Marsh looks down at the briefcase again.

She doesn't know why she ever thought it was the one Dylan gave her. It really looks nothing like it.

It couldn't, really. In this life, she may never have even *started* law school, let alone dropped out of it, and Dylan may never have bought her this gift.

When he quit the show at the midseason special, who knows what that changed about their past, in this path.

It's almost like he doesn't exist anymore.

SharpTruth17: <C:\ATAM\Bubble\directory\main_cast\access>
[Automatic security filters have deleted this account]
JesterG: <For %@&#'s sake, this guy again! Enough with this amateur hacking!>
TopFan01: <Hey all, while we work on a more permanent solution, remember our policy—don't feed the trolls!>
LunaMágica: <¡Sí, por favor!>

Marsh sighs as the comments quiet down. She looks down at the briefcase, which she was *sure* was Dylan's, but now is not, again.

Is the Bubble responsible for this? she wonders. A quick edit, to tie up a loose end? To keep things streamlined, once Dylan refused to participate in the season?

But is this really what Marsh wants—to have him *completely* erased from her life?

Or is it just what the show does?

"There's our star," Talia says, appearing beside Marsh. "We're ready for you."

Her jewelry tinkles as she takes the briefcase from Marsh and tucks it under her arm.

"Change is never easy," she says.

Marsh lets herself be guided over to the horse mural where she stands at the start of the masquerade romance scene, and places her over her tiny red X on the floor. Talia fixes a stray curl of Marsh's luxurious locks, and straightens the hem of her gown's neckline, admiring how beautiful Marsh is in this scene, how far she's come.

"But it's always worth it." She glances up at Marsh. "Don't you think?"

At last, Marsh nods.

Talia grins. "Take two," she says. "Let's make this one perfect."

Her host is right, she knows.

She puts her costume mask back on and turns to the mural as Talia steps off the set. Dylan made his choice, and she made hers. She can only worry about her life. She's only got one chance to make her life everything she wants it to be, and she has to keep going, to do as much as she can before the finale. In Tahiti, she resolved to do just that, and in Iceland, she succeeded at it. She can do it again here in Mexico, too.

And she *will*.

In her director's chair, Talia raises the black-and-white clacker.

"Action!"

TAKE TWO

The romance scene begins again as soon as the black-and-white clapper falls. The gentle *requinto* music starts up, guests begin to mill gracefully through the mansion, and Marsh tries to look extra dramatic in front of the mural.

She's not thinking about anything but this moment, she tells herself. She's going to live, breathe, and *be* this role.

This is her life. The one she's dreamed of, the one she's on *All This and More* to seize.

She's going to make it everything she wants.

"*Buenas tardes,* señora," Ren says again, behind her. "I haven't seen you here before."

This time, Marsh is ready for his reveal when he removes his mask.

They flirt, ad-libbing a bit, the conversation full of banter and tension. Ren mentions the painting in his room he thinks a sophisticated, gorgeous woman like her would appreciate.

"If it's so beautiful, why do you keep it hidden?" Marsh teases him as he leads her down the hall.

"I have many secrets," Ren replies, to a subtle exclamation of drums.

The door opens, and this time, Marsh walks in first. Ren is standing behind her as she looks at the painting, so close that his breath flutters across her earlobe, sending it tingling.

"Perhaps I have a secret, too," she tells him.

Ren's eyes are hungry. "I look forward to discovering it."

Marsh's hair tumbles sexily, and Ren's hands roam her body, finding their way down her gown and then up underneath it as they drift toward the bed again, locked in a kiss. Even though they're supposed to be playing two characters who have just met, they move in total, passionate harmony, almost like it's been choreographed ahead of time. It almost feels like Marsh has been in this exact moment before.

Actually, maybe she *has* been in this exact moment before, she realizes.

The longer the scene rolls, the more recognizable it becomes.

The layout of the place, the two of them together, the way they're holding and touching—it almost seems like a replay of when she and Ren hooked up in his Phoenix apartment for the first time.

That's weird.

"Is this all right?" Ren asks her as he buries his face in her neck.

Isn't that what he said to her the first time?

As he finally eases Marsh onto the bed beneath him, still locked in a passionate kiss, one of the sleeves of her dress slides from her shoulder, revealing the edge of a fancy bra beneath.

Even though it's just the corner, and even amid the intensity of the scene, she recognizes the familiar lace pattern at once.

She's wearing a Sharp Purple Le Fascination.

"Yes, it's all right," Marsh manages to say back to him, trying to remember her lines.

She's so mixed up, she can't focus.

"It feels so good, Dyl—"

She sits bolt upright.

"Cut!" Marsh shouts frantically. "I said, cut! Stop! Stop rolling!"

The overheads flash, brightening the bedroom immediately, and someone claps the black-and-white clacker.

"What happened?" Ren cries beside her, surprised. "I thought we had that take!"

"I'm sorry," Marsh apologizes. She pulls her gown back into place as she scoots off the bed. Her eyes dart, looking for Talia, but it's darker off the set than on it, and there are so many crew hands moving around that she can't spot her.

"Ready to go again?" Victor asks as he arrives, as a makeup artist appears to touch up the bronzer on Ren's chiseled abs.

But Marsh shakes her head and waves off another artist who wants to fluff her hair. "I need to talk to the director first."

"Everyone, take five!" Victor calls. The crew relaxes, and the scramble of logistics eases a bit as Marsh weaves through clusters of people and props, seeking her host.

Being an actress had seemed incredible at first, even better than Iceland, but everything about that last scene was way too weird. Maybe she made a mistake by allowing Talia to convince her to come to Mexico. Maybe this place has too many memories wrapped up in it to be the real fresh start she deserves.

"Talia," Marsh says as she reaches the director's corner behind a bunch of video monitors, from where she can watch every angle of filming. Talia's tall Sharp Purple–colored folding chair appears from behind the screens as she turns it around. "We need to talk. Did you see—"

"That was beautiful! Just beautiful!" Talia says as she settles down into her seat again—but Marsh recoils as if slapped.

Because it's not Talia Cruz in the director's chair.

It's Alexis Quinn.

"What the—?!" Marsh gasps, stumbling backward and nearly tripping over a page boy.

She knew it! She was right!

Marsh *did* spot Alexis Quinn in the Bubble, after all!

Before, it had been too dark, or too quick, and she'd convinced herself that she'd just been seeing things. But now, she's certain.

It's unmistakably Alexis.

But how is it possible that Alexis is here, on *All This and More*? She doesn't work for RealTV, and isn't involved in the show anymore. That's why Talia is the host—because it's a whole new crew this season. A whole new everything.

So why *has* Alexis been turning up randomly? What's she doing here, now?

But most importantly . . .

"Where's Talia?" Marsh cries.

She's hoping that Alexis will say that Talia will be right back—she's in the restroom, or on a quick call, or giving directions to some extras—anything to explain why she's not here, and Alexis is.

But to her surprise, Alexis just cocks her head.

"Who's Talia?" she asks.

Huh?

Marsh stares at her, bewildered.

Alexis Quinn was Talia's producer. During their season, there was no one closer to her than she was. They were together every step of the way, in almost every scene together, just like Marsh and Talia are now.

So why is she acting like she doesn't know who Talia is?

"Talia, who was just sitting here before we started that last take!" Marsh says, gesturing at her director's chair.

Jo and Victor have followed Marsh from the set and are now standing on either side of her, watching the exchange.

"Malvavisca, what are you talking about?" Jo asks. "Who's Talia?"

"Talia Cruz," Marsh says weakly to her. "The guest director. She was *just* here. Remember?"

Victor frowns, confused. "Alexis has been directing the whole time."

"No. No," Marsh whispers. She closes her eyes and shakes her head.

Alexis checks her clipboard. "If she wants to be an extra, there's a list for friends and family. I'm sure we can get her into an episode or two for you," she offers.

Marsh takes a deep breath, trying to stay calm. At first, she thought maybe the show was trying to plant an Easter egg for eagle-eyed fans by having Alexis make a couple cameos. But it doesn't seem like Alexis is here to play a part—on *Un Juego Peligroso* or *All This and More*. She's acting more like she doesn't know she's inside the show.

Or that it's happening at all.

The same way she didn't really seem to know when she appeared in the first half of the season, either. She's been acting more like she's part of the *cast*, rather than the *crew*.

"That last scene was nearly perfect. What do you say to one more try?" Alexis asks.

"I . . ." Marsh fumbles, as her eyes drift back to the waiting set. "I don't know if . . ."

"That's a wrap, everyone!" Victor announces suddenly, his lawyer voice booming across the set. "Cameras off, scripts down! It's a *party* now!"

"What?" Marsh asks, bewildered but relieved. "Party?"

"We just got the news," Ren says. He's holding a glass of champagne now, for some reason.

Everyone is holding a glass of champagne now, she can see as she spins around.

What's going on?

"Malvavisca," Alexis continues, ecstatic. "You've been nominated for the Nobel Prize—in acting!"

A burst of streamers pops to a chorus of whistles and applause across the set as the comments also go haywire.

Pollito: <¡INCREÍBLE!>
Notamackerel: <A Nobel? Are you kidding? This show has totally jumped the shark!>
JesterG: <I hate to agree with Notamackerel, but who could ever buy this twist? RealTV has seriously gone off the deep end!>

Marsh desperately snaps the stream of posts off as the party explodes around her, unfurling at impossible speed.

Everywhere she looks, her telenovela crew are singing, dancing, or climbing the sculpture props. Every inch of the cartel boss's dining table is covered with what Ren proudly announces is his cooking—platters of gorgeous, juicy lamb, sizzling roasted vegetables, crisp salad, freshly baked bread, cheesy pasta—the restaurant documentary he mentioned starring in earlier really did come in handy. The *Un Juego Peligroso* extras are acting like waiters, going around holding either champagne trays or plates of Ren's delicacies, and everyone is ravenous. *How could he have made fifty dishes all by himself, in mere minutes?* she wonders. But his food is Michelin-star delicious, and the music is so loud she can hardly hear herself think, much less worry about it. She's glad Harper isn't at this party—she's pretty sure people are doing lines of cocaine off the set bedroom's dresser, and there also might now be an actual white horse in the hallway, a live replica of the one in the mural.

Victor's verdict parties have nothing on this, she can't help but note.

Marsh does another lap, but she still can't find Talia. Eventually, she ends up back at the center of the party, where everyone toasts her again.

At last, she gives up. She still doesn't know where her host is, but she must be on her way. She figures she might as well enjoy herself until then.

She takes a sip of her champagne and dances a little to the music, which draws some cheers. She's almost not sure which show she's in right now— *All This and More* or *Un Juego Peligroso*. Everyone here is honoring Marsh's Bubble-manufactured Nobel nomination, but they're all still in their telenovela costumes, and they're celebrating on the cartel's opulent mansion set, the two productions blending together until they seem like one.

"*¡Felicidades!*" Jo cries as she finds Marsh in the crowd, and hugs her excitedly. "I'm so proud of you!"

"I can't believe this!" Marsh says back, just as a huge cloud of confetti rains down on them from a net in the ceiling and everyone shouts with glee. A billion little colorful snowflakes, twirling and sailing on the air—

Marsh catches one in her palm to inspect it as she laughs.

The confetti isn't just tiny squares of paper, she sees now. Every little piece is cut and folded into the same shape, a microscopic, intricate species of origami.

They're all tiny butterflies.

There are butterflies everywhere, she realizes now. As the shape of the food platters, printed on the napkins, as sculpture props, even newly in place of the white horse as the art of the mural.

"Amazing," Jo says, spinning around as the last flutterers fall.

"Hey," Marsh nudges her friend, and holds out the confetti in her hand. "Butterflies?"

"¡La Mariposa, Malvavisca!" Alexis answers, arriving beside them. "The name of our cartel in *Un Juego Peligroso*. It means 'The Butterfly.'"

Notamackerel: <Again??>

LunaMágica: <¡Dios mío! It's followed her from Iceland, and found a way into Mexico!>

Marsh nods slowly as this revelation sinks in.

Chrysalis is here.

But why?

What does it want?

"You okay?" Jo asks.

"I'll be right back," Marsh tells her. "Just going to run to the restroom."

She fights her way through the party, signing autographs as she goes. The line at the door to the restroom is long, but her cast and crew wave her to the front—*This party is for you! A star shouldn't have to wait!*

The door opens, and out falls Ren—laughing a little too loudly, moving a little too quickly. His eyes are wide, but there's a slight glassy quality to his gaze when it lands on her.

"Malvavisca," he croons, reaching for her. "My Malvavisca. Is this incredible, or what?"

Marsh falls into his hug. It's tighter than she expects it to be, and the force of it squeezes the breath out of her lungs for a moment, surprising her. Behind him, the extras who were also in the restroom with him are huddled together, doing something at the sink.

"If only this party never had to end," Ren says. "Maybe it doesn't."

Marsh frowns as he sways. "Are you on something?" she asks him.

"I *am* playing a bad boy in this series." He winks, with a shrug. "I figured, hey, why not get into the role a little?"

A flash of irritation strikes her at that, and she can't help but grimace. This is bad boy Ren? She'd been thinking more like smoldering, flirty looks and trendy leather jackets, not a forty-five-year-old party animal who still takes it a bit too far at parties. She has a teenager in the house! She doesn't want Harper finding his cigarettes, or whatever else he's got.

"Hey," he's saying now. Behind the drowsy stare, there's a twinge of concern. "Are you mad?"

Marsh sighs. It's not his fault that the Bubble nudged him a little too far down this edgy path for her exact taste.

"No," she finally tells him. "Really."

There's no point in being mad, because it'll never happen again. Or ever have happened, for that matter. She can fix this right up.

"Malvavisca—"

But his friends have come out of the restroom now, and are carrying him away toward the crowd. He blows her kisses over their shoulders, until she finally laughs and blows one back at him.

Once she's locked the bathroom door behind herself, she puts the toilet lid down to make a solid seat, and sinks onto it with an exhausted sigh.

So much is going on, it's hard for her to sort out how she feels. For every unsettling anomaly in one part of her life, there's a stunning improvement in another area, causing her to lurch back and forth between uncertainty and euphoria in a quantum whiplash.

Is Dylan watching, wherever he is?

She wonders what he thinks of this new version of her life in Mexico, full of screaming fans and Nobel Prize nominations. And what he must make of Chrysalis. Of how it's grown, and what it's done, since he walked off *All This and More.*

Marsh can almost hear him now, saying that he told her so, that he knew something was off, and that she should have listened to him, his tone more like he's teaching a lecture in one of his college classes rather than having a conversation.

But she has to admit, she'd take the *I told you so,* if only he were here.

Before she realizes it, her phone is ringing against her ear.

What is she doing? She's flourishing as an actress in Mexico, changing her whole life. She should be out there enjoying her party, and her ridiculous Nobel nomination! Hell, maybe she should even be trying some of those drugs! After all, she can do anything she wants here. Nothing matters until the finale.

But her call goes to voicemail anyway.

She sighs.

Typical Dylan.

He was the worst at answering his phone when they were married. What made her think he might actually pick up now?

As if in response, one of the sad, wet little paper butterfly decorations in the sink slides all the way down the porcelain, toward a foam hill of soap.

Maybe the champagne has gone to her head, or maybe it's because she can just edit these calls into oblivion later—Marsh lifts her phone to try again.

Except when she goes to her call log, his name isn't there at the top of the list.

Weird, she thinks.

She tries again, tapping in his number from memory. Even though she's barely had to call him for the last two years, she's had twenty where she constantly did before that.

The line rings as before, and he still doesn't pick up, as before.

"Really?" she grumbles. What if this had been about Harper? Wasn't it, in a way?

But as she lowers her phone, she sees that this second call to him is also not in her call log.

Marsh frowns.

She manually scrolls to *D* in her contacts, searching for him. But the list goes from Donovan's Italian to a friend named Eddie Vuong, with no one in between.

Dylan's entry is gone.

Now, *that* is very weird.

Marsh knows that she would never do that.

She's standing now, having risen from the toilet lid without noticing. *It must be the Bubble,* she tells herself. Trying to keep things clean. Removing variables, streamlining storylines. She dials him again from memory, and the signal hangs for a moment, as if searching.

"Come on, Dylan," she mutters, willing the call to go through. *"Come on."*

Just then, there's a hurried pounding on the door. Marsh is so startled, she drops the phone as she shrieks.

"Malvavisca?" someone shouts. "Malvavisca? Are you in there?"

"What?" she snaps back angrily. "I mean, yes! Just a minute!"

The door pounds again. "We don't have a minute!"

She can tell the voice is Jo's now. She sounds hyper, excited, the way she always does right before she launches into a winning rebuttal in court.

"Come on!" Jo yells, and jiggles the doorknob furiously. "The Nobel committee is announcing the winners right now!"

"What?" Marsh cries. She scrambles to the door and fumbles with the lock.

By the time she gets it open, it seems like the entire party has gathered in front of the door.

"Congratulations, Malvavisca," Alexis says, standing at the very front.

Beside her, Ren and Jo are hugging each other, crying tears of happiness.

"You won!"

TopFan01: <HOLY MACKEREL!!!>

LoboAzul: <¡El mejor programa de la historia!>

Notamackerel: <This is totally unbelievable!>

Monsterrific: <For $$%#'s sake, man, just shut up, no one cares that it's not realistic!>

ChilangoCool: <¡Malvavisca, te amamos!>

"What?" Marsh falters, still awestruck. She can't believe it. "I won? Me? A *Nobel Prize*?"

A burst of light from deeper within the mansion sets off a bluish glow across its gleaming surfaces, and Marsh turns toward the light. Someone has turned on the giant flatscreen in the fake house's living room, where *Un Juego Peligroso*'s latest episode is now playing on every channel, in response to Marsh's win.

"Turn it up!" Jo orders, and everyone cheers.

"*You're very clever, but unfortunately, not clever enough,*" cartel-Ren is saying to Marsh's character on-screen as the volume increases.

It's still the bedroom scene, but farther in the script than they must have gotten, because she doesn't remember this part of the story. When did she film this? How did it get finished?

"*I know who you are.*" Ren leans in, his voice barely a whisper. The tone is still sensual, but the words feel threatening, somehow. "*Who you really are.*"

"*I don't know what you mean, señor,*" Marsh replies. "*My friend invited me to this party. This is the first time I've met you.*"

"*Come, now,*" he says. "*You're acting, but you're not an actress.*"

His eyes narrow.

"*You're a lawyer. Aren't you?*"

Marsh suppresses a small shudder at that echo. The entire telenovela is turning into some kind of strange callback. It's like the Bubble is pulling its plot from a warehouse full of her discarded paths, but glitchy, each resonance more corrupted than the last.

"*Perhaps this little game of yours was fun at first, but did you really think you could dip your toes into these waters without danger?*" Ren sighs. "*And now look at you. You're in over your head, too far from shore to swim back. You'll never get out.*"

The title of *Un Juego Peligroso* is apt. This is turning out to be quite a dangerous game, indeed.

Marsh turns away from the screen, but Alexis is there now, standing beside her with a dreamy grin on her face.

"Is it everything you've ever wanted?" she asks Marsh, the same way she used to ask Talia the exact same thing, in her own season. "Is it perfect?"

Marsh studies her for a long moment, waiting for a flicker of something behind her eyes. A subtle wink, a small nod, a tell that she knows she's here in Marsh's season. But there's nothing. No indication at all that Alexis is working for *All This and More,* not *Un Juego Peligroso.*

"No," Marsh finally says.

Alexis's brow furrows. "Do you want to redo the take?" she asks. "What do you want to tweak? Do you want to change the mansion? Or the dress? Maybe the lighting?"

Alexis is asking about the last episode of the telenovela that they just filmed, but she might as well be talking about the other show—the one they're really in.

Maybe Marsh *should* change things. This path was thrilling at first, but now everything has gone a little too far. Ren is too much of a bad boy, the life of a famous actress is so intense, and the telenovela is too close to home in a way that's not poetic, but slightly scary. Maybe acting isn't for her. She's learned what Talia wanted to teach her, to be confident and brave, to shine as the center of attention, and she's proven to herself that she can do it. She can command that stage. But maybe she doesn't want it to be a stage. She doesn't want it to be pretend.

She wants it to be real.

As Marsh's eyes drift across the raucous party, she spots a familiar face in the crowd. That shining golden hair, that warmly bronzed skin, that flawless makeup.

Talia's finally back.

Their gazes meet, and Talia's face lights up. But she also catches sight of Alexis with Marsh, and her expression pitches into shock—then something like terror.

Marsh stares, confused, as Talia waves desperately at her, but the room is too loud for her to hear what Talia's shouting. But she's jerking her head back and forth, and then draws a perfectly manicured set of nails across her throat in a sharp, unequivocal sign.

Stop, she means. *Now.*

Marsh watches her for another moment, trying to decide what to do.

Then she turns to Talia's old producer.

"Alexis," she says quickly. "I need you to send me somewhere else. Fast."

Alexis is baffled by the question. "What? Like another party?"

"No," Marsh replies. "Another path. Another choice."

Alexis is staring at her like she's lost her mind.

Talia is pushing her way through the crowd now, picking up speed as she heads toward them. She doesn't stop to say hello to fans, or apologize for bumping shoulders. She's not smiling anymore.

Marsh whirls back to Alexis, frantic. She doesn't quite understand what's going on—why it's bad that Alexis is here, and why they shouldn't be speaking—but she knows something is off.

"I need you to get me out," she repeats.

"Are you saying that you don't want to work on *Un Juego Peligroso* anymore?" Alexis asks, still not understanding.

"No!" Marsh grabs her shoulders. Talia is almost on them now. "I mean, get me out of this *life!*"

"What—"

"Anywhere, I don't care. Just get us out of Mexico," Marsh begs. "Get us away from *Chrysalis.*"

As that word slips from Marsh's lips, something changes in Alexis. A light goes on in the back of her eyes. A waking, or a realization. Lucid at last, she turns and looks at Marsh with dazed, grim amazement.

"This . . ." Her eyes drift again, taking in the party. "This is . . . season three?"

"Yes," Marsh says quickly. "It's my life. I'm the star."

Alexis seems lost for another moment, still trying to process what's happening. Then she spins quickly to Marsh.

"Where is Talia?" she asks.

"There's only one way you can survive this," cartel-boss-Ren tells Marsh's character above them, on the telenovela mansion's giant flatscreen. *"If you give La Mariposa what we really want."*

"But, señor," Marsh protests dramatically. *"I really don't know what you mean! I'm just a guest at your party—"*

"Por favor," he replies, cutting her off. *"Enough pretending."*

He rolls up his sleeves in a slow, casual manner that doesn't seem charming so much as menacing. There wasn't before, but in this scene, now there's definitely a pistol holster hanging off his half-unbuckled belt, glinting dully in the dim light.

"You know you can't stop me."

His forearms are covered in tattoos of butterflies, Marsh sees.

"So why don't you just give me what I want?"

SharpTruth38: <Don't you all see now?? I'm telling the truth!>
[Automatic security filters have deleted this account]
SharpTruth39: <There's a problem with the Bubble, and—>
[Automatic security filters have deleted this account]

The butterflies ripple on cartel-Ren's forearms as he cracks his knuckles.

Marsh turns to Alexis, who's still staring at the flatscreen in awe, completely mesmerized by something that Marsh can't determine.

"What is Chrysalis, Alexis?" she asks her desperately.

"*Marsh!*" Talia cries, pushing through the last cluster of people between them. She's dragging the Show Bible under one arm, and snatches at Marsh with the other.

Alexis grabs Marsh's shoulder and pulls her, just as Talia's hand misses her other elbow by mere inches.

"You have to find it," Alexis whispers, in the last second they have. "It's the only way."

"Whatever she's saying, don't listen!" Talia orders as she closes the distance again.

But Alexis doesn't pull Marsh away again. Instead, as Talia reaches a second time, Alexis lunges for her, and grabs one end of the Show Bible.

"Hurry," she says, as Talia gasps.

"Malvavisca," Ren cries, unsure of what he's just come upon. The book opens, caught between the two women. "What—"

But Marsh is slammed roughly out of Mexico and into the darkness between episodes by Alexis's and Talia's struggle.

To escape into Alexis's choice:
Turn the page

To follow Talia's choice:
Go to page 405

EPISODE 8

MISSION POSSIBLE

Marsh has no idea where she is. Alexis and Talia were wrestling over the Show Bible so fiercely as that last episode ended, both struggling to flip to different parts of the book, there's no telling where Alexis's finger randomly landed in the nearly endless stack of pages.

So, as the scene opens and Marsh finds herself looking through a telescope, studying a building site on the other side of the street, she doesn't think it's odd at first.

But then as she pulls back and sees what's actually in front of her, it suddenly is.

It's not a telescope, she realizes.

It's a sniper rifle scope.

Uh . . .

Marsh looks down. There's no telenovela set, no raging party, no fancy masquerade gown. She's in a quiet, nondescript apartment, and dressed in all-black tactical gear. Jo, who's seated on a folding chair next to her, nods grimly.

Where did Alexis send her?

In the stillness of the room, the little buzz in her ear pierces like a siren.

"Report in," Victor's voice says, and Marsh gingerly touches the small device nestled there.

"Target acquired," Jo answers for her, into her own earpiece. "Marsh and I are going in."

"You're our only hope, agents," Victor replies to them both. "We're counting on you. *America* is counting on you."

Marsh lurches as the pieces finally fall into place.

Is she . . .

TopFan01: <Marsh is a secret agent in this episode?????>
Loulou22: <C'est ridicule !>
WarszawaMan: <Wy bałwany, to najlepszy odcinek!!!!>

The comments positively explode, word shrapnel covering everything in her view until all she can see are letters and exclamation points.

Marsh's heart is still racing, from the last jump or from her new environment, she's not sure. She didn't really have much of a plan at the end of that last episode beyond asking Alexis to get her out of Mexico as fast as possible. But now that she's here, she's not actually sure what to do. Alexis wanted her to find Chrysalis, but how can she do that if she doesn't even know what it is?

She wonders if that's why Alexis tried to pick this path.

So she can find out?

"Roger that," Marsh replies, finally figuring out how to make the device work. "Agent Marshmallow out."

Every spy movie trope Marsh can think of, this path has it. In just the time it takes her and Jo to get out of their safe house and across the street to the target site, they crawl through air-conditioning vents, hide around corners from bad guys, crack a safe, outmaneuver a car chase, and even triumph in hand-to-hand combat. Marsh herself is incredible, somehow proficient in computer hacking, karate, and throwing knives all at once.

She wants to be embarrassed by how over-the-top everything is, but she's having too much fun to care. Obviously, she's not going to make this path her permanent one and become a secret agent—but to see herself kick so much ass, to succeed even at this, makes her giddily proud. She's gone from lonely, sad background character who was convinced she was too late to change her life to finding love again with Ren, reigniting her professional passions, and proving to herself that she can not only survive, but *flourish,* in places like Iceland and Mexico . . . hell, even as a super spy! She hasn't found her perfect forever path yet, but she's starting to believe that when she finally does, she's going to be brave enough to actually seize it.

She and Jo infiltrate the half-finished construction site while trying not to marvel at Washington, DC's dramatic skyline in their background. Marsh kicks down the door to the room where Victor tells her that Ren is being held hostage through her earpiece, and Jo gets shot!—but she's wearing a bulletproof vest, Marsh realizes with overwhelming relief.

"Objection!" Jo shouts hoarsely, as she tries to get her wind back. "Badgering the witness!"

Despite the adrenaline of the situation, Marsh stumbles to a stop and looks back at her. "What?" she asks.

Wait.

She spins around, bewildered, as she realizes that they're not standing in a partially built building anymore. They're in a courtroom now!

Suddenly, all the walls are warm wood, with rows of pews lining one side. A sharp crack startles her as a gavel drops from above and smacks against the ground. A supervillain sporting a blond mohawk and a pin-striped suit is standing in the judge's place, brandishing a pistol and a threatening-looking remote, and below, Ren is strapped to a chair on the witness stand.

"Marsh, hurry!" he cries as he works the gag out of his mouth.

What the—?!

"Jo," Marsh says, nervous. "What's going on?"

"I don't—I . . . I meant to say, stop them!" Jo coughs and manages to yell again, looking rattled.

Marsh turns back, but the room is suddenly an abandoned building site again.

What was THAT?

"Marsh, don't let the virus upload!"

"It's too late." The villain laughs, standing on construction scaffolding instead of the judge's chair now, and Marsh finally recognizes them.

Is that . . . Sarah? She blinks.

Talia's makeup artist from season one?

It has to be. Marsh remembers Sarah revamping Talia's entire look during the makeover episodes, turning her from drab to fab!

But Sarah was part of Talia's team, not Marsh's.

Frantic, Marsh stares down at the gun in her hands. Why is Sarah in this episode? Are there even *more* people from Sharp Entertainment's old crew hiding in her Bubble?

But why?

"Alexis?" she calls, starting to panic. "Alexis? Are you there?"

But the action is too loud, too fast, and she can't even hear herself.

"Marsh!" Ren yells again.

He's older in this life, his hair shot through with streaks of gray and his brow creased with lines. More like he's a mentor of Marsh's than a contemporary. Perhaps he's an older spy, brought out of semiretirement to teach a new crop of agents the secrets of their trade, and somewhere along the way the sharp new recruit and jaded, wise veteran fell in love . . .

"The terminal!" he yells.

"What?" Marsh stammers.

"The terminal!!"

He jerks his head toward a gigantic computer server on the other side of the room, bursting with ports and cables and flashing lights. It's plugged into the incomplete building's power grid, and there's a little Sharp Purple memory stick jammed into one of the inputs. On the status screen near the top of the device, a graphic of a progress bar ticks up slowly, three-quarters complete.

The virus!

"If the virus finishes uploading, the whole city will collapse!" Ren explains. "Traffic systems, subway control, electricity, everything! Thousands will die!"

"Hurry!" Jo adds.

Marsh remains frozen a moment longer. There's so much happening, she can't figure out what it all means.

Is the virus Chrysalis, in this path?

What happens if it uploads?

But there's no way to pause the episode to figure it out.

"Time to light this on fire!" Ren shouts her tagline at her, and the Bubble responds. Everything cuts to slow motion, the scene readying itself for something dramatic, and Marsh realizes that she's already moving. She's whirling, her gun raised, taking aim—

She fires straight into the terminal.

The machine shatters theatrically into a million pieces, as if she shot it with a rocket launcher instead of a mere handgun. The progress bar flickers, then darkens as the remnants of the terminal crumple into a heap—the upload thwarted.

"Go, Marsh!" Jo cheers.

"Noooo!" Sarah wails, their chance at an evil monologue squandered. "You haven't won yet!"

Marsh helps Jo up as the construction site threatens to collapse, and the two of them free Ren from his ropes as Sarah escapes, likely to allow a sequel episode, if Marsh decides she likes this life and wants to stay. Together, the three of them hobble-run through the smashed door and down a few flights of steps as bits of drywall and concrete sprinkle their path.

Victor is waiting for them outside, surrounded by a team of men and women in suits and sunglasses and earpieces.

"Status?" he asks tensely as they reach him.

"We stopped the upload," Marsh says. "The city is safe."

"Marsh!" Ren cries. "You're a *hero*!"

Then the building explodes in the background behind them, turning itself into fireworks.

StrikeF0rce: <I'm back on board with this show now! Marsh is such a badass!>

Frónverji: <This is better than any of the spy movies!>

SharpTruth99: <Don't any of you see what's happening??!?>

"Where's Alexis?" Marsh asks as she waves the comments away.

"Who?" Victor asks.

"Someone get that man to a hospital," a voice orders, and Marsh turns around to see Talia, in a general's uniform, striding over.

Marsh supposes that she's not surprised.

It took Talia a minute, but her host was always going to find her star again.

Victor salutes Talia crisply. "Roger that, General Cruz!" he agrees, and Jo springs into action to wave down a crew of paramedics for Ren.

"I'll handle Agent Marsh's debrief," Talia says, and earns another salute and a "Yes, ma'am!"

She keeps her steely expression in place until Victor runs to help Jo with Ren, but as soon as they're alone, Talia grabs Marsh into a hug.

"Whew! I've been racing through the Bubble as fast as I could, looking for you everywhere!" She gasps. "Are you all right? I can't believe that Alexis did that! Anything could have happened. I mean, look at how dangerous this path is!"

"I'm fine, I'm fine," Marsh says, to quiet her. "But how did that even happen? What is Alexis doing in the Bubble?"

"I don't know," Talia says. "She's not part of the crew, that's for sure. I'm definitely going to have a word with the team that runs our security. That kind of tampering is unacceptable. It's sabotage!"

Behind them, Victor is supervising Ren's loading into an ambulance, and Jo hops in to accompany him to the hospital. He looks weak but proud, his gaze distant as if he's replaying every significant moment he's ever had with his protégé over the years, culminating in this defining, heroic scene.

He raises his head from the gurney, and when he spots Marsh, he waves slowly to her.

Marsh waves back, hoping that she's doing it poignantly enough.

"There's something I want to show you," Talia says, once the emotional moment has passed. "Let's go back to headquarters."

Marsh is expecting a drive in a sleek, unmarked car, but instead, Talia snaps her fingers. Suddenly, there's no crumbling, smoldering building, no scrambling news crews, no crowd of onlookers. They're both standing in a drab, government-looking office.

"Whoa," Marsh murmurs. "Is that how you do that?"

"Comes with being the host," she says. "It's second nature after a while."

There's only one thing in the room besides them, which is a serious-looking desk. On it, the Show Bible is waiting.

"There are so many paths left to choose from, I doubt we'll have to worry about Alexis ending up in the same place as us again," Talia says, looking relieved. "But I wanted to show you that the Show Bible is safe."

"I still don't understand," Marsh says. "It almost seemed like she was trying to help."

"How?" Talia replies. "By flinging you through the quantum universe completely at random, without a clue as to where you'd land? She risked your life, and your loved ones' lives, carelessly."

Marsh frowns at that. Talia does have a good point—what Alexis did *was* risky.

But she also knows that Talia didn't hear what her old producer said, before she sent Marsh here. That she has to find the source of Chrysalis. She was so desperate, she put them all in danger to give Marsh the chance to do it.

Just what does Alexis think Chrysalis could be?

And why does Talia seem so unconcerned?

"Whatever Alexis was trying to achieve, it doesn't matter," Talia continues. "I promised you at the beginning that I'd do everything I could to make your life as perfect as mine is by your finale, and I'm going to keep that vow."

The words are so comforting. Even with so many unanswered questions, Marsh just wants to sink into them. To forget the strange things that happened in Iceland and Mexico, and what Alexis said. She didn't join the show to track down whatever Chrysalis is—she came to fix her life! That's hard enough without trying to solve a mystery that's not even hers to begin with.

She's spent so much of her life doing what everyone else wants, she almost forgot she doesn't have to.

Especially not on *All This and More*.

"This is your season. Not Alexis's," Talia reminds her. "This is about what *you* want."

"Yes," Marsh echoes. "This is my season. And what I want."

Talia beams back and turns Marsh gently toward the waiting Show Bible. It is, as usual, even more monstrous than the last time Marsh has seen it. It's so tall when closed now that Talia needs a step stool to reach the cover.

"This was a fun diversion, but let's get you back on track. Let me send you somewhere else. After all, we don't have much time left, and there's so much more for you to do!"

Despite her lingering unease, just the mention of a new life makes Marsh's pulse quicken with excitement. It's still a thrill—all the things she could try, all the places she could go.

"Hey, Marsh," Talia says. "You could have *All This* . . ."

Marsh smiles as she watches her beautiful host cling to the massive book for balance, teetering in her stilettos as she climbs toward its cover.

"*And More*," she replies.

ALWAYS ONE MORE

Marsh opens her eyes slowly, both hesitant and excited to see what new possible future is laid out before her this time.

This one will be it, she tells herself.

And if not this one, then the next one will be.

Or the one after that.

There are infinite paths inside the Bubble, and all she needs is one perfect life by the finale. How hard could that be, to find just one?

She tries everything, because she can. Marsh is an haute couture fashion designer, a painter in Paris, a senator, a wine vineyard owner. Her faithful cast follows her through every life: Victor always her boss, Jo always her colleague, Harper always her daughter, Ren always her partner. The scenery changes so quickly, it's like reading a pop-out flip book, where from every page springs a new cardboard cutout. None of them can tell except for Marsh, although there are more strange contradictions—Victor and Jo lose themselves in conversations, or appear wearing suits and holding court papers when they should be clad in park ranger uniforms or carrying firemen's gear, and Harper keeps talking about the violin and then getting confused, even though with every new scenario, she has a different area of musical expertise. Sometimes the background flickers, replacing itself with a new environment that makes no sense, then flickers back again.

Ren bears the brunt of it, though. Out of all of them, he changes the most each time, morphing into some updated incarnation based on the previous episode, edging ever closer to Marsh's ideal man. He seems downright exhausted, at times—maybe because of all the transformations he's being put through, even if he doesn't know it.

Still, Marsh can't stop. It's simply too addicting.

A marine biologist. A world-renowned sculptor. An architect for the first permanent moon base.

Notamackerel: <Marsh is losing control of her own show! How many lives is she going to try?>

Moms4Marsh: <As many as she needs to find the perfect one!>

Marsh nods. That's right. Every new life is close, nearly right, but not exactly so. It amazes her now to think that at midseason, she almost thought she was close to done. Her life has become a thousand times better since then—she's ambitious and successful at whatever job she tries, her love life is blossoming, her makeover and her new closeness with her daughter have stuck around past the next commercial break—far more than she ever could have hoped for.

But the more places she visits in this montage episode, the more things she tries, Marsh starts to *really* understand what this show is all about.

Her family, her career—heck, even her bold new personality and style . . . those things are the big pieces. The broad strokes.

But broad strokes only do not make a masterpiece.

They don't make *perfect*.

And that's what Marsh is here for.

She won't rest until she gets it.

It seems ungrateful at first, to discard a path for a mere detail. But didn't Talia tell her that nothing, no matter how small, is out of reach on *All This and More*?

She leaves one life because the house isn't big enough, and the one after because it's monstrously big. Another time, it's because of the wrong city; the next, the wrong job. Once, Harper seems bored, then the weather isn't good. Then Marsh doesn't like her hair.

Each time, it gets a little easier.

"Sorry, can we cut?" she asks, as she stands at the edge of a hot air balloon's basket, gazing out over the gorgeous, golden Serengeti. The swelling music cuts off abruptly. "I just—I really want to be able to enjoy this moment, and the light was kind of in my eyes. Can we redo it?"

"Absolutely," Talia says, and gives the burner a little more gas to lift them back to their original position again, before the close-up started. The zebras seem to also turn around, to head back to where the herd was before they started galloping.

The Serengeti is incredible, and so is the romantic, candlelit dinner Ren has prepared for them in their luxury safari tent later that evening. Although she wishes it had been a pasta dish, not a salad. That there had been a few more candles, and that Ren's hair had been a little longer and more touchable.

And that hints of Chrysalis would stop popping up at the periphery of every other scene.

A path in which she's a famous author lasts for half a day, a life as a white water rafter for an hour. At a break in the river, Marsh sets down her paddle and waves away a butterfly, more forcefully than she ordinarily would if it had been just an insect and not a strange saboteur, doggedly pursuing her across the quantum universe.

"You know, this is great, but I feel like Ren's footwork wasn't quite as snappy as it could be," she says as they hand her a trophy for first place in the national ballroom dancing championship. "Do you think it's worth redoing?"

"We can do anything you want, Marsh!" Behind her graceful posture, it's clear that even the world's most unflappable host is exhausted, although she'd never admit it. "Or, something else! There are millions of lives here in the Bubble."

Talia's right, that there may be nearly infinite paths for her to try, and infinite details to tweak, but in the back of her mind, Marsh knows there's a limit to it. She might be able to keep going forever if it were just up to her, but it's not. It's about her happiness, but also about episodes. And there are only two of them left before the finale.

She has to pick something eventually.

Things go fuzzy around the edges as the Bubble prepares to shift to somewhere new yet again, and Marsh grins.

But not yet.

THE BIG TOP

As darkness lifts, Marsh finds herself standing inside of a giant red-and-white-striped tent, wearing a glittering gold leotard and stage makeup. Spotlights swing near, plunging everything from dark to light to dark again, and the roar of a crowd all around rushes her ears.

"Marsh, there you are!" Talia cries over the drone, waving. She's in a black top hat, a blue, festooned coat with tails, and bright crimson pants. "You're up next!"

Marsh looks down at her leotard again, baffled, but then the giant poster hanging behind her finally comes into focus.

WELCOME TO THE BIG TOP!
LAS VEGAS HOSTS THE GREATEST SHOW ON EARTH!

"A circus. I ran away and joined an actual circus in this episode," Marsh says to Talia, smiling at the joke. "A little on the nose, don't you think?"

Talia winks at her. "It's a stereotype for a reason," she replies before spinning back to the crowd, to announce the next act. "You have to admit, it's pretty fun, isn't it?"

It is.

Marsh discovers that she's an acrobat now, as she nimbly flips and twists through the air across trapezes and trampolines. She enjoyed her total makeover, but this is downright thrilling, to be strong enough now to whip around like she has wings. *How can I be this flexible at forty-five?* she wonders as she executes a quadruple backflip that makes even her jaw drop along with her audience's own. Maybe she's just that in shape. Or maybe she's not forty-five anymore.

Who even cares?

Her routine is stunning. When she lands from her last twirl off the trapeze—which the Bubble rewinds and does twice for her, sensing that she wants the spin even tighter, even more impressive—the crowd gives her a standing ovation so loud, she can feel her teeth vibrating in her smile. And the rest of the performers are just as impressive. Talia is the ringleader, of course, Victor and Jo are the clowns, Harper is a tightrope walker, and Ren is the lion tamer.

Marsh watches him run around the ring shirtless, his muscles glistening with sweat, bravely commanding the roaring beast this way and that with nothing more than confident posture and a sweep of his hand. He's darkly tanned in this episode, with long, curly hair that's been bleached blond for some inexplicable reason, but his butt has never looked better than it does now in his little red-and-blue spandex costume. He's also less talkative than he has been before, Marsh notices, although no less happy to be with her. So happy he seems the opposite, somehow—so desperately joyful that he can't control it. He looks maniacal in the ring, like he'd almost prefer it if the lion turned on him, and they could wrestle to the death.

The only thing constant about Ren is that he's always different, Marsh thinks as he and the lion play patty-cake as they each stand on one foot. It's nearly too much for her to keep all his versions straight. She can't imagine how confusing it would be for Ren if he could remember each of his incarnations.

The flaming hoops come out next, and despite the excitement, Marsh's attention wanders to the dark recesses of the big tent, to see what other acts are up next. It's dark and cramped, but she can make out a few silhouettes. There's a ribbon dancer, a man on tall stilts, a fortune teller . . .

Zauberfee: <Ich liebe den Zirkus!>
SharpTruth104: <I'm begging you all to look at what's happening to the Bubble!>
[Automatic security filters have deleted this account]
StrikeF0rce: <How many attempted hacking offenses before this guy gets permanently banned?>
SharpTruth105: <Screw this>
SharpTruth105: <***MARSH!*** If you're seeing this, look at the fortune teller! LOOK! You—>
[Automatic security filters have deleted this account]

The comments continue to harangue the troll who's now taken Notamackerel's place as most-hated commentor, but SharpTruth's panicked, direct request startles Marsh enough to seize her attention.

Has that ever happened before? she wonders.

Her viewers often shout all kinds of encouraging things at her, but it's always with the understanding that she'll almost certainly never notice any particular one, not with the millions of posts streaming by every second. But SharpTruth has not only also noticed that something's off about her season—her Bubble—but is trying to *tell her* something about it directly now.

Marsh peers across the darkened, crowded tent.

Wait.

It's hard to tell with so many people in such a small space, but is the fortune teller actually Talia's lighting tech from season one?

Is that really Jillian?

Her eyes snap back to the comments, but SharpTruth is gone, locked out until they can figure out how to get around the Bubble's security filters once more.

It doesn't matter. She's sure that it's Jillian—and now, certain that something very strange is going on.

For some reason, part of the old crew is in the Bubble with Marsh.

How did SharpTruth know that?

Who *is* her mysterious viewer?

SharpTruth106: <C:\ATAM\Bubble\episode_8\access>
[*Automatic security filters have deleted this account*]
SharpTruth107: <Marsh, I'm trying, but you have to—>
[*Automatic security filters have deleted this account*]

The applause draws her attention back to the main ring in time to see Ren bow and then dash out of the spotlight with the lion as Victor and Jo rush in to take their places.

"You all right tonight?" Ren asks her once he's out of view of the audience. He tosses his golden locks. "You seem disappointed or something."

The lion is not in a cage, as Marsh assumed would be legally required, but leaning against Ren like a terrifying pet. Harper squeezes past on her way out of the tent, and dribbles half of her water bottle into a steel bowl on the ground as she goes, which the lion eagerly laps up just like a dog.

Just like one very particular dog, actually, Marsh realizes with a start.

"A little," she admits. Slowly, she touches lion-Pickle's mane, and he licks her with a huge, rough tongue. "I enjoyed today, but I just thought it might be . . . more."

The circus was indeed a fun diversion, but of course, it's not the *perfect* life for her.

The music blasts as the clown segment draws to a close. The curtain rustles again, and a tall man with a reddish beard carrying enough bricks on one shoulder to build a house ducks in and lines up for his strongman act. His arms are tree trunks, like he's used to twirling dumbbells over his head all day long.

Or holding up a bunch of heavy sound equipment next to Jillian's lights, Marsh notes with an uneasy squint.

Hello, Charles.

She casts around, scouring the rest of the darkened big top as the next act begins. During Talia's season, her crew were as close as family. So if Talia's lighting and sound techs are in the Bubble, then surely their lead camera operator will turn up, too.

Elyse must be here somewhere.

"Well, that's all right if today was a little disappointing," Ren finally says to Marsh.

She's not really listening, she's still looking for Elyse, and it takes a second for what Ren says next to land.

"The next one will be better."

The next one.

She turns to him, uneasy. The hairs are standing up on the back of her neck.

What an odd thing to say, she thinks.

Does Ren . . . know something?

"What do you mean, the next one?" Marsh repeats.

"You know." Ren shrugs. He gestures to the tent around them. "The next show. We're in Los Angeles tomorrow."

Marsh watches him closely—but Ren's gaze is steady, his expression innocent. He doesn't know about the show, about the choices.

He's just trying to cheer her up.

"Great," she replies at last. "I'm looking forward to it."

Ren grins. "I hear the audience is very lively!"

After the show is over—the crowds gone, the empty cups and popcorn cleared away, the animals fed and asleep in their transport carriages, Harper in bed, and the tent broken down and rolled up at last—Marsh, Ren, Victor, and Jo gather in the caravan's main trailer to eat a late meal.

It's not the circus itself, but this part, all of them relaxing after the hard day of work, that she values most about this path. It's romantic. Not in an amorous way, but in the poetic sense of the word. It's just what Marsh, as a kid, imagined running away and joining the circus might be like. Being part of a tight-knit crew, living on the road, staying up late playing cards together at every stop, dazzling crowds, seeing the world. She tweaks the regular lamps to become lanterns with a wink, to make it even more cozy.

"Wait, it's already ten o'clock!" Jo shouts suddenly, lurching to her feet. "We're late!"

"Late for what?" Ren asks her. "The show's over."

"The bar!" she cries, banging into the table and sending the cards fluttering. "We're going to miss our reservation!"

The dread that Marsh feels this time isn't sudden, but subtle, sinking.

Jo means the Chrysalis bar.

"We have to go!" Victor demands, and then parrots himself yet again. "What good is a private table on the balcony if you never use it?"

"What are they talking about?" Ren asks.

"They're not talking about anything," Marsh insists. "There's no reservation."

"What am I even wearing?" Jo asks, looking down at her sweatpants and tank top. "I can't go out like this."

"There's no bar," Marsh says, but Jo and Victor don't hear her. The two of them seem so confused, so unmoored, as they pace the trailer uselessly, trying to figure out why they want to go to a place that doesn't exist in this path, to celebrate something that never happened anymore.

Marsh can't deny it any longer. The farther into the season she gets, the more unstable things grow. Breaks in continuity, fragments of memories left over in her cast members, old pathways encroaching on new ones.

She can even run away to join the circus, and Chrysalis will still find her.

"You look great, Jo," Marsh finally says, her voice softer this time, sadder.

Jo looks up at her friend, her throat tight, as she clutches her baggy shirt in her hands like she's never seen it before.

"Marsh," she whimpers. "I just, I don't . . ."

"All right, I think someone's had a little too much," Ren comes to the rescue, seizing her beer from her good-naturedly. "Let's call it a night. We've got a long drive to LA tomorrow."

"Come on, Jo," Victor says, seemingly back to his usual self. "I'll walk you to your trailer."

Marsh waves them all out and says she'll clean up before bed. But after she's alone, she doesn't collect the cards or gather up the dirty plates.

Instead, she slips out of the main trailer and heads for one of the smaller ones, in the opposite direction of her and Ren's cabin. She hesitates, then pulls her hoodie tighter around her and knocks.

"Yes?" the fortune teller says as she slowly opens the door.

"Jillian, right?" Marsh asks. "Can we talk?"

Inside Jillian's trailer, the room is set up just like her stage act. The lighting is low and moody, crystal balls adorn every surface, and there's a velvet blanket draped over a low table. A tarot deck waits at its center. On the back wall, there's a cheesy poster from a past show with bright colors and a cursive font that reads: JILLAXTRICA, THE ALL-SEEING ONE!

"Do you want a reading?" Jillian asks.

"No," Marsh says. "I mean, maybe. I just have one question."

"Ah." Jillian nods. "Love. The cards will tell us."

Marsh shakes her head. "Not love."

Jillian arches a brow, and her giant teal turban shifts slightly. "Money?"

Marsh takes a breath.

Here we go, she thinks.

"Chrysalis," she says.

She waits for a reaction. Jillian doesn't move at first—but then the word seems to do something to her, like magic, the way it did for Alexis. Jillian blinks, and when she opens her eyes again, she seems different.

"You can keep running," she finally says, lucid for the first time. "But you won't find Chrysalis that way."

Marsh takes Jillian by the shoulders. "What?" she asks. "What did you say?"

Jillian glances around the trailer like prey in a snare. "What *is* this place?" she whispers, awestruck, horrified.

"What is Chrysalis?" Marsh asks, ignoring her question. In this episode, it's the memory of a bar again, but Marsh knows that's just theater now. Chrysalis has worn a hundred disguises since the season started.

Jillian shrugs helplessly. "I don't know."

She drops her voice.

"But it's not part of your season."

Marsh falters.

Not part of her season?

She doesn't know what to make of that. How could something happening in her own Bubble not be part of her season?

How else did it get inside, then?

But Talia's lighting tech is fading. Her gaze is growing vaguer by the moment, her focus loosening, the distance growing.

"Jillian," Marsh says, trying to draw her back.

"It's Jillaxtrica, the All-Seeing One, my dear child," Jillian says suddenly in her stage voice, and pulls her sequined sleeve dramatically across her face like a cape. Whatever clarity she had, it's gone now. Marsh has lost her again, back into her role, a puppet whose strings are pulled taut once more. "Are you ready to see your fate in the cards?"

"No," Marsh says. "I . . . already have."

Ren is asleep when Marsh finally comes inside. She keeps the lights off and crawls into bed quietly, and in his slumber, he throws an arm over her with a satisfied snore.

She tries to relax into his embrace. But hours later, her eyes are still open, still fixed on the same spot of their low ceiling.

Finally, after midnight, she sits up.

Her heart is racing so fast, she's afraid it'll wake Ren.

Of course.

In the dark, her hands find a T-shirt, then jeans.

She can't believe it took her this long to realize it, but she's so glad she did. She knows what to do.

SharpTruth217: <Marsh, the desk>
[Automatic security filters have deleted this account]

Her gaze leaps to the little table bolted to the wall. A set of car keys is now waiting there.

SharpTruth218: <It's all I can do right now>
[Automatic security filters have deleted this account]

Her hands shaking, Marsh grabs them before they can disappear. There's no time to think. As quietly as she can, she slips out of the trailer and creeps out to the parking lot, where she climbs into the sedan whose lights flash against the dark when she presses the UNLOCK button on the little fob. The engine rumbles as it starts, and Marsh winces, her breath held—but nothing moves, no one has followed. After a moment, she edges out of the parking lot and onto the street. A few turns later, she's at the freeway.

But she's not heading deeper into the gaudy Las Vegas Strip. Those sparkling lights are in her rearview, not in front of her.

There aren't many people out to begin with, and soon, Marsh is the only car on the road. The freeway turns from urban thoroughfare to bare highway, and then to a single-lane road, leading out into the desert.

Her eyes desperately scan the harsh landscape as it rolls past, flat and parched and shadowed in deep purple beneath the night sky. A rusted highway sign listing the next cities and how many hundreds of miles away they are whizzes by her window, and she grips the wheel harder, determined.

This latest life has placed Marsh closer to Phoenix than she's been since the second half of the season started.

Closer to *Dylan* than she's been since the second half of the season started, to be exact.

THE LOCKED DOOR

Marsh speeds across the desert, her gas pedal permanently jammed to the floor. She keeps waiting for something to prevent her from leaving—for police cars to appear out of nowhere, for the road to veer in a wrong direction, for her car's battery to spontaneously die—but nothing does. Mile by mile, she rushes ever closer to Phoenix.

After another hour, dawn peeks over the horizon, a peachy orange glow that turns the windshield into a mirror. The road widens, and the glint of Phoenix's skyline begins to shimmer in the distance. By the time the sun is fully up, Marsh is entering city limits, and buildings replace the cacti.

She speeds down the freeway, dodging pickup trucks and semis as the glare bounces harshly off their polished hood medallions. The asphalt ripples with heat, and she almost starts to sweat before the Bubble upgrades her car's air-conditioning so it blows arctic cool.

How strange it is to be back here, she can't help but think as she drives. Already, this old life of hers seems as far away to Marsh as another planet.

Like it was all a dream, perhaps.

A new life is where she belongs.

But in order to make her new life everything it should be, she has to escape Chrysalis. And to do that, she has to find Dylan.

Because regardless of the form, Marsh knows that whatever's happening to her season isn't a narrative problem.

It's a quantum physics one.

And that makes Dylan Marsh's best chance at understanding how to fix it.

Her tires squeal as she pulls into the old apartment complex. It's the same one that Dylan lives in now outside of the Bubble, and also in the first half of her season. It looks exactly the same as it did then, she notes, encouraged, as she flings herself out of the driver's seat and sprints toward the stairs without bothering to close the door.

He *has* to be there.

But what will he say when Marsh tells him she finally believes that something really weird *is* going on inside her Bubble, and that it's only gotten much, much more intrusive after he left at the midseason special? Will he let go of his ego for one second, instead of starting a fight over how he knew better all along? Will he, for once, not pretend their life is a college classroom, that everything is a teachable moment? Will she have to strangle him first?

"Dylan!" Marsh shouts as she reaches the concrete landing. She throws herself against his door. "Dylan, it's Marsh!"

She waits, but nothing happens.

"Please, open the door. I know you don't want to talk to me anymore, but this is an emergency!" Marsh slaps the wood with her palms, rattling the whole door in its frame. "Dylan!"

For an instant, she wonders if he's not home, but it's very early morning on a weekday. Where else would he be but here drinking his coffee and getting ready for work?

Marsh suddenly stops her assault, and then rips open her purse. When they divorced, because they shared custody of Harper, they traded house keys with each other. For use only in emergencies.

This might not be entirely about Harper, but Marsh would bet that Chrysalis tampering with her Bubble, the Bubble that their daughter is in, definitely qualifies as an emergency.

The keys jingle on Marsh's key ring as she flips through them to find the one she's never had to use before. It slides into the lock with a metallic scrape and turns.

"Dylan, I'm sorry, but I need to talk to—" Marsh says as the door swings open.

But the sentence dies on her lips. She stares into the apartment, surprised.

Because it's not Dylan's apartment inside.

It's not *anyone's* apartment.

". . . Dylan?" Marsh calls in confusion.

The whole unit is completely empty. There's not a single piece of furniture inside of it.

"Dylan?" Marsh calls again, her voice small.

She steps cautiously inside and lets the door swing shut behind her. She touches the light switch on the wall, and the room is suddenly pitched in a quiet, yellow glow.

When he quit *All This and More*, did he . . . move out?

But that's not it.

As she studies the brightened room, she realizes that something is off. Even more than that Dylan isn't here.

Silently, she inspects the floor where his couch used to be—but the ground is perfectly clean there. There isn't dust on the counters in the kitchen or bathroom. There are no indentations where a bed frame would have rested on a carpeted bedroom floor, nor any other indication that objects have been recently moved out of any of the rooms.

At last, after she's scoured the entire place top to bottom, Marsh finds herself back in the living room again. She's trembling, and crosses her arms to be still.

If Dylan had merely moved, there would be signs here. Dings, nicks, spots, dust rings. But his apartment looks more like no one was *ever here* to begin with.

How is that possible?

He can't just vanish from existence.

Right?

Regardless of what kind of a husband he was, Dylan has always been a devoted father to Harper. Maybe he and Marsh couldn't make it work together, but she knows he would never give up on his daughter. No matter what, he would never let anything—even his anger over this show—stop him from being there for Harper.

But then . . . where *is* he, if not here?

As Marsh stands lost in the center of the empty living room, for the first time in what feels like a hundred lifetimes, the *All This and More* jingle finally begins to tinkle quietly in the background.

She must finally have reached the end of her eighth episode, she realizes, as she watches a little Sharp Purple butterfly flutter past the window and alight on the bare sill.

Marsh has walked so many paths here, and lived so many lives, and all of them have ended the same way.

With Chrysalis finally catching up to her.

Maybe Alexis was right, after all—maybe she can't outrun Chrysalis, even with infinite tries. And maybe Talia was wrong—that whatever it is, it's far more than just a benign quirk to be tolerated or ignored.

Maybe the only way to make her season everything she wants it to be is to stop running, and face it head-on.

She knows which path she has to choose now.

The one that Talia first offered her after the midseason special, which Marsh turned down. The one in which she was supposed to be a lawyer,

Ren a journalist, and Harper a violinist, not some other kind of musician or artist. It was the nearest version to true—and also the one in which she could have gotten close to Chrysalis, if she'd been brave enough to try.

Marsh looks up at the edges of her world, as they slowly blur and darken, the Bubble whisking her away, across an ocean of water and to another reality.

She doesn't know what could be waiting for her in Hong Kong, but there's only one way to find out.

EPISODE 9

DEADLINE

Marsh's arrival into the next episode isn't seamless as usual, but rather like a badly timed splice, off by just enough to jar. She appears a few inches above the floor and then drops the rest of the way, already moving before anything else. The force of her landing scatters a few papers off the desk in front of her as the scene rushes to catch up.

"Marsh!" Ren cries, lurching up from his chair behind the desk, and Marsh grabs his hand at the last second, barely avoiding a wipeout. "Are you okay?"

But she's too busy studying her new scene to answer. It's morning, she can tell from the light, and the two of them are in what must be Ren's office—where he must be back to being a journalist again, if what he said all those episodes ago is still true.

Her eyes drift to the window as the music swells triumphantly. Far below, the beautifully orchestrated chaos of Hong Kong and Kowloon Bay sprawl, a tangled web of concrete, water, people, and green.

SagwaGold: <嗰度喺我條邨!>
TopFan01: <Here we go, everyone . . . Welcome to Hong Kong!>
ChaoFeng: <九龍!九龍!>
SharpTruth299: <We're in the home stretch now>
[Automatic security filters have deleted this account]

Marsh grimly notes SharpTruth's scrubbed comment. But even so, she can't resist admiring the breathtaking view for a moment.

Hong Kong.

She finally made it. She's really here.

This was the place she dreamed about seeing as a child, then the ultimate adventure she'd someday take as a teenager, then the romantic, once-in-a-lifetime trip she and Dylan had planned for their twenty-fifth anniversary, if they'd made it that far. For as long as she's been able to read its name on a map, Hong Kong has been a symbol for Marsh. A way for her to prove to herself that she was *alive.*

"I thought that if I could make it there, I could make it anywhere," she confessed to Talia, just before all of this began.

And now she can. *All This and More* has made it possible.

Despite everything that's happened so far, Marsh can't help but feel a surge of hope as she looks out at her new path, her new life.

She's on top of the world—literally.

Ren's office appears to be on the south side of Victoria Harbour, staring out across the water toward Kowloon's vibrant Tsim Sha Tsui, with its tightly packed skyscrapers and crush of colorful multilevel mansions, each floor full of different vendors hawking their own wares. Even in the day, everything is lit up in neon. Marsh can't wait to see how electric the energy must be in the evening.

Having steadied her, Ren lets go of Marsh's hand and gives her a peck on the cheek.

"I'm surprised you're here," he says. "I thought you had a meeting about that big client Victor's been talking about all week."

"Big client." She nods at last. "Of course."

Everything is lining up again as it should. Marsh as a lawyer is the right version of her. The true one. It was an adventure to try out those other careers, but it had started to feel like she was losing control. Things were getting too fantastical, too far-fetched, even as incredible as it all was. But she's back on track now. She's changed her whole life—found her passion, saved her relationships, transformed her personality and style. She's already fiercely protective of this path, of everything in it. There's just one loose end to tie up before the finale, and then everything can be perfect, can be hers.

A big loose end.

She already knows it's here. Just not where.

Slowly, Marsh scans Ren's office. Her eyes fall across his cluttered desk, where a folder of handwritten notes rests atop of the mess. The title on the front, printed in Ren's neat, capital letter scrawl in red ink, stops her cold.

Chrysalis.

There it is.

Ren's notes for the article he mentioned so long ago, back in Tahiti.

"Is this the new story you're writing?" she asks, pointing at the folder.

Ren shakes his head. "You know I can't discuss confidential sources," he answers. "Even with you."

"This is different," Marsh says.

He shrugs, apologetic. "Sorry. Journalist's code. But it's really important. Career-defining important. If I can get it published in time, it'll change the world."

He looks excited. Like he really means it.

Finally, Marsh gets a proper look at him. Ren is cute and tousled now, with slightly unruly hair and a pair of chic geeky glasses that fit his journalist character—but he also looks a little haggard. He's got dark circles under his eyes, and there are more creases in his brow. His clothes are clean but rumpled, and his office is a mess of papers and books. He must be working very hard on this article.

This article about Chrysalis.

"Come on, I don't want you to be late for your meeting," Ren says, giving her another kiss. "Or me for mine! I'm still not used to how formal our editorial discussions are here. The *New York Times* Asia bureau operates at a whole new level!"

TopFan01: <Wow, Ren works for the New York Times now? Talk about a promotion!>

He leans over to his desk and grabs the Chrysalis folder. "Harper has violin, so I'll pick her up on the way home. We'll see you later tonight!"

Marsh stares at the unassuming manila cover as he heads for the door. At that word upon it that keeps following her, that just won't leave her *alone*, no matter what she does.

"You know I'd tell you, if I could," Ren says when she looks up at him again. "Right?"

"I know," Marsh replies. She smiles, and it must be convincing, because Ren looks relieved. "But you don't have to."

Because if he can't tell her what Chrysalis is in this episode, she'll just figure it out herself.

Her firm's new offices are in Central, just off Admiralty station, so Marsh is there in a flash. The buildings there are grand and modern and towering, and there are banks, consulates, and restaurants galore on every corner. Mendoza-Montalvo and Hall is located in one of the swankiest-looking high-rises, and as the elevator doors open to their floor, it's already busy, even at this early hour. First-years are scurrying everywhere, arms laden with binders and case files, and every conference room seems to be full.

Marsh ducks left down the hall, checking her watch. Even if she can't tell Jo directly what's going on, she needs a friendly face right now.

"Hey, Jo, do you have a sec—" but Marsh stops short as she enters Jo's office.

"Hello, Marsh," Adrian says politely.

"Uh. Adrian. Hi," Marsh says.

"Forget where you were for a moment?" he asks.

Marsh glances around the room, trying to get her bearings. Come to think of it, this *doesn't* look like Jo's office.

It's because it's not decorated like Jo's office. It's not Jo's stuff that's in here, Marsh realizes with a start.

It's hers.

"Adrian, where's Jo's office?" Marsh asks quickly, before she realizes what an odd question that probably is.

"South corner," he replies. "Like in every one of our locations. Victor's north, you're east, and Jo's south."

"I'm east," Marsh repeats slowly.

"Better morning light, you said. So whenever we open a new location, we always put the second partner's office on the east corner."

Wait.

Marsh gasps out loud.

She isn't just one of her firm's best lawyers in this episode—she's a goddamn partner now!

And it seems like the firm itself has also gotten a serious upgrade. The Phoenix headquarters wasn't a shabby setup by any means, but every inch of this new office drips with impressive details. The gold lighting, the wood paneling, the desks, the windows . . . even the paper looks twice as thick.

And Dylan's briefcase.

It's there, on the desk. Her desk. Back, at last—waiting for her.

She's smiling, she realizes.

Adrian clears his throat politely. "Can I help with something?"

Marsh turns to him again. Adrian's standing beside the row of filing cabinets on the far wall, and had been carefully dropping folders into them according to client name until Marsh stormed in—a strange job for a lawyer. He's also dressed more modestly than he was before. The quality of his suit's fabric is not as rich, and the fit is standard, an off-the-rack rather than bespoke.

But his tone is the most different of all. There's not a hint of flirtatiousness in it. It's polished, polite, and very, very deferential.

Is he . . .

Is Adrian Jackson Marsh's *paralegal* now?

"Are you all right?" Adrian asks as she stares.

"Busy morning," she finally replies.

"I'll say," he says. "I'm surprised you're not already in the conference room."

Victor's announcement!

"Going now," Marsh says, rushing out.

Then she rushes back in and takes the briefcase.

"I might need this," she says.

She squeezes through the heavy glass door just as Victor waves to quiet the crowd. The conference room runs the length of one wall of their floor, and is entirely glass, too, and Marsh momentarily gapes at the sweeping views of the harbor again. It seems like every lawyer, from partner to first-year, is crammed into the space, all of them chattering excitedly until Victor shushes them.

Whatever this is about, it's important.

Very important.

"Thank you all for coming," Victor says, his voice carrying effortlessly across the giant space. "We're going to keep this quick because I know we're all very busy, and that a bunch of you need to get back on the first flights out to Singapore and Tokyo to make your evening meetings."

"What's going on?" Marsh squeezes between bodies to whisper to Jo as Victor continues his brief introductory remarks.

"There you are. New development with our big potential client," Jo whispers back.

"How big?" Marsh asks, unable to help it.

"Huge," Jo whispers, giving her an odd look, like she should know this. "If we land them, we'll be set for life."

Marsh arches a brow.

"*Life,*" Jo repeats, with a nod. She glances sidelong at Marsh again. "Nice briefcase. Very retro."

"I want all hands on deck," Victor is saying. "If you're not on a case, you're assigned to this, immediately. Nondisclosure agreements are waiting for all of you outside this room. You will sign right after this meeting."

He glares around the room at the first-years, who visibly wither beneath his stare.

"I wouldn't have hired you if I didn't trust you, but let me say this once," he rumbles. "If there's a leak before we win or lose this bid, believe me: I will find you."

One of the newest recruits actually whimpers.

Victor takes a breath, and the room practically contracts around him.

"The client we're in the running to sign is Sharp Incorporated."

A shocked cry rises from the crowd in unison—and then a rolling wave of voices. Everyone is talking at once, some people looking stunned, some euphoric, some terrified.

These are now seasoned lawyers at one of the best firms in the world, thanks to Marsh's choices. They've worked for movie stars, political power-houses, billionaire business tycoons, and corporations with more money than most sovereign nations. Their reactions at this moment are so extreme, it's as if Victor just told everyone that humanity had definitively made first contact with extraterrestrials.

Sharp Incorporated is *that* big.

Except—it doesn't exist. Not anymore.

The entire Sharp conglomerate famously folded and its eponymous founder withdrew from the public eye after season two of *All This and More* collapsed disastrously.

So how can Marsh's firm be vying to represent them?

"All right," Victor says, trying to quiet them again, but everyone is too excited. "All right! We have twenty-four hours left to prepare our bid. All of you will contribute if needed, but Jo, Marsh, and I are apparently the only three who have been invited to take the test to see who runs point."

A test?

Marsh doesn't like the sound of that.

"You got it!" Jo calls to him from where she is midway across the room, and Marsh manages a weak wave of support.

"What test?" she whispers to Jo.

"Didn't you see the encrypted email that came in this morning? They sent it to just the three of us, apparently," Jo replies. "It's only one question. The answer is due by the end of the day today."

"One question?" Marsh repeats.

Jo shrugs, mystified, but as she whispers back, Marsh's stomach twists into a sickening knot.

"It's just: 'What does Sharp Incorporated want?'"

The harbor view is typically the most desired in any Hong Kong building, which is why Marsh's new corner office faces that way, but she actually prefers to look inland toward the looming Victoria Peak, so she changes it, so Jo's office faces east and hers faces south. It's a small detail, but she likes it better this way. Compared to the bustling water, the mountain is dark, heavy, unmoving. Its calmness feels like an anchor.

At last, Marsh leans back in her chair and sighs. It's late, and she's kicked off her heels and tucked them beside her desk to be more comfortable. She sets down a little crystal tumbler of Japanese whiskey from her bar, accidentally nudging a framed photograph of Harper, her, and Ren, plus Pickle—all together at a beach in California.

Marsh picks up the photo. It looks like a nice memory.

But something's strange about it.

Marsh, Ren, and Harper look happy, and Pickle is a black Lab as usual, thank goodness, not a hamster or a parrot or a goldfish. Everything seems to be in its right place.

It's strange *because* everything is in its right place.

Marsh took this exact photo on a vacation with Harper, Pickle, and *Dylan,* the year before they separated.

That's a very weird thing for the Bubble to have done.

Marsh looks away, trying to ignore the photo, but a few moments later, her eyes have crept back. Eventually, she gently turns the frame face down on her desk.

"Okay." She pulls her laptop closer. "Time to figure out what's going on."

She puts just one word into the browser's search bar and waits for the results to load.

Let's see how far down the rabbit hole this goes.

Chrysalis, now, is a giant pharmaceutical company based in Shenzhen, a massive Chinese city right across the narrow Sham Chun River from Hong Kong. And it's also the name of their flagship drug—a sleeping pill that promises to cure insomnia.

"'Chrysalis in your dreams,'" she mumbles as she reads.

That's a little creepy.

She skims the corporate website, but it's all marketing jargon and flashy graphics. Undeterred, she opens another search, and a few minutes of scanning recent news stories and articles finally gives her a first clue. Apparently, the Chrysalis pill is still unreleased, pending FDA approval, but during its most recent trial, an unintentional secondary effect was discovered.

The pill allows people who take it to lucid dream.

Interesting.

So, this must be what Ren is after. The big thing that will "change the world" if he can be the one to publish his profile of this company and its incredible new drug first. A sleeping pill that also allows people to have lucid dreams whenever they want.

It's odd, for sure. A little creepy—but also, judging from the wonderful, enlightening, even healing experiences the beta testers describe in these articles, maybe a little magical. But why does Ren think that this secondary application would be so incredible that it actually could change the world? Lucid dreaming doesn't really seem medically useful, but it also doesn't sound particularly dangerous, as far as side effects go.

But Ren is smart, Marsh knows. There must be some reason he's zeroed in on Chrysalis with such fervor in this episode. There must be something else buried here, beneath a medication that can induce positive lucid dreams.

"Knock, knock," Jo says, poking her head into Marsh's office. "I know we're sworn enemies now, but want to grab a drink before you head home?"

"Next time," Marsh replies. "Promise."

"Holding you to it," Jo says. She lingers, her hand on the door. "You send your answer in yet?"

"Not yet. You?"

Jo shakes her head. "Neither has Vic. He went home hours ago to meditate on it in his private Zen garden, he said."

"I doubt that's going to help." Marsh chuckles.

"Not like anything else will, though. There are just too many possibilities!" She groans, exasperated. "Security, privacy, public image management, tax and financial advice, assistance complying with international regulations . . . How can I pick just one? How can a corporation want just *one* thing?"

Because this isn't about business, Marsh wishes she could tell her. *It's about the show.*

"This is the strangest client interview I've ever had, that's for sure," she finally says.

Jo nods slowly, lost in thought. "Maybe we'll guess the same thing, and they'll have to hire all three of us," she suggests.

Marsh smiles. "Let's hope."

The idea seems to make Jo happy.

"Well, don't stay too late," she calls as she turns for the elevators. "What am I saying? Of course you will."

Marsh waits for a moment, until she hears the doors ding, and knows she's finally alone in the office.

On her laptop, she opens the encrypted email at last. Just like Jo said, there's only one line, and then a small space for Marsh to insert an answer.

What does Sharp Incorporated want?

Marsh stares at the question for a long time. But she's not trying to come up with an answer.

She already knows it.

At last, she puts her fingers on the keyboard and types.

She's done almost immediately. It's a short answer, just two words long.

If Marsh could tell Jo and Vic what was really going on, she'd explain that their guesses—security, revenue, public image—are all logical, but not correct. Of course Sharp would like to maximize its profits, or branch out into new markets, but that's all secondary.

What it really wants is the thing that became its downfall, then disappeared with all the answers. And now, whose fragments keep appearing in Marsh's life.

What Sharp is really after is . . .

Season two.

Marsh clicks SUBMIT.

It's breakfast time the next morning, and sunlight is streaming in through the huge windows over Marsh's sink. From their ultra-high-rise pent-house apartment—in a towering spire that looks more like a glass sculpture than something hundreds of people can live in—she can see across the peninsula, over Victoria Harbour and to the entire Hong Kong island. The world is quiet at such an early hour, but there are still a few traditional Chinese wooden junk boats out on the calm water, their signature red sails glowing warmly in the dawn light as they slowly sail toward the open sea.

The kitchen was already incredible, but Marsh has made a few upgrades overnight, and is positively overjoyed at the result. It looks like a room in a designer catalogue. Better, even. The ceilings are now at a perfect height, and all the hardware has become warm brass instead of chrome. Even the marble on the counters is infinitesimally whiter.

She can't wait to fine-tune the rest of the apartment.

Marsh looks up from rinsing off some berries at the sink as Harper comes into the kitchen. She's trying as hard as she can to act normal—to not think about Chrysalis, or Ren's article, or her firm's bid—but Harper still picks up on the unease bubbling beneath her calm exterior.

"You okay there, Mom?" she asks as she pours herself some granola from a container.

"Absolutely," Marsh says. "Big day at work is all." She holds out her hands, each with a different kind of berry in them. "Bilberries or crow-berries today?"

Harper stares at her. "What?"

Marsh jerks her hands back, shocked.

Bilberries and crowberries are native to Iceland!

"Blueberries!" she cries. "I meant blueberries!"

She looks down at her hands again. Now each one is holding a small pile of blueberries.

". . . sure," Harper finally says, giving her mom a strange look. "Next time, let's just do bananas."

Marsh manages a weak chuckle and dumps one cluster into Harper's bowl. On the floor next to her, Pickle stares up, his black tail wagging desperately, and she lets him have one, too.

It's fine, she tells herself. *Everything is fine.*

It will be soon.

"Good morning, ladies," Ren says as he glides into the kitchen, saving the conversation.

"Good morning," Marsh replies as he gives her an energetic peck on the cheek. "You look like you slept well."

"Fantastic!" he answers. He pours himself a huge glass of orange juice, ignoring the brewing coffee completely. "I honestly can't remember the last time I've felt so rested. I don't even need the caffeine!"

He does seem refreshed, Marsh thinks. His eyes are so bright and his skin is so dewy and smooth, he almost looks airbrushed. It's *quite* the turnaround from his chronically exhausted appearance just one day ago.

She studies him intently.

It almost seems like . . .

"See you two later!" Harper shouts as she bolts for the door.

"You didn't finish your breakfast!" Marsh yells.

"No time, I'm late," she calls just before the door slams. "I'll grab a *boh loh yau* from the corner bakery on the way!"

"I'm late, too," Ren says, giving Marsh another kiss on her other cheek. "I have to hit this deadline!"

"Wait," Marsh insists. "We need to talk."

"Tonight," Ren suggests, putting his orange juice glass in the sink and grabbing his satchel. "You've got to get to work, too. I have a feeling that today's going to be a big day for us both!"

The instant Marsh walks into the firm, it becomes a celebration. Every paralegal, first-year, and senior lawyer she passes congratulates her or stops to shake her hand. They're beaming at her like she's some kind of personal savior.

After the eighth or ninth encounter, Marsh begins speed-walking toward her office, and dashes inside with a quick jerk of her chin at Adrian to follow her.

"The adoration all a bit much?" he says jokingly as he closes the door behind them.

"I'll say," she mutters. "I thought I was going to have to elbow my way here."

"I mean, you did just set the firm up for life," Adrian replies.

Marsh nods slowly, taking in this news.

So, my answer was right, she thinks with a chill.

But the rest of the day is nothing short of incredible. Between commercial breaks, the firm doubles in size due to Marsh's victory, and Marsh herself earns even another promotion. At this point, her standing is higher than Jo's—than Victor's, even. She's not just a partner now. She's the top dog.

To think that she started this journey hoping just to become a lawyer. Now she runs the whole firm. Just a short while ago, she never would have imagined she could handle this amount of responsibility, but if anything, Marsh is already thinking what else she can do. What more to want, what more to pursue, what more to make hers.

The afternoon and evening rush by in a blur. She's so busy accepting congratulations all day and outlining the firm's new ten-year plan, it's almost midnight before she gets home. As the doors to her private elevator open to her penthouse, Marsh is so giddy with exhaustion, she almost curls up right there on the antique Persian rug. She creeps into the kitchen for a snack, hoping not to wake Ren or Harper, who probably have been asleep for at least an hour by now.

But to her surprise, the kitchen isn't empty. Ren is slumped over the table, pen still in his hand. He's fallen asleep on top of his notes that he brought home from work.

Marsh watches him for a moment as he snores lightly.

He really does look like he's sleeping well, she thinks. *So deeply.*

So deeply, in fact, that she could probably steal a glance at his research right now, and he'd never know.

Marsh's smile fades as the idea occurs to her.

As quietly as she can, she creeps over and crouches beside Ren. Most of the papers are hidden beneath him, but there are a few pinned down by his elbow at just the corner. She grasps the one and pulls gently, holding her breath.

The paper doesn't move at first.

She grits her teeth.

Come on. Easy does it.

Then it slides free.

Marsh sighs as Ren doesn't stir, and then turns her attention to the page. Time to see what he's been working so hard to reveal.

His notes are a mess, but slowly, Marsh pieces it together. Chrysalis is in the final stages of approval, and will be available with a prescription within the next few weeks—around the time that Marsh's finale should occur, co-incidentally, she notes with an uneasy shiver. But his shorthand seems to indicate that he's interested in a much earlier time period, all the way back to the very first volunteer trial the company conducted for the drug.

Even at that stage, there were no negative side effects for any of the volunteers, and they all reported falling asleep faster, enjoying their dreams, and feeling refreshed when they woke up, but something strange also happened.

Something *even stranger* than all of the patients having lucid dreams, rather.

The research supervisors realized that when they said things around the sleeping patients, they *also* could influence what happened in the dreams—without the patients knowing it.

The first time, it was an accident. While watching Patient A nap, the head doctor mentioned to one of the other researchers that Patient A should quit smoking, for his health. A few hours later, when that patient woke up, he reported that while in his lucid dream, he was smoking a cigarette, and chose to put it down. In fact, he resolved to quit smoking altogether, and happily threw out all his remaining cartons in his dream.

What made you decide to do that? the head doctor asked him, expecting the patient to remark that he'd heard the doctor say it, or that he'd felt suggested to, but Patient A didn't. He said he decided to do it all on his own. In fact, he was so adamant it was his idea, he thought the researchers were lying when they tried to convince him that they'd accidentally suggested it to him.

Marsh stares nervously at the paper.

What has Ren gotten himself into?

SagwaGold: <Omg, look!>
Moms4Marsh: <He's gone!>

Marsh jerks her head up—but her viewers are right. Ren isn't at the table anymore.

"What?" she whispers, spinning around just as a sound comes from the living room.

She darts out into the main hall in time to see Ren set a couch cushion into the dark, cold fireplace, and then step back to admire his handiwork. He holds out a pencil over the imaginary flames.

"R—" she starts to say, but as soon as he turns around, she realizes that he won't be able to hear her, even if she calls his name.

Because he's still asleep.

Marsh watches him intensely. She *knew* something was off this morning.

Outside the show, Ren isn't a sleepwalker. He just doesn't have that tendency. He sleeps like a log, barely moving even to roll over or adjust his limbs—let alone stroll the apartment.

Something would have to make him do this.

She hopes she's wrong.

But she doesn't think so.

Ren's eyes flutter, and his lips move clumsily.

"S'mores . . ."

"What? S'mores?" Marsh repeats. "Ren—"

"But I don't want to," he murmurs. "I want . . . to keep . . . kayaking . . ."

She gasps.

Is Ren . . .

Is Ren hallucinating her recap footage?

What's going on here?

"Ren?" Marsh finally says, very softly. "Honey? Wake up, honey."

Ren waits listlessly for another few seconds, and then instead of turning to Marsh, he moves forward and slouches in front of the fireplace. He paws the pillow away, now covered in old soot, and begins searching aimlessly through the thin layer of ash at the bottom of the pit.

"Where is it . . . ?" he murmurs. "Where is it . . . ?"

"Where's what?" Marsh asks him, deciding to see if playing along helps.

"My notes," he says.

"Your notes on Chrysalis?" Marsh asks.

"Yes," he replies blankly. "I had to hide them . . . but there were too many."

"They're on the kitchen table," Marsh adds.

"No," Ren says. "No. Not those. The ones . . . from before . . ."

Marsh stiffens.

What notes from before? When did Ren ever take notes from before?

When was Ren ever taking notes on Chrysalis, other than here in the Hong Kong path?

"Ren," Marsh asks, taking hold of his shoulders firmly. "What notes from before? When is before?"

Ren snorts suddenly, startling.

"What?" He's awake but disoriented now, and he tips groggily over onto his haunches. "Marsh?"

Across the room, Pickle scrambles on the couch, awakened by the commotion, and trots happily over to sniff him.

"You were sleepwalking," she says.

"What . . ."

He blinks slowly, and gently pushes Pickle away.

"Where am I?"

"The living room," Marsh answers. "You were sleepwalking, honey."

She coaxes him from the floor and up the stairs of their penthouse, Pickle now in tow. In their room, Ren crawls into bed and falls back asleep in seconds. Eventually, Pickle yawns and goes to his dog bed in the corner of the room, too, but Marsh stays by Ren's side, perched on the edge of the mattress, watching him snore softly.

After a few minutes, she leans forward and opens his nightstand drawer. Inside, next to a pair of old reading glasses, is a small prescription bottle of pills. Slowly, Marsh picks it up, and in the light of the bedside lamp, studies the symbol on the front of the Sharp Purple label with dread.

A small, delicate butterfly stares back at her.

She knew it.

Ren's devotion to this article is nearly as religious as his devotion to their relationship. There was no way he wasn't going to do absolutely everything he could to make sure his article is perfect—including taking the Chrysalis pills himself as the ultimate guinea pig.

And he knew Marsh would never agree to it.

So he went behind her back and started taking them in secret.

Marsh is a wreck the next day at work. She still looks fabulous, of course, but she's been at her desk for an hour, and has barely made any of the tweaks she wants to the decor at all, even though this would be a great time to have the Bubble fix the drapes and change the wood grain on the bookcases. She just keeps staring at the Chrysalis articles from yesterday on her laptop, until the words blur. Even her normally chatty commenters are quiet, perhaps too unsettled by this turn of events to be in the mood for chitchat.

What happens now? she wonders.

Should she confront Ren about this betrayal? Is it already too late, now that he's started taking the pills?

Should she tell him what's really going on—with the show, with his article?

With Chrysalis?

Her desk phone rings.

"Good morning. Your ten thirty is here," Adrian says.

"My ten thirty?" Marsh repeats, quickly pulling up her calendar on her laptop, panicked. Is this it? Has Chrysalis come to meet her at last?

But she's relieved to see the name waiting for her there in the little colorful rectangle.

Talia Cruz.

"Send her in, thank you," Marsh says, and hangs up.

"Your view! Incredible," Talia chirps as she sweeps into the room. Her elegant gait falters slightly as she catches sight of the briefcase beside Marsh's desk, but she recovers. "I love what you've done with the place. And this new art on the wall! Gorgeous. When did you acquire those paintings?"

"I've been busy," Marsh replies, and thanks Adrian on his way out.

As soon as he closes the door behind him, both of them spin toward each other.

"So!" Talia says brightly. "Hong Kong! How incredible. It looks like it's really everything you imagined, and more!"

Marsh falters, surprised.

After everything she just found out about Chrysalis's latest incarnation, can her host really be serious?

"I know we're almost out of time, but I'm really worried about this path," she says. "I don't know if it can be salvaged now."

"But, out of every life you've explored, isn't this one the closest to what you want?" Talia asks, aghast. "Isn't that why you chose to come to Hong Kong?"

It is, Marsh knows. She knows it so deeply that her heart aches to think about it.

"But what about Chrysalis?" she asks. "If Ren publishes this article in support of this strange medication . . ."

"Let's set that aside for a moment." Talia shrugs. "Everything here is basically a dream come true! Is it not? Harper is flourishing at Pallissard's Hong Kong branch, Ren is working for the actual *New York Times,* and you're crushing it here at the firm! I mean, it's all yours now! Overall, things seem pretty close to perfect, don't they?"

Talia punctuates the question with a twirl, so she can gesture to everything Marsh has achieved.

"Also, we should change that briefcase," she adds, unable to stop herself. "It doesn't match your wardrobe."

"You know, I think I'll keep it," Marsh says curtly. "So, you're really not worried about Ren's article? About letting him publish a profile on Chrysalis, and make it an integral part of the Bubble's world?"

"As your host, it's my job to be supportive, but also honest with you," Talia replies. "I know you've been concerned about this little Chrysalis thing, but I don't think it's something bad. I think it's actually rather good."

"What?" Marsh gasps.

Talia nods. "Think about it. It almost seems like it's been trying to *help* you all along."

Moms4Marsh: <Ooooh, that's an interesting point!>

Notamackerel: <I still don't trust it>

TopFan01: <There's no one with more All This and More experience than Talia, though!>

"What do you mean?" Marsh shakes her head. "It's been forcing me into things! Like the gala auction!"

"Where it paid millions and millions of dollars for your photograph, and would have set you up for life," Talia counters.

"And Mexico? Creeping into my telenovela?" she asks.

"Where it helped you win a Nobel Prize, for crying out loud," Talia says.

Marsh balls her fists, frustrated. "Well, what about now, then? In this life, it's basically a mind control drug!" she rebuts.

Talia clicks her tongue at her dramatics. "Or it's a way to make Ren an award-winning journalist, with an article about a miracle medication that's going to change the world for the better."

She motions for them both to sit, and clasps her hands calmly.

"I know you're concerned, but I don't think you need to be. If you look at it objectively, it really seems like, whatever Chrysalis is, it wants the same thing you do," she says. "Why not just let it help?"

Over Marsh's office's private intercom, the show's familiar jingle begins to play, this time like 1940s jazz elevator music, and both Talia and Marsh look up at the speaker for a moment, then back at each other.

"Actually, I have another idea," Marsh replies.

She waits, but Talia doesn't say anything at first. Gracefully, she rises and goes to the window again, to stare out at Marsh's gorgeous view.

"Talia," Marsh urges.

Talia continues to study the mountain for a moment longer. Almost like she doesn't want to hear Marsh's plan. Almost like she thinks it's the wrong choice.

Finally, she sits down again and smooths her skirt.

"Tell me," she says.

Marsh presses on, determined. "It came to me last night. How to fix everything wrong with this path, and make it perfect. A way to keep this life *and* make Chrysalis go away—for good."

Despite her misgivings, Marsh's host looks impressed with her certainty.

"Oh?" Talia asks.

"Well, as part of his research for this article, Ren started taking those Chrysalis sleeping pills at night, in secret," Marsh starts.

"Because the pills can cause lucid dreams as a side effect?" Talia asks.

Marsh nods. "I think he wants to write the piece with firsthand experience," she says. "But I found out that the pills don't just cause lucid dreams. They cause a very special type of lucid dream. A *suggestible* lucid dream."

A Chrysalis dream, she doesn't say.

Talia doesn't get it at first. But then her eyes snap wide as she understands what Marsh is getting at.

"I don't know, Marsh," she frets as the overhead tune draws to a close. "This is a very risky gamble."

Marsh sets her jaw.

It *is* a risky gamble.

But it just might work.

A GOOD DREAM

The only light in Marsh's bedroom is from her nightstand lamp as she gently lifts the covers and snuggles in next to Ren. He's already taken his Chrysalis pill and is lost amid some dream, a faint smile on his lips.

He looks so peaceful, Marsh thinks as she watches him.

SharpTruth356: <It's now or never, Marsh>
[Automatic security filters have deleted this account]

Marsh blinks away the posts. SharpTruth is right, but even though this is the smartest move, she really doesn't want to do this. It feels more wrong than the end-of-episode choices, somehow. Maybe because she'll be the one manipulating something this time, rather than the Bubble.

But this is for the best. She's doing this because she cares about Ren. How many times has she left an incredible path because something wasn't quite right for him? Or Harper, for that matter? Hell, even for Dylan, before he completely disappeared? She's not just in this for herself. She's trying to make everything in the Bubble right not just for her, but for everyone she cares about.

Ren mumbles in his sleep, and Marsh gently brushes a lock of his hair off his forehead.

What would he say, if she admitted to him what she admitted to Dylan in the midseason special? She can't help but wonder again. Would he panic the same way Dylan did when he found out he's part of *All This and More*? Or would he help her make the rest of the choices, to work toward the same perfect future together?

What a dream that would be.

"Ren," she whispers. "Ren, can you hear me?"

Ren doesn't move, but he sighs lightly in response.

Marsh hesitates, and takes a deep breath.

"Ren, you shouldn't write this article about Chrysalis," she says at last. "You don't want to write this article. You want to write something else instead. In fact, you should forget all about the article—like you were never writing it in the first place. Like it never existed."

She breaks off there and waits, her lips pursed tensely.

Ren doesn't really react, but then again, he's asleep. She's not sure what kind of sign he could give her right now anyway.

"Well, I guess we wait and see now," Marsh muses softly. After another long moment, she scoots down on her side of the bed and nestles into her pillow. She looks at Ren one last time, and then rolls over to turn out her light.

Just as she does so, Ren sits up in bed.

Marsh rolls back. "Ren?" she asks.

As soon as she does, she spots that familiar glazed look in his eyes, that telltale slackness in his jaw.

Ren's about to sleepwalk again.

Marsh scrambles out of bed and follows as he shuffles out of the bedroom, slowly down the stairs, and into the living room.

Notamackerel: <Is this it? Is it happening already?>
N3vrGiv3Up: <SHHH! Don't wake him!>

Everyone in the comments is tittering excitedly, trying to guess what weird thing Ren will do tonight. Some are warning Marsh not to wake him up like she did last time, that it can be startling for the person sleepwalking, flooding her with so many helpful tips that she's worried she's going to trip and tumble down the stairs into him, rendering the advice useless.

Together, the two of them move around the main level, Ren leading, Marsh following, until he ends up wandering into the kitchen—where all of his research on Chrysalis is still spread out across the table.

Marsh hangs back, holding her breath.

Ren stares at the table for a long time. He picks one page up and stares at it, his eyes unfocused, more like he's looking through it than at it. Then, slowly, he folds it in half, and tears it.

And then he tears those pieces again.

And again.

He keeps going until he's made confetti out of the page. The fragments flutter to the floor like falling snow.

For the next ten minutes, Marsh watches in open-mouthed amazement as Ren works his way through every single sheet of paper in his research this way, and the kitchen looks like someone left the window open during a blizzard.

Part of her is relieved, but another part is a little horrified. All that pains-taking work Ren did, gone in an instant.

And he doesn't even know he's doing it.

Finally, Ren finishes shredding the last page. His hands drop limply to his sides, and he stares without seeing at the destruction.

He looks so lost, she thinks.

His eyes slowly grow even more glazed, as if he's slipping even deeper into slumber, and his feet turn and shuffle him out of the kitchen with a mind of their own.

Marsh peeks after him to make sure he's heading back up to the bedroom, and then returns to the mess.

She stares for a whole minute longer, with dreadful wonder.

Then she yanks a garbage bag out from under the sink, and begins shoveling every last speck of shredded paper into it as fast as she can.

In the morning, Marsh is up first, wired with energy even though she didn't sleep a wink the whole night. Every time her eyelids grew heavy, Ren would sigh or roll over, and she'd snap to attention again, ready for him to have another strange dream or take a second sleepwalking stroll. By the time dawn finally broke, she was already downstairs.

Hopefully now that he's forgotten about the article, Ren will forget about the sleeping pills, too, she prays.

"Whoa," Harper says as she comes into the kitchen.

Marsh turns around, coffeepot still in hand, to see her daughter staring at the suddenly bare kitchen table.

"Where's the mess?" she asks. "What happened?"

"Shh," Marsh replies quickly. "He's putting the article aside for now. Politics at the office or something," she lies. "But I don't know how sensitive he is about it yet, so let's not say anything unless he does. Okay?"

Harper nods. She looks back at the pristine wooden surface again. "It's just so weird, to see it look like a table again, instead of a dumping ground. I almost got used to all those papers heaped there. It looks . . . sad now."

"I know," Marsh says. "Maybe let's keep sitting on the stools at the kitchen island for now, too."

Harper smiles and hops onto one of the high seats with a wink.

A few minutes later, Ren comes downstairs, looking as rested and refreshed as usual. He wishes both of them good morning, and then pads over to the coffeepot. Marsh and Harper exchange a silent look. Harper's eyebrows seem to say, *He really isn't going to mention it, is he?*

In response, Marsh's own warn Harper to keep mum.

Because it's not that Ren's avoiding the subject of the Chrysalis article; she wishes she could tell her daughter. It's that he might not remember he was ever working on it at all.

"So, I was thinking we could go to that new outdoor film festival this weekend," Ren says after a sip of coffee. "How does that strike you two?"

"Sure," Harper says. "Sounds fun."

"What about you?" Ren asks Marsh.

She smiles. "It does sound like fun," she says.

Yes, it does.

Marsh feels as if she's holding her breath for four straight days—but they make it to the end of the week without Ren remembering that he was working on the article. And at the firm, Chrysalis has paid its retainer fee, but no further meetings are scheduled. The happy family explores the Hong Kong International Film Festival on Saturday, where Marsh adjusts the weather so it's pleasantly cool enough that no one sweats, and then goes out to dinner at one of Marsh's favorite dim sum restaurants, where she curates the menu so all the specials are available. On Sunday, the day Ren was originally supposed to submit the final draft to his editor, he entertains himself by cooking a complicated French duck recipe for dinner, and Marsh invites Victor, Adrian, and Jo to join them.

"Hi!" Victor says as the elevator doors open into her penthouse. "Thanks for having us!"

As Marsh scoops Jo into a hug, Pickle comes crashing straight into the knees of a woman with them who Marsh doesn't recognize, but who greets Marsh with an easy, familiar smile, and also seems to know Pickle very well.

"You're my favorite, too!" she cries, bending to pet him.

"Everyone loves Bex," Jo says, and puts an arm around Bex's waist once she stands up again.

TopFan01: <Wait . . . that's the woman Jo took home from the fancy Phoenix bar, in the first half of the season!>

Moms4Marsh: <Did that actually happen in this path? I can't keep track!>
LittleXoài: <Cô ấy đẹp!>
SagwaGold: <Go, Jo!!!>

It's definitely the woman from the bar, Marsh decides with a casual blink to free her vision.

"I'm so glad you could make it," she says to them both. She knows she's grinning too wide—but she's so excited to see Jo's new partner, and can't wait to gossip over all the details of their romance the way that she and Jo gossiped over Marsh's budding relationship with Ren, just before the show started.

"I am, too," Jo replies. Beside her, Adrian rubs his hands together like a greedy kid as they all laugh. "We all know how legendary Ren's duck is!"

"I aim to please," Ren replies, with a proud bow. "The recipe takes hours, but it's worth it."

"Hey, we also worked hard. We went *all the way* down the street to buy this bottle of champagne," Bex teases. "Two hundred whole meters!"

"Let's get that on some ice," Ren replies, and sweeps his arm to welcome them into the apartment. "Come with me! You can get a sneak peek of the duck before anyone else gets to taste it."

Everyone protests jokingly and crams themselves down the hall after him, Pickle barking excitedly along, like an adorable scene from a family sitcom.

The evening is wonderful. Everything Marsh has ever wanted. They all toast their new lives at her massive, meticulously decorated dining table, and the glaze on the duck practically sparkles as she cuts into it. Victor and Adrian are fawning over their new boss, Ren is beaming with love, Jo and Bex are making jokes, and Harper hangs on every word as Jo tells her about how her mother was when she was just a wee little Marsh, only a bit older than Harper is now herself.

In these stories, Marsh blazed through law school at the top of their class, traveled all over Europe and Asia on her summer breaks, and was responsible for setting up Jo and Bex in the first place. Instead of Marsh meeting Dylan on a camping trip, it was Jo who was starstruck by Bex near the kayaks, and Marsh who sneakily bundled up a s'mores kit and gave it to Bex as an excuse to talk to Jo after dark. It's then that Marsh notices gold rings on Jo and Bex's fingers as they mime sticking the sweets on a stick.

LunaMágica: <Omg, the show is like Jo's Cupid!>
Moms4Marsh: <This is so sweet!>

Marsh tries not to burst into happy tears for her best friend. Outside the Bubble, Jo's relentless energy for work always made it hard for her to make a relationship stick for more than a few months. She covered it up with fun flings and enjoyed her freedom, but Marsh knows she's always wanted a long-term partner who would understand and support her career, just like Ren now does for Marsh—and now it's finally happened.

All This and More made it happen.

As they all eat and talk, Marsh's cheeks burn, sore from how long she's been smiling. This is what she's been working so hard to achieve. This kind of love and joy.

This kind of perfect.

"So, Ren," Victor asks innocently as they pass the serving platters, "how's work?"

Marsh and Harper both freeze and look at him.

"It's great," he says affably. He seems as oblivious as ever. "I'm really enjoying this new position at the *Times*. The hours are pretty good. For a journalist."

Everyone laughs at that.

More champagne goes around, and as half the group retires to the living room while Harper, Ren, and Bex volunteer to get dessert ready, Marsh slowly relaxes again.

She can see SharpTruth in the corners of her vision, still begging her to locate the source of Chrysalis before the end of her season, just as Alexis did—but she ignores him. She doesn't need to do it anymore. She's finally solved the problem. And things are working out exactly how she wants in this path at last. She only has to make it for one more episode.

Perfect really *does* seem almost within her grasp.

Victor convinces everyone to play one round of charades, but partway through, Harper appears in an apron, holding a spatula like a trophy.

"Dessert is ready!" she reports proudly, before scrambling back to the kitchen. "I did the frosting!"

"Well, that's clearly going to be the best part, then!" Jo calls after her as they all stand up, the game forgotten. Everyone heads back to the table, excited to try Ren and Harper's dessert, but when they reach the dining room, Marsh pauses, surprised.

The room is completely empty.

"Hello?" Marsh calls.

"Almost ready!" Harper calls back, and a second later, she and Bex appear with a gorgeous dark chocolate cake.

"It took both of us to get it onto the serving platter," Bex jokes. "Ren's cake is so beautiful, we didn't want to mess it up!"

"Looks delicious," Victor says.

"Where *is* Ren?" Marsh asks.

Harper looks around. "I don't know," she replies. "He said he'd clear the table while we did the frosting."

"The restroom, perhaps?" Jo offers.

They all sit down to wait—but after a few minutes of making small talk and staring eagerly at the beautiful dessert on the table, Ren still hasn't appeared.

"I'll just go check on him," Marsh says, rising.

"Tell him I'll eat his serving if he doesn't hurry," Harper adds.

"Ren?" Marsh calls as she ascends the stairs. "Honey? Need anything?"

But no one answers.

Marsh pokes her head into the bedroom, but the master bathroom is empty. So is the bathroom down the hall, and the study, the guest bedroom, and even Harper's bedroom.

Where is he?

"I . . . can't find him," Marsh admits when she returns.

"What?" Jo asks. "He's not upstairs?"

Marsh shakes her head.

"Well, that's weird," Adrian says.

Harper has explored the entirety of the first level of their penthouse in the meantime. She arrives back in the dining room with an equally perplexed expression.

"He's not downstairs, either," she says.

Everyone looks at one another.

"Hmm." Jo frowns. "Why would he leave without telling anyone?"

"And especially so late at night," Bex adds. "He was practically dozing in his chair as Harper and I got the cake ready."

Marsh turns, suddenly laser-focused on her.

"What did you say?" she asks.

That's not good.

Very not good.

"All that cooking must have taken it out of him. He did seem very tired tonight," Victor adds.

"You're sure he's not just asleep upstairs?" Jo asks.

Slowly, Marsh's eyes drift to the back door of the penthouse. The one that leads to the service elevators, and out the resident-only exit to the streets far below.

Ren is definitely asleep, she knows.

Just not upstairs.

SNOOPING

Marsh waits impatiently for the elevator to open, and then dashes out into the hallway. The lobby's grand glass doors are to the left, but that's not where she's going.

She cuts right, and heads downstairs into the basement. The door to the building's trash room squeaks as she opens it.

Marsh deliberately closes the comments, then flicks on the light.

She hauled the garbage bags she'd filled with Ren's shredded research down here the night he had his dream, almost a week ago. By now, they're half-buried in the blue eco dumpsters under even more recyclables, if they're still there at all.

But there's no time to waste. If there's some clue about where Ren may have gone in his discarded notes, she has to find it. And fast. She dives in with a grunt, and begins tossing piles of plastic wrapping, empty cartons, and flattened cardboard boxes until she locates her discarded bags.

When she opens the first one, she has to push down a wave of panic. She'd forgotten how severe Ren's destruction was. He didn't just tear the pages in half, but shredded them into confetti. She has no idea how she's going to use any of this. Even so, she starts digging, desperately seeking a piece of evidence that he didn't shred that night.

Finally, mid–third bag, Marsh pauses. She almost tossed a scrap of paper away, but something—she's not yet sure what—caught her eye upon it. She pulls it back to read it again.

Talia works at RealTV—can she get me access to the producers there to publicize this feature?

Hm, that's odd, she thinks.

Talia has *never* worked for RealTV—inside the Bubble. She's always played other parts in Marsh's episodes. Even when she was part of *All This and More* for her own season, Sharp Entertainment was running things. The only place she's ever been connected to RealTV is as Marsh's producer for this current season.

But how does Ren know that, if he's here inside the Bubble?

Marsh is sure that Talia hasn't slipped up. She would never make that mistake. She's too polished, too professional. And she's sure Ren has never caught the two of them discussing Marsh's possible choices at the end of an episode, either.

But it's right here in Ren's writing.

He knows that Talia is connected to RealTV, somehow.

She digs deeper, until she finds a Sharp Purple Moleskine notebook, torn in half down the spine. It must have been mixed in with Ren's research, and he ripped it up along with all the rest.

The cover is scratched, and the corners battered. Like he's been keeping this journal for a long time.

Dream one: Central Park. I have the ring in my pocket, but I can't remember if Azalea Pond is left or right. Try to text Jo without it being obvious, but Marsh doesn't notice.

Dream two: Roommate broke up with college girlfriend, bought a bunny as a pet because he was lonely. I hate him. Named Pickle, just like our dog now.

Marsh sets the front half of the diary down for a moment, chilled.

It seems that Ren had been journaling about his sleeping pill–induced dreams. But the dreams are . . .

They're all moments from her recap. Moments that he's not supposed to remember, because he wasn't there.

How is that possible?

Too hard to keep track

Is Ren aware that choices are being made?

Does he know that he and everyone else are in *All This and More*?

Need to get to the source

The source?

What's the source?

Possible that D is still here

"D?" Marsh whispers to herself. The hairs on her arms stand on end.

Does *D* stand for Dylan?

Has Ren been searching for Dylan this whole time, ever since he disappeared after the midseason special?

But why didn't he tell Marsh, if so?

Maybe not place, but time

"Not place, but time?" Marsh repeats hoarsely.

What does *that* mean?

She stares at that last line with pure bewilderment.

Marsh turns the page so quickly it almost tears—but that's where Ren's scribbles cut off. She's run out of this half of the notebook.

She looks up, her eyes skimming over the mountain of trash bags.

If she found the first half, the second half has to be in one of them.

A few minutes later, in another bag, she unearths the remains. Same color, same shape, same frayed partial spine.

Slowly, Marsh begins flipping through the second half of Ren's journal.

What she sees chills her.

Ren has drawn a flowchart of some kind. At first glance, it looks like an org chart for a company, or a family tree, perhaps. But the longer Marsh stares, she begins to realize what every bubble in his diagram represents.

An event.

An event that happened *this season*.

The brunch date Ren and Marsh had together. The disastrous threesome. Harper's meteoric rise at Pallissard. The marriage proposal at the theater. The gala in Iceland, the telenovela scenes, even, somehow, the dinner party they just had here in Hong Kong . . .

It's all there.

Some of the little squares have symbols next to them, and there's a haphazard legend meant to help decipher his code. A star means that Ren thinks the event might have been a dream, an underline means he thinks it might be a memory, and a circle drawn around the square means he's just not sure. Some of his events have multiple symbols beside them, and others he's clearly gone back and changed, over and over, until the square is just a gray pencil splotch.

JesterG: <Oh my God, it's like Ren has been tracking the whole show!>
SagwaGold: <我唔明喎! How did he start to figure it out?>
Monsterrific: <I don't know what's going on anymore!>

Marsh doesn't, either—but one thing is for sure.

Ren knows something is wrong with reality.

And he's been trying to figure out what it is.

She's still staring at Ren's writing when a squeak on the basement stairs startles her. As fast as she can, Marsh shoves the halves of the notebook deep into the nearest garbage bag, hiding them from view.

"Find anything?" Harper asks as she comes into the trash room.

"I thought I told you to do the dishes," Marsh chastises her gently.

"I did," Harper replies, crossing her arms. Jo, Bex, Victor, and Adrian appear behind her.

"We got them done in record time," Jo says. "So, did you find anything?"

"Maybe," Marsh allows. "I think Ren was investigating . . . another story," she settles on saying. "About . . . missing persons. He's been trying to find Dylan—"

"Who's Dylan?" Victor asks.

Marsh sighs in frustration and motions to Jo to fill him in. She doesn't have time for this.

"Why are you looking at me?" Jo asks, confused. "I don't know a Dylan."

That finally slows Marsh down. Her hands pause midway through a stack of notes, and she closes her eyes for a moment.

Deep breath. Don't panic.

The show is still working hard to scrub his existence clean, and has made yet another person forget him. It's happened before, but it's still deeply unsettling to watch Jo—who was there the day Dylan and Marsh met—act like she has no idea who he is.

If the Bubble can remove even Jo's memories of Dylan, she dreads whose it will alter next.

"Dylan is Harper's father, but that's not important right now," Marsh finally says. "What I need to—"

"What?" Harper cuts her off. "What do you mean, my father?"

Moms4Marsh: <Oh no>

Time freezes. Marsh's heart stutters.

Slowly, she turns to Harper, full of dread.

"Ren is my father," Harper says.

Moms4Marsh: <No, no, no>

Marsh's knees wobble. The room is tilting slightly, or maybe she's lightheaded.

"Harp," she murmurs, clinging to hope.

She tries to speak calmly, praying that her confidence will help Harper remember, but the fear throttles her voice.

"Ren is your stepfather," she warbles desperately. "Dylan is your biological father."

Harper is staring at her in horror now.

"What do you mean, my biological father? *Ren* is my biological father, Mom. I only have one dad. What are you talking about?"

LunaMágica: <This can't be happening>
Fortunata111: <How can the show do this to her?!>

"Marsh!" Jo cries, catching Marsh as she stumbles.

Marsh pushes her off. She can't breathe. Her throat is tight, working itself up and down as she refuses to let the sob come free.

"We have pictures of Dad—*Ren*—at the hospital with you, holding me," Harper says, frantic. "He always teases you about how you craved sardines and peanut butter during your pregnancy. It was the most disgusting thing."

Marsh shakes her head helplessly.

This can't be real, she tells herself.

"That wasn't Ren. It was Dylan," she tries to say.

Moms4Marsh: <Oh, I can't bear this! If something stole my children's memories of me, or their father . . . >

Harper is on the verge of tears now.

"Please," Marsh begs. "Remember."

"You're scaring me, Mom," she whimpers.

Someone, do something! she wants to scream.

She could have borne anything for a better life, Marsh knows. Any change, any pain, any loss.

Any price—except one that touches her daughter.

"I think we should call a doctor," Victor offers.

"No doctor," Marsh says. "There's no time."

"Marsh, if you're . . . I don't know, having a stroke, or something . . ." Jo starts.

"I'm not having a stroke," Marsh snaps. "I need—"

What *does* she need? She doesn't know. What was she doing before this horrible moment? Her mind has been wiped blank by shock. She was looking through these papers, and saw Ren's strange notes, and—

That's right! She remembers now.

She was looking for Ren.

He's lost, maybe in trouble, and she has to find him. And then maybe Ren can help her find Dylan.

She can make everything right again.

She can make it perfect for everyone.

"I need to find Ren," she finishes. "He's on medication, and isn't safe out there alone."

"What kind of medication?" Jo asks.

"Sleeping pills."

"He's been having weird dreams ever since he started taking them, he told me," Harper says.

They all look at Marsh.

"Did you ever try any, Mom?" she presses. "Maybe you dreamed this 'Dylan' person?"

Monsterrific: <Oh no>
StrikeF0rce: <Marsh needs to get out of there>

Marsh shudders as she backs away from her best friend and daughter.

"Marsh, we're really worried about you," Jo says. "Let us help. Just talk to us."

Marsh shakes her head, trying not to cry.

SharpTruth387: <Marsh, please. Let me help>
[Automatic security filters have deleted this account]
SharpTruth388: <You know where you have to go>
[Automatic security filters have deleted this account]

"I love you, Harp," she says fiercely. "Everything is going to be okay. I promise."

Every cell in her body is telling her not to leave her daughter.

But if she's going to help her, she has to find Ren. And if Ren somehow has figured out that he's in *All This and More*, then there's only one place he could be sleepwalking toward now.

RealTV's offices.

A FAMILIAR FACE

Marsh's shoes echo on the asphalt as she runs across the empty parking lot toward RealTV's looming front entrance. The moon is just a crescent tonight over Kowloon Bay, and it almost seems like she's flickering in and out of existence as she passes through each streetlamp's yellow pool of light and then plunges into darkness again, over and over.

Even though RealTV is now located in Hong Kong, the building itself still looks mostly the same as its original location. At last, Marsh reaches the curb, and quickly surveys the manicured walkway and entrance. As she does, a shadow on the concrete just before the giant glass doors begins to work itself into a solid shape, something large and horizontal, like a miniature mountain range—until at last, she recognizes the maroon shirt Ren was wearing before he disappeared from their apartment on his sleepwalk.

"Ren!" Marsh gasps, dashing forward. "Thank God. Are you all right?"

She kneels and gently rolls him onto his back so she can see his face. His eyes are lazy, drooping, and his mouth is slack and his expression relaxed.

Still asleep.

He must have sleepwalked all the way here along Austin Road or Hung Hom South and tried to get into the building, but then ran out of steam because it was locked and curled up on the bristly entrance mat, all without knowing he'd done any of it.

Thank goodness she's found him before he could have gotten into *real* trouble.

Marsh lets out an exhausted sigh and sits back.

That's one problem solved, at least.

In the silence, she studies Ren as he sleeps. Out of all the episodes since the midseason special, Ren might look the most like his original self, for once, except there's something a little off. Almost like he's a little bit . . . undefined. It's as if he's just slightly out of focus, his outline fuzzy, like the Bubble can't quite capture him with the same sharp, crystalline detail it can everything else.

How strange.

She doesn't know what to make of it, but as she looks up at the RealTV building they're sitting beneath, her musing comes to a screeching halt.

She stares, petrified, at the giant, glowing REALTV NETWORK sign above the door.

It doesn't say *RealTV* anymore.

It says *ChrysalisTV* now.

Just then, the glass doors shudder, then begin to swing outward, like someone is pushing them open from the inside.

SagwaGold: <Run!!!!!>

The comments explode, but she's still crouched beside Ren, unwilling to flee without him. The glint of the lights around the entrance have turned the glass into mirrors, and she can't see who—or *what*—is opening them.

"Stay back!" Marsh shouts, but it's too late.

The doors open, revealing a figure cloaked in the darkness of the inner hall. Slowly, he steps into the light.

SharpTruth400: <At last>
SharpTruth400: <Thank God>
[Automatic security filters have deleted this account]
SharpTruth401: <There he is>
[Automatic security filters have deleted this account]

Huh?

Marsh uncovers one eye.

"Hi, Marsh," the man now standing there says. He's tall and lanky, with dark hair and eyes. Marsh has definitely seen him somewhere before, she knows.

SharpTruth402: <Lev>

Lev?

She realizes at once.

The twins.

Lev and Ezra Hoffman. The brothers who helped invent the technology that the Bubble runs on!

The memories come rushing back. Dylan went to school with Lev, before he and Ezra were hired at Sharp Labs and eventually discovered quantum bubbling. Lev was the one who told Dylan and Marsh to watch *All This and More* in the first place, way back when it had just gone on the air with Talia Cruz as its star.

SharpTruth402: <We found you>
[Automatic security filters have deleted this account]
[Additional security measures implemented]

Marsh stares long after the words have been erased.

It all makes sense now. How SharpTruth knows so much about how the show works, and how he can keep evading the security filters.

And why he's so desperate to help Marsh figure out what's going wrong in her Bubble.

Ezra? Marsh wonders.

It has to be.

"It's good to meet you, at last," the man in front of her finally says.

"Lev Hoffman?" Marsh asks. "What are you doing here?"

"I've been here since the pilot episode," he replies. "This office is where I run everything from."

"Where you run everything from?" Marsh repeats. "But I thought your brother was running things this season."

Lev's eyes widen.

"Ezra works for *All This and More* now?" he asks. "Where is he?"

"At—"

Marsh pauses.

It's not called RealTV anymore in this episode—but she refuses to call it ChrysalisTV.

"—at the office outside the Bubble," she finally says. "They put the science team on the outside this season, instead of on the inside like it used to be."

Marsh watches Lev as he tries to absorb this information. He's surprised and confused.

Something is very off about this.

She turns on the comments, but Ezra is still banned, and she snaps them off again.

Why doesn't Lev know that his brother is also working for the show this season? Even if they once had a falling-out over quantum bubbling—if they're both now part of the crew, didn't they communicate before her first episode? And why aren't they communicating now? Why is Ezra sneaking around in Marsh's comments, whispering secrets to her, instead of going directly to Lev?

"Lev, what happened during season two?" Marsh asks him.

Lev looks at her and, after a moment, shakes his head.

"That's just it," he finally says. "I don't know."

"You don't know?" Marsh repeats.

"I've tried to recall it, but it's all just a blank. I remember working on Talia's first season, and I know that I also worked on season two. But when I try to think about it, it's all vague. Like my memory was wiped or something." He sighs. "Talia's finale is clear in my mind, and then the next thing I remember is your first episode."

Marsh stares, rattled.

It doesn't make any sense. Why can't Lev remember anything from the last season, if he worked on it before production shut down? And why didn't Talia or anyone else on the new crew mention that Lev was back this year?

"I don't . . . I don't understand," Marsh says.

Lev shrugs helplessly. "Me either. But I'm trying to figure it out. And I do remember all of this season, so far."

"Then you must know about Chrysalis," she replies.

Whatever's gone wrong between Ezra and Lev, and whatever happened to Lev's memory of season two, they can figure that out later. Because in *this* season, Marsh is fast running out of time.

Lev nods. "I've been tracking it since your first episode."

He looks around, and then crouches beside a still-slumbering Ren.

"Come on," he says, helping Marsh to lift him up. "Let's talk inside."

The two of them stagger into the lobby, Ren slung between them. They carry him into the conference room and gently set him down behind the big oak table. Marsh sees that Lev has set up his workstation all across it, having turned the space into a web of laptops, empty snack wrappers, and a collection of RealTV—now ChrysalisTV—coffee mugs.

"Whew!" A musical gasp breaks the silence as the door swings open behind them.

Marsh lurches upright to see a new figure rushing in.

"Marsh, there you are!" Talia cries when she sees her. "Thank goodness you found Ren. I was so worried! I—"

Talia's relieved monologue cuts off abruptly as Lev also stands up from behind the table.

"Lev," she says, surprised. "You've been at RealTV this whole time?"

"Yep. Trying to figure out what's going on with Marsh's season."

"That's right!" Marsh says, shaking off the distraction of Talia's appearance. "Lev was telling me that he noticed Chrysalis right at the start of my first episode. So you must know more about it than we do," she prompts him.

Lev nods again, but he's frowning. He beckons them over to his laptops.

"I don't have all the answers, but I have some theories," he says.

"Well, this is good news, right?" Marsh replies, hopeful. "Can't you just tell the tech team outside the Bubble what to search for, so they can patch the glitch? If they can locate Chrysalis, they could—"

"They can't," Talia says.

Marsh pauses. "Can't? What does that mean?"

Lev seems to agree. "It's a security feature. Once the Bubble starts running, you can't alter its code from the outside. It's an automatic defensive strategy against hacking." He sighs. "Unfortunately, we never anticipated tampering from the inside."

Well, that explains why Ezra can't reach Lev directly, either, Marsh supposes.

As Lev begins typing again, Marsh spots a familiar purple font on his screen.

It's the same one that's been on her own laptop lately, thanks to her new client.

"Is that Sharp Entertainment's website?" Marsh asks.

"I've been trying to hack into their databases," Lev replies. "Well, not the real Sharp Entertainment, but what little of Sharp Entertainment exists here in the Bubble. I'm hoping that maybe I can find the answers there, if I can't remember them myself." He frowns. "But so far, I haven't gotten anywhere."

"But RealTV bought the rights to *All This and More* after Sharp Entertainment folded, and took over everything for Marsh's episodes," Talia says. "You won't find any data from this season there."

"You're right—but I'm not looking for data from this season," Lev says.

Talia cocks her head, as if not expecting that response. "What do you mean?"

"This Bubble we're in now is the one I created for you, Talia. I know, because I recognize all my code." He points to an incomprehensible matrix of numbers on his screen. "I think that once I perfected the first Bubble, Sharp Entertainment—and now, RealTV—didn't make a new one for each season. They kept reusing the same one."

He glances sidelong at Marsh, his fingers on the keyboard never slowing.

"Whatever Chrysalis is, it's here inside the Bubble, with us," he says. "Which means, if there's only one Bubble . . ."

"You're after data from season two," Marsh gasps suddenly, understanding. "From the mysterious contestant's life that never aired."

Lev looks at her.

"Bingo."

He finally stops typing, and turns to her.

"Whatever happened in those lost episodes that no one ever got to see . . . I think that's where Chrysalis started."

Marsh stares.

"Holy mackerel," she finally says.

Notamackerel: <This is . . . I mean, I knew something was wrong, but
    this . . . >
N3v3rGiv3Up: <What does it mean??>
StrikeF0rce: <It means that Marsh might be in a lot more trouble than we
    thought>

"So that's what you've been working on all season," Talia finally says, equally stunned.

Lev nods. "If I can find something in Sharp Entertainment's files, I might have a better idea of how to resolve this glitch." He grimaces at his screen. "*If.* I've been searching since the end of Marsh's first episode, and I've found nothing so far. What little record of Sharp Entertainment that exists here in RealTV's—or, I guess, ChrysalisTV's—databases, it's been wiped pretty clean."

Marsh leans closer to his herd of computers. "There must be something I can do to help," she says.

Suddenly, a huge rumble startles them all, and the room wobbles violently.

"What's happening?!" she cries.

Marsh, Talia, and Lev stumble, and then drop to the floor as the shaking continues.

"I think it's an earthquake!" Talia says.

"In Hong Kong?" Marsh asks, bewildered.

"It's not really an earthquake . . ." Lev says. "It's the Bubble! It's struggling to . . . resolve the conflicts!"

They grab Ren and drag him under the conference table, holding on to the legs for safety. The whole building is groaning now, rolling in waves, and Marsh screams as the chairs around them topple over and the big flatscreen bolted to the wall jerks threateningly.

"What was that?" she wails as something glass crashes to the floor outside the conference room, sending a spray of shrapnel across the lobby.

"Come on!" Talia lunges from her crouch toward the door, and manages to wrench it open amid the shaking. "Let's get out of the building!" she shouts.

But Marsh shakes her head. "We can't leave Ren!" she says. "We have to make the choice here!"

Talia looks at Ren, still trapped in his slumber, then at Marsh before another crash nearly sends them all flying against the wall. "With everything so unstable, there's no telling where we'll end up!"

"I think I know where we're all going to end up right now if we stay another second," Lev replies.

As if in response, the angular chandelier overhead snaps its chain and smashes into the top of the table.

"Fine! Everyone, hang on!" Talia orders as she throws herself back under the table with them. Marsh can't tell what she's doing at first amid all the shaking, but then as a thump even louder than everything else pummeling their building rattles her teeth in their sockets, she knows.

The Show Bible.

It's so monstrous now, Talia can't even hold it up. She has to leave it on the floor and crouch over it to flip through it.

"Let me read it," Marsh begs. "Let me read it, Talia!"

"Marsh, you know this already," Talia says, hovering protectively over it. "Contestants *cannot* see the Show Bible, or read ahead in it before they make choices. It's cheating."

"I know, I know!" Marsh replies, furious. "But this isn't about the show, Talia. This is serious. It's my safety. It's my *life*!"

"All the more reason not to risk it!" Talia argues. "Trust me!"

Moms4Marsh: <Come on, Talia! Let her see it! This is serious!>

Marsh hesitates, on the verge of panic. She's frozen, her mind gripped by fear—but suddenly, an idea strikes her.

"We have to jump back!" she cries.

"What?" Talia asks. "We're almost at the finale, Marsh! Why do you want to go *back*?"

"Because then, I'll already know how everything happens," Marsh says. Ezra was right all along, she can see now. "I can go straight to Chrysalis from the start, when it's still small, and figure out what's going on, once and for all!"

Talia is shaking her head, shouting something about episode constraints or viewership numbers, but Lev is deep in thought despite the chaos, considering her logic.

"It could work," he says at last. "If the Bubble holds long enough."

"That's a big *if*!" Talia protests. She flinches as a piece of drywall dislodges and lands right next to them in a spray of white sand. "What are you even going to do, once you get there?"

"I don't know yet," Marsh says. "But I'll figure it out!"

"Marsh, this is ridiculous," Talia replies. "Let's finish strong. You love your Hong Kong life, don't you? Why do you want to leave it? Let me take you to your finale, where we can make every last thing perfect."

Marsh shakes her head, desperate. The building is collapsing around them, and yet her host refuses to budge. Another minute, and they could all be buried in the rubble!

There's only one way she's going to be able to find out what Chrysalis really is.

Finally, instead of arguing, Marsh looks at Lev.

Lev sees her expression and nods back.

"Now," Marsh says.

"What?" Talia asks—and then yelps angrily as Lev grabs her and Marsh dives for the Show Bible.

"Hurry!" he urges as Talia struggles.

"No!" she says. "Marsh, seriously, don't do this!"

Marsh throws her whole body into it, and manages to muscle open the cover. Instantly, text overwhelms her, the font tiny and dense, every page packed to the margins, the words nearly impossible to read without a magnifying glass.

What does it say? She flips wildly as the building wavers. *What secrets are there?*

As Talia begs her to stop, Marsh finds the current scene. It almost looks like it's writing itself in real time, words printing themselves upon the paper to record that Marsh has commandeered the Show Bible, that the end-of-episode music has just begun overhead. The book bloats even more, growing a little larger, as Marsh hovers over her next choice.

EPISODE 6: PARADISE

EPISODE 9: DEADLINE

Marsh frantically tries to remember. "Paradise" was the name of her Tahiti vacation episode, wasn't it? Should she go back to search for Chrysalis in Tahiti, or to the start of this episode, in Hong Kong? Is Tahiti too far? Is Hong Kong not far enough?

"What should I do?" she asks Lev.

"Neither," Talia demands coldly.

She's going for intimidating instead of beseeching now, cycling through every tactic. Even amid the chaos, her voice cuts, low and sharp, like the edge of a knife.

"It's not safe, Marsh. You can't just flip like that, without me. You don't know what you're doing. You don't know what *could happen.*"

Marsh's hand wavers, hesitant.

What is Talia hiding? Or is she just protecting them? Will Marsh make an even bigger mess than the one she's already in if she tries to do this alone?

"Let me guide you." Talia reaches for her. "We can do this together. We can still make this life perfect."

SharpTruth499: <Perfect for who?>
[Automatic security filters have deleted this account]

Just then, Ren finally begins to stir beside Marsh as the end-of-episode song jingles in garbled bursts over the building's failing speaker system.

"Did I miss it?" he mumbles, his eyelids fluttering. "What did she choose?"

Marsh stares at him with terrified wonder.

"You could have . . ." he hums. ". . . *All This* . . ."

"No, Marsh!" Talia shrieks, breaking free from Lev. "You can't—"

Marsh makes her choice just as the ceiling splits open.

To jump back to
Paradise:
Turn the page

To jump back to
Deadline:
Go to page 381

EPISODE 6

PARADISE

When the lights go up, Marsh is already moving, even though she doesn't know where the show has planted her for the starting scene. The ground is soft—*sand!*—her feet sink, and she nearly topples.

"Oh!" Ren gasps. "Did you step on a seashell?"

Marsh lurches upright and stares.

She can hardly believe it.

Everything is exactly like before. The peaceful sky, the clear water, the warm air. Marsh and Ren on the beach, Harper with the other kids at the shore, the hotel looming up from between the palms.

Moms4Marsh: <Whoa, she actually did it!>
LunaMágica: <She made it back to Tahiti!>

The waves crash, thunderous, as Marsh spins around.

SharpTruth509: <Marsh, the Bubble's not stable>
[Automatic security filters have deleted this account]
SharpTruth510: <Find Chrysalis>
SharpTruth510: <Hurr—>
[Automatic security filters have deleted this account]

He doesn't have to tell her twice.

Marsh takes off running.

"Where are you going?" Ren calls, baffled.

But Marsh leaves him behind. She sprints straight across the beach, up the sidewalk, and into the lobby of the gorgeous hotel, where she takes the stairs two at a time until she reaches the floor where her and Ren's room is located.

There's an odd sound in the background, almost like a baby crying, but she ignores it.

She remembers he brought his laptop on the trip, and she knows the password. All of his research is torn to shreds in Hong Kong now, but if Ren was working on his article while they were on vacation here, then his notes on Chrysalis would still exist, she reasons midsprint down the carpeted hall. All she has to do is find them. And then she'll see.

Their door!

She throws herself against it to burst through—and smacks her forehead so hard she sees stars.

"What the . . ." she whimpers, stumbling backward, and realizes her mistake.

Of course the hotel door would be locked.

She checks the pockets of her beach sarong, and comes up empty-handed. *Damnit!*

Ren must have their key.

Marsh lets out a frustrated growl. But she doesn't have to run around looking for Ren among all the holidaymakers. She can just go to the front desk and get a key of her own.

The attendant behind the desk startles as she rushes down the stairs, but Marsh doesn't care. The shrill whine is louder down on the ground floor, and she has to raise her voice to be heard over it. Behind her, a group of guests—moving as fast as she is, oddly—dash out of the front doors.

ChilangoCool: <¿Por qué corren los otros huéspedes del hotel?>
TopFan01: <Does anyone else hear that weird sound?>

"Hi, I—"

"Ma'am! Are you a guest here?" The clerk cuts her off.

"Yes. I need to get into my—"

She grabs Marsh's arm.

"Wait," Marsh stammers. "Are you . . ."

There's no mistaking it. She has the same friendly face, the same thick dark hair and freckles.

The hotel clerk is Elyse. Talia's lead camera operator from season one.

"What are you doing here?" Marsh asks.

"Ma'am, there's no time to waste," Elyse says, pulling her around the counter by the elbow as she walks. "You shouldn't be here. This is an emergency!"

The whining peaks—and suddenly, Marsh recognizes the sound for what it is.

"Is that an air siren?" she asks.

"A tsunami warning!" Elyse shouts at her over it.

"A *what*?" Marsh cries.

"The hotel is going to be destroyed!"

Moms4Marsh: <OH NO!!!>

If Chrysalis was trying to obscure itself so Marsh wouldn't find it before, now it's outright on the offensive.

If it can't hide, it's going to *fight*.

"You!" Elyse waves rapidly, and two hotel security guards rush over. "Is there still a jeep? Help me get this guest to emergency evacuation!"

"No," Marsh says, pulling away from Elyse, but the two guards are ushering her toward the door now, speaking into walkie-talkies. "I need to go back to my room!"

"You can't; there's no time," one of the guards says. "The last jeep is leaving in five minutes!"

Marsh yanks her arm away.

"Dan? Sergio?" she stammers.

The two of them were season one's special effects coordinators, responsible for all the fireworks and fanfare at the end of every episode. Her eyes dart as the panic rises. Is everyone in this hotel someone from the old crew? And why can't any of them remember?

"Hurry!" Dan urges as Sergio rushes ahead to open the door.

But Marsh rips away from them and runs for the stairs again, ignoring their calls for her to come back. But instead of heaving herself against the door again, she swipes the little plastic rectangle she managed to lift from one of the guards' belts as they struggled.

The master key.

Her door opens, and Marsh lurches in.

The bed has fifteen luxury pillows, there's a cut pineapple on a platter on the coffee table, and orchid petals sprinkle the carpet, just like last time.

She ignores it all and dives for Ren's suitcase.

She can do this in time.

"Where is it?" she demands as she digs. "Where's the goddamn laptop?!"

"Marsh!" Ren shouts. She whirls to see him standing in the open doorway, alarmed. "What are you doing?"

"I'm sorry," she apologizes, but doesn't stop searching. "I can explain later, but I'm not spying on you. I mean, maybe I am, but not like—"

"Stop!" Ren grabs her arm and drags her to her feet. "Whatever you're doing, stop right now."

"Ren!" She wrenches free. "I just want Chrysalis."

Ren grabs her again. "We're leaving, now."

"Not without Chrysalis!" she says. "What is Chrysalis, Ren?"

"Just leave it, Marsh!"

"What is it? Why are you hiding it?"

"I'm not hiding anything!" he replies, and points at the window. "There's a goddamn *tsunami*!"

"Mom!" Harper screams, in the doorway, too, now. "We have to go!"

The sight of her daughter stops Marsh like a brick wall. She turns, riveted, every fiber of her being attuned to the terror in her voice.

"It's going to be okay," she promises.

"Marsh, we're evacuating right now," Ren declares, but she pushes him off.

"You go, take Harper, I'll be right behind you."

"What?" Ren is hysterical. "That's not happening!"

"Just go!" she says.

Ren grabs for her again. "We're all going together, right now!"

"What are you even *doing*?" Harper cries.

"Ren, please," Marsh demands. "Get Harper to safety."

She's terrified for her daughter, but she also knows that running isn't going to stop anything. It'll put off the tsunami, but then what? What next? If she can find Chrysalis, if she can just figure out what it is, she'll finally know what to do, and everything will be okay.

Won't it?

"Help me!" she bellows, and Ren angrily yells, "*I'm fucking trying!*" at her, but she's not talking to Ren.

SharpTruth520: <Marsh, I can't fix it!>

SharpTruth520: <I can try to reset the episode, but you'll have to find Chrysalis agai—>

[Automatic security filters have deleted this account]

Marsh looks up. Through their huge ocean-view window, she sees the wave.

It's so massive, so horrifyingly beautiful, that even as afraid as she is, she can't stop herself from staring at it. It's so tall, it blots out the sun. A mountain range of blue. Has she ever seen something so big in her life? The roar of it is deafening, the only sound in the world.

"Marsh, *please*," Ren begs her.

"Mom!" Harper wails.

"Do it now!" Marsh screams at the ceiling. "Do it now!"

SharpTruth521: <I'm tryin—>
[Automatic security filters have deleted this account]

Harper is hugging her now, too frightened even to cry. Breathless, Marsh watches the wave crest, taller than the hotel. All they can see is the wall of water, the foaming white crown. The glass buckles in anticipation.

SharpTruth522: <Now, Marsh!>
[Automatic security filters have deleted this account]

At last, there's that familiar tinkling chord, piercing through the roar like a bolt of light from heaven. An opening in the scene, a way out.

SharpTruth523: <JUMP!>
[Automatic security filt—

EPISODE 6

Marsh is holding her breath as she plunges into the next scene—but there's no wave now, no hotel room.

"*Bara nokkrar mínútur eftir!*" A booming voice garners applause.

Marsh spins, her green gown twirling.

Ezra managed to save her just in time—he's skipped her to Iceland. She's at the gala.

Moms4Marsh: \<Whew, this is so much better!>
Notamackerel: \<Wake up!>

"This is so exciting!" Ren says beside her, staring at the stage.

Marsh takes a couple of gulping breaths, trying to calm herself down to match the new, sophisticated ambience. There's no siren, no encroaching wall of watery death.

"You want a drink?" Ren asks.

Marsh shakes her head, and tries to smile. The excitement in the ballroom is palpable, just like the first time. The grand hall is even more beautiful, and everything glitters. But up front, it's not Talia holding the microphone and waving to the smitten crowd.

It's Alexis.

"There's still a little time to get your bid in!"

SharpTruth534: \<We came in late>
[*Automatic security filters have deleted this account*]
SharpTruth535: \<The auction's almost over>
[*Automatic security filters have deleted this account*]
TopFan01: \<Is there not a permanent way to ban this guy?!>

"Mom!" Harper laughs as she rushes over. "Your Ísvængur is the highest-earning lot in the whole auction so far!"

"Incredible!" Ren says. "We're so proud of you!"

Marsh studies the room as she hugs Harper back, trying to figure out what to do. She didn't manage to find Chrysalis in Tahiti before she had to flee, but that's because she didn't know exactly where it was hiding. Here, she does.

The Ísvængur.

She has to get to her photograph.

"Harp, let's go," she says. "I need your help with something."

"Marsh!" Ren cries. "There are only a few minutes left. They'll be waiting for you onstage, to thank the high bidder!"

"Then stall for me," Marsh tells him, and disappears with Harper into the crowd as the applause continues.

This time, the photos up for auction aren't displayed just in front of the stage. Instead, the exhibits are locked safely in the facility's basement vault, "for everyone's security," the guard posted at the elevators says.

Why would the originals be dangerous to people? Marsh wonders as the sliding door opens to the basement, a partially unfinished level with low ceilings and harsh lighting. *They're just pieces of paper!*

But as soon as they enter the vault, Marsh understands.

Monsterrific: <Holy mackerel!!!>

Marsh shouts the same thing as a bloodcurdling snarl makes her lurch backward, bumping into Harper and nearly toppling them both.

"Is that a . . ." Marsh gapes. "Is that a snow leopard in that cage?"

The photographs of various endangered animals aren't just photographs anymore.

They're *real animals.*

Instead of easels with gigantic prints set upon them, each lot is now a cage containing a live incarnation of its portrait. There are predatory cats slinking back and forth, eagles flapping their wings, snakes hissing, a tank with a dolphin, and more.

"What is going on?" Marsh whispers, still stunned.

"Hey," Harper murmurs, surprised. "Where's the Ísvængur?"

Marsh whirls toward the center of the room, where her Ísvængur should be waiting in the middle of the alphabet. Sure enough, the pedestal is there where her butterfly should be.

But the cage is gone.

SharpTruth536: <Uh-oh>

[Automatic security filters have deleted this account]

Suddenly, a blaring alarm goes off, and the room is bathed in a red glow.

"What's happening!" Harper gasps, scampering to her mother.

"This is an emergency alert!" a robotic voice drones over the intercom. *"Extreme volcanic activity detected. Repeat, extreme volcanic—"*

"Mom!" she cries.

Again? Marsh wants to shout.

"It's okay," she says desperately. "Everything will be okay."

The room plunges into darkness, and then the emergency lights kick on.

"What do I do?" she yells. "How do I stop it?"

SharpTruth537: <Find the Ísvængur!>
[Automatic security filters have deleted this account]

"Come on!" Marsh says, dragging Harper toward the elevators.

As the doors open to the main ballroom, she can see the elegant mood has evaporated. It's chaos now. People are crying and screaming, knocking chairs over and scattering plates and glasses everywhere as they panic.

Where's Ren? she wonders. *Is he looking for me and Harper?*

"What's going on?" Marsh grabs the nearest frantic guest. "Why isn't anyone evacuating?"

"The doors locked because of the emergency alert! We can't get out of the Harpa!"

"What?" Harper screams.

"Which volcano is it?" Marsh asks as her daughter clutches her. "Öræfajökull, again?"

"All of them!" he shrieks. "The whole island is erupting at once! There's nowhere to evacuate to!"

"Emergency alert! Unprecedented volcanic activity detected over all of Iceland. Repeat, unprecedented—"

"It's the end of the world!" he screams before he runs.

"What do we do?" Harper wails.

Moms4Marsh: <How can this be happening?!>
StrikeF0rce: <Everything is collapsing!>
LunaMágica: <It's not fair!>
SharpTruth538: <Marsh, the roof!>
[Automatic security filters have deleted this account]

"Come on!" Marsh orders. She drags her daughter back into the elevator, and sends it much higher this time—all the way up.

As the doors open and they scramble out, all she can hear is the shrill wail of the emergency sirens from every corner of Reykjavík. Around the Harpa, in every direction, the horizon is ablaze with an exploding volcano, a dozen peaks encircling the city in an apocalyptic ring.

Frónverji: <My God . . . it's like Ragnarök . . . >

"Marsh! Harper! Thank goodness!" Jo says as she hugs them. "We couldn't find you in the ballroom; we didn't—"

"The volcanoes!" Victor cries. "We can't get out!"

More desperate guests are crowding onto the roof now, everyone fleeing to the highest point. Screams alternate with shouts of horrified awe as each new wave of arrivals encounters the view.

But there's still one person Marsh doesn't see.

"Stay with Harper," she orders them, and throws herself into the throng, searching for Ren.

SharpTruth539: <It's here somewhere. I'm tracking—>
[Automatic security filters have deleted this account]

Finally, she spots him. Ren is on the far side of the roof, alone. All the way at the edge, right up against the safety railing. There's something in his grip.

A small glass cage, no bigger than a shoebox.

His hand is on the little door.

"Ren!" Marsh screams. "*No!*"

But just before she reaches him and slams the door shut, the Ísvængur flutters free—and disappears into the blazing night in a streak of blue.

No.

"Why?" she gasps, breathless with despair.

That was it.

Chrysalis is gone.

She grabs his arm fiercely. "Why would you do that?"

"What do you mean?" Ren asks, shouting over the melee. "For you, of course!"

The Ísvængur has flown so fast and far, she can't even see it anymore against the molten orange skyline. Marsh sinks to her knees in exhausted despair.

At last, Ren lowers himself beside her.

"I'm sorry," he says. "I thought you would want me to."

She snorts. It's so absurd, it's funny. "You thought I would want you to rob a gala?"

"No. Want me to free it." He looks out, at the burning sky. "It's the last of its kind. Even if we're trapped on the roof, it has wings."

Marsh sighs.

Tahiti turned out to be a bust, and Ren has just ruined her only shot at catching Chrysalis here in Iceland with his misguided noble aims.

There's only one place left she can think to find it now.

SharpTruth540: <C:\ATAM\Bubble\episodes\la_estrella>
[ERROR]
SharpTruth540: <C:\ATAM\Bubble\episodes\la_estrella\safemode>
[ERROR]
SharpTruth540: <Shit>

Marsh sits up straighter as her vision flashes.

"Hurry," she urges. The night air has grown so hot, her face is flushed, and sweat is running down her brow.

SharpTruth540: <I'm trying. I'm having trouble accessing Mexi—>
[Automatic security filters have deleted this account]

"It's all right," Ren says, soothing her. He's leaned back against the railing to allow her to cuddle into his chest. The look on his face is impossibly serene.

Marsh stares at him, her unease growing. Around them, people are falling to their knees, calling their loved ones' names, praying to their gods. They don't know this isn't real, that she can undo it—hopefully. Marsh can see the lava now, glowing white-hot at the periphery of the city, oozing ever closer, obliterating everything it touches.

"Why aren't you afraid?" she asks him, no more than a whisper.

There's a pop, almost like a sink stopper being pulled out, and then a flare of music, as everything goes dark.

EPISODE 7

LA ESTRELLA

Marsh screams like she's on fire, and falls over onto the cool, soft, safe couch.

She sits up. She's in her telenovela trailer, the way the first episode in Mexico started. But the couch is pure white now. Like someone forgot to dye it.

Wait.

She looks around.

Most of the furniture and decorations are missing this time, in fact. The little room looks colorless and empty.

"Ezra?" she whispers, hesitant.

Lito555: <Parang may kakaiba>

Monsterrific: <It's almost like the Bubble is still trying to fill in the details of the scene or something>

It doesn't matter. Marsh lurches up from the plain couch. If Chrysalis was trying to interfere with the telenovela storyline in this path, she knows where to start. She has to get to the set, and then find the director's copy of the *Un Juego Peligroso* script.

"Wait, where are you going?" Ren asks as he appears spontaneously—*what?*

Marsh startles, surprised, but doesn't slow.

"I want to finish blocking the romance scene befo—" he continues, but Marsh is already to the door. She opens it and steps out before her eyes catch up.

She was expecting to land on a busy street somewhere in Condesa or Polanco, but what's outside now is nothing like that.

Because it's literally *nothing*.

The door opened up to an endless void.

SharpTruth541: <Look out!>

[Automatic security filters have deleted this account]

But Marsh's foot is already dangling in the air, past the trailer's metal steps, and she begins to plummet.

Just before she hurtles into the blackness, she grabs the last rung to stop her fall.

Moms4Marsh: <MARSH!!!>
LunaMágica: <NOOOO!>

"Help!" she screams as she hangs on for dear life.

"Malvavisca!" Ren howls. He throws himself to the ground and leans out of the open door, reaching desperately.

"Ren!" she shrieks.

"Grab on!" he begs, his hands stretched as far as they can go. "Quick!"

Marsh lets out a fearful grunt, and swings one arm up. She almost misses, but then her fingers graze his, and she grabs hold. She seizes his wrist with her other hand.

"I've got you!" Ren grunts as he begins to haul her up. Her legs dangle and she screams again. "Don't let go!"

As soon as her head appears, Ren snatches her shoulders and yanks her inside the trailer. Together, they collapse in a heap on the floor as the door slams shut.

"*What was that?*" Marsh cries, terrified.

SharpTruth543: <Shit! I can't get the rest of the scene to load!>
[Automatic security filters have deleted this account]
SharpTruth544: <It's too unstable here>
[Automatic security filters have deleted this account]

"I don't know where else it could be," she replies aloud, before she can help it. She's still too rattled to pretend everything is normal in front of Ren. Tahiti was a bust, and so was Iceland, but whatever is happening here seems really off. "Should we go forward? Or back?"

"Go forward or back? What are you talking about?" Ren asks, as she blinks through the frantic comments still screaming about her near-miss with death. "You want to redo an episode?"

Marsh is about to call for Ezra again, but the shout dies on her lips.

She turns to him slowly.

Is she misunderstanding?

"What?" she asks.

"What?" he repeats.

But she doesn't give up. "What do you mean, 'redo an episode'?"

"Like we always do!" he says. "To make each one better. Each one perfect."

Her chest feels as if it's in a vise. Her breath is shallow, nervous. Out of the corner of her eye, she sees the doorknob on the trailer door go fuzzy, then crisp again.

SharpTruth545: <Marsh, get out of here>
SharpTruth545: <It's glitching—>
[Automatic security filters have deleted this account]

"How do you know about the show?" Marsh presses.

But Ren just laughs. "I'm *in it*, Malvavisca!" he says. "I've been a series regular ever since they revealed me as the cartel boss."

Marsh puts her head in her hands and sighs, frustrated. Everything is so mixed up now—so many things getting scrambled, bleeding over, repeating themselves—she can't tell what's suspicious and what's just the paths scrambling anymore.

"I know this is hard," he says, his voice gentle. "But you've wanted this for so long. I know you can do it. You were made to be a star."

Marsh opens her eyes. As quickly as it was gone, the dread is back again. Is Ren talking about *Un Juego Peligroso*? Or *All This and More*?

SharpTruth546: <Something's very off>
[Automatic security filters have deleted this account]

"What is Chrysalis?" she asks shakily.

Ren cocks his head. "What?"

"What is it, Ren?"

"I don't have the script. We only get it the day of."

"It's not a script," she insists. "You know that."

She knows she's not making any sense to him, but something is different about this argument. Ren never understands what she's talking about, but as they argue now, she realizes that rather than bafflement, he's watching her with what almost seems like fascination. His eyes are glittering, the way that a child might study a magician at a magic show.

It almost looks like he's . . . *smiling*.

"I know how important this last episode is," he finally says. "Let me help you. That's why I'm here."

Over Ren's shoulder, the doorknob goes fuzzy again, and stays that way. The rest of the door slowly warps.

He takes her hand. "Everything is going to be okay."

"Will it?" Marsh asks.

"It will," he says. "I promise."

"How do you know?"

"Because I want the same thing you do," Ren says.

The door vanishes, the blackness gapes.

Marsh looks up at him. Her stare is both a challenge and a plea.

"And what do I want?" she whispers.

SharpTruth549: <Marsh—!>
[Automatic security filters have deleted this account]

"To make this show perfect," Ren answers.

Marsh watches him as he holds out a Nobel award to her, that famous giant golden coin nestled in its velvet box, as the trailer starts to pixelate.

"Isn't it?" he asks, his eyes eager, full of hope. "Pretty damn close?"

CHRYSALIS

When the episode opens, the scene is entirely silent and still.

In the gentle dark, Marsh closes her eyes and takes a deep breath.

SharpTruth599: <Marsh? You okay?>

For once, the comment box is deserted but for him, and the words hover for longer than she's used to. Perhaps Marsh has run far enough that the Bubble is still catching up.

"I'm okay," she says.

SharpTruth599: <Thank goodness>
SharpTruth599: < . . . Where are we?>

Marsh looks around the quiet room. The familiar wallpaper, the old, ugly carpet.

"My house," she says. "From when I was a kid."

It's funny how small it all looks now. She doesn't know if it's simply because she's older now, or because of everything she's seen and done as part of *All This and More*. But she doesn't mind. Smallness is exactly why she came here. She just needed something manageable. Something safe. A place away from everything. No wild scenarios, no over-the-top adventures, no Chrysalis, no Talia, even no Ren or Harper. A place where she can hide for just a minute.

A place where she can *think*.

"Ezra," she says to the quiet living room. "Do you know where Lev is?"

SharpTruth599: <I can't see him right now>

"I'm sorry."

SharpTruth599: <I'm sure he's somewhere>
SharpTruth599: <He has to be>

Marsh hopes it's true. Even though they got separated in Hong Kong, Lev has managed to survive in the Bubble so far. She's sure he's on his way.

"Can you see Dylan?" she finally asks.

The answer is a long time coming.

SharpTruth599: <I can't find him, either>

Marsh nods grimly.

She wants to lie down on the couch, pull her mother's crochet blanket over her legs, and close her eyes to all of this. What she wouldn't give to let all of this be someone else's job, someone else's problem.

But hiding here won't solve anything. This season is about Marsh and her life.

In the garage, she finds her old bicycle. It still looks the same, a red frame with a green basket, but it's big enough that she can ride it as an adult. It's only a few minutes down the road to her old school anyway.

The campus is deserted, but Marsh knows that the side door to the teachers' lounge is always unlocked. A student accidentally broke it during a prank several years ago, and the school never fixed it.

The halls are covered in colorful flyers and overstuffed bulletin boards, and the linoleum squeaks. It's strange to be back, after so long. After she was laughed off the stage, she quit theater, and never set foot in the arts wing again. Drama club had loomed like a fortress in her mind, impenetrable and cruel. Now, she can see that it was just a small, slightly damp room. The faint musk of old textbooks and stale socks makes it seem even more benign.

There's a rustle, and Marsh turns to see her old music teacher, a slightly stooped, graying man with thick glasses and a Santa Claus beard, shuffle into the doorway from the hall.

Except in this episode, he's taller and younger, and his face looks different. He still reminds her of her old teacher, but he also reminds her of someone else. He looks kind of like Lev.

"Ezra?" she asks, surprised.

Ezra shrugs, a little sheepish. "Best I could do under the circumstances. Sorry."

"Don't be." She marvels. "I'm glad you're here."

Ezra looks around. "Your middle school?"

"That's right."

It takes him a moment to understand, but Ezra has seen all of Marsh's bonus footage, including this place.

"You think Chrysalis is hiding within your biggest regret," he finally muses.

Marsh nods. "Somewhere I'd never want to face."

She turns, and looks down the long hallway lined with lockers.

"This way."

Ezra falls in beside her, their footsteps echoing in the quiet.

"Why did it take you so long to reach out to me?" Marsh asks as they walk. "If you knew from the start something was off."

"I didn't know from the start," he answers. "I had my suspicions, but until I was certain, I didn't want to show my hand. And then, well. You've seen how robust the Bubble's automatic security systems are."

"Did Lev tip you off?" she asks.

"Yes and no," Ezra says. "We fought over quantum bubbling's applications, so we haven't been on the best terms ever since Sharp Entertainment green-lit Talia's pilot episode. But when Lev disappeared partway through filming season two, I knew something was off. He'd never do something like that, even if we disagreed. But then when everything folded, I couldn't find anyone from Sharp to tell me where he, or any of them, had gone. The deeper I dug, the weirder it seemed."

There's a fizz of pixels on the wall, but Ezra crushes them back into place with a grimace, and his face is clear again.

"When I heard that RealTV was restarting the show for a third season, I knew I had to get myself hired onto the crew."

"I'm glad you did," Marsh replies. "I'm sure Lev is, too. Even if he doesn't know you're here yet."

Ezra sighs.

"The last time we talked was when he showed me season one," he says. "I mean, you saw it. The world did. It was amazing. But I was still mad, and I couldn't admit it. We argued, and when he said he was staying on for season two, I stormed out. But then . . ."

Marsh understands.

"I couldn't let that be the last thing between us," he finishes. "I had to right the wrong."

"I understand," Marsh says as they pass her old English classroom. "Believe me."

Ezra smiles and puts his hands in his pockets. He looks around the dark hallway they've just turned into.

"So, what are you doing here, exactly?"

"The same as you," she answers. "Righting a wrong."

Ezra seems to understand. He's seen every frame of her recap, every one of her episodes. He remembers the flashbacks to her talent show. "Shouldn't we be in the auditorium, where the stage is, though?" he asks.

Marsh shakes her head and keeps walking.

"You'll see," she says, as she doesn't resist the memory, for once.

It's the night of her disastrous talent show performance again. After she'd fled midsong, Marsh was too embarrassed to be seen in the costume, even for a second. The only thing worse than what just happened to her would be to have to run out of the school and all the way home still wearing it, where even more people could laugh at her.

While the next act performed, she changed back into clothes in the drama room as fast as she could. She could barely see for all the tears, but she didn't make a sound, terrified that someone might hear her and know where she was. Once she was dressed, in her rush to escape, Marsh forgot the rumpled cloud on the floor in the corner.

The next day, everyone in the school had heard the story—and seen the costume. Because the older kids had found it, and hung it up in the gym locker room to taunt her.

"Kids can be so mean to each other sometimes," Ezra says, shaking his head.

Marsh pushes open the door to the basketball court.

"I'd hoped that if I just kept my head down, I could wait it out," she says. "I sat alone at lunch, and skipped after-school sports. I even pretended to be sick to stay home for a few days. But the kids just wouldn't stop. I'd wanted to be noticed, but then all I wanted was to be forgotten. To disappear."

She sighs.

"Became the story of my life."

She and Ezra are standing in the locker rooms now. Her costume is hanging in the back of the changing area, impaled on hangers and broom handles high above her head. The last bell rings, and the hallways slowly quiet. Then the lights go off.

At last, behind them, her child-self slips into the room, her breathing quick with desperation. She creeps forward and stares, her eyes stinging.

"A character-defining moment from childhood," Ezra says as they watch. "Great for ratings. Talia would be proud."

Marsh snorts, despite the somber scene. "Where is she, by the way?"

"I don't know. But probably close, if not already here."

Marsh nods.

"Just wait," she says. "It's almost over."

For a moment, it looks like young Marsh is going to lose her nerve. But she knows that as long as it hangs there, the other kids will never let her live it down.

With a frightened gasp, little Marsh rips it from the hangers and shoves it deep into the garbage.

Marsh waits until her younger version has escaped back out the door, then reaches into the trash. She pulls out the battered, dirty costume and holds it up. It's so little. It wouldn't even fit Harper, now.

"Marsh," Ezra urges, his voice gentle. "If you still want to find Chrysalis, we don't have much time. Even though you escaped for a moment, Hong Kong was your ninth episode. The next one will be the finale."

Marsh checks her watch.

There are only thirty minutes left until this one ends.

"So, this is really it, then?" she asks.

"I'm afraid so."

Marsh takes a deep breath.

"I still have time," she tells herself.

Time to quash Chrysalis, and save her season. Time to make everything perfect.

She folds the costume and tucks it under her arm.

"Take me back home," she asks Ezra. "I know where Chrysalis will be."

Suddenly, she's not at school anymore, but on her front stoop. Ezra's gone, unable to follow in his music teacher form, and Marsh is alone again. But this time, the street isn't as quiet as before. At the far end of the sunny front yard, a pair of landscapers mow the lawn and trim the hedges with unnerving slowness. Rafael and Bryn, the *All This and More* composer who created the show's signature song and Talia's former hairstylist, have the right tools and are standing in the right place, but the two men barely move, and their eyes never leave the house. Across the way, the old location manager and

HR director, Mike and Linnea, pretend to gab at their mailboxes, but they were never Marsh's neighbors, they have never lived on this block.

<Get inside,> Ezra says, words scrolling across her vision. <Lock the door.>

Marsh slides the dead bolt for good measure, and dashes up the stairs. She takes them two at a time, in socked feet, the way she used to as a girl. She slams the door and hangs the PRIVATE BEDROOM! KEEP OUT! handwritten sign she once believed would actually deter her parents, then crouches in front of her bed.

Slowly, she pulls out the box.

The sight of it takes her back. It was her mother's old wedding dress box, made of sturdy cardboard and decorated with a faint floral pattern on all sides. When she was a toddler, she was small enough to curl her entire body inside, which used to make her mother laugh. After she got a little too old to do that, her mother let her have it to use as a treasure chest, to store all of her valuables.

Over the years, it held many things. At first, rocks, seashells, pinecones, and dried flowers. Later, notes from her elementary school crushes, an autographed photo from her first concert, her old college study abroad brochures for Iceland and Hong Kong. The one thing it's never contained is her cloud costume.

Until now.

Marsh nestles the old outfit inside. As she does, the other items shift, until they're new. Marveling, she pulls each thing out and studies it. Her law school diploma, her photographs from Iceland, her *Un Juego Peligroso* masquerade mask. A dozen mementos from the adventures she's experienced here, the lives she's led.

And one more thing, most precious of all.

Marsh smiles as she picks up the lawyer's briefcase that Dylan tried to give her countless times.

She pops the clasp and opens it to reveal a Sharp Purple–colored folder.

<A client file?> Ezra asks.

"Yes," Marsh says. "From Mendoza-Montalvo and Hall. It's mine—for the bid I just won in Hong Kong."

The title across the top says: *Sharp Incorporated*.

<But Sharp doesn't exist anymore,> Ezra types.

"Exactly. Because it folded during season two," Marsh agrees. "Which is when Lev thinks that Chrysalis *started*."

She taps the folder.

"Whatever happened to Sharp back then, I think it was because of Chrysalis."

The silence in the room hangs heavy as she and Ezra consider her theory.

<Only one way to find out,> he replies at last. <Ready?>

Marsh shakes her head. "Here goes nothing."

And she opens the folder.

"It's not just a client. It's a case," she confirms as she sees the formatting, the legalese.

Her eyes widen.

"It's *my* case."

It's true. All of the quick scribbles are in her handwriting, somehow.

She reads as fast as she can.

"It's a lawsuit," she says when she realizes it. "The plaintiff is . . . Claire Sharp herself."

Claire Sharp, billionaire owner of Sharp Labs, the original discoverer of quantum bubbling technology, and Sharp Entertainment, the original creator of *All This and More*.

<But you didn't film a case scene in this episode,> Ezra says.

"Because the case is old," Marsh says as she skims. "The hearings all took place during season two."

She pauses suddenly.

If the suit is from season two, and it was Marsh's case . . .

Marsh was a lawyer before?

But that's impossible.

Wouldn't she remember?

<What else?> Ezra urges. <What was the suit for?>

"Damages to the show," Marsh continues as she reads. "We alleged that the season two contestant tampered with the Bubble, and that caused it to become too unstable. So unstable . . . that it collapsed."

<Collapsed? With everyone still inside?!>

Marsh nods, looking pale.

"They got stuck here, with no way out," she says. "Until my season started."

She covers her mouth, aghast.

It's true. The crew of season two have been trapped inside the Bubble this whole time.

That would explain why RealTV needed a whole new team for season three, why there was no one from the original crew anywhere to help with the transition, and why they're all here now.

The silence lingers as they both try to absorb this terrible revelation.

"I can't believe it," Marsh murmurs. She's trying to count everyone she's discovered so far, but there are too many to keep track. "Alexis in Mexico, Jillian and Charles at the circus, Elyse at the hotel, and Mike, Linnea, Rafael, and Bryn just now . . ."

<And Lev,> Ezra adds.

Everyone from the old Sharp crew, imprisoned here and their memories wiped, all so they couldn't warn RealTV what had happened in season two before it launched Marsh's episodes . . .

Marsh puts the paper down suddenly.

"Ezra."

She can hardly say it.

"And me too," she whispers. "Right?"

If Marsh was the lawyer for Claire Sharp's case, then it stands to reason that she also was in the Bubble during season two, somehow.

Which means that she also has been stuck in here with them.

"I might be sick," she says. "I don't understand."

What *did* happen in that season, that would be worth all this to hide?

Who would go this far?

<Keep reading,> Ezra begs.

Slowly, Marsh looks back down at the folder.

Just as she reaches for the next page, a sharp, grating tone rings out across her empty house.

<Marsh!> Ezra types. <The finale!>

Her eyes wide with terror, Marsh turns the sheet over as fast as she can.

There, on the last page, is the answer to all of her questions. Why Chrysalis has been determinedly inserting itself into her paths, in whatever form it takes. Why it's tried to influence her choices, no matter how she tried to avoid or thwart it. And why it's grown only more insistent the closer to the finale Marsh draws, before her chance to change her life forever is complete.

"Ezra," Marsh says weakly.

She can hardly breathe.

The mysterious season two contestant . . .

was Ren.

She looks up in horror just as the episode goes black.

WE'LL BE RIGHT BACK, FOLKS!

The screen stays black for a moment. Everything hangs, silent, still.

"Incredible! Just incredible!"

Talia singsongs as she bursts forth in a flurry of Sharp Purple swirls and trumpets—as if Marsh has just won the lottery, not discovered that *Ren himself* was the long-lost season two contestant whose season mysteriously vanished without a trace.

"What an exciting cliffhanger before our season finale!"

JesterG: <Cliffhanger?! Don't you mean train wreck??>

LunaMágica: <I can't believe it! Ren has been the season two contestant all along!!!>

Notamackerel: <The show is totally out of control!>

TopFan01: <Come on, friends. We're all on the same side—Marsh's! Her most important episode is up next. Let's stay supportive!>

"Life has just gotten better and better for our heroine, even as it's gotten more complicated. It wouldn't be worth it otherwise, right?" Talia winks. "In the second half of her season, Marsh has embraced the magnificent power of *All This and More* to the fullest. She's visited a hundred different paths, and tried a hundred different things, to discover the best possible version of her life at last."

Monsterrific: <Wait, Talia is seriously not going to address that last twist?!>

YanYan242: <Maybe she doesn't know?>

StrikeF0rce: <How could she not?!>

LunaMágica: <Maybe Ren tricked her, too?>

JesterG: <I dunno—but I have a bad feeling about this . . . >

"And now, the time has come for Marsh to make her final choice, and return the new, amazing life she's built to the real world!" Talia cries desperately, and a montage of the last few episodes begins to play behind her, heavily sanitized—all mentions of Chrysalis scrubbed and clips where Marsh looks the most confused or afraid conveniently cut. It ends with Marsh, Ren, and Harper on the summit of Victoria Peak, awestruck by the panorama of skyscrapers and color and lush green below them, Ren's engagement ring sparkling on Marsh's finger as she puts a hand over her heart.

Notamackerel: <We can't let the show send her into the finale like this!>
Moms4Marsh: <For the love of God, shut up and leave Marsh alone!
   These are her choices, not yours!>
LunaMágica: <Her choices? What about Chrysalis?>
Notamackerel: <What about DYLAN???>

Suddenly, everything inverts like a photograph negative, and Talia becomes a ghost of herself as the *All This and More* scrolling marquee behind her turns into a flickering roulette of random symbols.

StrikeF0rce: <What the—?!>

The music screeches, but Talia snaps into action, bending everything back into place with just a slight falter in her normally polished expression.

"With only the finale episode left until her season is over, will our darling Marsh manage to get everything she's ever wanted? Or will she run out of time before she can make her life as perfect as it can be?" she asks, tossing her hair slightly so it falls just right again.

TopFan01: <Quick, visit our fan page to enter your guess for what Marsh's final choices will be!>

"Hold on to your hats, loyal viewers, because you're about to find out!" she cries as everything judders again, static snow falling as the background fractures into multicolored bars.

Notamackerel: <The whole thing is glitching out! Marsh is in serious danger!>

Talia's red nails dig into the edges of the frame as she wrenches it back into focus, her dazzling smile clinging fiercely to her lips.

"Stay tuned for our exhilarating season finale!"

EPISODE 10

THE SEASON FINALE!

When the world brightens again, Marsh's quiet refuge has been transformed completely.

A full production stage, complete with lights, sound speakers, confetti, and possible pyrotechnic effects, has risen around her like an unearthed buried city, trapping her inside.

"Marsh!" Talia calls.

Marsh turns and spots her host waving from the center of the commotion. She's all dolled up for the finale, in a sparkling gold dress that compliments her blond hair and catches every flash and flicker of celebratory color from the roving spotlights. Behind her, her own gigantic face grins from a screen the size of a building.

"Welcome to your season finale!" both Talias boom, and the show's opening tune pours out of the speakers. "The time has come!"

TopFan01: <This is your last chance to wish Marsh luck!>
Moms4Marsh: <You can do this, Marsh! We know it!>
Notamackerel: <How can we stop this? It's not too late!>

"Talia," Marsh gasps. Her host—possibly the only person who can help her—is finally here. She rushes for the low stage Talia is standing on and clumsily pulls herself up onto it. "We have to cut. This is important. I know what Chrysalis is. I—"

"—was almost late to your own finale!" Talia finishes for Marsh, and a laugh track plays in harmony with her giant face's deafening laughter. She's got that look in her eyes, that unstoppable glint when she's after a perfect shot.

"Talia, please, listen," Marsh tries again. She checks the euphoric comments once more, but there's no sign of Ezra yet. "This is serious."

"So is this," Talia replies, refusing to break character. "This is your finale, remember? Your last chance to get everything just right."

This is not working. Marsh frets.

She has to try something else.

She leans in, drops her voice. "Talia, I'm really sorry about in Hong Kong, when I grabbed the Show Bible from you," she says.

"That was quite the surprise," Talia agrees. She sighs. "I'd thought that telling you about it before your very first choice would comfort you, but it clearly complicated things. But don't worry. We don't need it anymore."

"What?" Marsh wails, horrified. "But—"

"This is the finale, Marsh!" Lights flare behind Talia, making her glow. "We don't need to keep notes or flip pages anymore. Everything ends here. You only have one choice left to make."

Marsh reels, panicking. The thought of her finale choice has always been terrifying, but it's even more so now without the Show Bible! How could Talia do this to her, in the final hour?

"Talia, the whole time, you've been telling me the Show Bible is the linchpin of my season, the map holding everything together, and now you want me to just—"

"Trust me. This is better. Simpler," Talia says.

She's almost too afraid to ask.

"What did you do with it? Did you . . . destroy it?"

"Don't be silly! That would be catastrophic. I've left it locked up at RealTV for safekeeping."

She winks—not to Marsh, but to the cameras.

"Also, at this point, I'd need a whole second van to get it here anyway."

Marsh pushes down a wave of dread as more confetti, more streamers, rain down to punctuate her joke.

Either Talia can't stop the finale, or she's under Ren's control, Marsh figures. She doesn't know which, but it doesn't matter, because the outcome is the same.

She can't help Marsh now.

"We can't film the finale yet," Marsh insists. "We have to—"

"You're right! There *is* something we have to do first!" Talia agrees. She spins toward the edge of the stage, and sweeps her arm grandly. "It's time to bring out our incredible cast! We know they wouldn't want to miss this very important moment!"

A blare of trumpets ushers Victor, Adrian, Jo, Bex, Harper, and Pickle—who's a potbellied pig now—onto the stage. They're awestruck, gaping at the fanfare, exclaiming things that Marsh can't hear over the music. With terror, she scans the rest of the stage as her friends and family spin around to take everything in.

Where is Ren?

"Oh my God, Mom," Harper cries, her mic finally kicking in. "You're the season three contestant? This is so cool!"

"*Harp!*" Marsh yells desperately. "Come here!"

She runs toward her mother—but Talia cuts her off halfway across the stage.

"Isn't it?" she gushes, and holds her own microphone to Harper. "Tell us how excited you are for your darling mom!"

Harper excitedly obeys, mesmerized by her giant face on the screen as she compliments her mother while Talia grins dazzlingly beside her.

"Talia, you have to stop the show," Marsh says. "I don't know where Ren is, but we have to find him. He's the one who—"

But a clash of music drowns her out, no matter how loud she yells.

"I can't believe it," Jo is repeating, over and over. "How are we supposed to find the Ísvængur here? The climate is all wrong!"

"Where's my clipboard? I don't remember this in the script . . ." Victor says, but they all scream and duck as a volcano goes off in the distance somewhere behind the screen, and the sky turns orange, then molten red.

"Holy mackerel, holy mackerel!" Pickle screeches, a parrot now, as he takes flight and tries to reach Marsh. "Holy mackerel!"

"Pickle, silly boy," Harper says, reaching up to give him a place to land on her hand as he passes, and he takes it.

Talia sends Harper back over to the rest of the cast, who now are all dressed like orchestra musicians. Pickle has become a monkey who can play a harp. Harper takes her place as the lead violin, and they begin to play the score for the episode as Talia turns to Marsh.

"Can we cut?" Marsh calls out to anyone who will listen, her voice barely controlled. "I need five with Talia. I can even change into better clothes and redo the entrance if you want!"

"I know it's scary, but we've been preparing for this since the very first day," Talia says, putting a comforting hand on her arm. "I promised you I'd be with you at every step, all the way through to your final decision, helping you make the best choices possible, so your life could be as wonderful as mine. All we have to do is make one more."

"Talia, you have to listen to me," Marsh begs again, even though she knows it's futile. Nothing she can say will stop her immaculate host from urging the show toward its conclusion before she can stop Chrysalis and make everything perfect, the way it should be.

She got so close, *so close,* but it wasn't enough. She's out of time.

What can she do?

Think!

"We've been hard at work behind the scenes, combing over every single page of your Show Bible, and we've come up with an incredible ending episode!" Talia's recording booms on the screen above them.

A huge spotlight pours down on Marsh, and the music shrieks. She watches as the gigantic screen she's standing in front of starts to change. The *All This and More* title disappears in a burst of confetti, and a beautiful, glittering image appears.

"Is that . . ." Marsh asks, recognizing the famous skyline.

"Your life has gone from good to great to *even better,*" Talia continues, as the image on the screen flashes between various famous buildings and landmarks. "You've managed to take hold of your career and are pursuing your passion at last, and you've built a happy, loving family. And now, it's all going to culminate in this final, epic scene."

Actual fireworks explode overhead.

"You've had the incredible chance to be a lawyer, and then law partner, with Victor and Jo. And now you can start a brand-new firm of your own in one of the most vibrant, exciting cities in the world—New York City!"

"New York?" Harper cries.

"It's incredible, right?" Talia agrees. "This could be the pinnacle of your career, Marsh! Everything you've ever wanted! Ren could transfer to the *New York Times* headquarters, and think of the access to music Harper would have. She could attend university at the legendary Juilliard School, and see live shows on Broadway!" She hugs her handheld microphone to her chest for a moment as she stares at Marsh. "Just think how happy she could be."

"But that's not all!" Talia's giant face shouts overhead.

The screen changes again, and this time, Marsh recognizes the image of this second place instantly. How could she not? It's one of the most picturesque, beloved cities in the world.

"Is that *London*?" Marsh stares.

"Exactly!" Talia cheers. "You could still be a lawyer—a scholar of international law, to be exact—but *here!*"

She points dramatically at the huge screen.

"Imagine how glamorous and romantic a life in such a historic, gorgeous city could be," she says. "You and Ren could stroll through Kensington Gardens every morning, have high tea, and visit some of the best museums and galleries every afternoon, and take Harper to see the London Symphony Orchestra every evening. She could get her degree from the Royal Academy of Music, Ren would be an award-winning international journalist, and you, an illustrious professor at the prestigious King's College!"

The music trills hysterically, earsplitting.

"What do you think?" Talia asks excitedly.

"I . . ." Marsh stares at the screen, absolutely confounded. Too much light, too much sound. She can't think through these options, much less figure out what to do. "I don't . . ."

Talia leans in. "You'll be on top of the world no matter what. All you have to do is choose."

Two short sentences appear in Sharp Purple lettering on the giant screen's deep black background.

Open up Marsh's own law firm in New York
Move Marsh's family to London

Marsh swallows nervously. She knows that billions of eyes are on her right now. Viewers all around the world have slid to the edges of their seats, and are holding their breaths as they wait for her to make her final decision. She remembers this moment well from season one, when she was watching Talia's finale episode of *All This and More*. How hard she was clutching the armrest of her couch, and how fast her heart was beating.

K8theGr8: <Please please please, choose New York!>
Melekbebek: <No, London!>
RedMoon: < لندن بتحبك! >
LoboAzul: <¡Ven a Nueva York!>

The words explode like fireworks in her vision. Marsh scans the comments yet again, but there's still no sign of Ezra.

"Thank you, everyone, for tuning in with us this season! As we prepare to open the Bubble and rejoin the world, we must suspend the comments, but we've loved sharing every minute of Marsh's journey with you!" Talia says, waving like a beauty pageant queen.

Notamackerel: <No! They can't turn us off! Where's SharpTruth when we
    need him??>
Moms4Marsh: <We love you, Marsh!!!>

It's the last thing Marsh sees before the comment window closes with
terrifying finality.

She waits nervously, but it's true.

Gone—all of them.

Even Ezra.

It's just her now, alone, facing this impossible final choice.

"Remember, Marsh . . . you could have *All This* . . ." Talia singsongs. The
whole set presses in around her.

"*And* . . ." Marsh tries.

Talia's eyes grow even larger, encouraging her.

"*And* . . ."

She can't do it, she knows.

This isn't right!

She's not ready.

Not to make this choice, and not to end her season.

Not like this.

"What?" Talia asks.

"I can't," Marsh blurts out. "I can't do this."

Talia looks tense. The TV-glamorous smile on her face is growing more
strained by the second, struggling to remain plastered serenely across her
face.

"What do you mean, Marsh?" she asks. "You have to. This is the season
finale."

Marsh shakes her head. "No. I'm not ready."

"You have to be," Talia replies through gritted teeth. She scoots a little
closer to her and puts a hand on her shoulder.

"After all, look at your new life! With the choices you've made, you've
managed to find true love again with a great guy! Viewers absolutely love
Ren, Marsh. He's a total crowd favorite. And you managed to completely
overhaul your career, and you're now doing what you've always wanted to!
Not only that, but I know how much it means to you that you were able to do
so much for Harper," Talia continues. "She's on fire—such talent and passion
for music! It's incredible."

Another round of fireworks goes off to punctuate her speech.

"I think you did pretty good, Marsh," Talia continues at last. For a moment, her expression isn't the TV-glamorous one, but softer and kinder, more like how it was the first day she—nervous, excited, and totally out of her depth—began her own journey as the very first episode of *All This and More* aired, and changed the world forever. "I might even say it's perfect."

Her eyes glint hungrily as she says the word, her polished expression failing for just an instant before becoming serene again.

"Wouldn't you?"

Marsh hesitates, helpless.

It's true that Ren did make a mess, and nearly destroyed the Bubble a second time, but it's also undeniable that he did help her improve her life. He supported her through law school, he became a parent to Harper, he gave up careers, he moved countries. He changed everything about himself— hundreds of times. He did everything he could to try to make Marsh happier.

And he *did* make her happier.

Part of her wonders, could she have accomplished everything she has in her season *without Ren*?

Overhead, euphoric music booms.

"Now, let's see those options again!" Talia's giant face exclaims.

Marsh spins around as the Bubble's cameras appear, and all loom in on her. The cheesy music crescendos, and the lenses press in so close that her breath fogs all the glass.

"What'll it be, Marsh?" Talia asks Marsh. "What do you choose?"

SharpTruth601: <Marsh, I'm here>

The comment fizzles and glitches, a kaleidoscope of fonts, but it's there, briefly. Her heart soars.

SharpTruth601: <I think I know what you're—>
[ERROR]
SharpTruth601: <I can't go with you>
[ERROR]
SharpTruth601: <But I can open the way>
[ERROR]
SharpTruth601: <Just give me a sign>

Finally, Marsh turns to Talia.

"Okay," she says. "I know what I choose."

"That's the spirit, Marsh!" Talia says. "For the last time this season, let's remind our awesome viewers that . . ."

Her voice rises slightly, taking on a musical quality as she begins to sing-song the show's name. Words that have become a prayer chanted by billions of people in the world, a dream desperately held by nearly every living soul.

"You could have *All This* . . ." Talia sings.

Marsh grins, determined.

". . . Or *light it on fire* instead," she answers.

Talia, confused, opens her mouth to reply.

But Marsh takes off at a dead sprint.

"No! Wait!" Talia cries, but she's so startled, she can't leap into action to stop Marsh before she's already run past. *"Marsh!!"*

SharpTuth602: <Go!>
[ERROR]

Marsh throws her whole body into it, her legs pumping and her lungs heaving, running like her life depends on it, because it does.

SharpTruth603: <Go! Go! Go!>
SharpTruth603: <You can do this, Marsh!>
SharpTruth603: <And when you find Lev again, tell him I—>
[ERROR]
[WARNING: BUBBLE UNSTABLE]
[EMERGENCY PROCESSES ACTIVATED]

If Talia catches her, it's over. Marsh will never have another chance to make this life right—to make it *hers*—before it's over.

This show was already impossible, and it was even more impossible that Marsh managed to get so far, despite all the obstacles.

This finale is her one, only shot in the world to make everything *perfect*.

And she will not give that up.

JUMP CUT

Marsh lands hard midrun, and the sticks and leaves slide beneath her feet as she scrambles, then trips. Trees loom in overhead, and the air is turning to white puffs in front of her lips in the chill.

She made it.

She puts her head to the ground and thanks Ezra silently.

He sent her exactly where she was trying to go.

"Are you okay? I told you not to wear those shoes!" Jo calls.

Marsh stands and brushes off her knees. Behind her at the car, Jo is holding a duffel bag and a big plastic cooler. Birds scream as they tear across the sky.

She smiles as she stares back at the woods.

She couldn't find Dylan in the regular season episodes, but she'd forgotten about the recap—that all-important bonus footage that's also in the Bubble with her, containing the most significant moments of her life, and their relationship. Places and times where she knows for *certain* that he was with her.

Marsh is finally going to find him here—at the camping trip from her sophomore year of college where they first met.

Jo bumps the door closed with her hip. "Come on, I want to get a good spot."

"I'll get it!" Marsh grabs the cooler from her. She rounds a tangled cluster of pine and bursts into the campsite clearing.

"Finally!" one of their classmates says. "If you're the ones in charge of bringing the booze, you have to get here first, not last."

"Those roads are snowy in some spots!" Jo shoots back, dragging their fold-out chairs into the circle of seats and blankets already there. "We should have done this spring semester, not fall."

Marsh opens the cooler and passes the beers around. Someone tells her to take a can, but she waves them off absentmindedly.

Where is he?

"Marsh," Jo says. "Help me with our tent before it gets dark."

A sack of poles and folded fabric drops into Marsh's arms, and Jo drags her to a spot of firm ground, just like she did the first time. Marsh is still scanning the crowd as she opens the sack, and everything slides out in a clanging tumble, which makes Jo laugh.

Where is Dylan?

Marsh and Jo did arrive last out of everyone, which means Dylan already has to be here somewhere, maybe trying to start the campfire, or maybe over by the cars, helping Mateo to get the food they're going to grill for dinner ready.

Mateo, she realizes. Dylan's roommate.

She just has to find Mateo.

Marsh sprints away from the almost-finished shelter back toward the group before Jo can even register what's happening. Most of the other tents are already set up, and she darts between them, peeking inside each open flap, but Mateo is nowhere to be found. She goes faster and faster, until there are no more left, and her heart might hammer itself right out of her chest.

Then at last, she spots Mateo! He's holding one side of the big inflatable raft a group of guys is carrying to the lake just past the trees.

"Mateo!" Marsh cries, so happily that it makes him laugh. She and Mateo knew each other, but they weren't close enough friends to warrant the crushing hug she envelops him in now.

"Someone's excited for camping!" He laughs awkwardly, straightening his flannel shirt once Marsh releases him.

"Mateo, let's go!" someone shouts. "The lake waits for no one!"

"Quit your whining!" Mateo shouts back, hefting his yellow handle higher. "Want to come?"

"Yes," Marsh says, even though she didn't want to the first time.

Mateo gives Marsh his spot. "Stand here, I'll go to the other side." Then he stops to catch the attention of someone else who's approaching.

Yes, Marsh prays. *This is the moment!*

"Oh, by the way, this is my roommate this semester," Mateo says.

"Finally," she sighs, and turns to practically collapse into Dylan's arms.

Thank God.

"Uh, hi," Ren says, holding out a hand. "Nice to meet you."

No.

No, no, *no.*

Marsh doesn't realize she's tripped until her elbows hit the ground, the dried pine needles like hot pins against her skin.

"Marsh! Are you hurt?" Mateo asks.

"No," she says, but that's not what she means.

Dylan's not here.

Ren has replaced him in her recap, too.

It can't be. She refuses to believe it. There *must* be somewhere else . . .

"Here, take my hand," Ren says.

"Get away from me," Marsh says as he reaches out, lurching to her feet before he can help her up. "Get away."

"What?" Ren asks, but she's already running, as far and as fast as she can. Branches whip her face as she weaves between the trees. She doesn't know what's happening, but she does know that she has to get out of here. If Dylan isn't in this moment, she'll just have to find him in another.

But he's not in the next jump. Or the next.

Or the next.

Family vacations, long car rides, Dylan's proposal, their wedding, Harper's birth, a vet appointment with Pickle, a surprise birthday party, watching the first episode of Talia's magical season one together, a winter holiday in front of a campfire. Marsh flashes through more memories than she can count. No matter where she goes, Dylan is nowhere.

But Ren, in some form or another, is in all of them.

She spots him in one corner of one moment, and then walking toward Marsh waving in the next. There he is again in another, and another, every time waiting for her, ready to welcome her with open arms, until Marsh is moving so quickly, everything is just a blur.

To go to the moment that

She jumps before she can even read the rest of the choice, trying not to waste even a minute.

To go to

But then she's gone again.

To g

And again.

Because Marsh refuses to believe that Dylan is just gone.

He has to be *somewhere*. She just has to find him.

And at last, she thinks she knows where to look.

The last place she'd ever want to.

As soon as she jumps, the light turns yellow, and Marsh slams on the brakes. The tires squeal frantically, searching for purchase—her car skids to a jolting stop just before the intersection.

Marsh relaxes her death grip on the steering wheel. It's night, and the sleepy road is empty except for her. She waits impatiently as the red drags on and on, almost as if taunting her.

Come on, she urges the light as it glares back, refusing to change.

She doesn't have time for this.

Marsh edges off the brake and creeps into the intersection, braced for another car to suddenly appear. Then she floors it and disappears across the double white lines and down the lane. She doesn't let off until she whips into the parking lot and skids into the first spot.

Her hand shakes as she turns off the engine.

This time, it's too dark to see if there are two cars huddled at the far end of the community college lot, glistening with rain, or not. In front of her, the familiar lobby doors loom.

No matter where she's looked, Dylan's nowhere to be found. But maybe it was because she was searching in the wrong places. In the wrong kind of memories.

Marsh regards the still, silent building for a long time, terrified. Because if he's not here . . .

She doesn't know where else he could be.

With a deep breath, she pops the door, and begins the long walk.

At last, at the top of the stairs, Marsh pauses just like she did last time. She takes out her compact of powder and looks at it, wondering if it matters or if she has to put it on to make the rest of the moment match.

She does, just in case.

She hurries down the seventh-floor corridor to Dylan's office. There's no reason she needs to hesitate—she already knows what's in there—but she still does. Her hand still trembles on the cool metal doorknob, her fingers still refuse to close and turn it so that the room will open to her. Her stomach still feels slick with dread.

But she has to do this.

She has to find Dylan.

Marsh throws open the door and bursts into the room, ready to grab him and run.

Except Dylan isn't there—again.

Only the woman is.

She's sitting in his chair, legs crossed as she looks out the window, facing partially away from Marsh. Her dress is black and tight. A delicate jasmine perfume hangs in the air.

In person, and during the recap, this moment was too raw and awful for Marsh to watch. This really is the first time she's *really* looked at Dylan's mistress. Or the side of her, rather. Even so, she doesn't know how she didn't recognize her, even as shocked as she was.

But as Marsh stares at her now, at that familiar, famous face, that powerful outfit—and most of all, that slice of signature Sharp Purple dye down one side of her glossy dark bob—the resemblance is unmistakable.

"I was wondering when you'd finally show up," Claire Sharp says.

Her voice is soft, sensual, as if she's been expecting Marsh, or maybe she thinks Marsh is Dylan, by accident. Marsh stares, spellbound, struggling to understand.

None of it seems possible. How would Dylan even meet Claire? And even if he did, how could it have ever come to this? Why would a billionaire businesswoman like Claire give a complete stranger like Dylan the time of day—let alone an illicit night?

Something feels so off about this, even more off than an affair could feel, but she can't put her finger on it. It's wrapped up too neat, the bow tied too tight.

It's too *perfect,* she can't help but think.

As she stares in horrified awe, Claire slowly begins to turn in her chair.

Marsh wants to run, but she's rooted to the spot. She watches Claire's expression change from seductive to surprised as she completes her graceful spin and their eyes meet.

"You," she says, and for a moment, Marsh thinks she means that she recognizes *Marsh,* too, even though that's impossible. "You're not Chris."

"Chris," Marsh repeats. "Who's Chris?"

"We thought it would be sexier not to use each other's real names."

Of course, Marsh realizes.

Chrysalis.

She doesn't know where Ren is, whether he's not in this jump cut or still on his way, but it doesn't matter. It's clear that Dylan's not here, either.

"I think Chris isn't coming," Claire says, growing more uncertain by the moment of what's going on.

Marsh shakes her head sadly. She's not even mad. Claire might not know what's happening right now, just like the rest of the trapped season two crew.

"He's not," she says.

Because he's not anywhere.

Did she miss him somehow, in an earlier jump when she went too fast? But she looked everywhere in those memories. She's sure. She knew exactly where he'd be in each, and yet he wasn't. Every significant moment, every important kernel of history, and he's been erased from them all.

This moment was Marsh's last chance, her best bet, and still nothing.

But if Dylan's not here, in this last possible place—where can he be at all?

"Maybe I should go," Claire adds, rising from her chair.

"No," Marsh says. "I'm the one who should go."

She doesn't know what else to do, or where else to jump. She just knows she can't stay.

Marsh stumbles through a set of heavy wooden doors and trips over a rug, throwing a tumbling echo of footsteps across the stone floor.

"Shit!" she curses as she catches herself on her hands and knees, and winces at the way the walls bend her voice back at her in the broken silence.

After a few moments, she picks herself up from the rug.

Now what?

She's exhausted, out of ideas, and almost out of time. But she can't give up. She has to find Dylan. She has to fix this. She *has to.*

But what can she do?

Then she hears it.

One small word that only she and one other person know, and said in a voice she'd recognize anywhere, anytime.

". . . Mallow?"

Marsh turns around.

Dylan.

He's here—he's *here*—standing in front of her, in the flesh.

"Dylan!" Marsh shrieks, launching herself into his arms.

"Mallow? *Mallow!* Oh, thank God!" he's shouting back, and then he's holding her, familiar and crushing as he clings to her in a desperate embrace.

"I've been trying to find you everywhere, and everywhen!" Marsh wails into his shoulder. "Everything about you—our photos, our friends' memories, all gone! Then I tried to call you, but your phone number disappeared from my contacts, and then—"

"What? Disappeared?" He gasps, pulling back to stare at her.

"Yes! Like you never existed! You just *vanished* after the midseason special!" she yells at him through tears. "Why did you leave like that?"

"I didn't leave!" Dylan says. "I mean, I did—but I didn't mean to leave for *good*! I was mad about the show, and just wanted to go home and clear my head. Then, when I tried to go over to your house the next day to talk about it, things were . . . They were *different*. I couldn't find you or Harper. I couldn't find anything, the harder I tried."

"What?" Marsh asks, confused.

"It was like the more I tried to reach you, the harder it was to move,"

Dylan says. "Things were closing in. Streets turning around on me, buildings disappearing . . . someone following me, it felt like! So I ran. I finally thought I might be safe here, but then when I tried to leave, I couldn't get out." He waves his arms around. "I've been stuck here ever since."

Finally, Marsh has calmed down enough to look around for the first time.

Where is *"here"?* she wonders as she examines the scene. Where are the two of them? And why would it be where Dylan got stuck?

They're in a big, multistory building, with shelves full of books all around them. The walls are stone, the light is soft and gray through the tall windows, and the air is even stiller than usual for a grand, serious place like this.

"Are we . . ." Marsh furrows her brow. "Are we in our old university library?"

Dylan nods. "Yeah. The day before our freshman year." He points at the wall clock behind them. "Welcome orientation is supposed to start in an hour. But the time never changes."

Marsh shivers. "Weird."

"Yeah," he agrees. "But thank goodness you chose this moment. We never would have found each other otherwise."

"It was a fluke," Marsh admits. "I didn't know where I was going. I was just looking for somewhere safe."

"Somewhere safe?" Dylan frowns. "Marsh, what's been happening out there, the second half of this season?"

Marsh takes an exhausted breath.

How can she even *begin* to explain?

"Try me," Dylan says, reading her expression. "I do know a thing or two about quantum bubbling."

"This is about so much more than just the Bubble now," she replies.

She sighs.

"If you say, *I told you so,* I swear, I will leave you here."

Dylan holds up a solemn hand. "Just tell me what's going on."

She has to close her eyes to say it.

"It turns out that Chrysalis . . . is Ren."

For once, instead of firing back with a witty rejoinder, Dylan bites his tongue and waits.

Quickly, she explains everything that happened after he disappeared—that Ren has been sneaking around behind the scenes this entire season, pulling strings and trying to influence Marsh's choices, the same way he did in his own season.

"Harper," Dylan says, as soon as she finishes.

"She's safe," Marsh replies. Ren would never hurt her. "And she doesn't know. I tried to tell Talia, but she wouldn't listen. That's why I ran. To find you."

Dylan's shoulders sag, heavy with relief. "I'm glad you did."

"But I almost couldn't! I've been everywhere in our life together, and you were nowhere," she says, shuddering at how close she came to missing Dylan before her time ran out. "I even . . . I even went to your office, that night. And nothing. I'd run out of places to try, and was just running. I didn't know you were even here on this day!"

"I think that's just it, though," Dylan says softly.

"What do you mean?" she asks.

"You said Ren had found a way into every significant life moment you could think of with me, including that day camping, when we met for the first time. At some point in your relationship, Ren must have asked you, or you must have told him about that first time you saw me. That's how he knew how to get there and replace me."

Dylan points up to indicate the library all around them.

"But, this is the first time *I* saw *you*. You didn't know about this moment, either—and so neither did Ren. Only I did." He swallows. "I could never forget it."

Marsh looks at him. Slowly, she turns around to face the quiet library, to take it in.

She remembers the day now, sort of. There were hints of this moment in the recap, but only from her perspective, of course, not his. Marsh had slipped away from the orientation tour to come into this room to look at all the law books. They were so mysterious and imposing, such huge leather-bound tomes stacked from floor to ceiling, with gold-leaf lettering on all the well-worn spines. She just wanted to run her fingers along one of the shelves, to feel the supple material of the covers and dream of the day when she'd soon start reading them all, as a prelaw student.

She hadn't known anyone was watching her.

But apparently Dylan had been.

"Mallow," he says, when she turns to him.

But before Marsh can respond, there's a boom—the big double doors that lead out of the library being thrown open.

"Damn," Ren pants, and leans over to put his hands on his knees, apparently winded from running. He checks his watch. "The finale's half over. We're almost out of time."

Dylan is in front of Marsh now. He's trying to push her away from the main doors, back toward the study areas, where there's a secondary exit.

"Marsh," he says under his breath. "On three, when I say go—"

"Calm down. I'm not going to hurt you," Ren says, waving a hand.

"You expect us to believe that?" Dylan shouts. "You trapped me in this frozen scene for who knows how long! You erased me from the show! You—"

"It wasn't like that, I swear," Ren says, looking at Marsh. "I was just trying to simplify things. To make the paths easier."

"By manipulating me?" Marsh counters. "How could you?"

"Please. Don't you see?" He shakes his head, frustrated, overwhelmed. "I thought you'd understand."

But Marsh is too angry to listen.

"Understand? You tricked me!"

She stabs an accusatory finger at him.

"My life was part of your *fucking season*."

Everything—not just what happened to Marsh here, in her episodes, but also what happened in *Ren's*—was all planned. The hundreds of bad Love-Match dates, the loneliness, the inescapable rut she couldn't climb out of alone, was all him. Carefully, purposefully engineered to lead her to him.

Even . . . even the affair.

"Chris," Claire Sharp had called Dylan when Marsh stumbled upon her in his office.

Like Chrysalis.

It was ultimately Dylan's fault that he chose to cheat, but was the fact that it was Claire he met more orchestrated than she'd known at the time? Because it seems impossible that in the real world, Dylan would ever have been able to cross paths with a woman like Claire, as powerful and rich and busy as she is, let alone get to know her and convince her to have an affair with him. The founder of Sharp Incorporated would have given him one second of attention, if even that.

But if you could redo that one second a million times, putting things together *over and over again,* until everyone finally does exactly what you want, and you get it exactly the way you like . . .

Until it's perfect . . .

"They weren't your choices to make," Marsh finally says.

"Were they yours, either?" he asks.

Marsh glares.

"What's the difference, anyway?" Ren asks, throwing up his hands. "Everything I did, both seasons, was all for you."

He sighs and wavers slightly. He looks exhausted, worn to the bone, like he might collapse at any moment.

"I've never stopped loving you, all these years," Ren finally continues. "But I waited too long to tell you, and then it was too late. You'd met Dylan, and then you were married, and then you had Harper, and then it was decades too late. The show was *it*. My last chance to fix our lives. To make you as happy as you were always supposed to be."

He closes his eyes and shakes his head.

"But it's one thing when you're just trying to improve your own life. The more people you add, the more complicated it gets. So many threads to unknot, so many strands to follow."

"What did you do?" Dylan demands. "What did you *do*?"

"I just—I was desperate," Ren answers, but he's looking at Marsh. "There was so much I had to accomplish, and too many rules in the way."

"Ren," Marsh repeats. "What did you do?"

"It took an entire episode, but it was worth it," he says. "I made myself a journalist—went back and sent myself around the world after school where I knew there had been big stories, backfilled my résumé with clips, turned it into my whole career. Then I wrote a big piece on quantum bubbling and Sharp Entertainment."

Of course, Marsh remembers.

The big article he told her about in her recap, that made his career take off.

"You could pretend to need expert interviews," she says at last, understanding now.

Ren nods. "Before your season, the crew was always in the Bubble, too. The low-level coders at Sharp Labs gave me a tour, and showed me how everything worked," Ren continues. "How the Bubble closes and opens, how they change scenes, how the security filters are triggered."

He can't help but smile.

"I snuck back in at night and made myself the system administrator, so I could edit every aspect of every episode. Then I changed the password, so no one could undo it."

"You idiot. You fucking idiot!" Dylan shouts. "It could have been so much worse. It could have been the actual end of reality!"

"Or not!" he yells back. "Or it could have been everything I wanted!"

Marsh puts her head in her hands.

"You changed the password to 'Chrysalis,' didn't you?" she finally asks.

"That's how I thought of the Bubble," he tells her, his voice full of wonder. "Like our little cocoon, from which this perfect butterfly could emerge, at the end."

"Or like the butterfly effect," she can't help but say.

"Small, seemingly innocent changes that can lead to unpredictable consequences," Dylan murmurs. It was one of his favorite remarks to make about *All This and More,* every time they watched Talia make a choice.

Back when they were just viewers of the show—not contestants.

"That isn't fair," Ren rasps, his words like acid. "Of course everything was going to be messy at first! What rough draft starts out error-free? Especially one as important as this? This was about happiness, about *life*. It was going to require risks."

His eyes darken.

"But I didn't get the chance. When Alexis realized what was going on, she told Claire, who filed the lawsuit. Alexis and Claire said that what I'd done was too dangerous, and decided to pull me out at the midseason special, and cut the show prematurely. I begged her and Claire to reconsider. I was at the start of my season—everything had been pulled apart, but I still needed to put it back together! But they wouldn't listen. They wouldn't let me finish. They were just going to leave all of our lives in pieces."

His hands curl themselves into fists.

"I couldn't allow that to happen. Not when we could have had so much more," Ren says. "My last choice was to make you the season three contestant."

He looks longingly at Marsh.

"So that we could try again."

For a long moment, none of them say anything. The silence is so intense, it has its own atmosphere, like a heavy, dark fog.

Despite how angry Marsh is, it hurts her to see Ren so despairing. After not one, but *two* seasons, of trying everything he could think of to win her over, no matter the cost, he's nothing left to give. He's a tree hollowed out, a heart bled dry.

And she knows that even so, if ten more episodes magically appeared right now, he'd do it all over again for her.

That's how much he loves her.

"You're a monster," Dylan says.

"Oh, am I?" Ren snorts. "You're not perfect, either. Far from it. You're telling me you wouldn't undo all the bad—all the pain—you've caused the people you love, if you had the chance?"

Dylan scowls, but Marsh can see by the guilt on his face that what Ren said cut deep.

"Even if you had succeeded in season two and gotten everything you wanted, none of it would be real," he says at last.

"'None of it would be real,'" Ren repeats, rolling his eyes. "Grow up, Dylan."

"It's selfish," Dylan says.

But Ren simply turns to Marsh. "I was just trying to make you happy. In my season, and now in yours. I did everything I could. To make your life—our life—better. Is that selfish?"

"Marsh, let's go." Dylan takes her hand.

"No, don't look at him," Ren demands. "Look at me. Stay with me. We can still fix this, Marsh. Ignore how angry you are at me for a second. Just think about the show, and everything we accomplished. Where you started, and where you are now. Everything I did for you. Everything I changed."

His stare is so desperate, so determined, that despite everything that's happened, it's hard not to listen to him.

"We don't need Chrysalis anymore, now that you know everything," he says. "We can choose each other, and everything we've built here, at the finale. Everything you've wanted, your whole life. You can be the incredible lawyer you deserve to be, Harper can stay at Pallissard, and we can be together. We can have perfect."

His eyes shimmer, huge and dark, as he smiles.

"Or pretty damn close, right?"

Marsh looks down. She doesn't want to recall that line, but it was true when she said it half a season ago, just before the midseason special.

She doesn't want to admit that Ren is right.

Because she really *is* happy.

Things *are* pretty perfect.

Ren is pretty perfect.

Suddenly, her arm almost yanks out of its socket.

"Now!" Dylan yells, hauling them toward the back exit of the library before Ren can react.

"Marsh!" Ren cries.

"Run!"

Marsh lets Dylan drag her away, faster in his terror than Ren is in his dogged determination. But even as the two of them lurch through the old, musty corridors, passing genre after genre, shelf after shelf, Marsh can't deny that even though Ren did a terrible thing, deep down, she can understand why.

She knows things about the show that Dylan never can, even with his fancy physics degree. Because the show isn't about fairness, or realness, when it all comes down to it. The show is about life. Her *life*. The only one she's got.

Ren was acting out of desperation and love. Can she really blame him for what he did?

If she'd had his chance, could she have resisted the same temptation, either?

THE PLAN

"I think we lost him," Marsh finally says as she and Dylan stumble to a halt, her voice ragged with exhaustion. Her legs wobble, and Dylan doubles over panting.

"Who knows for how long, though," he says once he's gotten his breath back. "What do we do now?"

"I have no idea!" Marsh replies. "I was hoping you would! You're the physics genius, aren't you?"

"But this is *your* show!" he replies, glancing around. "Why does it look like this?"

"I don't know," Marsh admits.

They're standing on their old street in Phoenix, in front of their suburban house, but everything looks like it's two-dimensional—the homes, the trees, the cars—like a wooden, wallpapered backdrop on a movie set instead of the real thing.

"I think we're behind the scenes or something," she finally says.

Dylan shudders. "That's creepy."

Marsh nods.

Even as grim as the situation is, she can't help but notice that the flower garden next to their front door would look better with pink or yellow blooms, not red. The urge to tinker prickles, a thorn in her side.

"How much time do we have left?" she asks, turning away.

They're just flowers. But they do look better now, vibrant fuchsia and marigold against the light blue wall.

Dylan, oblivious, checks his watch. "Fifteen minutes, maybe," he answers. "Twenty, if they've cut the commercials."

"Shit," Marsh frets, tangling her fingers in her sweaty hair.

"They wouldn't just . . . end the show without letting you make your last choice, would they?" Dylan asks her.

She shrugs nervously. "I don't know."

Dylan rubs his face. "Great," he mutters. "Just great."

Marsh fidgets as he begins to pace.

"I'm so sorry," she finally says, but it comes out weakly. "I just thought, there were so many things I wish I'd done, and . . ."

"No, I'm sorry," Dylan cuts her off. He faces her square on, and looks her in the eyes. "For a lot of things. But especially the affair."

Marsh is so surprised, she can't speak. She actually can't remember now—did he never apologize for it? If he did, not well enough, anyway.

"Part of it was Ren's fault," she offers, a small olive branch.

"Maybe." He shrugs. "But the rest of it was mine. I should have been better."

She makes a small sound, like the start of a cry being smothered, and bites her lip to stop the tears from escaping.

"I hurt you, and I hurt Harper. I was weak, and greedy, and wrong. I . . ."

But suddenly, Dylan trails off midsentence.

"Goddamnit, Dylan," Marsh snaps, throwing up her hands in disgust. "Are you kidding me? I mean, what did I expect? That you were actually going to take the blame for something, for once? That—"

"Shh," Dylan interrupts, waving his hand.

Marsh gasps, floored. She's about to unload on him for that, but she stops short when sees his expression.

He doesn't look upset or guilty anymore. He looks *excited*. His shoulders are hitched up right around his ears—just like whenever he's mid-lecture at school, or hovering over his research, and has just thought of something new.

"Tell me you have a plan," she says desperately.

Dylan turns to her.

"What if instead of trying to escape Ren, we beat him at his own game?" he proposes.

"What do you mean?" Marsh frowns.

Dylan is pacing again, faster now, deep in thought.

"What did you say, back in the midseason special?" he asks. "That Talia has some kind of book that contains every choice you've made, or could make?"

"The Show Bible," Marsh answers.

Yes! she realizes.

Dylan wants the two of them to steal Marsh's huge binder from RealTV. With that book, they would have access to every single piece of information from this season to help make Marsh's final choice. And with Dylan's understanding of physics, they might still be able to pull off a perfect ending after all!

"But it's a mess, because of Chrysalis," Marsh frets. "Thousands of pages, so big that Talia can no longer move it around. Who knows what it looks like now. Even if we can reach it, what if we flip to the end, and the choices there are—"

"No, no," Dylan says. "Not the end of the Show Bible. I want us to do the opposite."

"Flip to the beginning?" Marsh asks. "But why? We're in the finale. We're out of time. Don't we want to change the end?"

He shakes his head. "I mean, maybe we could do that, but with only one choice left, even with the book as a reference, we still run the risk of having some of these other negative changes remain when the Bubble opens."

Marsh studies him for a moment.

"You think there's a better way out," she says.

"Maybe." He pauses. "This whole mess we're in is because Ren tried to cheat the system by manipulating your season three, right?" He takes a breath and steps closer to her. "But what if he hadn't?"

"Hadn't cheated?" Marsh asks.

Dylan shakes his head. "Hadn't made a season three."

Marsh stares at him, trying to follow his train of thought, but she doesn't get it at first.

Then she understands.

Holy mackerel.

"If we can get ahold of the Show Bible, instead of trying to control the path forward like Ren did, we can use it to go *back*." He makes a fist. "All the way back, Mallow. All the way to the pilot episode. To . . . reality."

"Before I made any choices," Marsh says.

He takes Marsh's hand. "We could undo everything that's happened. Our lives will be back to the original version again, and you and Harper"—he looks hesitantly into her eyes—"and me. Imperfectly, but together at least, could start over again. We could have a chance."

He stares at Marsh, begging her to agree, as her heart hammers in her chest.

It's a ludicrous plan. Ren is still chasing them, they're almost out of time, and RealTV is on lockdown.

It seems impossible. And probably very dangerous.

"You're sure this will work?" Marsh finally asks him.

"No," he confesses. "But do you have a better idea?"

ALL THIS . . .

The RealTV studio has transformed again since Marsh saw it last.

The roof is at least twice as tall, and every surface is now made of tinted reflective glass, turning the building into an ink-black mirror in the night. Across the front, the network's logo is lit up in full neon—the dark sky glows with the sizzling red lights.

The word CHRYSALISTV glares back at Marsh, each letter taller than she is.

"That does not look very inviting," Dylan says. "At all."

"Nope," she agrees nervously.

Up close, she can see through the window tint that the lobby looks empty inside. Nothing moving, nothing making noise. A camera in the corner of the awning watches her and Dylan with a dim crimson eye.

Marsh tests the door, but of course, it's locked.

"Don't suppose Talia gave you a key?" Dylan asks.

She shakes her head. "Should we try to pick the lock?"

"Not enough time. I think we should just break the glass."

"What if there's an alarm?"

He shrugs. "Then we'll have to move fast."

Slowly, they both look back at the door.

Marsh picks up a brick-sized rock from the Zen garden–style landscape beside the concrete walkway and hands it to Dylan.

He passes it hand to hand, testing.

"Well, here goes nothing," he says.

Marsh expects a blaring siren as the rock crashes through the glass, but the night remains quiet after the shatter. Or maybe it's just a silent alarm. Either way, after a few moments, she lets out the breath curdling in her lungs, and they inch forward.

Dylan chooses another rock to scrape away the remaining shards so Marsh can stick her arm through and unlock the door from the inside.

"Ready?" he asks.

"As I'll ever be," she says.

In the foyer, the lights are low, everything just an outline of itself.

Somewhere, a clock is ticking, and the computer at the receptionist's vacant desk hums in its electronic slumber.

Marsh half expects Talia to be waiting just inside the entrance, all of the set pieces of her finale transported with her, grinning maniacally as she holds out her microphone.

But so far, the room remains empty, and she and Dylan are alone.

"Where to first?" he asks.

"Maybe Talia's office," Marsh suggests. "It's this way."

But the Show Bible isn't there—or at the hair and makeup counters, or in any of the greenrooms, or the conference area. Marsh begins ducking into every door she passes as she and Dylan work their way toward the back of the studio, just in case, but the nearer they draw, the more she knows there's only one place the Show Bible could be.

Marsh grips the metal handle of the door to the soundstage, and jumps at how cold it is. The darkened ON AIR sign at the top of the wall looks strange in its sleepy, standby state.

Slowly, she lets Dylan and herself in.

The stage is silent and still. Only the safety lights are on, but it's enough to see. Cameras, duct tape, gauzy light diffusers, and some discarded pages of Talia's script from the preseason teasers slowly come into focus in the dimness of the frame.

The two of them creep to the edge of the black curtain wings and stop there, listening for movement before they emerge into the open. Quickly, secretly, Marsh makes the stage just a little bit bigger. This is the first time Dylan's seeing it, and she wants it to seem grander, more important.

"So, this is where it started?" he asks softly.

Marsh nods. She can't help the flicker of nostalgia that finds her, in the darkness. Every moment of that first episode is viscerally fresh. She points to the fraying X of tape at the center mark. "I made the first choice right there."

She's sure Dylan is wondering what that decision was.

"I, um . . ."

"It doesn't matter." He turns to look at her. "None of it was real."

Marsh hesitates, unsure of what to say to that. She's glad that it's too dark for him to see her expression.

Because . . . the adrenaline rush, standing in front of the other lawyers in her firm's boardroom. The electric, thrilling shiver on her skin whenever Ren touched her. The desperation every time she hurtled herself backward in time, earlier and earlier in her marriage, searching for a way to save all of the history she and Dylan had built together. The pride she felt while watching Harper raise her bow at the head of the orchestra . . .

All of that certainly *felt real.*

"Come on," Dylan whispers. "Let's check the producer's booth."

Together, they creep out of the wings, onto the stage. Just beyond the top row of the audience, Marsh can see it—a giant black cubicle where the sound mixer, lights manager, and director sit during filming. It's an imposing structure already, but even in the semidarkness and from this angle, it's clear that there's something huge hulking over the edge of its vast desk.

A monstrous, book-shaped something.

"There," Marsh points.

"We've only got a few minutes," Dylan says.

"Let's make this fast, then."

They take off across the stage at a run. But before they reach the edge of it and drop down into the audience, all the lights come on at full blast, a garish swirl of color and shapes flooding the stage, and the *All This and More* music begins to blare.

"What's going on?!" Dylan asks as they cower.

The slow click of heels on hard floor echoes over the chaotic soundtrack. Marsh turns toward the wings to see Talia Cruz emerge from the darkness and saunter onstage. As she enters, the lights pause their flashing and the music suddenly shuts off, as if scared into silence.

"Well! This has been *quite* the finale," she purrs in the newfound quiet. "So many surprise twists."

"Talia!" Marsh exclaims. "Thank God! You have to help us. We—"

"Oh! And I'm *so glad* you finally found Harper's wayward father," she continues, her golden season finale gown sparkling as she turns to him. "Hello, Dylan."

Her voice is generous, but her eyes are too focused, too sharp. Marsh isn't sure she's blinked yet.

Back at the original finale set, Marsh assumed Talia was trapped in Chrysalis's thrall, unable to tell anything was wrong.

She seems different now.

"Let's jazz things up, shall we?" Talia suggests, and snaps her fingers.

Suddenly, the stage shifts. It's no longer a TV studio. Everything is dark, and there's a disco ball rotating overhead, casting little flecks of rainbow light across the dim room. Crooning music swells. Marsh, Dylan, and Talia are standing at the center of the dance floor, surrounded by a crowd of couples—all from the season two crew—slowly swaying to the tune. Charles dips Alexis; Julie waltzes with Claire. Sarah and Rafael gently twirl.

"What?" Dylan gasps over the song. "What's going on? Where are we now?"

Marsh stares down at the Sharp Purple chiffon dress now on her body.

Oh no.

"It looks like my senior high school prom," she says.

"Very good," Talia replies, pleased. "Almost perfect! But we're still missing one very important person."

She turns and beckons.

"We can't end your season without your dream guy here!"

"Talia, *no!*" Marsh cries with horror—but it's too late.

The couples jostle slightly as Ren steps forward from the crowd. He's in the tuxedo he wore to their senior prom, holding a flower boutonniere.

"Marsh, I know you're scared, but we're almost out of time. Please, just think about this," he says.

But Marsh rushes to Talia before he can.

"Talia, listen," she begs desperately. "Everything that's been going wrong, he's behind it. He's the mastermind."

"Mastermind!" Talia trills. "Don't be silly."

Marsh tries to grab her host's flawlessly smooth arm.

"He's Chrysalis, Talia," she shouts as she grabs for her again—to shake her, to drag her to safety, to force her to warp them elsewhere. "Ren is *Chrysalis!*"

But Talia's response stops her cold.

"Marsh, *I know,*" she says.

Everything freezes.

Huh?

Marsh stares at her, confounded.

". . . What?" she finally asks.

Talia sighs. She snaps her fingers again, to transform her outfit. The gold dress replaces itself with a dark silver one, her hair slicks back, and her nail polish turns gunmetal gray.

If she was glamorous before, now she looks . . . formidable.

Oh no.

"Marsh, Marsh, Marsh."

She shakes her head, as if bored, exhausted.

"Do you really think Ren could have pulled any of this off on his own—let alone all of it? And without me noticing?"

She glares, imperious.

"I'm your producer. I know everything about your season."

No, no, no.

Marsh is backing up now, dragging Dylan with her. She can hear his racing breath, feel the tiny beads of sweat flick from his brow as he shudders.

"I can explain," Ren starts.

"No," Marsh says, drawing back.

But even as she refuses to believe, she knows it's true.

How did she miss it? she wonders with sickening dread.

It's so obvious now.

Ren could not have engineered all of this on his own. Collapsing the Bubble before Alexis could pull him out, trapping his crew inside without their memories so they couldn't warn anyone of what had happened, getting a new third season picked up by RealTV, and making the episodes air live this time, so that nothing could stop the show early . . .

He had to have had help.

"I don't know where you think you're going," Talia says. "This is a Bubble, Marsh. Remember?"

Marsh faces her duplicitous host at last.

"You betrayed me," she accuses.

"Betrayed you?" Talia feigns amazement. "Is that what I was doing, when I was busy making you a lawyer, and changing Ren's personality, and improving your relationship with your daughter? When I was creating your new life in Iceland, and Mexico, and everywhere else you wanted to go, so you could stomp through and pick it all apart? When I painstakingly tweaked every last detail for you, until everything was exactly how you'd dreamed, and you were happy?"

She snorts, disgusted.

"You should be *thanking* me."

Marsh reels, startled by the vitriol. She's lost in her shock, unable to make sense of this revelation.

Talia Cruz already got everything she ever wanted. Her season was perfect.

Why come back, then? Why do it again?

Talia, meanwhile, is preening for some invisible camera as Marsh flounders.

"When Ren used one of his last remaining episodes to find me and ask for my help, at first I thought he'd just chosen poorly, and ruined his own season," she says. "I was about to turn him away to live with the consequences of his choices."

"But then I told her about you," Ren adds, still staring at Marsh eagerly, beseechingly.

Talia nods. "And my interest was piqued."

Marsh shudders.

"Why do you think I chose you?" Talia asked her on the very first day, as she stood there unable to believe someone as shy and unsure as she could be chosen out of millions to be the season three star.

If only she'd understood what her host really had meant then.

"Every time Ren tried to change something in his season, you resisted," Talia continues. She rolls her beautiful eyes. "Tweak after tweak, replay after replay, he could not get you to cooperate. You corrupted his episodes, rejected his decisions, mangled his paths."

"Because it wasn't my choice," Marsh says.

"No," Talia scoffs. "I don't believe that. It was just because you weren't satisfied with your options."

She grins.

"But I knew I could make you so—with your own season."

"So we're just pawns, and this is a game to you?" Dylan growls, but Talia barely looks at him.

"The opposite," she says. "It's so, *so* much more than a game."

Her eyes are locked with Marsh's.

"It's *everything*."

Finally, understanding dawns.

Talia was the first, and only one, when *All This and More* began. When her finale concluded, and she became the world's biggest star, she wouldn't have realized she had it backward until much later. It wasn't about how much the show still needed her, but how much she still needed the show.

Talia is afraid.

Not of herself, but of the other contestants.

Because if one of them isn't happy with their outcome—if they don't think their lives are perfect, too—then what does that mean about her own season? What does that mean about *All This and More*'s promise?

If the show isn't real, then how can Talia's life be?

"But the show *is* real," Talia replies, as if reading Marsh's mind. "Isn't it?"

She stares Marsh down, challenging her to disagree.

"You're going to tell me that I didn't succeed, even with Ren's continued meddling? That your life really *isn't* better than it was before? That you really *aren't* happier now?"

Marsh opens her mouth, and then closes it again.

She won't let herself agree with Talia. But she can't disagree with her, either, she knows.

At last, Talia checks her delicate watch, and claps her hands. The disco ball starts to spin a little faster; the music gets a little louder.

"So, now that we're all here together, and we all know everything," she says, her voice exaggeratedly, falsely bright, "it's finally, *finally* time to make your last choice, Marsh."

Dylan curses, but Talia talks over his affronted sounds.

"Do you want everything you've made for yourself here?"

She nods at Ren.

"Or, do you want to go back . . ."

She casts a disdainful glance at Dylan, to mean the life Marsh had before—no career, possibly no marriage, and certainly no adventures, no excitement.

". . . to that?"

Marsh looks at Dylan, and then at Ren.

She trembles, terrified.

Even if she had a whole entire new season, she doesn't know if she could answer that question.

Suddenly, a loud crack shatters the romantic song, and everyone turns toward the high school gym doors.

Something bangs on the door again—and then it bursts open.

"*Lev?*" Dylan asks.

"Lev!" Marsh cries, relieved.

"Hey, Marsh," he says. "Long time no see, Dylan."

He catches the door with his foot before it closes, and pushes it open again as more people crowd in behind him.

Marsh is confused at first, but then her heart soars when she sees who they are.

Jo, Victor, Adrian, Bex, Harper, and even Pickle—they're all here.

Lev winks as Talia glares at him.

"Wouldn't be a proper finale without the whole cast, would it?" he asks.

For a moment, nothing happens.

Then it does.

Lightning fast, Dylan tackles Ren. "Go, Marsh!" he yells as they tumble to the floor. "Now!"

The prom explodes into chaos. The season two crew stops dancing and lunges for Marsh, but her season three cast leaps into the fray. The mellow lights and music go haywire. Marsh screams as Talia's taloned hand lashes out to grab her, but Lev gets in the way.

"Get to the Show Bible!" he shouts. "We're almost out of time!"

Marsh leaps to action. She bounds across the dance floor toward the DJ's booth as quickly as she can, with the speakers wailing and disco ball whirling madly. The dance has become a mosh pit—she can even hear Pickle barking wildly somewhere as he runs through the season two crew, clipping them all at the knees, and Harper telling him he's a good boy—but she keeps going. Her hand strikes the platform, then she's hauling herself up, then she's over, tumbling into the DJ booth.

"I have it! Dylan, I have it!" she says as she drags the Show Bible off its pedestal and onto the floor with an earsplitting slam. It's so huge, it nearly comes up to her waist even sitting on the ground, and probably weighs several times what she does.

"Please!" Ren calls from a tangle of limbs. "Marsh! Think about this!"

"Shut up!" Dylan orders, trying to cover Ren's mouth.

"This is the most important choice you're going to make in the whole show," Ren says quickly, struggling to keep his head free. "You're really going to give up your chance at this new life and go back to what it used to be? Back to being unhappily married, or divorced? Back to being a paralegal instead of the lawyer you've always dreamed of being?"

"If it makes things right, then yes," Marsh says through gritted teeth.

"What about Harper?" Ren asks.

That slows her down.

"You're really going to take away everything she's accomplished at the violin? All her studies at Pallissard, all her breathtaking concerts, all the skill she's gained?"

Shit, she thinks. Her hands grip the book, lost.

"Wouldn't you do anything for her? To make her happy?"

Marsh grimaces. Harper lives for her music, she knows. She's never been more alive, more fulfilled, than she is now. And it's all because of the show.

Can Marsh really take that away from her?

Or is that just a convenient excuse?

"It's too late," she finally says.

"No, it's not," Ren argues. "It doesn't have to end like this. You can have anything you want."

"But it would be a lie!" Dylan cries.

Marsh knows the voice he uses in his classroom lectures. Even as tired as he is, Dylan's trying to give a big speech. If this were a scripted show, here would be his big moment.

But it's not. It's reality TV. And the struggle with Ren has exhausted him too much for eloquence.

She understands what he means to say anyway. That the point of these stories is always that your original life is the best one, after all. That's the warm and fuzzy moral they want you to take away, right? The hero or heroine goes out and tries on all these new lives, but always comes back in the end, because they realize it's not about the success, or the stuff, or the circumstances. It's about the self. That *you* are the thing that makes your life special.

Talia chuckles dryly as Dylan's voice peters out, spent.

"I'm sorry," she says. "But that is bullshit. And you know it."

Marsh looks down, so that Dylan can't see that it's true.

"No matter how good, it doesn't matter," he insists, dogged. "Because it isn't real."

Ren sighs, as though Dylan will never understand.

"What would you really rather have?" he asks Marsh as she stares at the Show Bible.

Her hands shake as she touches the cover.

"Something that's true? Or something that makes you truly *happy*?"

As if in answer to Ren's question, the chaotic music finally cuts off. In the hanging silence, a single tone rings soft and pure.

It's the opening note to the decision music.

The end of the season finale.

Dylan jams an elbow into Ren's neck, pressing him down. "Send us back, Mallow!"

"No! Come with me," Ren begs.

"Both of you, shut up," Talia says. "This is Marsh's finale. It's her choice."

Marsh clutches the Show Bible in a panic.

Can she really go back to how things used to be—with no marriage, no career, no way to support Harper's dreams, and no hope of ever getting there again—just because it was her original life? It would be *true,* but how could she ever be satisfied again like that, having had a taste of real happiness, of the way her life should have gone . . . and then being made to give it all up forever?

But if she stays with Ren and keeps the life she's built here, would she ever see Dylan again? Would Harper?

"There has to be some way to have both," Marsh tells herself as she clutches the Show Bible. It's what this show is all about!

To get *All This . . . and More.*

As the music peaks, rushing toward its conclusion, a thought occurs to her.

She looks down at the book again.

Maybe there is *a way.*

In season two, Ren failed because he was focused on the wrong thing. He was trying to control the Bubble so he didn't have to waste his precious few episodes cleaning up whatever unintended consequences each of his choices created.

But the trouble with trying to achieve perfection isn't the complications from each choice.

The trouble is *time.*

After all, what are a few curveballs in a scene when you have as many tries as you need to fix it?

The solution is so simple. It's been staring her in the face the entire season.

The Show Bible.

She thought she'd grasped its purpose. So did Dylan, clearly. But now, she sees why her host has been so protective of it, and why the show has rules against the contestant being able to use their own book. She truly understands its full power.

Because the Show Bible isn't just how Talia tracks all the choices. It's also how she moves the season forward—

Or not.

If Marsh were the one in control of her Show Bible, not Talia, then she could pause the finale. She could stay in the Bubble just long enough to have time to figure out how she really wants her season to end.

Or maybe a little longer.

Maybe until she straightens out every little kink and fixes every little detail she didn't get a chance to correct. Until she makes everything exactly the way she wants it. Exactly perfect.

Who knows how long that could take.

Maybe even . . . forever.

The thrill of that possibility startles her.

No.

Marsh can't just stay in the Bubble.

She can't keep bettering her position at the firm, or improving Harper's musical talent. She can't continue to tweak every single little thing—endlessly enhancing her vacations, her wardrobe, the spice in her bedroom, even the blades of grass on her dream house's lawn—until she reaches the absolute limit of her happiness.

Can she?

And then, another idea. Just a whisper of a hope.

Maybe, with enough time, she could even . . . find a way to make it work with Dylan, if she wants.

He's upset about her season now, and there's no one she knows who's more stubborn than he is, but he's still Harper's father. And was her partner, for half a lifetime. No matter what, they're still a family.

If she stayed in the Bubble, she could wait as long as he needed for him to come around. There would be no rush. She could introduce him to the magic of the show little by little, rather than as a surprise. Show him how wonderful things could be again. Teach him how he, too, could dream bigger than he ever has before.

And then, eventually, everything really would be perfect. She could have her career, her fabulous new life, *and* her family.

Isn't that exactly what *All This and More* promised her?

Marsh looks up to see the entire cast and crew of both seasons staring at her as she debates this final choice.

Every face wears a different expression. Confusion, intrigue, euphoria. Lev looks grimly determined. Harper—her darling Harper—full of trust. Dylan's eyes are terrified, and Ren's are desperate.

And Talia, surprisingly, is watching her with something approaching a smile.

Despite every horrible trick her host played on her, every subtle lie and manipulative nudge, Talia Cruz is still the only other person in the world who's faced what Marsh is facing now. The finale episode that will become the start of the rest of her life. The end of endless chances. The last decision before she must live with herself forever.

She knows what Marsh is going to choose, Marsh realizes.

"Congratulations," Talia says to her, for the final time.

The music runs out.

"You could have *All This* . . ."

You cannot simply turn the page to continue this time.

You must choose Marsh's ending:

| To go back to Marsh's original life with Dylan: Go to page 449 | To choose Marsh's new life with Ren: Go to page 457 | To stay in the Bubble until Marsh can make everything perfect: Go to page 465 |

STOP!

Don't turn the page!

To reach Marsh's final choice, you have to pick one of the three options at the end of her season finale.

If you want to explore Marsh's other episodes, return to the beginning of the story and make different choices to access what lies beyond this point.

ERROR

---

chrysalis (noun)
chrys· a· lis | \ ˈkri-sə-ləs \
plural *chrysalides*\ kri- ˈsa- lə- ˌdēz \ or *chrysalises*
1: a pupa of a butterfly
2: a protecting covering
also: a sheltered state or stage of being or growth

Well. Now you've done it.
  You've gone and gotten yourself stuck.
  You aren't supposed to be here.
  You aren't supposed to see this.

butterfly (noun, often attributive)
but· ter· fly | \ ˈbə-tər-ˌflī \
1: any of numerous slender-bodied diurnal lepidopteran insects with
broad and often brightly colored wings
2: something that resembles or suggests a butterfly
especially: a person chiefly occupied with the pursuit of pleasure
3: butterflies *plural:* a feeling of hollowness or queasiness caused especially by emotional or nervous tension or anxious anticipation

*Is it any wonder why the Bubble has become so unstable, with you break-
ing the rules like this on top of everything else that's going on?*

4: butterfly *effect:* a property of chaotic systems (such as the atmo-
sphere) by which small changes in initial conditions can lead to large-
scale and unpredictable variation in the future state of the system

You should get out of here—while you still can.

To get back on track: Go to page 351	To jump randomly and hope for the best: Go to page 727,659	To give up and start over: Go to page 1

SERENDIPITY

The old, dented bell clangs against the glass door of the bar as Marsh pushes it open and slips inside.

The bar is her local dive, a dark and stuffy place where she's always felt not cool enough to fit in. Tonight, she's got too much on her mind to notice. Or perhaps, she's learned to be a little bolder in this path, she imagines her lovely host would tell her.

In any case, there are only a handful of patrons, all of them sitting far apart at the beat-up wood counter, and Marsh chooses a stool in the corner where she can also be alone. She sinks into the ratty cushion with a sigh.

What a disaster.

All of that work to get her marriage back on track, pushing herself to places she never thought she'd be courageous enough to go—only to have the whole thing fall apart at the final hour.

Why would the show do that? she wonders, as she ponders Ren's surprise appearance in her bedroom. How handsome and eager and nervous he looked, standing there in the doorway, half in shadow.

She's purposefully not called Talia again yet, because the last thing she needs right now is a chipper pep talk, but she knows what she would say if she were here: that this is great for ratings! A little bit of drama will get viewers to invest in her character.

Stories have to have complications to be meaningful, she can imagine her host proclaiming. *That's just good craft!*

But that last episode wasn't just *any* episode. It was Marsh's big chance to change the course of her marriage—basically, her life, if it had worked.

She was so close.

Too close?

She shakes her head and pulls her cardigan tighter—under the sweater and jeans, she still has Le Fascination on—and dismisses that thought. Yes, *All This and More* might give contestants a gentle, encouraging nudge in one direction or another, but it would never do something as dramatic as trying to choose Marsh's life partner for her.

It must have just been sheer dumb luck that Ren ended up in that scene.

Coincidences really *do* happen in real life, sometimes.

As Marsh sits in exhausted silence, the bartender finishes mixing something at the counter, and then a dark, caramel-colored old-fashioned in a heavy glass slides just next to Marsh's hands atop a Sharp Purple napkin.

"Wow," she muses, pulling the glass closer to her as the dark, inviting liquid swirls. "My favorite. How did you know—"

But the words die on her lips as she looks up at the bartender.

"Lucky guess," Ren says, with a wink.

Marsh just stares, shocked.

JesterG: <Whaaaaat>

StrikeF0rce: <This guy is everywhere!>

"Okay maybe not *that* lucky of a guess." He chuckles. "You looked like you might need something strong, and I've got a personal spin on the old-fashioned that most people love. I just made you the drink I'm best at."

Ren smiles a little wider, charmingly. Marsh hasn't blinked yet.

One coincidence is just that.

But two?

She finally shakes her head, flabbergasted at this second surprise appearance.

Where is Dylan right now? she wonders. Sure, the threesome path was a long shot, but Marsh was willing to try even that for him, to save things. So why isn't he here now, commiserating with her? Laughing over what a weird disaster the night turned out to be? Promising that even though they didn't go through with it, he loved that they'd tried, and that the experiment had brought them closer together? That their love was stronger than ever?

Why is Marsh alone in their neighborhood bar in this episode?

But she's not actually alone, she revises.

Ren is here.

He's always here for her.

Maybe two coincidences aren't just two coincidences.

Maybe they're a sign.

"You all right, miss?" Ren finally asks. "I can make you something else, if you don't want an old-fashioned. It's on the house, don't worry about it. Anything you want."

"No, it's not that," Marsh finally says. She looks at him warily. "You don't . . . recognize me?"

"Uh." He shrugs, embarrassed. "Are you a regular? I just started here."

Marsh shakes her head, then nods. "No. I mean, yes, I'm a regular. This is my local spot. But I meant, do you recognize me from before?"

Is she asking about the last scene, or high school?

She did make a choice not to pursue the tryst—this episode probably erased that reality for him, as if it never happened.

Ren is studying Marsh intently, his face unreadable for a moment as he digs back through his memory. Then, a light goes on in his eyes, and he gasps happily.

"Oh my God," he cries. *"Marsh?"*

Despite the oddness of their last encounter still hanging over her, Marsh can't help but break into a smile as well.

"I can't believe it!" Ren says, slapping his forehead. "Wow, you look great. You look *amazing*! This is incredible. How long has it been? So, you live here now? What do you do?"

Marsh feels suddenly shy, but Ren is so enthusiastic, talking a mile a minute like a little kid who can't control himself, that it's hard to stay that way. After a few minutes, she's relaxed, and is alternating between trying to answer his rapid-fire questions and laughing at his antics.

She hadn't expected to be joking about anything tonight, but it's almost like the whole evening has been washed away, the slate wiped clean. It's just so nice to be with someone so thrilled to be in her presence, treating her like the interesting, gorgeous woman she wants to be—*will be, by the season finale,* she promises herself.

In fact, she feels happier than she has in a long time. Sure, she was excited to step out of her comfort zone with Dylan, but that was mostly novelty and nerves. Here, now, she's really having fun.

"So," Ren finally says, and she realizes he's looking down at her hands around the old-fashioned. At her wedding band.

"Seven years this month," she replies.

"Congratulations." Ren whistles.

Marsh manages a smile. "Thanks."

She would never cheat on Dylan. *That's his area of expertise,* she thinks, scoffing. But she just wishes the subject hadn't come up yet. She wanted to keep enjoying the innocent flirtation, that little buzz of electricity in every word and glance, that feeling of being attractive to another person, for a few minutes longer.

She doesn't want to lie.

Just pretend, for a little bit.

"Any kids?" Ren asks.

"One daughter. She's five. Her name is Harper."

"Marsh, that's awesome," Ren says. "Really awesome. I bet you're a great mom."

Marsh smiles again, more genuinely this time, but she knows her posture is still stiff. Any second, he'll pick up on it, and the whole mood will chill, that magnetic pull will vanish, gone as easily as it arrived. "What about you?" she asks, to turn the conversation onto Ren. "Anyone special in your life?"

Ren shrugs and turns back to the counter to make Marsh a second round. The stools have all cleared out, and she and Ren are the only two left in the bar, she realizes.

They've been talking for hours.

"Nope," he answers as he sets down another old-fashioned in front of Marsh, and then takes a sip from one he made for himself. He savors the drink, and then leans his elbows on the counter in front of her.

"Just 'nope'?" Marsh asks, smirking. "I haven't seen you since high school, and that's all I get?"

He laughs. "I spent a lot of my twenties traveling. I'd change places whenever I felt like it, and find a bar in that new city. Upscale clubs, quirky cocktail spots, dives, whatever I could find. I'd mix drinks, meet the locals, have conversations, learn the place. Then I'd pack up and move again."

As he describes his nomadic life, he gestures to a collage of weathered postcards tacked up behind the cash register. Places he's been, or wants to go, he seems to mean. One of them is especially eye-catching: a collage of sunny beaches and lush jungles, and the words *Come to Mexico!* beckoning near the bottom.

ChilangoCool: <¡Una pista!>

LoboAzul: <¡Ven a México, Marsh!>

Marsh sighs wistfully. "Sounds romantic."

"It was," Ren agrees. "But also a little empty. It took me a while to realize I kept moving so much not because the places got old after a while, but because I was lonely there."

"Wise words," Marsh says.

Ren shrugs. "I had to grow up a bit to admit what I really want."

"And what's that?" she asks. "What you really want?"

Ren looks at her. Suddenly, there's more of that pull in the air again. She can feel it between them, like they're two halves of a magnet, teetering.

"You know, you're different from back then," he says, grinning a little. "More . . ."

"Don't even say it," Marsh cuts him off. She takes a drink. "So are you."

"How so?"

Marsh chuckles. "Well, considering the last time we talked, you made me a mixtape and were sobbing about how your life was over if we didn't stay together through college—" she says, as he laughingly interjects, "Hey, I was seventeen!"—"and now you're this handsome wandering bartender hero, like the bad boy out of some romantic comedy movie . . ."

"Handsome, am I?" Ren teases.

Marsh goes red. "I mean, I'm just saying, well, you—"

"Hey, it's all right. Thank you for the compliment," he says, clinking his glass against hers. "You're even more beautiful than in high school."

Marsh blushes again, and tries to cover it with another sip of her old-fashioned, but the warming liquid hits her tongue funny, and she ends up coughing, which just makes Ren—and eventually her—laugh harder.

"You really are," Ren says.

"Oh, stop," Marsh replies.

But she knows she doesn't want him to.

Even if he was the puppy-dog desperate one who got his heart broken in high school, and has been carrying a little flame for her ever since, who cares? That just makes this chance meeting all the more sweet. It's like they're back on that incredible first date just before she was chosen for *All This and More,* right before she ruined everything. She's got butterflies, and Ren is practically beaming at her as they talk, unable to help it. Just being in her presence has transformed him, made him come to life. Everything she says is hilarious to him, every little gesture the most graceful thing he's ever seen. They're perfect for each other.

It's like the show designed him for her. She wants to laugh.

Maybe it's not fair to expect Dylan still to be as flirtatious and smitten with her as he was decades ago, when the two of them first met—but who said anything about fair? This is reality TV. This is a fairy tale. This is *All This and More.*

She can do anything she wants.

Including something drastic.

Maybe she's been going about this all wrong, Marsh considers as Ren laughs at yet another joke. Maybe she actually isn't supposed to save her marriage on this show. Maybe her marriage is the very thing that's been holding her back all this time.

Maybe she's supposed to let Dylan go—*permanently*.

To give up on Dylan and
pursue a relationship
with Ren instead:
Go to page 125

HIGH STAKES

At last, Marsh turns to Victor and nods, ready for him to deal the final card that will decide the tournament.

She doesn't know what Chrysalis might try if she attempted to escape in some way before the end, but she doesn't want to find out.

But how will she win? Nothing in poker beats a royal flush, and Ren's already got it. She doesn't see how there's anything that can save her.

She swallows grimly as Victor reaches for the deck.

SharpTruth217: \<Marsh\>
SharpTruth217: \<The cards\>
SharpTruth217: \<Something's—\>
[Automatic security filters have deleted this account]

But before SharpTruth can return, Victor flips the last card over.

Marsh blinks in disbelief.

. . . *What?*

"Holy . . ." Victor nearly curses by accident. "That . . . that . . ."

The crowd gasps in amazement.

Marsh looks back at her cards, and then to the first three that Victor dealt, certain that she's misremembered them.

But she was right.

All four aces are in play—two in her hand, and two on the table.

So how can the final card *also* be an ace?

PokerChamp888: \<Wait, WHAT??!?!\>
Moms4Marsh: \<Holy mackerel! Does that beat Ren's hand?\>
Notamackerel: \<No! I mean, yes—but it doesn't make sense!\>

N3vrGiv3Up: <What do you mean?>
PokerChamp888: <Because that card is impossible!!!>

It's not, if we're playing by Chrysalis's rules, Marsh thinks, as she stares at the wings of the Sharp Purple butterfly at the center of the card.

She waits—for someone to realize something is wrong, for the audience to accuse her of cheating, for the tournament to discredit her victory—her breath held.

At last, Victor raises a microphone.

"Ladies and gentlemen," his voice booms. "Coming in at the last moment with an incredible five-of-a-kind, the only hand in history that could beat Ren's royal flush . . . we have our champion!"

The whole casino explodes with raucous applause.

Marsh startles as whistles erupt around the room, and her opponents all swoon with anguished awe at how incredible her victory was.

Somehow, Chrysalis managed to tamper with the deck, and create a fifth ace.

She really wins after all.

"Let's hear it for Marsh!" Victor shouts.

"Marsh! Marsh! Marsh!" the crowd rallies.

Despite her shock, it's impossible for Marsh not to be swept up in the excitement. It physically presses itself upon her. Jo is shaking her hand and congratulating her, and row after row of fans are pressing in on their table, begging her to autograph their own card decks, their T-shirts, their bodies. Their jubilation is so wild, Marsh feels like she just hit the jackpot at a slot machine.

"You think you've won," Ren says over the commotion, tossing down his royal flush as the applause continues to thunder throughout the casino. "But just wait. It'll be me, next time."

Marsh waves him off at first. There's so much commotion and sound, and she's too distracted to hear him clearly, so it takes a beat for Ren's words to fully land.

Next time.

Marsh pauses.

What an odd thing to say.

Does Ren . . . know something?

She turns back to him, confused. "What do you mean, next time?" she asks. The hairs are standing up on the back of her neck.

But Ren just snorts.

"You know." He gestures to the casino. "Next time. It's an annual tournament."

He puffs out his chest.

"I'll beat you next year, and the year after, and the year after, until I break your record."

Marsh watches him closely—but Ren's gaze is steady. His expression is confrontational, but open. He clearly doesn't know about the show, about the choices. He's just talking smack.

"Next time," Marsh agrees at last, and Ren *hmphs*. "I look forward to it."

SharpTruth222: <Marsh, this is your chance>
SharpTruth222: <Find Julie>
[Automatic security filters have deleted this account]

Marsh whirls.

Of course!

Julie Pabst was a part of *All This and More* from the very start—when it was no more than an idea in development! If there's anyone who might be able to tell her more about Chrysalis, it could be her.

She scans the crowd eagerly, but Julie's nowhere to be seen.

Where did she go?

"Are you coming?" Jo asks her.

"What?" Marsh asks. "Where?"

"To the Chrysalis Tournament after-party, of course!" Jo says. "Everyone will be there."

So, it's called the Chrysalis Tournament now, is it? Marsh muses.

She's certain that if Julie is still in this path, she can find her there.

A DARK CLOUD

The after-party inside the private casino club is even more packed than the tournament, somehow. It's dark, humid, and punctuated with pulses of light, like an electric obstacle course. The cheers are so loud, Marsh can feel them reverberating in her gut. A live shot of her face is being projected on an even bigger jumbotron than the one at the tournament, her own nose as tall as her real body. She manages a wave, which elicits another round of teeth-rattling applause.

The bar is neon, and so are the drinks. Marsh eyes one suspiciously as a passing waiter leans close with a tray.

"I'll just have a glass of wine instead," she says to him.

Suddenly, he has one for her in his hand.

"Perfect." She smiles and takes a sip.

"Well, well, well," Ren says, and she turns to see him sauntering toward her in the crowd. His lips are stained faintly nuclear blue from his cocktail. "Even I have to hand it to you. That was a pretty impressive win."

Marsh waits to see if he says anything about how impossible the victory was, but he doesn't seem to know.

"Well, thanks," she finally says. She glances around. "Is Julie here? I should thank her for such a good match, too."

"I haven't seen her," Ren says. "But . . ."

Marsh looks down to see him slyly offering a hotel key card to her. He does his best roguish wink. "I have the penthouse suite. In case, you know, after the after-party . . ."

Marsh arches a brow.

"It has a private waterfall Jacuzzi," he adds.

He scoots a little closer.

"Also . . . I know we agreed to keep things on the down-low because the tournament circuit is so catty, but it's been years now." He peeks at her nervously. Suddenly the act drops, and he looks just as earnest and mushy as he always does. "Maybe we can go public?"

LunaMágica: <Awww, still the same, lovable Ren after all. I was starting to wonder if they weren't together anymore!>
BenzinhoGatinho: <Não fale isso! Don't even say it!>

On the jumbotron, highlights of Marsh's incredible—*impossible*—win are playing, spliced between shots of the euphoric crowd. Marsh definitely didn't feel as cool and confident in the moment as she looks in the footage, but it seems the Bubble has tweaked the replay a bit so she's steely in every single shot. She watches herself push all of her chips into the center of the table without a moment of hesitation just before her victory, fascinated by her own courage.

"You really had the crowd there," Ren says, and tips his glass toward the giant screen. "But then again, you're a natural-born performer."

Marsh snorts at that, unable to help it.

"What?" She laughs.

Is he somehow thinking of Mexico? Did some fragment of memory from that path carry over into this new life?

Because nothing could be further from the truth—the *real* truth.

"No, I mean high school!" he replies.

What?

"I never told you this story, actually," he says, and swirls his drink. "But what the hell."

Marsh stares at Ren, spellbound, as he begins to talk about Beaumont, Texas, and math class, and her parents' old two-story house with the ugly pink carpet.

How does Ren remember high school, in this life—their *real* high school? Did the two of them still meet way back then in this path, and have been dating ever since?

But what does that mean about Dylan?

About Harper?

"You remember, I came over to pick you up for prom? Anyway, while you were finishing your makeup, I was waiting with your corsage at the bottom of the stairs, where your mom had all those photos on that table. There was that one of you from your middle school talent show—you know! You're in the kitchen, trying out your costume."

It comes to her at once, an unbidden flash she can't drive out of her mind's eye before she sees it. The tacky gold picture frame, and the captured moment within it.

Marsh is ten years old. She's standing in front of the refrigerator, a huge grin on her face. Her costume is so big, she can't put her arms all the way down at her sides. She's a huge, billowing white ball made of cotton balls and basted with silver glitter, to make it all shimmer. It's the night before she goes onstage, and she's so excited, so free, so ready.

So *stupid*.

Ren laughs. "That's when I knew!"

Marsh's throat is tight as she stares at him.

"You knew what?" she finally asks.

"Your nickname!" he exclaims, so proud of himself. "That's how I came up with it. I saw that picture of you in your white costume, and thought, it's perfect! It's *you*."

As Ren continues to chatter excitedly, Marsh closes her eyes and shakes her head. She wants to laugh, or punch something, she's not sure which.

This whole time, all these years, the nickname she's never liked . . .

Ren based it on one of the worst moments of her life.

And it's not even *right*.

Not the nickname, not that version of herself, nothing. Not even the costume. She wasn't a marshmallow at all.

"Are you okay?" Ren asks. He's staring at her nervously, clearly concerned by her reaction. "You look a little faint."

Marsh turns to him.

"This is definitely something we're going to edit out," she says.

Ren gapes.

Talia will kill her for this, but she can't help it this time.

"What?" Ren stammers.

"I know you have no idea what I mean, but this isn't right," she continues.

"What part?"

"All of it."

He blinks, shocked. "Surely not . . . all of it?" He looks unmoored. "I mean, this was your choice, wasn't it?"

Marsh had been ready with a sharp comeback, but his words catch her off guard.

"What?" she demands. "What do you mean, my choice?"

But as soon as her suspicion flares, it's gone again.

"Not to tell anyone we're together, because we're rivals on the circuit," Ren says. He's not talking about the show itself. Just their current life within it. The only one he knows. "I understand your concerns, but I just—"

Marsh interrupts him by putting a hand on his.

She wants to tell him, even though the last time she confessed, the whole thing went down in flames. Dylan tried to quit, then disappeared, and now everything's gone off the rails. But poor Ren looks so desperate, so confused. He's become a hundred different people for her, and each one of them has loved her. He deserves to know. How can things be perfect if he doesn't?

But before she can speak, a flicker of movement over his shoulder stops her.

"I hear you," Marsh finally says. "I promise things will get better. Okay?"

He nods as she leaves him in the middle of the crowd, that hurt look still on his face. But she can't think about that right now. She only has so much time, and there's something far more important she has to do.

"Julie Pabst," Marsh says.

"Come to gloat, have we?" Julie asks.

Marsh shakes her head. "To ask you a question."

Julie hums, curious, and gestures for Marsh to continue.

Here we go, Marsh thinks.

It worked for Alexis—hopefully it does for Julie, too.

"Chrysalis," she says.

Julie doesn't move at first. But then the word seems to do something to her, like magic, the way she was hoping it would. Julie blinks, and when she opens her eyes again, she seems different.

"You can keep running," she finally says, lucid at last. "But you won't find Chrysalis that way."

Marsh takes Julie by the shoulders. "What?" she asks. "What did you just say?"

Julie looks around the raging party with a mixture of awe and horror. "What *is* this place?" she whispers.

"What is Chrysalis?" Marsh asks, ignoring her question. "What does it want with a card game?"

"Nothing," Julie says. "Chrysalis isn't really a card game. Not really."

Marsh knows what she means, even though she doesn't fully understand it. Chrysalis is just a card game in *this* path—but it's something much bigger than that.

"What should I do?" she asks.

But Sharp Entertainment's executive is fading. Her gaze is growing vaguer by the moment, her focus loosening, the distance growing.

"Julie," Marsh says, trying to draw her back. "Help me. Please."

"Listen," Julie says. "We always say, the most important thing about reality TV, the reason people watch it, is that parts of it *are* real."

She gestures at the club dismissively.

"All of this, it's just a formula. A distraction. Every episode has to be bigger, louder, more over-the-top. But this isn't why you came on *All This and More*."

Just then, a familiar jingle threads itself into the thumping beat of the DJ's club remix. That little tune that signifies the close of an episode, the encroaching end of Marsh's season.

She whirls to Julie, her eyes wide.

"You don't have much time," Julie says.

"You can hear it?" Marsh asks her, surprised.

"Yes," she says. She looks happy, yet saddened by that joy, at the same time. "I can now."

"What do I do?"

"You have to go back," Julie says.

"Where?"

"To wherever your life was most real. Wherever the show got closest to what you really want. That's where you'll find Chrysalis."

Marsh is about to panic, to beg Julie to tell her where that is—but she realizes that she already knows which path it has to be.

It's the one that Talia first offered her after the midseason special, which Marsh turned down. The one in which she was supposed to be a lawyer, Ren a journalist, and Harper not some other kind of musician, but a violinist. It was the nearest version to true—and also the one in which she could have gotten close to Chrysalis, if she'd been brave enough to try.

"You know, I'm the one who came up with the catchphrase, in one of our preproduction meetings," Julie murmurs, as the jingle draws to an end.

Marsh turns to her, her posture already tensed in preparation for the jump.

"Good luck," Julie says. Her voice shifts, faintly lilting. "You could have *All This* . . ."

Marsh looks up, at the edges of her world, as they slowly blur and darken, the Bubble whisking her away, across an ocean of water and to another reality.

She doesn't know what could be waiting for her in Hong Kong, but there's only one way to find out.

To go to Hong Kong:
Go to page 253

EPISODE 9

Marsh appears into the scene like she's still in the earthquake. She stumbles forward and grabs the edge of the dresser for balance, her feet scrabbling for purchase, until she realizes that nothing is moving in this new setting.

She's in her bedroom. Through the windows, the Hong Kong midnight skyline glitters.

Marsh lurches upright and stares.

Everything is just like before. The city, their apartment, their life. Leaning against her closet door is Dylan's briefcase, stuffed full of her court papers.

SagwaGold: <Whoa, she actually did it! She made it back to the beginning of the episode!>

Now she just has to get to Chrysalis.

There's the sound of water turning on, and light splashing. Marsh glances toward the bathroom and catches sight of Ren's pajama-clad leg at the sink. Then she turns to his nightstand.

As she reaches for the little brass handle, she sees it fizzle slightly—as if for a moment, it's not made of metal, but something else. Then it's normal again.

SharpTruth509: <Marsh, the Bubble's not stable here>
[Automatic security filters have deleted this account]
SharpTruth510: <Be carefu—>
[Automatic security filters have deleted this account]

Marsh hesitates, and then grabs the edge of the duvet. With it wrapped around her hand like an oven mitt, she gently tugs the drawer open.

The pill bottle stares back up at her.

"What do you think about going to the film festival this weekend?" Ren asks as he comes out of the bathroom, but then he stops as he sees her crouched over his nightstand. "What are you doing? Are you . . . spying on me?"

"What is Chrysalis?" Marsh demands, quickly reaching into the nightstand. Even if Ren doesn't know what's really going on, in their Hong Kong path he's her closest link to Chrysalis, and has been pursuing it doggedly for his article. He has to know what it is, even if he doesn't know *what* it is.

But Ren just blinks. "What?"

"Don't lie," Marsh says. As she stares him down, refusing to break eye contact, her hand shuffles through the drawer, searching for the bottle. "What is Chrysalis, really?"

"What are you talking about?" he asks, either confused or pretending to be.

"This new medication, for the big profile you're writing," she replies, irritated. Finally, still not able to find the bottle by feel, she turns to the drawer. "You've been taking the pills in secret, as part of your—" she starts to say, and then stops.

SharpTruth511: <Something's wrong>
[*Automatic security filters have deleted this account*]

She stares into the drawer.

TopFan01: <Wait, I'm confused>
TopFan01: <I could have sworn . . . >

All the usual things are there. Ren's second pair of reading glasses, a set of earplugs, his bookmark, some extra cash.

Everything but the pills.

She saw them. She knows she did.

They were just there.

But they're definitely not now.

"What are you talking about?" Ren throws up his hands. "Yes, I'm writing an article, but what pills?" He steps closer, more frantic now. "Are you going through my notes? Marsh, that breaks the journalist's code!"

SharpTruth512: <I don't know what happened>
SharpTruth512: <We might need to—>
[*Automatic security filters have deleted this account*]

Marsh continues to stare at the empty drawer as Ren demands to know what's going on.

What if I try again? she wonders, as he gesticulates in the periphery like a TV show on mute, his pleas barely reaching her ears.

Chrysalis was ready for her here, and managed to outsmart her once—but two can play at that game. Ren was already taking the pills by this point in the Hong Kong path, and must have hidden them somewhere else, but what if she stopped him even before this? What if she went back to before he tried the pills for the first time, and forbade him from using himself as a human guinea pig? Maybe if Ren never took the medicine at all, he'd never get close enough to Chrysalis to ever write the feature that would introduce their drug to the world.

Finally, realizing that she isn't really listening to him, Ren stops his barrage of questions.

"Whatever's wrong, I can fix it," he says. "I promise."

"No," Marsh replies. She picks up the briefcase and clutches it to her chest, a protective talisman. "I can."

EPISODE 9

DEADLINE

Marsh appears in her apartment again. She tenses her body, ready to reach out and grab the dresser for balance, but she's not beside the dresser this time, but rather in the doorway of her bedroom, and her hand swipes empty air. She pitches forward and trips over a bundle of something hard and heavy at knee height, dropping the briefcase.

"What the . . ." she groans, sitting up and rubbing her hip.

SharpTruth513: <I think we did it>
SharpTruth513: <I think we got you back further>
[Automatic security filters have deleted this account]

Maybe Ezra is right, she sees as she gingerly stands.

It's afternoon, not night. Toppled over in a heap in front of her are two big pieces of luggage, full of rumpled beach clothes.

If all this is here, it must mean that she's jumped back to the day that she, Ren, and Harper returned from Tahiti. Their actual first day in Hong Kong—earlier even than when the original Hong Kong episode began in his office the next morning.

"Whoa there." Ren laughs as he comes into the room behind her. "I didn't realize you wanted to start unpacking the instant we got home. Don't you want some lunch?"

"I'm not hungry," Marsh says.

On their bookshelf, the decorative lamp disappears for an instant, the room suddenly a little darker, and then reappears again. So fast, she can't be certain it was real or just her blinking.

"That's okay! I'm not really hungry, either," Ren says. He kisses her hand and keeps hold of it sweetly. "Would you mind if I did some work at the kitchen table for an hour or two, then? I have a new article I'm really, really excited about."

"Do you," Marsh replies, unable to muster false surprise.

Ren nods vigorously. "I can't talk about it yet, but it's going to be big," he says. "Life-changing big!"

But midway through his excited monologue, he pauses, then wrinkles his nose for a moment. He makes a face, then sucks a little breath of air in through his mouth.

Then he yawns.

He's sleepy, Marsh realizes.

"Sorry," Ren says. "Might need a nap first, actually."

Her eyes narrow.

"Didn't you sleep the whole way on the plane?" she asks.

His easygoing expression begins to fade.

SagwaGold: <Busted>

"Uh," he falters. Immediately, his eyes shoot to his nightstand.

She drops his hand.

SharpTruth514: <No, something's off>
[*Automatic security filters have deleted this account*]
SharpTruth515: <Not nightstand>
SharpTruth515: <Suitca—>
[*Automatic security filters have deleted this account*]

Marsh barely catches the words before they're gone, but it's enough. Instead of walking over to the bed, she slowly bends to look in Ren's suitcase.

"Marsh—" Ren starts, his eyes wide, but she ignores him. She shoves her hand into the mess of clothes.

Buried in the middle is a hard, curved shape.

She pulls out the bottle of pills.

Of course. She groans, squeezing the jar in her hand. Even though she jumped back, it wasn't enough.

He's already taking them.

"I can explain," Ren says, defensive.

But Marsh puts a hand up as something else occurs to her. She turns and looks at the nightstand, then back at Ren.

"Were you trying to mislead me?" she finally asks.

But how could that be possible?

How did Ren know that *she* knew about the pills in the first place?

She never revealed she did in the original episode. The only time she confronted him was just moments ago—and they're now even earlier than that. That scene now never happened.

"This isn't what you think it is," he insists desperately. "Please just listen to me!"

Marsh shakes her head. But instead of yelling at him for hiding this from her, Marsh just tosses the bottle onto the bed and grabs her briefcase from the floor.

"Where are you going?" Ren asks, startled.

"Back," she says, but she's not talking to him.

EPISODE 9

Marsh arrives in her bedroom yet again, this time right near the bed. No, *over* it. She's floating in the air, lying prone, as if she's supposed to be sleeping in the bed but has materialized a few feet above it. She gasps, and the duvet lurches, a flickering, glitchy burst of color. Suddenly it's draped over her, but before she can grab it, it disappears and reappears below her again, spread neatly across the sheets, as the Bubble shudders between trying to correct its error and accidentally creating more of them in its place.

She screams as she drops, but the mattress catches her and the briefcase with a cushioned thump.

SharpTruth516: <Marsh, something's wrong>
[Automatic security filters have deleted this account]
SharpTruth517: <It's even more unstable this tim—>
[Automatic security filters have deleted this account]

"No kidding," she whispers, scrambling free of the covers as they twitch and blink beneath her. Once on the floor, she turns around, but the bed is normal again. She can see now that she landed on top of piles of clothes, once neatly folded but now a mess. On the rug beside her, two empty, open suitcases wait, along with a pair of clear zippered pouches and a smattering of travel-sized toiletries.

She and Ren haven't even left for their Tahiti vacation yet, she realizes. They're preparing for it in this scene.

She's gone back as far as she can go.

"Okay, let's try this again," she murmurs, as one of the suitcases shivers ever so slightly, then snaps back to stillness.

"All I'm asking is for you to consider it," Ren is saying as he comes out of the closet holding two pairs of swimming trunks, but he comes to an abrupt halt as he sees the disturbed clothing.

Marsh rushes to think of an excuse, but before she can, Ren's demeanor changes. It's just some clothes, but suddenly, he looks frustrated, or upset. His brows knit together as he walks over to the bed and sets his swimwear down on the pile, and he takes a breath to steel himself before turning to her.

"Are you really that upset?" he finally asks.

What's going on? Marsh wonders.

Are we in a fight?

"Upset about what?" she asks carefully.

"About the pills," he replies.

YanYan242: <Oh no, it didn't work!>

Marsh sets the briefcase down on the dresser and puts her head in her hands.

No matter how far back she goes, it's never enough.

Ren is always writing about Chrysalis, and will always try the pills.

"I know it's risky, but this idea I have is really huge," Ren says. "It could change *everything* for us."

"Oh, I think it already has," Marsh replies. Her throat is tight, whether with sadness or anger, she can't tell.

"This article is so valuable, the research has to be airtight. If I can get my hands on a prescription, and try the pills myself, it might—"

"It doesn't matter what I think," Marsh cuts him off. "Why even ask me? I think you're going to take the pills, no matter what I want."

Ren frowns, confused at that response.

"Why would you think that?" he asks her. "That I would take them without asking you first?"

Because you already have, she doesn't say. *Every time.*

"Because you want to. This article is too important to you."

"It's not more important than us," he says.

Marsh hesitates. Something's different about this scene, but she can't put her finger on it. It's still an argument over the pills, but where she's upset, Ren is the opposite now. As they talk, he's watching her with what almost seems like fascination. His eyes are glittering, the way that a child might study a magician at a magic show.

"Really," he adds. "If you're sure you don't want me to take them, just say so."

March arches a skeptical brow.

He waits, but Marsh holds her ground. Her eyes drift down, to the nightstand, and Ren's gaze follows hers. Slowly, he walks over to his side of the bed, opens the drawer, and pulls out the bottle.

He already has them. Again.

"Hm," she sighs pointedly. "See?"

But this time, Ren turns the cap, and a sharp crack echoes—the bottle was still sealed.

He hasn't taken any yet.

That's a surprise.

"I told you, I want to make this decision together," he says, his eyes locked with hers.

Notamackerel: <Is it just me or does Ren look like he's . . . smiling?>

SharpTruth519: <Marsh, something's very off here>

[Automatic security filters have deleted this account]

"What is Chrysalis?" Marsh asks shakily.

Ren cocks his head. "What?"

"What is it?"

Ren steps closer to her, and his expression is concerned, placating, again. "Do you trust me?" he asks her.

"It doesn't matter," Marsh repeats. "You're going to take the pills, whatever I say."

"Please, trust me," Ren begs. "I wouldn't do this if I didn't think it was worth it."

Marsh closes her eyes, and lays her exhausted head against his chest.

She doesn't know what to do. She doesn't want to leave this loop without figuring out what Chrysalis really is, but no matter what she tries, he always seems to have the pills, and always takes them.

Monsterrific: <How is she going to make this right by the finale?>

"I'm doing this for us. I can make all of this right, if you let me."

Ren rattles the bottle softly.

"I *know* I can."

Marsh pulls back to look at him. The dread is a cold weight deep in her gut, like she's swallowed a chunk of ice.

"You can't *know* that," she replies.

"Yes, I can," he swears. "I do."

"How, exactly?" Marsh asks.

Behind him, she sees the dresser where the briefcase is resting go fuzzy and vague. For a moment, it's just pixels, then yawning, empty space.

SharpTruth520: <Marsh, get out of here>
SharpTruth520: <It's glitching>
[Automatic security filters have deleted this account]

"How do you know?" she insists.

"Because I'll never stop trying," Ren replies. "No matter how long it takes."

The emptiness expands, the dark void growing. Around the dresser, the wall starts to warp.

"I mean it," he insists as Marsh lunges.

She reaches out, her hand plunging into the gap, desperately grabbing hold.

"I'll do whatever you want. Anything for us. And what the *hell* is with that briefcase?!" he snaps furiously as he sees it in her hands now, yanked back from the void.

Her grip on the handle tightens protectively.

"Because I'm a lawyer," she says.

Ren shakes his head. "But why *that* briefcase? Why *that* one?"

She doesn't answer. As if in response, the rug twitches, then becomes transparent.

"It's mine," she says.

The floor starts to dissolve as Marsh backs up, but Ren doesn't seem to notice.

"It's not even in style!"

"Ren," she whispers. "The room—"

"You want a briefcase?" he asks, ignoring her. "I'll get you a briefcase. Any one you want."

"The *room*," she repeats, staring, but he doesn't seem to be able to break out of his role.

SharpTruth521: <Marsh!>
SharpTruth521: <We can't wait>
SharpTruth521: <I have to—>
[Automatic security filters have deleted this acc—]

"Fine, I'll let the article go again," he says at last, throwing up his hands. "Would that make things perfect?"

A BAD DREAM

Marsh is at her Hong Kong dinner party.

Again.

She, Jo, Bex, Harper, Victor, Adrian, and Ren are all gathered around her gorgeous dining table just like last time. At the center, the French duck waits, succulent and spiced, amid a heap of delectable side dishes. The comment box is completely still for once, as if locked. Soft jazz is playing in the background from their expensive stereo. The briefcase is gone.

Marsh looks around, her expression tense.

"I'm so glad we could do this," Ren says as he settles into his chair and scoots himself in. "It's so nice to have everyone here."

The camera pans to the rest of the table as he talks. Everyone else at the party is happy—frozen midlaugh, their cutlery partially raised or their napkins halfway shaken out.

Except the scene has already begun.

And no one but Marsh and Ren is moving.

"Don't you think?" Ren asks.

She stares, unable to speak.

"Marsh?"

She nods at him at last. Manages a weak smile.

"Yes," she says. "It's very nice."

Ren grins back. Oblivious, he pops the champagne cork and carefully fills Marsh's crystal flute, then his own.

"A toast," he says. "To you."

"No," Marsh says.

Ren sets the bottle down and studies her.

"You've been under so much stress lately," he says. "Let me help you. That's why I'm here."

Marsh looks around the table again, at the utterly still scene. Jo is reaching for Bex's cheek, a lock of Harper's hair hangs in midair. Even Pickle, begging for scraps beside Victor's elbow, is stone still. None of them are blinking, or even breathing. It's like someone pressed PAUSE on a remote, for everything in the Bubble but her and Ren.

Is this Chrysalis?

"I don't think you can help me," Marsh finally says.

Ren reaches over and puts a hand on hers.

"I know this is hard," he says, his voice gentle. "But it'll all be okay. I promise."

Marsh closes her eyes, as if she can't bear any more. "Will it?" she asks.

"It will," he says. "Because I want the same thing you do."

Marsh opens her eyes and looks at him. Her stare is both a challenge and a plea.

"And what do I want?" she whispers.

"For everything to be perfect," he answers.

Marsh watches as he reaches back to his champagne glass, and picks it up. As he raises his arm to toast her, everyone else around the table suddenly turns and raises theirs, too, perfectly synchronized. Their glasses are full now. The bubbles hiss and pop against the crystal. Marsh watches, both fascinated and horrified, as six flutes go up, then come back down.

"Cheers, Marsh," they all say as Ren does.

"Cheers," she whispers.

Ren tilts the rim to his lips, and the rest of the party does the same. They put their glasses down together, six light thuds that sound like one. He reaches for his napkin, and everyone flicks their own at the same time, in the same way, six fancy squares of cloth smoothed identically onto six laps.

"Isn't it?" he asks her, his eyes eager, full of hope. "Pretty damn close?"

Marsh stares for one more long moment.

Then she stands up from the table.

"Where are you going?" Ren asks, surprised. "Dinner just started."

Marsh walks out the door.

CHRYSALIS

When the next scene opens, everything is entirely silent and still.

Marsh is now standing in the hallway of a deserted, aging municipal building. She waits, taking in the low ceilings, the muted beige walls. The flecked tile on the floor has lost its sheen. It's quiet because it's late evening, after hours, but even so, the place still seems even smaller and shabbier than she remembers. Perhaps it's because she's older now. Or because of everything she's seen and done as part of *All This and More*. But she doesn't mind. Smallness and quiet are exactly why she came here. A place away from everything. No wild scenarios, no over-the-top adventures, no Chrysalis, no Talia, no millions of viewers, even no Ren or Harper. A place where she can hide for just a minute.

A place where she can *think*.

In the gentle dark, Marsh closes her eyes and takes a deep breath.

Just then, a single sound, a soft crack, breaks the silence.

What was that?

She's not waiting to find out. She spins around and begins to sprint, terrified. Her shoes slap down the hall like thunderclaps. In response, another set of shoes answers from the direction of the original sound, heading for her, and she screams.

"Marsh! Wait! It's me!" Lev calls at last.

"Lev," Marsh gasps. She's so relieved, she nearly collapses. "Thank goodness."

Lev emerges from the dark of the hallway, where Marsh is now crouched on her hands and knees as she waits for her panic to subside.

"Sorry," he says. "After the earthquake, I ended up . . . I don't know where. I had to build a tunnel through the code." He points into the blackness behind him, at who knows what.

"It's okay," Marsh says. "I'm glad you're here."

Lev helps her to her feet.

"Back at RealTV's offices," he starts. "You said that Ezra is running the Bubble for this season."

Marsh nods. "I saw him on the outside, just before my first episode started. I didn't think much of it at the time. But since the midseason special, he's been using back doors to communicate with me." She looks at Lev. "He's been trying to find you, ever since the second season was canceled. I think he got himself hired for season three because he was suspicious that something strange was going on."

Lev looks shell-shocked. He has questions about Ezra and the Bubble, probably a million of them, but Marsh can tell that he knows she probably wouldn't be able to answer even one. She's the star of the show, not a physicist.

"Is he with us now?" he finally asks.

Marsh waits for a moment, but the air in front of her stays silent.

"No," she says. "But he saw you, before the earthquake. He knows you're here. I'm sure he's trying to reach us right now."

"He'll find a way," Lev replies. "I know it."

Marsh hopes it's true. Even if the Bubble's security filters have cut Ezra off again, he's always managed to sneak through. She's sure he will again.

Lev takes a steadying breath and looks around. "So, where are we, exactly?"

"Court," Marsh says. She looks at the fluorescent lighting, the cheap plastic waiting chairs. "The south tower of the Maricopa County Superior Court in downtown Phoenix, to be exact."

Lev studies the setting thoughtfully.

"I've seen this place before, in some of your recap bonus footage," he says.

Marsh smiles.

"Jo and I had a judicial internship here in law school," she replies. "Before I dropped out."

"Ah," Lev muses. "We're here because you think Chrysalis is hiding within your biggest regret."

Marsh nods. "Somewhere I'd never want to face."

She turns and motions for Lev to follow her down the hall.

"This way," she says.

He falls in beside her, and their shoes echo softly as they walk. As they pass the elevators, a cluster of pixels fizzles on the wall beside them, but Lev crushes them into the paint with a glare.

"I remember being so excited, and so intimidated, on our first day," Marsh continues. "We both were. I thought that if I said one wrong thing, or made one mistake, they'd throw me out or something."

"I felt the same way on my first day at Sharp Labs," Lev confesses. "Ezra was very confident, he liked to charm others, and I was the quiet one. My style was to keep my head down and do the work."

They pass a clerk heading the other way. During their intern days, it wasn't uncommon for Marsh and Jo to see others working late, but that's not what makes her do a double take. It's because the clerk looks suspiciously like Bryn, Talia's hairstylist from season one. The same tall build, the same dark curls.

Lev frowns subtly when she looks at him. They both quicken their pace.

"There was this one afternoon," she continues, her tone low. "They were going to renovate the judges' chambers, and all of the interns had to stay late to pack up the files and computers. One of the guys found Judge Lippincott's stash of booze."

"You drank it?" Lev asks.

"I didn't, of course," Marsh answers. "But Jo did. By the time the sun was down, they were all tipsy."

Marsh stops them in front of the biggest courtroom on the floor, and Lev arches an inquisitive brow.

"Then someone brought up the dare."

Although it's later in the evening than when they arrived, the hallway has slowly become even busier, somehow. At the far end of the hall, Alexis is standing with unnerving stillness beside season one's HR director, Linnea. Alexis is dressed in a judge's black robes, and Linnea in a court officer's uniform, but even though they're facing each other, their eyes never leave Marsh. Outside the adjacent courtroom, the music composer who came up with *All This and More*'s famous tune, a man with a buzzed head and quirky glasses named Rafael, is now sitting on one of the benches with a phone to his ear—but the screen is dark, and there's no one on the other end of the line.

"Get inside," Lev says softly but urgently. "Now."

Marsh moves as quickly as she can without appearing to scramble. Still, when she pulls the door open, Alexis and Linnea turn toward her, their shoulders swiveling at the same time, their heads tilting to the same curious angle.

"Marsh," Lev warns.

From the bench, Rafael begins to stand.

Marsh slams the door shut and locks it.

As the silence settles again, she and Lev sigh and lean against the door.

It's strange to be here again. After she dropped out of law school, she never came back to the courthouse—not even to watch Jo argue her first case. She said it was because Harper was too little to leave with a babysitter, but that was just an excuse. The longer she waited, the more forbidding this place became. It had grown in her mind into a fortress, a remote tower with no rope, no ladder, no way to climb. Now, Marsh can see that it's not a hallowed temple, not a closed palace. It's just a modest, slightly drab municipal office. There are scuffs on the baseboards and flecks of paint missing on the walls. The air-conditioning rattles ineffectually.

At last, her eyes drift to the first row of wooden pews.

"The dare was to etch our initials into the underside of the front pew," Marsh finally says, pointing. "Someone swore it was a tradition, that there were a hundred sets of initials hidden there. Another said it was good luck. That if we did it, we'd pass the bar and become lawyers."

Lev studies the pew, then looks back at her.

"I was too afraid of getting in trouble." Marsh sighs. "I didn't even look underneath to see if it was true. Over the years, I've always thought this was the instant I started to lose my way. That if I could go back and do this part over again, my life would have turned out right."

"A character-defining backstory moment," Lev says, with a wink. "Great for ratings. Talia would be proud of you."

Marsh snorts. "Where did she end up, after the earthquake?"

"I don't know." He points his chin at the door, to indicate the others in the hall. "But wherever she is, she's probably on her way here."

Marsh nods. Her expression grows serious, and she takes a breath to steel herself.

"This will just take a second."

Even with the subpar air-conditioning, the floor is surprisingly cold against her knees as she bends down. There's not much room, but after an awkward shimmy, Marsh manages to get her head and shoulders beneath the flat underside of the first pew.

Sure enough, the interns were right. The initials are there. Everyone from the semester she served, plus scattered clusters of dozens more. Jo's signature calligraphic *J*, twice as big as everyone else's and clumsier than usual since she'd been using a pocketknife and not a fountain pen, is right above her nose.

Even though Marsh didn't end up scratching her own mark with the rest of them that night, there's still a little space next to Jo, as if waiting for her.

"Do you have something sharp? A knife or paper clip, maybe?" she asks Lev.

He squats down. "A pen," he offers apologetically.

"That'll have to work."

She uncaps it and presses the tip to the wood until it makes a little dent. Slowly, she drags her hand back and forth, digging the first tiny line. She blows a little curl of splinter away, and grips the pen tighter.

As she finishes her initials, a thump beside her head makes her flinch, then smile.

She scoots out and sits up. Then she reaches back underneath the pew—and pulls out her lawyer's briefcase. The one that Dylan surprised her with, countless times, and the one that's followed her from episode to episode, refusing to give up on her.

Her hands run over the cool leather, the edge stitching, the square handle. *It's here.*

She lost it, both in her real life and in the Bubble, but now she's found it again.

Somewhere, a clock chimes, noting the late hour.

"Marsh," Lev urges. "We have to hurry. Even though you've escaped for a moment, Hong Kong was your ninth episode. The next one will be the finale."

Marsh checks her watch.

There are only thirty minutes left until this one ends.

"So, this is really it, then?" she asks.

"I'm afraid so."

Marsh takes a deep breath.

"I still have time," she tells herself.

Time to quash Chrysalis and save her season. Time to make everything perfect.

Finally, she pops the clasps and opens it to reveal a Sharp Purple–colored folder.

"A client file?" Lev asks.

"Yes," Marsh says. "From Mendoza-Montalvo and Hall. It's mine—for the bid I just won in Hong Kong."

The title across the top says: *Sharp Incorporated.*

Lev frowns. "But Sharp doesn't exist anymore."

"Right. Because it folded during season two," Marsh agrees. She turns to him. "And you said, based on what you could find in Sharp Entertainment's database fragments, that Chrysalis *started* in season two."

She taps the folder.

"Whatever happened to Sharp back then, I think it was because of Chrysalis."

The silence in the room hangs heavy as she and Lev consider her theory.

"Only one way to find out," he replies at last. "Ready?"

Marsh shakes her head. "Here goes nothing."

And she opens the folder.

"It's not just a client. It's a case," she confirms as she sees the formatting, the legalese.

Her eyes widen.

"It's *my* case."

It's true. All of the quick scribbles are all in her handwriting, somehow.

She reads as fast as she can.

"It's a lawsuit," she says when she realizes it. "The plaintiff is . . . Claire Sharp herself."

Claire Sharp, billionaire owner of Sharp Labs, the original discoverer of quantum bubbling technology, and Sharp Entertainment, the original creator of *All This and More.*

"But you didn't film a case scene in this episode," Lev says.

"Because the case is old," Marsh says as she skims. "The hearings all took place during season two."

She pauses suddenly.

If the suit is from season two, and it was Marsh's case . . .

Marsh was a lawyer before?

But that's impossible.

Wouldn't she remember?

"What else?" Lev asks.

"You're . . ." Marsh looks up. "You're named, too, as an expert witness. You don't remember, either?"

He shakes his head tensely. "What did I say?"

"Well, it looks like the suit was for damages to the show," Marsh relays as she reads. "You were brought in because we were alleging that the season two contestant tampered with the Bubble, and that caused it to become too unstable. So unstable . . . that it collapsed."

"Collapsed?" Lev cries, shocked. "No, no, no, that can't—" He paces away, then lurches back. "Collapsed? With everyone still inside?!"

Marsh nods, looking pale.

"Everyone got stuck here, with no way out," she says. "Until my season started."

She covers her mouth, aghast.

It's true. The crew of season two have been trapped inside the Bubble this whole time.

That would explain why RealTV needed a whole new team for season three, why there was no one from the original crew anywhere to help with the transition, and why they're all here now.

The silence lingers as she and Lev try to absorb this terrible revelation.

"I can't believe it," Marsh murmurs. She's trying to count everyone she's discovered so far, but there are too many to keep track. "Alexis, Julie, Rafael, Linnea, Bryn. . ."

"And me," Lev says, sick with wonder. "I've been in the Bubble . . . this whole time?"

Everyone from the old Sharp crew, imprisoned here and their memories wiped, all so they couldn't warn RealTV what had happened in season two before it launched her season—

Marsh puts the paper down suddenly.

"Lev."

She can hardly say it.

If Marsh was the lawyer for Claire Sharp's case, then it stands to reason that she also was in the Bubble during season two, somehow.

Which means that she also has been stuck in here with them?

"And you too," Lev says gravely.

Marsh reels, light-headed.

How?

How could she not know?

As she nearly topples, Lev catches her arm and steadies her.

"I'm sorry, Marsh."

She looks at him. "I don't understand."

What *did* happen in that season, that would be worth all this to hide?

Who would go this far?

Lev holds out the folder to her.

"Keep reading," he urges. "You have to do it. All I can see is a blank page."

Slowly, Marsh takes it from him.

Just as she looks down at the paper, a sharp, grating tone rings out across the empty office.

"The finale!" Lev says. "Hurry!"

Her eyes wide with terror, Marsh flips straight to the last sheet in the stack as fast as she can.

There, on the last page, is the answer to all of her questions. Why Chrysalis has been desperately inserting itself into her paths, in whatever form it takes. Why it's tried to influence her choices, no matter how she tried to avoid or thwart it. And why it's grown only more insistent the closer to the finale Marsh draws, before her chance to change her life forever is complete.

"Lev," Marsh says weakly.

She can hardly breathe.

The mysterious season two contestant . . .

was Ren.

She looks up in horror just as the episode goes black.

To begin the season finale: Go to page 322

EPISODE 8

BLASTOFF!

Marsh has no idea where Talia has sent her. She and Alexis were wrestling over the Show Bible so fiercely as that last episode ended, both struggling to flip to different parts of the book, there's no telling where Talia's finger randomly landed in the nearly endless stack of pages. Marsh doesn't know what to expect, and so is trying to expect nothing.

But even so, out of everything it could have been, total silence is the last thing she was ready for.

Slowly, she looks around as the scene brightens.

If her Mexico telenovela star trailer was small, the room she's now in is low and narrow to the point of being claustrophobic. The walls are white, and covered in screens, keypads, and other serious-looking equipment. There are rope tethers, tubes, cubbies, LED bulbs, and buttons everywhere, and there seems to be no natural light at all. Everything is bathed in a sickly fluorescent, artificial glow.

Is she in an underground bunker? A submarine?

But then Marsh notices a tiny porthole window in the wall, and catches sight of the view.

It's black out there.

Blacker black than she's ever seen.

And there are tiny pinpricks of white amid the darkness.

Is she . . .

In space?

JesterG: <Marsh is an ASTRONAUT????>

StrikeF0rce: <I can't believe they can do this! I'm back on board with the show now!>

SharpTruth99: <Don't any of you see what's happening??!?>

The comments have gone completely haywire, clogging up her view until all she can see are spaceship emojis and hearts.

Vadasz123: <Felháborító!!>

Mochiko5283: <いや、このエピソードが今までで1番いい!!!!>

Moms4Marsh: <Omg, do you think they'll do zero-gravity sex?>

Marsh's heart is still racing, from the last jump or from her new environment, she's not sure. She didn't really have much of a plan at the end of that last episode beyond trying to get out of Mexico as quickly as possible. But now that she's here, she's not actually sure what to do. Alexis wanted her to find Chrysalis, but how can she do that if she doesn't even know what it is?

She supposes she could find out, she thinks as her eyes drift to the little window again. In the cosmic distance, something glitters, a faraway comet or planet beckoning.

Or not.

At least, not *yet.*

She's so far away, Chrysalis won't find her here. Not for a while. Instead of chasing it, she could just take a breath. She could briefly enjoy how beautiful, how exhilarating, how *impossible,* being an astronaut on the International Space Station would be.

After all, as Talia's been insisting to her all along, there are infinite lives here in the Bubble for Marsh to enjoy. If something isn't quite right in one of them, like her career or her city—or Chrysalis—she can just choose another one.

She floats from room to room, giddy at her weightlessness. She does backflips, she swims, she spends an entire day doing everything "upside down," and marvels at how it makes no difference. She takes pictures of herself in every room of the ISS, to email back to Harper on Earth. She laughs at how whenever she's not taking a bite of something, she can just let go of it and it hangs suspended in midair. She gets lost for hours looking out of portholes at the great, mysterious expanse of the universe, awed by the magnitude of what the Bubble can do.

Finally, their crew captain Victor puts them to work, and together with him, Jo, and Ren, Marsh prepares to complete a daring space walk that will upgrade the ISS's satellite system—and she discovers that she's somehow proficient in mechanical engineering, advanced mathematics, and astronomy all at once.

Ordinarily, she'd be embarrassed by how unrealistic that is, but she's having too much fun to care. Obviously, she's not going to make this path her permanent one and really become an astronaut, but to see herself succeed even at this life makes her giddily proud. She's gone from lonely, sad background character who was convinced she was too late to change her life to finding love again with Ren, reigniting her professional passions, and proving to herself that she can not only survive, but *flourish*, in places like Iceland and Mexico . . . hell, even in space! She hasn't found her perfect forever path yet, but she's starting to believe that when she finally does, she's going to be brave enough to actually seize it.

As Marsh creeps out into the desolate, terrifying, beautiful obsidian vacuum in her poofy white suit and bulbous helmet, she's breathless with wonder. For as long as she lives, she knows that without a doubt, this will be the most magnificent thing she'll ever see.

Ren, on the other hand, is the nerdiest version he's been so far in any of the episodes, to fit with his new character here, she supposes. He's pale, and very slender—convenient for life on the ISS—his hair is thinning on top, and his glasses are twice as thick, so that they make his eyes seem giant at some angles. *He looks more like a stereotype of a scientist than a real one,* Marsh thinks, and rolls her eyes at the show.

But on the bedroom front, he's just as eagerly, nearly frantically, diligent as always—even with zero gravity. *All This and More* is smart enough to know not to tweak that detail.

Marsh has been doing everything she can to avoid it, but now that their mission is completed, and a shuttle is heading to the ISS from Earth to pick Marsh and her crew up, she knows she can't procrastinate any longer.

She has to talk to Talia at some point.

Even though they're in space, Marsh's team tries to keep pace with Earth, and all the clocks are set to US Central Time, where the Johnson Space Center in Houston, Texas, is. On their last night before the shuttle arrives to dock, she takes the late shift at their comms desk. She waits until the rest of the crew is strapped into their sleeping bags and all the lights are out. Finally, with a sigh, she opens up the long-distance satellite channel.

Houston—*Talia*—has called fourteen times and sent fifty emergency pings over the course of this episode.

"Uh, hi," she finally says, as a nearly hysterical Talia Cruz appears on the grainy screen.

"*Marsh!*" she shouts, gripping the sides of whatever JSC headquarters computer she's looking at Marsh from. "Thank goodness! I've been trying to reach you since Mexico! Are you all right? Is everyone else all right? Is anyone hurt? Do—"

"I'm fine. I'm fine," Marsh interrupts gently. "Everyone is okay."

"Oh, thank God. Whew!"

Talia, in rare form, sinks into her chair for a relieved moment before springing back to exquisite posture. Even dressed as a government administrator, and at four o'clock in the morning, she looks like a movie star.

"I can't believe Alexis!" she continues furiously. "That was so dangerous! Flipping through the Show Bible like that, trying to send you somewhere without a plan. Anything could have happened!" She balls her delicate fingers into charming little fists. "I'm just glad I could get you away from her, to somewhere safe!"

Notamackerel: <How far is far enough, she sent her to literal SPACE!>

"How did it even happen?" Marsh asks. "What is Alexis doing in the Bubble?"

"No idea," Talia says. "She's not part of your crew, that's for sure. Believe me, I'm definitely going to have a word with the team that runs our security. That kind of tampering is unacceptable. It's sabotage!"

"I don't know what she was doing, but it really didn't seem like sabotage," Marsh replies. "It almost seemed like she was trying to help."

"How?" Talia asks. "By trying to fling you through the quantum universe completely at random, without a clue as to where you'd land? Who knows what would have happened if I hadn't managed to reach you in time? She risked your life, and your loved ones' lives, carelessly."

Marsh frowns at that. Talia does have a good point. What Alexis did *was* risky.

But she also knows that Talia didn't hear what her old producer said, before she sent Marsh here. That she has to find the source of Chrysalis. She was so desperate, she put them all in danger to give Marsh the chance to do it.

Just what does Alexis think Chrysalis could be?

And why does Talia seem so unconcerned?

"Whatever Alexis was trying to achieve, it doesn't matter," Talia continues. "I promised you at the beginning that I'd do everything I could to make your life as perfect as mine is by your finale, and I'm going to keep that promise."

The words are so comforting. Even with so many unanswered questions, Marsh just wants to sink into them. To forget the strange things that happened in Iceland and Mexico, to forget what Alexis said. She didn't join the show to track down whatever this Chrysalis thing is—she came here to fix her life! It's already hard enough to do that without trying to solve a mystery on the side that's not even hers to begin with.

She's spent so much of her life doing what everyone else wants, she almost forgot she doesn't have to.

Especially not on *All This and More.*

"This is your season. Not hers," Talia says, like she can read her mind. "This is about what *you* want."

"Yes," Marsh echoes. "This is my season. And what I want."

"That's it, Marsh!" Talia replies, with double the verve. "Don't worry. You don't have to be concerned about Alexis. There are so many paths left for us to choose from, I doubt she'll ever end up in the same place as us again."

She bends down, reaching for something out of the frame.

"And," she says, as she sits back up with effort, and pulls the Show Bible into her lap. "Most importantly, the Show Bible is safe. We have it."

The book is, as usual, even more monstrous than the last time Marsh has seen it. It's so gigantic now that it's nearly as tall as Talia is, as it sits there on her thighs. It takes up more of the little video screen than her host does.

"So, outer space was a fun diversion—can we just pause for a second to say, *Wow! How incredible!*?" She continues as she opens the cover, struggling to keep her voice bubbly and easy as the weight of the pages nearly overwhelms her. "But it's time to get you back on track. Let me send you somewhere else. After all, we don't have much time left, and there's so much more for you to do!"

Despite her lingering unease, just the mention of a new life makes Marsh's pulse quicken with excitement. It's still a thrill—all the possible things she could try, all the possible places she could go.

"Are you ready?" Talia asks over the feed, her finger hovering just above some new future, some new life. "You could have *All This* . . ."

Marsh smiles.

"*And More,*" she replies.

ALWAYS ANOTHER

Marsh opens her eyes slowly, both hesitant and excited to see what new possible future is laid out before her this time.

This one will be it, she tells herself.

And if not this one, then the next one will be.

Or the one after that.

She tries everything, because she can. Marsh is an haute couture fashion designer, a painter in Paris, a senator, a wine vineyard owner. Her faithful cast follows her through every life: Victor always her boss, Jo always her colleague, Harper always her daughter, Ren always her partner. The scenery changes so quickly, it's like reading a pop-out flip book, where from every page springs a new cardboard cutout. None of them can tell except for Marsh, although there are more strange contradictions—Victor and Jo lose themselves in conversations, or appear wearing suits and holding court papers when they should be clad in park ranger uniforms or carrying firemen's gear, and Harper keeps talking about the violin and then getting confused, even though with every new scenario, she has a different area of musical expertise. Sometimes the background flickers, replacing itself with a new environment that makes no sense, then flickers back again.

Ren bears the most of it, though. Out of all of them, he changes the most each time, morphing into some updated incarnation based on the previous episode, edging ever closer to Marsh's ideal man. He seems downright exhausted, at times—maybe because of all the transformations he's being put through, even if he doesn't know it.

Still, Marsh can't stop. It's simply too addicting.

A marine biologist. A world-renowned sculptor. An architect for the first permanent moon base.

Notamackerel: <Marsh is losing control of her own show! How many lives is she going to try?>
Moms4Marsh: <As many as she needs to find the perfect one!>

Marsh nods. That's right. Every new life is close, nearly right, but not exactly so. It amazes her now to think that at midseason, she almost thought she was close to done. Her life has become a thousand times better since then—she's ambitious and successful at whatever job she tries, her love life is blossoming, her makeover and her new closeness with her daughter have stuck around past the next commercial break—far more than she ever could have hoped for.

But the more places she visits in this montage episode, the more things she tries, Marsh starts to *really* understand what this show is all about.

Her family, her career—heck, even her bold new personality and style . . . those things are the big pieces. The broad strokes.

But broad strokes only do not make a masterpiece.

They don't make *perfect*.

And that's what Marsh is here for.

She won't rest until she gets it.

It seems ungrateful at first, to discard a path for a mere detail. But didn't Talia tell her that nothing, no matter how small, is out of reach on *All This and More*?

She leaves one life because the house isn't big enough, and the one after because it's monstrously big. Another time, it's because of the wrong city; the next, the wrong job. Once, Harper seems bored, then, the weather isn't good. Then Marsh doesn't like her hair.

Each time, it gets a little easier.

"Sorry, can we cut?" she asks as she stands at the edge of a hot air balloon's basket, gazing out over the gorgeous, golden Serengeti. The swelling music cuts off abruptly. "I just—I really want to be able to enjoy this moment, and the light was kind of in my eyes. Can we redo it?"

"Absolutely," Talia says, and gives the burner a little more gas to lift them back to their original position again, before the close-up started. The zebras seem to also turn around, to head back to where the herd was before they started galloping.

The Serengeti is incredible, and so is the romantic, candlelit dinner Ren has prepared for them in their luxury safari tent later that evening. Although she wishes it had been a pasta dish, not a salad. That there had been a few more candles, and that Ren's hair had been a little longer and more touchable.

And that hints of Chrysalis would stop popping up at the periphery of every other scene.

A path in which she's a famous author lasts for half a day, a life as a white water rafter for an hour. At a break in the river, Marsh sets down her paddle and waves away a butterfly, more forcefully than she ordinarily would if it had been just an insect and not a strange saboteur, doggedly pursuing her across the quantum universe.

"You know, this is great, but I feel like Ren's footwork wasn't quite as snappy as it could be," she says as they hand her a trophy for first place in the national ballroom dancing championship. "Do you think it's worth redoing?"

"We can do anything you want, Marsh!" Behind her graceful posture, it's clear that even the world's most unflappable host is exhausted, although she'd never admit it. "Or, something else! There are millions of lives here in the Bubble."

Talia's right, that there may be nearly infinite paths for her to try, and infinite details to tweak. But in the back of her mind, Marsh knows there's a limit to it. She might be able to keep going forever if it were just up to her, but it's not. It's about her happiness, but also about episodes. And there are only two of them left before the finale.

She has to pick something eventually.

Things go fuzzy around the edges as the Bubble prepares to shift to somewhere new yet again, and Marsh grins.

But not yet.

A GAME OF CHANCE

Marsh can't tell if she feels the thunder of applause or hears it first. As the darkness lifts, she looks eagerly around the chaotic, bustling room. There are no windows, but lots of bright lights, neon signs, and wall-to-wall carpet in a terrible geometric pattern. Tables are everywhere, each one tightly packed, and people are laughing, crying, shouting, and everything in between. Somewhere, a bell begins to ring, and another excited cheer rises up from the back corner.

It's a casino, Marsh realizes.

Is she in Las Vegas?

"Ah, there you are!" a brown-haired woman in a fancy business pantsuit cries from the table nearest to her.

She looks familiar to Marsh, but amid all the chaos, Marsh can't place her. Is she from Mendoza-Montalvo and Hall? Or perhaps from Pallissard? She knows she's seen her somewhere before, but nothing seems right.

"We were about to finish the match without you!" the woman continues, gesturing to an open chair. At the same table, Ren and Jo are also waiting.

"We'd never finish without Marsh," Ren bellows, and slaps the green surface in front of him, more fired up than Marsh has ever seen him.

"That's right," Jo agrees. "It wouldn't be a proper victory if I won without beating the reigning champion."

"You wish!" Ren chuckles villainously. "That prize is all mine."

"Take your seats, please," Victor says. He's in a suit, standing alone on one side of the table, and holding a deck of cards. Marsh's eyes finally focus on the giant banner on the wall behind him.

ANNUAL WORLD SERIES OF POKER TOURNAMENT
FINAL ROUND

In this life, they're all world champion professional poker players?

Marsh grins as the casino roars.

This will be fun.

Still gaping at the sign, she manages to drop into her chair. She has no idea what all of the stacks of colored chips in front of her are worth, but if this is the final game, it must be millions. Another bell rings, another match won somewhere, and the crowd begins to gather around her table now. From the mezzanine above, even more onlookers lean over, eager to witness the final event.

Behind her, a tournament jumbotron broadcasting the action cuts to a tight shot on Marsh as she gets settled. As she watches, the Bubble senses the tweak she wants, and zooms so the close-up is even more extreme. She, as she always does now, looks fantastic—might as well enjoy it.

Victor clears his throat. "Now that all the players have returned, let us continue the final round of this tournament!" he proclaims—part dealer, part announcer, it seems. "Good luck to you all."

"Prepare your concession speech!" Ren crows at Marsh. Clearly, his tactic is to bluff his way to victory with that unshakable confidence. "Don't worry, you're all invited to my after-party!"

Marsh can't decide what to make of this new Ren. He's so much cockier and showier, which is interesting, but he's also obsessively competitive. She gets the sense that his ultimate goal in this path, the thing he's been working toward for decades, has been to be at this table, in this tournament, playing against her. Perhaps they're lifelong rivals? He's so happy to be here, he hasn't stopped grinning since the scene began. So much so, in fact, that he almost seems the opposite—so maniacally thrilled that he can't control it. Marsh is faintly concerned that, whether he wins or loses, he's going to flip the table and launch himself at poor Victor.

The only thing constant about Ren is that he's always different. She sighs.

It's nearly too much for her to keep all his versions straight. She can't imagine how confusing it would be for Ren if he could remember each of his incarnations.

"If you please," Victor says to him. "This is a tournament for professionals."

Jo snorts. She, at least, seems the way she usually does. She's got the same focused, lethal expression she has during closing arguments—it turns out being a lawyer makes one well suited to cards. It's impossible to tell whether she has a killer hand or just a killer poker face.

Well, it'll make it that much more fun to best them both, then, Marsh thinks.

Peace restored, Victor shuffles the deck dramatically, then assumes a stoic pose after he's dealt. Jo, Ren, and the mysterious pantsuit woman peek at their cards with polished nonchalance, and Marsh tries to keep her face neutral as she does the same.

PokerChamp888: <Pay attention, everyone! We might only get one look at their hands!>

Mysterious woman

Ren

Jo

Marsh

Fortunata111: <Wow! What great cards Marsh has!>
Moms4Marsh: <Awww, Ren has all hearts, because he's full of love!>

Marsh smiles. Her pulse is starting to quicken, and she's getting into the excitement. She tries not to look at the comments, but there are simply too many poker enthusiasts spouting off, and she can't help but learn what everyone else is holding.

Well, why not use her loyal viewers to her advantage? She shrugs as she and everyone else push a handful of chips forward as their starting blind. Her newfound expertise in this life ought to start filtering into her consciousness at any moment, but after all, wouldn't doing everything she can to push the odds even *more* in her favor be in keeping with the spirit of the show?

"Everyone's in," Victor announces, and then deals the three communal cards face-up on the table to start the round.

PokerChamp888: <Incredible! Now Marsh has four-of-a-kind with those two aces! She's practically guaranteed to win!>
Schneckchen: <Marsh ist die Beste!>

Marsh is certain she's going to give herself away, but it doesn't matter. There's so much energy buzzing in the casino, it's emboldened everyone at the table. She can feel the adrenaline in her own veins, urging her to play recklessly.

"Bets, please," Victor says, looking first to the mysterious woman.

Marsh holds her breath as the woman turns and examines her, rather than her own cards, with intense seriousness. At last, she pushes every stack of chips in front of her forward without a word.

"All in!" Victor cries, his voice hitching slightly at her daring. "That's all in."

TopFan01: <Wow, how bold!>
YanYan242: <This is a high-stakes game!>

"All in, too, then!" Ren shouts, with a slavering enthusiasm that makes the crowd jeer. He shoves forward all his chips—somehow, they each have exactly the same amount, Marsh notices—which makes her heart beat faster.

Next, Jo glares like it's a cross-examination. She doesn't have the cards to be competitive, Marsh knows, even as she still withers beneath her friend's intimidating gaze.

At last, she sits back.

"I fold," she says.

The mysterious woman chuckles haughtily.

Her business-y suit, the sensible heels, the short hair—it's all frustratingly familiar to Marsh.

She's got to be a lawyer, she thinks, still trying to place the unknown player. *Right?*

But now, it's Marsh's turn, and every gaze is riveted to her.

To stay in the tournament, she must match Ren's bet, and go all in herself. But she's not worried. With her four aces, she's got the best chance of winning out of everyone.

And, after all, this is *All This and More.*

The show would never let her lose.

"All in," Marsh finally declares, pushing every chip in front of her into the pot as the whispers of surprise at the drama swell.

Frónverji: <I thought there were still two more cards to go! What happens now that they've all bet everything they have?>
PokerChamp888: <The dealer will still deal the last two cards—and then, whoever ends up with the best hand wins!>
Moms4Marsh: <This is so exciting!!>

"As per the tournament rules, if at least one player is all in, all players participating in a hand must show their cards, because further betting is impossible," Victor announces for the benefit of the crowd, and then turns back to the table. "Players, if you please . . . show us your cards."

Marsh, Ren, and the mysterious woman all look at one another as they turn their cards over in unison.

"Damnit!" the mysterious woman wails, her smug expression crumbling into one of dismay as she sees that Marsh's aces have her queens beat. "I can't believe it."

Ren, in contrast, is still nearly vibrating with energy, despite having the worst hand of the three of them. He appears on the verge of either tears or laughter, he's so swept up in the game.

"So far, it looks like Marsh's victory is all but assured," Victor says, drumming up the audience.

His hand lingers on the deck.

"Are we ready?" he asks.

"Yes!" the crowd chants.

Yes, Marsh agrees.

At last, he deals the penultimate card.

"Ten of hearts, jack of hearts, queen of hearts—with this king, Ren now has a royal flush!" Victor affirms, to jubilant applause. "Incredible!"

LunaMágica: <Oh no! Ren now has the best hand possible!>

Moms4Marsh: <What does that mean???>
PokerChamp888: <It means that there's no way Marsh can win, no matter what the last card turns out to be>
N3vrGiv3Up: <What?? No!!! She has to win! I know she will!>

"Better luck next time," Ren needles Marsh, preening. At the center of the table, his towers of chips sway, and one falls with a rushing hiss, as if to punctuate his taunt.

Marsh is still staring at the king of hearts, stunned.

She can't believe she's lost the upper hand.

How could this happen? How could the show allow it?

And what is she supposed to do now?

SharpTruth104: <Ignore the game—I'm begging you all to look at what's happening to the Bubble!>

[Automatic security filters have deleted this account]

SharpTruth105: <Screw this>

SharpTruth105: <***MARSH!*** If you see this, look at your fourth player! LOOK at her! She—>

[Automatic security filters have deleted this account]

The comments continue to harangue the troll who's now taken Nota-mackerel's place as most-hated commenter, but SharpTruth's panicked, direct request startles Marsh enough to seize her attention.

Has that ever happened before? she wonders.

Her viewers often shout all kinds of encouraging things at her, but it's always with the understanding that she'll almost certainly never notice any particular one, not with the millions of posts streaming by every second. But SharpTruth has not only also noticed that something's off about her season—*her Bubble*—but is trying to tell her directly.

Marsh studies the woman in the pantsuit intently.

It was hard to see with all the commotion in the casino and the thrill of the game—she wasn't sure it even mattered, anyway. But if one of her viewers also has noticed something might be wrong, it must be important.

As Marsh stares again, curious anew, recognition finally hits her with the sudden force of a car crash.

She gasps.

Is the mysterious woman actually the old head of Sharp Entertainment?

Is that really Julie Pabst?

It has to be. Marsh recalls her face now. She was always behind the scenes, but is famous for being the executive that green-lit the idea for *All This and More* and got the show onto the air in the first place.

But why is she here, in this poker game? Are there even *more* people from the old crew hiding in Marsh's Bubble?

Her eyes snap back to the comments, but SharpTruth is gone, locked out until they can figure out how to get around the Bubble's security filters once more.

It doesn't matter. Marsh is sure that it's Julie Pabst, and now, certain that something weird is going on.

For some reason, part of the old crew is in the Bubble with her.

How did SharpTruth know that?

Who is this strange viewer?

Marsh furtively casts around, scouring the rest of the casino's audience. During Talia's season, the Sharp team was as close as family. So, if Sharp's old CEO is in the Bubble, then surely her handpicked composer—the man who became world-renowned for coming up with *All This and More*'s signature musical jingle—will turn up, too.

Rafael must be around here somewhere.

"I've been looking forward to this tournament for a long time," Julie says to Marsh, once she realizes she's being studied.

Marsh narrows her eyes.

"Ever since the first season?" she tries, even though discussing the show is against Talia's rules.

But Julie just cocks her head.

"Since when?" she asks. "The first *tournament*, you mean?"

Marsh frowns. Julie doesn't seem to know she's part of the cast, instead of the crew.

Just like Alexis didn't, either.

But the game has continued on. Around their table, the crowd titters excitedly as Victor prepares to deal the all-important last card.

SharpTruth106: <C:\ATAM\Bubble\episode_8\access>
[*Automatic security filters have deleted this account*]
StrikeF0rce: <This is unacceptable! Anyone who tries to hack the poker
    game should be banned!>
SharpTruth107: <Marsh, I'm trying, but you have to—>
[*Automatic security filters have deleted this account*]

Victor hasn't set the final card down yet, but Marsh looks up from the comments, confused, as a familiar jingle filters in over the casino's intercom system.

She knows what that sound means.

It's time to make a big choice.

But why here, why now? This is just a card game.

How is a poker hand going to significantly influence her season?

She looks back at the waiting deck as the chatter swells in anticipation. Or rather, at the paisley design on the back of its top card.

That's how, she sees now.

"You okay?" Jo asks her.

Even ferociously competitive Ren looks concerned.

But Marsh can't answer. She stares at the intricate pattern.

She doesn't know how she didn't notice this before, either, but it's unmistakable.

At the center of the design is a butterfly.

LunaMágica: <Dios mío . . . there it is again>

Marsh looks up, lost.

This path was supposed to be a fun diversion, a chance to get her thrills in before settling down into her final life. But now she can't deny it any longer.

No matter how far she runs, no matter what path she chooses, Chrysalis will still find her.

Would it be worse to keep playing now that it's here, or to quit the tournament? With Ren's royal flush, her commenters say that she can't win, but this is *All This and More.*

What if she manages to pull off a victory, somehow?

What if she can't?

To try to escape
the game:
Turn the page

To keep playing:
Go to page 373

"It's your turn, Marsh," Jo encourages as the whole casino holds its breath for her to reveal her cards and end the tournament.

But Marsh shakes her head.

She doesn't know what to do. Based on the cards, she's almost certain that she—or rather, Chrysalis—has the best hand. But there's no telling what will happen if she lets that victory play out. Or if she folds and forces Chrysalis to fail.

If only there were some way to get out of the tournament without having to win or lose.

"Are you all right?" Ren finally asks her, after she's been silent for too long. Everyone at the table is staring at her, waiting for her move. A pin drop would be like an explosion. "What's wrong?"

"I can't do this," she finally says.

Ren frowns. "You're not enjoying the tournament?"

"No," she admits.

He stares at her, trying to understand why Marsh is so upset. What she's saying makes no sense to him, she knows, but there's no point trying to explain.

"Don't worry," he replies at last, his voice much softer than before, the ridiculous bravado act dropped. "You'll get it right next time."

At first, it's such a relief to hear him try to comfort instead of compete with her, that it takes a beat for Ren's words to fully land.

Next time.

Marsh pauses.

What an odd thing to say.

Does Ren . . . know something?

She turns to him, uneasy. "What do you mean, next time?" she asks. The hairs are standing up on the back of her neck.

But Ren just shrugs.

"You know." He gestures to the casino. "Next time. It's an annual tournament. I'm sure you'll make the finals again next year."

Marsh watches him closely—but Ren's gaze is steady, his expression innocent. He doesn't know about the show, about the choices. He's just trying to show good sportsmanship.

"Yes," Marsh agrees at last, and Ren smiles. "Next time will be better."

"In the meantime, though." Julie clears her throat, and Marsh's heart jumps into her own. "We have *this* tournament to finish."

SharpTruth217: <Marsh, I can help>
[Automatic security filters have deleted this account]

SharpTruth is back! Marsh wants to jump out of her chair with joy. She doesn't know how they can help get her out of this, but she's so desperate, she'll take assistance from anyone at this point.

SharpTruth218: <Nod if you see this>
[Automatic security filters have deleted this account]

She nods as subtly as she can.

"We're waiting," Julie taunts, her patience running thin.

"Time to see your hand," Victor says.

SharpTruth219: <I'm trying, hang on>
[Automatic security filters have deleted this account]
SharpTruth220: <Got it!>
SharpTruth220: <Best I could come up with>

Marsh's breath seizes as she waits to see what her mysterious benefactor has done.

SharpTruth220: <Now, do—>
[Automatic security filters have deleted this account]
SharpTruth221: <Do a magic trick—>
[Automatic security filters have deleted this account]

What?

She blinks, confused, as SharpTruth's last comment disappears.

Do a magic trick?

What's *that* supposed to mean?

How is a magic trick going to save her?

Frantic, Marsh looks down at her cards.

She's still holding them. In fact, she's holding the entire deck now, she realizes.

And she's still in the casino, but they're all not at a poker tournament anymore.

They're at a magic show.

And Marsh is the magician.

"What an incredible illusion!" Victor, dressed in all black, like her assistant, perhaps, cries into a microphone from the corner of the stage—*they're on a stage now*—and the audience below roars with applause at whatever she just did. "Let's hear it for the Great Marshmallow!"

Marsh flinches as the spotlight on her grows even brighter to match the rising sound. She glances down at her sparkling black-sequined tuxedo, and then touches the brim of the black top hat on her head. The stage is emitting some moody fog from the bottom vents now, and it's swirling around her feet, the cool mist licking at her ankles.

"Now, are you all ready for tonight's last trick?" Victor asks the rapt crowd, once they've finally quieted. "We need one volunteer."

"Oh, choose me!" Ren waves enthusiastically from the front row, where he's seated next to Julie and Jo as part of the audience now. "Choose me!"

Marsh swallows and points at him. "The gentleman in the front," she says. Her voice wavers, but her lips pull into a rictus stage grin.

Elated, Ren bounds out of his chair and rushes to climb the stairs onto the stage. A spotlight finds him as he approaches, and guides him to her.

"I love card tricks," he crows, and the audience chuckles.

"Well, then . . ." Marsh holds out the deck in a fan, and tries to look confident. "Pick a card. Any card."

Ren stares intently at the crescent of Sharp Purple butterflies on the backs of all the cards, trying to decide. Finally, he eases one from near the middle out, and cradles it dramatically in his palms as he raises it to his eyes.

"Now, remember your card," Marsh instructs, and holds the deck back out.

Ren slides it back into the rest, and she collapses the fan into a single block.

She shuffles once, twice, her breathing shallow and fast.

"Abracadabra," she whispers—and disappears.

When Marsh appears again, she's still in the casino, but not onstage anymore. She's several levels down—below hotel rooms, below the stage, below the gambling hall—in a basement service corridor that the maintenance staff use.

SharpTruth did it.

She actually escaped the tournament.

Her heart is thundering so loudly, she's afraid it's echoing all the way up to the gambling levels for everyone to hear. Her eyes drift down the plain white walls to the end of the empty hallway.

What now? she wants to ask.

SharpTruth222: <Quick, pocket>
[Automatic security filters have deleted this account]

She jams her hand into one pants pocket, then the other. A set of car keys is now tucked into the fabric.

SharpTruth223: <All I can do right now—>
[Automatic security filters have deleted this account]

Marsh pulls the little key and fob out and stares at them, her hands shaking.

She understands SharpTruth's plan now.

She knows what to do.

As quietly as she can, she opens the rusty service door. A blast of hot, nighttime desert air hits her, and she stumbles through it into a casino parking lot jam-packed with darkened cars. She smashes the UNLOCK button on the plastic fob repeatedly, until a few rows away, a sedan's lights flash against the dark. The engine rumbles as it starts, and Marsh winces—but nothing else moves. No one has figured out yet that her magic act was an escape plan.

After a moment, Marsh edges out of the parking lot and onto the street. A few turns later, she's at the freeway. But she's not heading deeper into the gaudy Las Vegas Strip. Those sparkling lights are in her rearview, not in front of her.

There aren't many people out to begin with, and soon, Marsh's is the only car on the road. The freeway turns from urban thoroughfare to bare highway, and then to a single-lane road, leading out into the desert.

Her eyes scan the harsh landscape as it rolls past, flat and parched and shadowed in deep purple beneath the night sky. A rusted highway sign listing the number of miles to distant cities whizzes by her window, and she grips the wheel harder, determined.

This latest life has placed Marsh closer to Phoenix than she's been since the second half of the season started.

Closer to *Dylan* than she's been since the second half of the season started, to be exact.

To find Dylan:
Go to page 248

EPISODE 1

THE VERDICT

Marsh's heart is thudding in her chest as the camera fades up from black and the episode crystallizes around her.

It's dark, and at first, she can't tell where she is—but then she recognizes the room.

It's late evening, judging by the dark horizon and twinkling city through the window, and the overhead lights are off, but there's no mistaking that she's in Victor's office at Mendoza-Montalvo and Hall.

Marsh lets out a slow breath, relieved.

"Hello? Victor?" she calls, but the hall beyond the doorway remains silent. It is late, after all. Victor must have gone home already.

Marsh is standing by his desk, and it takes her a moment to figure out what she's supposed to be doing. Dropping off a file? Picking one up? Finally, she realizes that she's holding a wooden box.

His cigar box, which he opens only for special occasions.

There's only one reason Marsh retrieves his cigar box for him—because he's celebrating a landslide victory with the other lawyers in the conference room.

"Hi, Marsh," a voice says, and Marsh nearly jumps out of her skin.

"Oops." Behind her, Talia scrunches her shoulders apologetically. "I didn't mean to surprise you."

"Sorry," Marsh manages, once her voice won't give away how fast her heart is racing.

It comes out as a mumble, but Talia has more than enough pep to carry the scene until Marsh gets her act together. "Welcome to your first choice!" She beams and executes a twirl.

TopFan01: <Here we go, y'all!>

The words appear in the air right in front of Marsh's face, a stream of hearts exploding all around them, and she screams, nearly dropping her phone.

"Wonderful. The chat roll is online already!" Talia exclaims, delighted.

YanYan242: \<TopFan01, you're back!\>
Fortunata111: \<Our favorite moderator!\>
JesterG: \<All hail the voice of reason!\>
TopFan01: \<Thanks, y'all. Happy to be here, too! Are you all ready to root
    for Marsh as she makes her life perfect??\>

"The . . ." Marsh pauses. "Chat? Roll?"

"It's a new feature this season, now that the show is live!" Talia sings. "It's
amazing. Sharp Entertainment used to host an Internet forum where fans could
gather, but this year, RealTV has created a direct line between you and your
millions of dedicated, passionate viewers! You'll be able to see their comments
in real time during key scenes." She clasps her hands together. "Amazing, right?"

"Uh." Marsh stares at Talia long enough that any normal person's smile
would waver. "Y-yes," she stammers at last. "Amazing."

Talia rewards her with a comforting squeeze on her arm as more hearts
flood across her field of vision.

N3vrGiv3Up: \<I can't wait!\>
Schneckchen: \<Ich liebe diese Sendung!\>
Moms4Marsh: \<Go, Marsh, go!\>

There are hundreds of posts every second, far too many to catch, let
alone remember, every name, but inevitably, some stand out.

Notamackerel: \<YAWN! I can already tell this is going to be the most
    boring season ever!\>

Thousands of cartoonish middle fingers obliterate Marsh's view, until
she nearly staggers.

Monsterrific: \<Oh, of course. Our favorite troll had to find his way here, too.\>
StrikeF0rce: \<Couldn't find any friends of your own during the hiatus?\>
Notamackerel: \<Got tired of your mom!\>

The thumbs-downs overwhelm Marsh so quickly that she actually
swipes at the air in front of her. "How do I . . ." Every word is like a fleck of
dust stinging against her eyes. "How do I make it stop?"

Talia giggles. "We never want our viewers to stop, Marsh! But they'll of course understand that sometimes you need a private moment. If you ever do, you can just go like this . . ." Talia closes her eyes for a second, a slow, deliberate blink. "And the comments will minimize for a little bit."

Marsh copies her, and everything goes mercifully silent.

"Wow" is all she can finally manage.

Talia, unfazed, pulls Marsh closer to her, likely so they're centered in the camera frame. "So. Talk to me. What do you think of your new life so far?"

"Uh." Marsh is still too rattled from the comments to focus. "I mean, I don't even know what's happening yet."

Talia is always ready to help. She points to the box under Marsh's arm. "Well, what's this?"

"The party!" Marsh gasps. "Come on, this way."

She tucks the box under her arm and hustles toward the conference room at the end of the corridor, Talia following close behind. As she nears, the echoes of a raucous conversation crest and ebb, punctuated by bursts of laughter. Through the glass wall, she can see that the entire ceiling is covered in balloons, and everywhere there isn't a bottle of champagne or a platter of hors d'oeuvres on the great oak table, the lacquered wood is sparkling with confetti.

Marsh hasn't been to every victory party, just the ones where Victor asked her to stay late to help set up the champagne and hors d'oeuvres, but she's seen enough to know that this particular celebration seems even *more* lavish than they already are.

"Sorry about that," she says as she pushes the door open, but before she can finish her apology for taking so long, everyone in the packed room suddenly stands up and starts clapping.

"There she is!" one of the senior lawyers cries, and a couple of the first-years jump up to blow a piercing whistle amid the cheering.

Marsh stands frozen to the spot, her eyes wide like a cornered animal's.

Why is everyone at the firm clapping for her for bringing a box of cigars?

As Talia beams at her, Marsh spins toward the giant table, where she knows the congratulatory cake will be. She looks to see whether Victor or Jo's name is written in colorful frosting on the side of the towering pastry.

But this time, the letters spell out *M-A-R-S-H*.

The party is because *she's* the one who just won what seems to be the biggest case their firm has ever had.

Marsh is not just a lawyer for Mendoza-Montalvo and Hall now, she realizes.

She's a superstar there.

"What do you think?" Talia giggles. "Pretty awesome, huh?"

Marsh just stares.

Is this real?

It can't really be real.

Talia grins at her dazed expression. "It is."

SagwaGold: <我們愛你, Marsh!>
LunaMágica: <She is so adorable!>

Talia grabs Marsh's hand before she can bat the words away on instinct, and Marsh manages to smile appreciatively instead.

Her host winks at her, and Marsh blushes.

You're getting the hang of this, it means.

"You're looking very starry-eyed." Jo chuckles as she appears, and hands her a glass of bubbly. "The victory's finally hitting you?"

On her other side, Talia takes the opportunity to lean in. "Enjoy your party. You've earned it!" she whispers, and lets the crowd overtake her as she scoots back into it. "I'll be around, don't worry."

Marsh finally stops staring at the cake and toasts Jo as nonchalantly as she can manage. "Used up all my steely veneer in court," she says.

Jo takes an appreciative sip. "I'll say. I've never seen a jury come back so fast in my life. I hadn't even finished my lunch when we heard they were filing back in, and I had to stuff my face and run. I was still chewing a bite of sandwich as I slid into one of the pews!"

Marsh bursts out laughing as Jo mimes how she tried to hide her mouth as she huddled in the last row of the courtroom earlier that afternoon.

"I can't imagine what Judge Chopra would have thought if he saw me, but I wasn't going to miss the verdict for anything," Jo finishes, still chuckling. "I'm so proud of you, Marsh."

"We all are," a familiar voice says, and Marsh turns to see Dylan standing behind her.

What's Dylan doing at Mendoza-Montalvo and Hall? She gasps.

Her left thumb darts furtively forward to stroke her ring finger, to confirm there's no ring there. How could there be? In this episode, because

Marsh put her career first over everything else, her path would have followed Jo's much more closely than it followed her original life. She and Dylan would have divorced just after Harper was born, and she would have gone on to finish law school and become a lawyer, like she'd always wanted.

Already, her head's starting to spin a little keeping track of the details. When she and Dylan split up in each reality, how old Harper is, if there was ever a Ren. Marsh is glad that Talia has the Show Bible to make sense of it all.

"There's our woman of the hour," Victor Mendoza-Montalvo declares, then a friendly thump lands on Marsh's shoulder as he joins their little circle. "Ah, a visitor?" Victor asks, seeing Dylan.

Marsh freezes for a moment, unsure of how to introduce him, because she still doesn't know who Dylan is to her in this reality, but Dylan is already shaking Victor's hand.

"I'm Dylan, Marsh's ex," he says casually, as if he's completely comfortable with it.

"Oh, yes," Victor replies, as if he faintly recollects this information. Marsh's suspicion that she and Dylan have been divorced a long time must be correct, then. "The two of you have a daughter, right?"

"Speak of the devil," Dylan replies as Harper appears from the crowd at the same moment.

"Hi, Mom," she says as Marsh joyfully cries, "*Harp!*"

"I wanted to bring her by for a little bit," he explains as Harper, self-conscious around so many adults, gives her mother a shy hug. "I thought you might like for her to see what an incredible job you did."

The rush of pleasure at his words surprises Marsh. She'd always told herself that Harper's passion for the violin was proof that she'd been a good parent, wasn't it? That she'd taught her daughter that she could have anything she wanted, if she worked hard enough.

But it was one thing to tell her, and another thing entirely to be able to *show* her.

"Thank you," Marsh replies at last, and means it.

"Speech! Speech!" the junior associates are chanting now.

Marsh tries to wave them off, but the cheers just get louder, and Harper is pushing her forward gently, until she finally gives in.

"I . . . uh . . ."

An embarrassed blush is threatening at her cheeks. She can feel the cheap stage makeup on her face again, hear the whisper of the old drama teacher giving directions from the wings. So many eyes on her, so much attention.

But it's different this time.

They're not all staring at her with ridicule.

They're looking at her with *awe*.

"The very first day of my Introduction to Constitutional Law class . . ." Marsh stammers—and the whole room leans in. They're smiling, waiting for the funny anecdote, ready to laugh.

They want to hear what she says, she realizes.

And when the crowd erupts into whistles and thunderous applause at the end of her speech, Marsh is stunned to find that she's not shrinking away anymore, not hunching her shoulders and casting her eyes down. Instead, she's actually *grinning*.

Maybe she really can do this.

"You've outdone yourself this time," Jo says as Marsh rejoins them. "We should have told the interns to get even more balloons!"

"I'll have to give the cleaners a bonus this year, for all the times we've destroyed this room with a party." Victor winks at her. "It's worth it, though. Keep on winning like you are and I'll happily hire a full-time second cleaning crew just for your celebrations."

"That's our Marsh," Jo says. "Any more landslide verdicts and we're going to have to change the name of the firm."

Marsh almost chokes on her champagne—*Is she that close to being considered for partner?* She's afraid to even *hope* that it's already possible for her so early in the season, but Victor is looking at Marsh expectantly. Her stomach loops itself into excited knots.

"I'll leave you to catch up," Victor finally says, nodding politely to Marsh, Dylan, Harper, and Jo as he starts to move toward another cluster of lawyers. "Enjoy the party, Marsh. You've earned it!"

"I'm off, too," Jo says as she air-kisses Marsh's cheeks, then Harper's, to the girl's delight.

"Take care," Dylan says to her, shaking hands.

"You too. And, Marsh, I'll see you later!" she shouts at Marsh over the crowd as she departs. "This is your night. I'm not letting you stop celebrating until dawn!"

As Jo waves from the door, Marsh spots a little poster hanging on the bulletin board beside her—it's a sign-up sheet for a company retreat to Hong Kong.

Is that a clue? A teaser for what's still to come? Her heart flutters with excitement.

"Meet me in an hour! You better be there!" Jo says, and disappears.

"Does she ever slow down?" Marsh laughs.

Dylan shrugs back. "Do you?"

There's no trace of jealousy or bitterness in his voice, but still, the words catch Marsh off guard. She looks at him more closely, trying to see this version of his life instead of the original.

"So, how's your work going?" she asks.

"Good," he says. "And it's been fun to have Harper in my class this year."

"What?" Marsh asks, confused. Harper is only in her teens—does this mean Dylan doesn't teach at the college level in this life, but rather at a high school?

"Yeah." Harper shrugs. "I was going to take biology for my science requirement, but physics is kind of interesting."

"She's doing pretty well so far," he says proudly. "Maybe she'll even get the PhD I never did!"

Marsh laughs at his joke, but the sudden drop in her gut makes the sound come out funny.

Dylan never finished his PhD in this life?

In the real world, Marsh was the one who gave up her career to raise Harper, both because it felt cruel to ask Dylan to do it and because she'd thought she wanted to, at the time. But in order for this reality to have worked out the way it has for her, it must have been Dylan that had to pick up the parental slack when they separated.

Did he choose it happily?

Or does he regret it here, just like Marsh does outside the Bubble?

"Do you ever wish you'd finished your PhD?" Marsh asks him, softer.

Dylan smiles. "Oh, I don't know. It was so long ago. And Meadows High is great."

"And he gets to see me all day," Harper teases, then grows awkward once more.

"Want some of the cake?" Marsh offers as she studies her.

"It's eight o'clock! She'll never sleep tonight," Dylan cries.

"But we're supposed to be celebrating," Harper counters, giving him puppy-dog eyes. "You're saying that Mom's big win isn't worth just *one* sugar high?"

Dylan chuckles. "Touché. You really drive a hard bargain, missy. Clearly you learned from the best."

She smiles, shy all over again at this reference to her mother.

Marsh frowns. In this life, there's definitely a difference between how Harper is with her father and how she is with Marsh. She clearly *likes* her mother—but isn't as comfortable with her as she is with Dylan.

Maybe Marsh has been so busy climbing in her career that the two of them didn't spend enough time together to grow as close as they should be.

"Fine, but no extra frosting!" Dylan insists as their daughter scampers off.

Marsh wants to ask him more about her, but once she's gone, Dylan's gaze unfocuses, his thoughts drifting somewhere distant.

"You know, sometimes it sort of feels like I did," he says, almost more to himself.

"Did what?" Marsh asks.

"Finish my PhD. There are these moments—of course they never happened, but they feel so real that sometimes, I forget they actually didn't. Almost like in some alternate universe, I managed it, or something. I don't know if that makes any sense."

Marsh tries to come up with a response, but she doesn't really know what to say to that. In another version of this moment, she might find it funny that her own personal physics expert is talking about quantum bubbling without any idea how relevant the subject really is, but in this version, she can't summon the humor. Not when he looks so lost in it.

Dylan laughs, his gaze returning to the present. "Who knows, maybe it's just a coping mechanism. But it works. I'm happy with my job."

"Hey." Marsh waits until he looks at her. "Your job is important. Seriously."

He taps her glass gently with his own. "Well, thanks. But we're not here to talk about me. We're here to celebrate you. Speaking of, I have something to show you."

"A gift?" Marsh asks, surprised.

"Sort of." Dylan is chuckling to himself and shaking his head as he unzips the backpack he must use to cart his teaching materials to and from the high school. "You'll think it's sentimental, but that's me." He pulls out a medium-sized rectangular box, sort of like what a dress shirt might come in.

Marsh takes it from him, still a little mystified. "Can I look at it now?"

"If you want."

Marsh unwraps it, and a smile catches her as she sees what's inside.

"It's a briefcase," she says. "For a lawyer."

"Okay, there's a story to this, I promise. I didn't just buy you a super outdated, cheap messenger bag earlier today as a joke," Dylan laughs. "I originally bought it to be a surprise gift, for when you passed the bar. But then—well, you know." He shrugs.

Marsh touches the gold front clasp on the leather softly, moved. If Dylan had gotten the briefcase before she'd dropped out, that meant he'd purchased this gift when she was pregnant, probably for a fortune neither of them could afford at the time, and kept it all these years.

Even after they'd separated, and then divorced. Even after their lives had diverged dramatically. Even after they'd lived more time apart than together. He'd still kept it.

"You've had this the whole time?" Marsh finally asks.

"At first, I think I was holding out hope we might reconcile. But then after I realized we wouldn't, I started to get another idea." He nods at the box. "I watched you do so well here, climb the ladder so quickly, and I knew you were where you were supposed to be, doing what you were supposed to be doing. Even though things didn't work out how we planned, they're still pretty good. We've got Harper, and we're still friends."

"I'm so glad we are," Marsh says. Her voice is genuine, earnest.

"Me too," Dylan agrees. "I know you've got a much better briefcase now, probably one that cost as much as my car, but Harper's birthday is next month, and I was just thinking, maybe we could tell her that I bought this for you when you were just starting out, and now we're giving it to her, to use for school if she wants. Kind of like a good-luck talisman. Something to remind her that she can go as far you have, if she works just as hard."

Marsh looks at the bag again, overcome. She touches the tacky, gold-plated front clasp on the leather.

"If you use it for just one day, it'll technically be true," Dylan says, misreading her expression. "You don't even have to take it out of your office, so no one will see it."

Marsh shakes her head. "It's not that."

She looks back up at him, unsure of what she wants to say. Her throat is tight, and she's on the verge of tears.

"I really am happy for you," Dylan says. His voice is soft, and without a trace of defensiveness. "I know how much it cost you to achieve this. The choices you had to make, the sacrifices you had to endure. I—I'm proud of you, Mallow. I think Harper is, too. Even if she's too embarrassed to admit it."

Marsh flinches as a sudden prickle stings her eyes.

Has she ever heard Dylan talk this way before? She did such a good job of hiding her disappointment over her lost career from him while they were married. It was a point of secret pride for her—as if hiding it from him could also hide it from herself. Knowing that he'd still glimpsed it somehow was almost more startling than even the affair.

An affair that actually never happened, in this version.

The question is there before she knows whether she wants it to be or not.

Was this path the right one?

"Do you ever . . ." she begins.

In response, Dylan clucks his tongue and holds his glass up to her. "All the time. But that's what I do. Not you. Don't go soft on me now, Mallow. Not after all it took for you to get here. Besides, there are no redos in life anyway, right?"

Marsh doesn't quite trust herself to speak. She steels herself and accepts the toast, and hopes Dylan can't see the tightness in her lips as she tries to smile.

As she takes a sip of her champagne, her phone lights up suddenly, jolting to life where she's got it pinned between her thumb and the briefcase in its box with her other hand.

"It's Jo," she says, skimming the text message. She clears her throat quickly. "She's over at Chrysalis now, and is demanding I join her."

"Of course, your celebration continues at the most exclusive bar in the city," Dylan says. "Those views must be to die for."

So, Chrysalis is the name of a bar, Marsh muses. And if it's the most exclusive bar in town, it must be on top of the Vanguard skyscraper, and is called Skyline outside the show.

She knows because, outside the Bubble, that's the bar where the two of them celebrated their last anniversary, before everything fell apart. It was make or break, and Dylan had gone for the grand gesture. But Skyline was so exclusive, he couldn't get a reservation, and they had to wait in line for two hours outside. Then, they couldn't afford seats, and had to huddle at the standing-room-only bar, where they paid so much money for just one round of drinks that it pretty much ruined the whole evening.

And look at her now.

She's a regular at this place, in this life.

Even so, Marsh can't help but wonder what subtle ripples this choice sent through the Bubble to have caused the bar's name to change in this reality. But perhaps it doesn't matter. If her life ends up perfect, who really cares what one exclusive bar ends up being named?

"Chrysalis! You should go," Victor says as he passes by Marsh and Dylan again. "What good is a private table on the balcony if you never use it?"

Marsh blinks. Not only does she have enough power to get past the red velvet rope at Chrysalis, but she also has a private table there, apparently. The surprises just keep coming.

A phone buzzes again, but it's not Marsh's this time.

Victor pulls his own phone out of his pocket, and then chuckles at the screen. "Jo's texting me now, to tell you to get your workaholic ass over there."

"She never gives up on a good time." Marsh rolls her eyes, but inside, she's glowing to be so familiar with a titan like Victor that she and Jo would be on social text chains with him.

"Seriously, go," Victor is saying as he pockets his phone and waves at someone across the room. "We'll carry on here for another hour, but you deserve far more celebration than that for this case. Jo will make sure you get it."

"I'll think about it," Marsh says. "I will."

"I don't want to see either of you roll in here tomorrow until at least eleven o'clock!" he demands as he departs.

"If you're on your way to another party, I've got to get my congratulations in now!" another voice says, and Marsh looks up to see Dylan's jaw drop open as Talia joins them.

She enjoys watching him cycle through his emotions. It's the same process she went through the first time she saw Talia in person: surprise, disbelief, shock, euphoria, shock again.

"Dylan, this is—"

"Talia Cruz," he says, starstruck.

"Charmed," Talia says.

"It's an honor," he manages as he shakes her hand. "Wow, the people you rub shoulders with these days," he adds to Marsh, and she tries not to flush with pride.

"We're old pals," Talia adds with a little wink. "But Marsh is really the star here tonight! What a victory!"

As they chat, Marsh's phone buzzes impatiently once more, a string of emojis from Jo lighting up the screen. Marsh deduces from Jo's choice of pictures that the crowd at Chrysalis tonight is very attractive.

"Looks like you're going to have a good night whether you stay or go," Talia says as she sees what Jo's texted, and winks again. "That guy's also been looking at you all evening."

Marsh glances over her shoulder to see a man about her age in a sharp blue suit standing with another group of colleagues.

Adrian Jackson is looking at her. One of Mendoza-Montalvo and Hall's best lawyers, after Victor and Jo. Although in this episode, maybe he's also behind *Marsh*, now.

Moms4Marsh: <Omg, he's gorgeous!>

He *is* gorgeous. Tall, athletic, with dark brown skin and a goatee. When he sees Marsh meet his gaze across the room, he raises his glass subtly to her and winks without missing a beat of conversation.

Marsh whips around again, flustered. She glances at Dylan, unable to help it, but he's shrugging casually like this is entertaining for him, not hurtful or embarrassing. In this life, they've been amicably separated since Harper was a baby, after all. Any sadness over their divorce has long since faded, and been replaced with a comfortable co-parent relationship, she supposes.

But flirting right in front of him feels like a step too far.

Talia, however, seems to have other ideas.

"Well, I think I'll go freshen up my drink," she says pointedly, and Dylan takes the hint.

"Here, allow me," he offers. "Would you like anything, Marsh?"

Marsh shakes her head, even though her mouth is suddenly cotton.

As Dylan heads to the bar, she stares at his back. He's always carried his stress in his shoulders, and after decades, she could read his mood in the slope of his trapezius, the pinch of his scapula. Sometimes his mouth would say one thing, and his deltoids another. One could hide things, but the other never could, she knew well by now.

Talia clears her throat and giggles. "So, is this night just perfect, or what?"

She looks confused when Marsh throws up her arms.

"I don't know!" she cries. "Everything feels so strange!"

"I understand," Talia says, giving Adrian another appraising glance from across the room. "It must be hard to fully enjoy yourself in this scene with Dylan hanging around."

Marsh's gaze follows Talia's, to Adrian's blue blazer, his dark goatee—

Wait a second.

She looks again, confused.

Is that . . . ?

"What?" Talia asks.

"Sorry." Marsh shakes her head. "It's nothing."

For a second, she thought Ren was at the party—even though that would make no sense.

But it was just her imagination.

Her phone buzzes again. A string of joking profanity has unfurled itself across the screen, along with a pair of lips and a bunch of hearts.

That's right! Jo's still waiting for her at Chrysalis!

"What if we go to the bar?" Talia chirps, seizing the opportunity. "You can spend some time with Jo, let loose a little, enjoy yourself without your ex peeking over your shoulder . . ."

"It's more than just that," Marsh says. "Maybe I started off this show with the wrong choice. I'm finally a lawyer now, but at what cost? Harper's whole childhood was with us separated, and Dylan's career, totally rewritten. This is too far."

"It's all right. These are big changes! There are going to be a few kinks to work out in every path," Talia says.

"But this?" Marsh shakes her head. "I wanted to make my life better—not ruin Dylan's. It's not fair to him."

N3vrGiv3Up: <We love you, Marsh! Always thinking of others!>
Notamackerel: <She's just a coward!>

Marsh pushes away the comments, frustrated.

It *isn't* fair—that she put two decades of labor into something now not over, but erased, that Harper didn't get to grow up with the family she had outside the Bubble, that Dylan's life is hollow, diminished.

It isn't fair that even if she'd choose to leave this path for all those reasons, the trolls still may be right.

Talia holds her gaze calmly. "A little panic is normal in the beginning, but let's not jump the gun. You've wanted to be a lawyer for so long, and now you finally are! You want to give it up again so easily?"

Marsh frowns, but finally shakes her head. "I don't," she says.

"Of course not!" Talia agrees.

Marsh looks up as the show's familiar jingle cuts gently in through the party stereo's speakers, announcing her next choice.

"This is all part of the process," Talia promises her. "You're so early in your season. Just give this path a little more time. See how you like being a lawyer at the top of her game! And then if you *still* decide you want something else, we can do that. Deal?"

Marsh nods. "Deal."

Talia knows what she's doing. And she's right. What *would* be the harm of staying in this version a little longer, even if things are a little skewed? Hasn't she had to skew her own life for everyone else's, for years? What's another episode or two?

"Remember, Marsh—"

Marsh turns to see Talia wink at her.

"You could have *All This* . . ."

Marsh smiles back. "*And More*," she replies.

To stay in this path and
meet Jo at the bar:
Go to page 79

STOP!

This is the wrong way!

You must return to the beginning of the story and make different choices to access what lies beyond this point.

ERROR

---

chrysalis (noun)
chrys· a· lis | \ 'kri-sə-ləs \
plural *chrysalides*\ kri- 'sa- lə- ˌdēz \ or *chrysalises*
1: a pupa of a butterfly
2: a protecting covering
also: a sheltered state or stage of being or growth

Well. Now you've done it.
You've gone and gotten yourself stuck.
You aren't supposed to be here.
You aren't supposed to see this.

butterfly (noun, often attributive)
but· ter· fly | \ 'bə-tər-ˌflī \
1: any of numerous slender-bodied diurnal lepidopteran insects with broad and often brightly colored wings
2: something that resembles or suggests a butterfly
especially: a person chiefly occupied with the pursuit of pleasure
3: butterflies *plural:* a feeling of hollowness or queasiness caused especially by emotional or nervous tension or anxious anticipation

Is it any wonder why the Bubble has become so unstable, with you break-ing the rules like this on top of everything else that's going on?

4: butterfly *effect:* a property of chaotic systems (such as the atmo-sphere) by which small changes in initial conditions can lead to large-scale and unpredictable variation in the future state of the system

You should get out of here—while you still can.

To get back on track: Go to page 44	To jump randomly and hope for the best: Go to page 727,659	To give up and start over: Go to page 1

∘ ∘ ∘ AND MORE

The room is quiet and still, and everything is bathed in a gentle pink glow from the sun through the blinds.

Lazily, Marsh stretches, and adjusts the covers. The nightstand clock reads after nine. In the bathroom, the shower turns off, and damp feet gently slap the tile floor.

After all this time, here she is again.

She smiles and wiggles her fingers against the pillow. Her ring is back on her hand this time.

"Did I wake you?" Dylan asks when he comes out of the bathroom and sees her eyes open. "Was I too loud again?"

It had used to drive her mad every morning. But it doesn't have to. Not this time through.

"I think it's cute," she says.

Pickle awakens with a snort as Dylan hops onto the bed beside her, still in his damp towel, and scrambles off the rug to put his two front feet on Marsh's belly for morning kisses.

"Good morning, buddy!" Dylan laughs at his eager panic, and Marsh hugs his big black dog head. "Yes, we love you!"

In his excitement, Pickle drools all over the blankets and her arm.

"Pickle!" Marsh squeals. She gives him another pat and flops back against the pillow—pulling the blanket up, closing her eyes, putting herself back into place.

Waiting for someone to say, *Let's cut.*

"What are you doing?" Dylan asks.

Marsh sits back up.

Dylan is still next to her, not back in the bathroom. The drool is still on her wrist.

Nothing reset.

Everything is real.

"You okay?" Dylan looks at her oddly.

She grins.

The world feels new again. It's a rush to realize that she can't simply whisk something away with a snap of her fingers. That she can't repeat a conversation a hundred times until it's exactly right, but boring and overdone. Marsh only has one shot at everything, every moment, and suddenly every second is precious and rare. Her life may not be perfect, far from it, but it's *true*. The colors don't need the show's enhancing filters; the sounds don't need mixing. The imperfections delight her anew.

For a time.

Marsh adjusts her shawl against the theater's over-cranked Phoenix air-conditioning and crosses her legs the other way in her seat. All around, a smattering of attendees mill, and a teenage usher walks the aisles, passing out programs.

A thump lands beside her, and she turns to see Dylan sliding into the stiff audience chair.

"Okay, I paid for two hours," he says, a little out of breath from the hurry. "I had to find quarters. I really thought you'd fed the meter."

He had, and she'd thought he had, and they'd only realized once they were inside, which led to an argument.

"Thank you," Marsh says instead. She gives him a peck on the cheek, and then looks down at the paper program in her hands. Right by her index finger is Harper's name, and the Beethoven piece she'll be playing tonight. Not at Pallissard, but as part of her regular high school band.

"Are those two seats taken?" an elderly couple asks, and Marsh turns her knees to make room for them to sit on the other side of her and Dylan.

"Our grandson is performing tonight," the woman says as they settle. "I think he's a little nervous."

"This is also our daughter's first big performance," Dylan replies. "She's got the jitters, too."

"They're all going to do great," Marsh agrees.

"What's your daughter's instrument?" the man asks, politely making small talk.

Marsh nods along with the conversation, but as it drags on, her attention starts to drift. Her *hmm*s grow fainter; her eyes start to wander. Her gaze fixes somewhere in the middle distance.

She's doing it again.

She can't help it.

That joke Dylan just made could have been funnier. Their seats could be a little closer to the stage. There could have been less traffic on the way here. They could be in San Francisco instead. She could be wearing a more stylish dress.

"Marsh?" a voice calls.

Things are good here. They always were.

But they're not perfect.

Stop.

"Marsh," Dylan is saying as she finally snaps back. "Everything okay?"

"Yes," Marsh replies.

She chose Dylan, not Ren. She wanted this life, not her fabricated one.

She pulls her shawl higher on her shoulder against the chill as the lights blink overhead, warning that the show will start in a few minutes.

"Do you ever think about what it would have been like, if we'd moved to Denver instead after graduation?" The question slips out before she can help it. "Or if we'd both gone to different colleges? Or chosen different majors?"

Dylan shakes his head. "I wouldn't change a thing," he says, absentmindedly shifting in his threadbare seat so his ass won't fall asleep. "Would you?"

"No," Marsh answers.

She pats his thigh firmly.

"No," she tells herself.

But as the lights go down, and all that's left of her is just the faint glint of the stage lights catching in the whites of her eyes, Marsh's gaze begins to drift again. Exploring the dimmed theater, roaming over everything that's here—and everything that's not.

Everything that *could be.*

She doesn't know she's uncrossed her legs in the darkness until both of her feet are on the floor. Until she's already beginning to stand.

"I'll be right back," she whispers to Dylan.

"Hurry," he whispers back. "Harper will be on partway through the first half, before intermission."

Marsh slips across the aisle and out of the theater, then down the empty hall, to the little theater lounge.

The audience are all in their seats to enjoy the concert, and the normally bustling space is completely still.

There's just one person there, this time.

"Took you long enough," Talia Cruz says from a barstool, with a little wink.

Marsh studies her for a long, silent moment. That perfect glossy hair, that flawless posture. The way she knew Marsh would come back, eventually. Inevitably.

Nothing would make her happier than to turn and leave.

Instead, Marsh slowly drapes her shawl over the stool next to Talia, and slides onto it.

Her former host passes her the glass of champagne beside her own. They toast, and drink, humorlessly.

"So," Talia says, setting her flute down. "How is it, being back in your original life? Is it everything you hoped it would be?"

"Yes," Marsh replies.

"You're happy," Talia adds. "No regrets."

"None," Marsh says.

Talia watches her as Marsh takes another drink, and then takes a sip of her own. As she does so, she shifts slightly, revealing her purse resting on the stool on her other side.

There's something inside of it.

Something large, and heavy, and book-shaped.

Marsh turns back to the counter, and stares intensely at her champagne. She watches the bubbles fizz like they're the only thing in the world.

"Who's the lucky season four contestant?" she finally asks.

Talia smiles.

"You're going to love them," she says.

She turns to her purse and lifts the Show Bible out. It's pristine, the edges not yet scuffed, the corners not yet softened from episode after episode of being dragged around and flipped through. On the spine, it says, *Powered by Hoffman Labs*.

"Your episodes are being hailed as some of the best television of the last century," Talia tells her. "RealTV can't wait to get the next season on the air—and a hundred more after it. The show is going to be bigger and better than ever before. All thanks to you."

Marsh shakes her head.

"I think you're going to love what I have to offer," Talia chirps, as if there are still cameras on them. "It's an incredible opportunity. A chance to put everything you learned to use, a chance to do some good. A chance to help someone else."

Faintly, from down the hall, the sound of applause reaches them.

"How would you like to be our new host?"

Marsh can't tell what it is, that feeling that has her throat in a crushing vise. Hate or understanding. There's the click of a door, footsteps, a clink of bottles in a cardboard box. The bartender arrives from the back room and sidles up to the counter.

Marsh stares, breathless.

"You two look like you're celebrating something," Alexis says as she refills their glasses.

Talia tips her head in thanks.

"I'm not sure yet," she replies, and looks at Marsh. "Are we?"

Marsh doesn't say anything for a long time. Finally, Talia lifts the Show Bible from her lap, and pushes it onto Marsh's. She feels the weight of it settle on her thighs, and her hands automatically move to stabilize it so it doesn't slide off, but she doesn't look down at it.

She can't. She won't.

"You still could have *All This* . . . ," Talia says.

She angles her delicate head expectantly, waiting to hear Marsh say the rest of the phrase and complete her sentence.

But Marsh stays silent. Her jaw is clenched tight to resist the urge.

"Come on," Talia chides. "I know you want to."

"No," Marsh refuses—but she doesn't give the Show Bible back.

It's still in her lap, still in her grip.

Her former host waits, her beautiful eyes sharpened, her delicate lips curled.

"The show must go on," she says at last. "Some things we have no choice about."

She leans a little closer, and puts one of her graceful hands on top of Marsh's. Gently. Encouragingly.

Together, the two sets of fingers curl around the edge of the book's cover.

"And others we do."

Acknowledgments:
Go to page 471

About the Author:
Go to page 472

STOP!

You've reached the end of the story!

If you want to explore Marsh's other episodes, return to the beginning of the story and make different choices to access what lies beyond this point.

ERROR

chrysalis (noun)
chrys· a· lis | \ 'kri-sə-ləs \
plural *chrysalides*\ *kri- 'sa- lə- ˌdēz* \ or *chrysalises*
1: a pupa of a butterfly
2: a protecting covering
also: a sheltered state or stage of being or growth

Well. Now you've done it.
You've gone and gotten yourself stuck.
You aren't supposed to be here.
You aren't supposed to see this.

butterfly (noun, often attributive)
but· ter· fly | \ 'bə-tər-ˌflī \
1: any of numerous slender-bodied diurnal lepidopteran insects with broad and often brightly colored wings
2: something that resembles or suggests a butterfly
especially: a person chiefly occupied with the pursuit of pleasure
3: butterflies *plural:* a feeling of hollowness or queasiness caused especially by emotional or nervous tension or anxious anticipation

Is it any wonder why the Bubble has become so unstable, with you breaking the rules like this on top of everything else that's going on?

4: butterfly *effect:* a property of chaotic systems (such as the atmosphere) by which small changes in initial conditions can lead to large-scale and unpredictable variation in the future state of the system

You should get out of here—while you still can.

To get back on track: Go to page 351	To jump randomly and hope for the best: Go to page 727,659	To give up and start over: Go to page 1

○ ○ ○ AND MORE

Her new firm is quiet at such a late hour. Marsh stands beside the imposing oak desk in her corner office, one hand on the polished wood. At the window, Ren watches the tower lights on top of the Empire State Building turn the majestic stone structure a brilliant Sharp Purple against the night.

Beyond her closed door, faintly, is the echo of laughter and celebration. Another victory party, for another legal case she's won.

"I'm surprised," Ren admits.

She turns to him.

He looks, at last, the way he looked when he first came into the bar in Phoenix and she saw him again for the first time in decades. He's even wearing the same smart casual outfit. It's a parting gift from *All This and More*. A touch of familiarity, a tiny anchor.

"I thought you might try to keep us in Hong Kong."

Marsh smiles.

"I chose New York for Harper," she says. "I knew that you and I could be happy anywhere."

"That we can," Ren agrees, nodding.

He comes over to take her hand. Together, they admire the famous view.

New York was the only choice, in the end. It's where Juilliard is, and it's closer to Dylan than any of the other places she could have gone. Not for her own sake—of course, he'd never have been able to accept the show and live this life with Marsh—but she hopes that in time, he'll realize that their daughter still needs him in hers.

She did the best thing. For everyone.

At last, she looks back to Ren. He's gazing at her hand, at the beautiful ring he gave her during the midseason special, with misty eyes, overcome. She tilts her finger, and the diamond sparkles brilliantly.

"I know you never want to say that things are absolutely perfect, but . . ." he says.

Marsh knows that he wants her to reply, *It's pretty damn close.*

She opens the side drawer of her desk and pulls out the box of celebratory cigars they've come to retrieve. Her box, her victory.

Her new, real life.

"Actually, I think it is, after all," Marsh finally says, instead.

Ren's face lights up—surprised, relieved, overflowing with love—as she winks at him.

"Perfect."

The first few months are a whirlwind, even more than the first few episodes of *All This and More*. Although she watched Talia's season, Marsh still can hardly believe at first that everything that happened in the Bubble persisted once she and Ren clasped hands and faced the cameras. She remains a sharp-witted lawyer at the top of her game; Ren writes more articles, each one better than the last; and her daughter's first solo concert earns a standing ovation. When they announce during her encore that Harper's going to be named a Living National Treasure, the tears of joy that Marsh cries are the deepest, purest pieces of her soul.

All the uncertainty, all the struggle—it was worth it, to have everything she has now.

She keeps waiting for the other shoe to drop.

But it never does.

The show has kept its promise.

And everywhere she goes, she's famous. People name their children after her, leave flowers outside her law firm, beg for her autograph in the streets. She seems almost more beloved than Talia now, if that's possible. The colors of the world are better than any painting, and every sound is in perfect symphony.

At the one-year anniversary special, sponsored by the newly created Hoffman Labs, Marsh and Talia sit together on a grand stage before an audience of thousands, and within the screens of millions more.

"It's incredible," Marsh says of her postshow life, as the crowd cheers and sobs with joy for her. "It really is everything and more."

"Marvelous," Talia agrees. She leans in, pressing for the last sound bite. "You really wouldn't change a single thing?"

Marsh faces the audience.

"Nothing," she says, to resounding applause. "Nothing at all."

It's true.

Not her inspiring, interesting career, not Ren's excitement and dedication to their relationship, not Harper's boundless, nearly superhuman musical talent. Not their gorgeous apartment, not their neighborhood, not

New York's sweltering, then blizzarding seasons. Not their vacations, not their favorite restaurant.

Not her sex life.

Not her wardrobe.

Not even the kitchen dish towels.

On a Friday night, the elevators to their Manhattan penthouse open seamlessly, and Ren goes first, turning on a few lamps to illuminate the darkened living room. Through the floor-to-ceiling windows, the city dazzles, glittering angles and pinpricks of light against the inky black sky.

"That was amazing," he says as she slips out of her dress heels. "Humanitarian Lawyer of the Year! I'm so proud of you."

Marsh looks down at the award in her hand as he talks. It's a dinner-plate-sized slice of crystal, carved into some exquisite shape. Her name and honor have been lasered onto its sparkling surface.

"And the dinner, just delicious," Ren continues happily. "Did you try the dessert? So decadent!"

Marsh is still staring at the award. At her reflection bent across its sculpted edges.

It's beautiful.

Perfect.

It's instantaneous, the swift jerk of her arm.

"Marsh!" Ren cries, flinching in shock as she smashes the award against the wall. "What are you doing?!"

She pulls her arm back, smashes it again.

And again.

And again.

She drives the heavy crystal into the drywall until it finally strikes a metal stud and shatters, a starburst of light and shards across the floor, and only the bare platform base is left in her hand.

"Marsh!"

At last, panting, Marsh stops. She turns to Ren, where he's still staring at her, frozen in the center of the room.

She grins.

In the morning, the apartment is just a little quieter than usual. The floor has been swept clean, and a piece of art taken from the hall and hung over the gaping hole in the wall. Ren is all smiles again. He doesn't bring up what happened, and she doesn't explain. She wins another case at work, and Harper's solo performance in the evening is even better than the first.

That night, as Marsh is brushing her teeth in the bathroom, she slowly, quietly snaps the pump of the soap dispenser, so no one can hear.

"Hey, what happened to your favorite flower vase?" Ren asks a few days later, staring at the empty spot on the mantel.

Marsh shrugs. "Don't know," she says.

The scratch on her brand-new car is next.

And more.

She burns dinners, tears up papers at work, breaks every gift she receives. She doesn't know why she's doing it, but she can't stop. This isn't the Bubble anymore—she can't simply rewind the mistake; she can't scrub the damage from existence—the pain she feels each time sends a shiver of perverse delight through her.

Everything she worked so hard to change in her episodes. Everything she ever wanted for her life. Every desperate, unrealized dream she carried heavy within her, then impossibly, made come true.

She imagines herself almost like a miner, chipping away at a wall of rock with her chisel. How much can a mountain take before it crumbles? Where is the granite? Where is the gold vein? How deep can one go?

Where exactly is that weakest spot, that if struck just right, would cause the avalanche that would crush her?

"Why are you doing this?" Ren begs, at his wits' end, unable to keep pretending he doesn't notice, he doesn't see. "What is *wrong*?"

"Nothing," Marsh says.

That's just it.

"Nothing at all."

Acknowledgments:
Go to page 471

About the Author:
Go to page 472

STOP!

You've reached the end of the story!

If you want to explore Marsh's other episodes, return to the beginning of the story and make different choices to access what lies beyond this point.

ERROR

---

chrysalis (noun)
chrys· a· lis | \ ˈkri-sə-ləs \
plural *chrysalides*\ kri- ˈsa- lə- ˌdēz \ or *chrysalises*
1: a pupa of a butterfly
2: a protecting covering
also: a sheltered state or stage of being or growth

Well. Now you've done it.
You've gone and gotten yourself stuck.
You aren't supposed to be here.
You aren't supposed to see this.

butterfly (noun, often attributive)
but· ter· fly | \ ˈbə-tər-ˌflī \
1: any of numerous slender-bodied diurnal lepidopteran insects with broad and often brightly colored wings
2: something that resembles or suggests a butterfly
especially: a person chiefly occupied with the pursuit of pleasure
3: butterflies *plural:* a feeling of hollowness or queasiness caused especially by emotional or nervous tension or anxious anticipation

Is it any wonder why the Bubble has become so unstable, with you break-ing the rules like this on top of everything else that's going on?

4: butterfly *effect:* a property of chaotic systems (such as the atmo-sphere) by which small changes in initial conditions can lead to large-scale and unpredictable variation in the future state of the system

You should get out of here—while you still can.

| To get back on track: Go to page 351 | To jump randomly and hope for the best: Go to page 727,659 | To give up and start over: Go to page 1 |

. . . AND MORE

The screen stays dark for so long, it seems like this might be it. The show might really be over, never to return.

Viewers everywhere hold their breath, desperately hoping.

It can't end like this.

Not another season squandered, another star lost.

Again, the world waits. Every evening, millions rush through their dinners and scramble to their living rooms, where they sit all night, keeping that same stubborn hope, that same determined certainty, that the show will come back if they don't give up.

It finally happens again one Friday night. But this time, it's no accident.

The music starts anew.

On every street, traffic stops as cars pull to the shoulder, and balls roll forgotten in the grass in sports stadiums. Meals burn on restaurant grills, but no one is eating them anyway now. Every screen, everywhere, public or personal, has tuned itself to the only thing that matters, and every set of eyes are watching.

As the episode opens, the set is positively glittering in high definition, every inch of the RealTV stage covered in cameras and teleprompters and boom mics. There are wardrobe racks stuffed into every wing, and a dozen specialty lighting configurations are clipping through their routines as *All This and More* gets ready to go live.

"Let me get a look at you," Marsh's host says as the main camera zooms close on them. Talia's just as glamorous as always, her grin just as dazzling. She gives Marsh's sleeve a little tug, then winks. "Don't worry, you're going to be great. This is all about you. You're the story."

"I'm the story," Marsh repeats, just like she did the first time, and looks down at the all-important binder—not tucked under Talia's arm, but her own, now.

This time, she'll make sure that she gets everything she wants. That she gets *perfect* after all.

Because now, Marsh has infinite tries to get it right.

Things are already better, in fact. The original time through, Talia was wearing red, which clashed with Marsh's complexion. Now, she's in a much more suitable blue dress that makes them both glow. It's a small thing, but that's what perfect is all about. There are other differences, too. The lights are better layered, the music is faintly orchestral, and the *All This and More* logo is a little less garish, a little more sophisticated.

"We'll start really general," Talia repeats her line, like a replay, as the swing cam arcs across the stage to get a dynamic reveal of the opening set of choices. There's something else about Marsh's host that's different, too, it seems. Something more than just her dress.

Something subtle, but definitely there.

But it's a joy to see how much more smoothly the next episode flows, compared to before. Marsh doesn't immediately panic that she's chosen the wrong thing, and Talia doesn't have to talk her down. She glides from decision to decision effortlessly, confident in her choices, and even more confident in her revisions. By the time she makes it to the midseason special, Harper has become the world's youngest musician to ever perform at Carnegie Hall, and Pallissard names their largest scholarship after her. Mendoza-Montalvo and Hall has grown into the biggest, best law firm in the world, and Ren has founded his own newspaper and been nominated for the Pulitzer. Marsh visits the RealTV studio, and Lev can't but comply when she asks him to adjust a few settings. It's a breath of fresh air when the pesky comments feature disappears permanently, unable to be reopened even by Ezra's clever hacking.

And every time Chrysalis manifests, it's smaller and smaller, until it turns into a delicate gold necklace with a butterfly-shaped gemstone charm, which Marsh spots in a shop window and Ren offers to buy for her on their second "first" date—this time set in colorful, floating Venice, just because she can.

"*Bellissima*," Alexis the jeweler says as she loops the chain around Marsh's neck and hooks the clasp.

"It's perfect," Ren says nervously. Desperately.

Marsh touches the butterfly charm and smiles.

"Pretty damn close," she says.

It really is. Little by little, every errant quirk gets rewound, every less-than-ideal side effect buffed away. The only stubborn detail is Dylan, who's barricaded himself in the university library again, and refuses to leave—but Marsh isn't bothered. He's angry at her for this choice, but she knows that it's only a matter of time before he comes around, and finally sees that she's been right all along about everything that the Bubble has to offer. Not just to her, but to Harper, and to him, too.

In the meantime, she'll entertain herself on fun, romantic adventures with an eager suitor who will do anything to woo her, spend as much time as she wants with her amazing daughter, and continue to improve every facet of her life.

And then, when Dylan finally does join her, Marsh really will have everything she could ever dream of. It really will be *perfect*.

She's well aware how obstinate he can be, and how long this plan will take to work. But she's confident that it will.

After all, she has forever to wait . . . and no one can stay mad *forever*.

Not even Dylan.

"Wow! Our beloved heroine has really lit this season on fire so far, hasn't she?" Marsh's lovely host exclaims as the episode breaks for some commercials. Everything has improved so much faster, and by such orders of magnitude that she's having trouble coming up with dramatic tidbits to tease the audience during her *We'll Be Right Back, Folks!* segments.

Talia turns to gaze adoringly at a floating graphic of Marsh's grinning face next to her.

"I can't wait to see what's next!" she trills as their two faces align side by side on-screen.

That's when it finally becomes obvious.

A feeling that's been there all along, too subtle at first to pinpoint. But as the season has progressed, the sensation has grown stronger—like a filter slowly being turned up—until it's impossible to ignore.

It almost seems like the longer the show goes on, the more Talia looks . . .

. . . Like *Marsh*.

Can that really be?

But it's unmistakable. The change is minor, but it's there. The tint of her hair, the way she moves, her tone when she speaks. It's all shifted slightly, and is shifting still, more and more with each passing scene.

It's not just Talia, either.

Of course, Harper has always looked like her mother, but now it's apparent in Jo, Victor, and Ren, too. It's even visible in the supporting cast, like Bex and Adrian. Their features are slowly harmonizing, as if they're all musical instruments in an orchestra being carefully brought into tune.

In fact, almost everyone in each scene, no matter how peripheral their role—the coffee shop barista, the receptionist at Marsh's law firm, the entirety of the audience at every gala and fundraiser that she attends—looks more and more like Marsh.

And that's not all.

Even things outside the show are starting to look more similar to things within it. People are finding it hard to say for sure that their living rooms are the same as when they started watching the new season three. They look more like Marsh's now. The couches, the patterns on the rugs, the layouts of the furniture, are eerily familiar. It's strange, to see the same color on a wall as on the screen just in front of it, blending together. Like every television isn't so much a television, but a strange funhouse mirror.

"Our best episode yet!" Talia cheers, as Marsh poses victoriously on the top of Mount Everest, her cheeks lightly pink from the climb and her hair exquisitely tousled in the artificially gentle breeze. "I can't imagine anything more perfect! Can you?"

But Marsh doesn't answer immediately. The show waits, and the whole mountain hangs with her. She looks down, lost in thought, as the clouds shift against the piercing blue sky.

Then she looks right at the camera.

Right at *you*.

"What do you think?" she asks. "Was that take really perfect, or would you do it again?"

You watch, spellbound.

Is she really talking to *you*?

It should be impossible—but she's looking straight into your eyes. Her own pair moves when yours move, tracking. Like she can really see you.

"Come on. Don't leave me hanging," she says, even though there's a plate of glass between you.

Or maybe there's not.

"This is what you wanted," Marsh tells you.

Isn't it?

"All of it," she clarifies, and sweeps her arm across the screen. "*All This* . . . ?"

You're not sure where everything suddenly went too far. Where the line blurred, on what side of it you've fallen. If you've become part of the show, or the show has become part of you.

Maybe there's no difference.

Maybe it doesn't matter.

Marsh is still waiting for your response. She smiles at you, inviting.

You can feel the words pushing up from within you. Automatic, instinctual, like a spent breath wishing to escape.

The voice that emerges from your lips no longer sounds entirely like your own.

"*And More,*" you finally say.

Acknowledgments:
Turn the page

About the Author:
Go to page 472

ACKNOWLEDGMENTS

Writing this novel was as dizzyingly complicated as it was joyfully fun, and would have been impossible without a lot of help. Many thanks are in order.

I'm eternally grateful to my editor, Emily Krump, and my agent, Alexandra Machinist, for believing in me and pushing me to write the stories I want to write, no matter how weird they may be. To Danielle Bartlett, Deanna Bailey, Kaitlin Harri, Stephanie Vallejo, Janet Rosenberg, Tessa James, Ploy Siripant, Nathan Burton, and everyone at William Morrow, thank you for bringing *All This and More* to life and supporting it so passionately.

This book was written across five countries and nine cities, and with the help of even more friends. Thank you to Jillian Sleutzkin, Elyse Klein, Naomi Kanakia, Sarah Gailey, Charles Soule, Rafael Roa, Linnea Hartsuyker, and Bryn Dodson for your support, encouragement, and keen eyes on my unruly drafts. Thank you to Rafael Roa, Daniel Sleutzkin, and Mike Chen for designing the poker game that Marsh plays. And thank you to Hildur Knútsdóttir, Ewen Ma, Sergio Rosales, Lorena Zúñiga, Renate Landsgesell, Mari Yamamoto, Jonathan Michalczyk, Ngan Le, Mark Le, Joy Dai, Prashanth Srivatsa, Gary-Ronald Garcia, Matteo Maillard, and Athar Fikry for your help with the many languages that appear in the text.

Thank you to my mother, Lin Sue Flood, who taught me to read and to love stories, and has always been the first one to see anything I write. Mom, there's not a better first reader out there. To my dad, Sean Cooney, for letting me turn half of your living room into a temporary writing station and library over one summer. And to Adam Bryant, for running every single errand, doing every single chore, and taking Goose for every single late-night walk so that I could hit my final deadline. You refuse to accept thanks for this, but in here, I make the rules, so—thank you. This book would still be a draft without you.

Last, but never least, thanks to Pinkin, because he's perfect.

ABOUT THE AUTHOR

Peng Shepherd is the nationally bestselling, award-winning author of *All This and More*, *The Cartographers*, and *The Book of M*.

Her novels have been acclaimed as a "Best Book of the Year" by the *Washington Post*, a "Best Book of the Summer" by the *Today Show* and NPR, and featured in the *New York Times*, the *LA Times*, and on *Good Morning America*, as well as translated into more than ten languages. Her work has also been optioned for TV and film.

A graduate of New York University's MFA program, Peng is also the recipient of a National Endowment for the Arts fellowship. She was born in Phoenix, Arizona, where she rode horses and trained in classical ballet, and has lived in Beijing, Kuala Lumpur, London, Mexico City, and New York. When not writing, she can be found planning her next trip or haunting local bookstores.

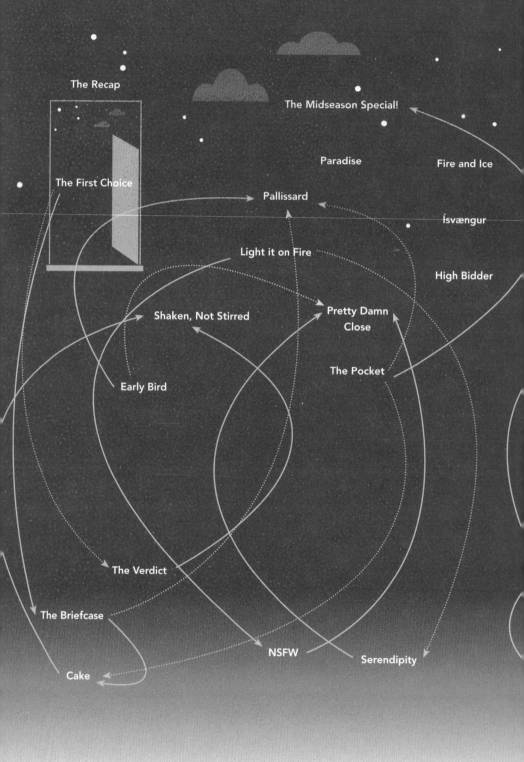